ALLAH'S
SCORPION

ALLAH'S SCORPION

DAVID HAGBERG

A TOM DOHERTY ASSOCIATES BOOK
NEW YORK

ALLAH'S SCORPION

Copyright © 2006 by David Hagberg

This book is printed on acid-free paper.

A Forge Book
Published by Tom Doherty Associates, LLC
175 Fifth Avenue
New York, NY 10010

www.tor.com

Forge® is a registered trademark of Tom Doherty Associates, LLC.

ISBN-13: 978-0-765-30623-4
ISBN-10: 0-765-30623-9

First Edition: January 2007

Printed in the United States of America

0 9 8 7 6 5 4 3 2 1

This novel is for Lorrel.

My apologies to the men and women serving at U.S. Navy Base Guantanamo Bay, and especially Camp Delta—fact is, I made some deliberate errors in the layout of the facility, especially the security arrangements. I did not want to make this a blueprint for escape.

If *We* had prescribed for them: Lay down your lives or go forth from your homes: they would not have done it except a few of them; yet if they had done what they are exhorted to do, it would surely have been better for them. . . . We would then bestow upon them a great reward from Ourselves. . . . Whoever so obeys Allah and the Messenger shall be among those upon whom Allah has bestowed His favors.

THE QUR'AN, Al-Nisa, 4:67–71

If they turn back [from Allah], seize them and kill them wherever you find them. . . .

THE QUR'AN, Al-Nisa, 4:89–92

ALLAH'S SCORPION

PROLOGUE

□

GUANTANAMO BAY, CUBA

Under an overcast moonless sky, a rubber raft came ashore three hundred meters east of the U.S. Naval Base Guantanamo Bay's outer security fence. Four men dressed in U.S. Navy SEAL night fighter camos, their faces blackened, Heckler & Koch suppressed baseline carbines strapped to their backs, jumped out of the boat and quickly carried it ten meters up the beach to some tall grass. They moved swiftly, efficiently, as a well-practiced team.

Their leader, who'd entered Cuba with his operators ten days earlier under a French passport identifying him as Pierre Halille, raised a pair of Steiner Mil Spec binoculars to his eyes and scanned the beach in the direction of the U.S. Navy Base and the sprawling Camp Delta detention facility situated on a bluff that rose nearly fifty meters above sea level. He was sweating lightly even though the night was relatively cool. He was not used to the humidity, and a great deal was at stake this morning, not the least of which was his life and the lives of his men.

The fence was six meters tall and was topped with coils of razor wire. Strong searchlights atop guard towers at one-hundred-meter intervals lit the no-man's zones like day. Nothing could get close without being spotted, either by the American military guards on the inside or the Cuban Frontier Brigade patrolling the outside.

Other lights were on throughout the sprawling camp, but very little activity went on at this hour. The main part of the base, with its hospital, schools, barracks, dining halls, and recreation centers, was to the west, along the bay, housed mostly in prefab buildings, large air-conditioned tents, and a collection of white-walled concrete-block buildings with red roofs. Base headquarters, the hospital, the school, and several other facilities were housed in more substantial buildings, yet even from here the installation looked temporary.

Farther to the west, on the other side of the bay, Leeward Point Field served as Gitmo's airfield, while on this side were eight separate detention areas, each within its own fenced and heavily guarded compound. Three were for high-security-risk prisoners, another three for medium risk, one for minimum risk, and the eighth, Camp Echo, outside the main detention area, was used for low-risk inmates selected for hearings before a military tribunal. These were the prisoners who would be the first to be released and returned to their home countries.

He lowered his binoculars and raised his watch. It was 2:18 A.M. He held his breath and cocked his head to listen for a noise, any noise that might indicate their presence was known. U.S. Navy and Coast Guard fast-attack boats patrolled these waters to prevent escapes from the base by sea. But the only sounds were the small waves sighing ashore.

In twenty-two minutes a diversion would begin five kilometers away at the northeast perimeter. They had to be in place before it began. It was the only way in which they had even the slightest chance of reaching Echo. A Cuban Frontier Brigade combat unit would make one of its routine probes on base defenses. This evening the attack would be more intense than usual, and would last much longer than normal, drawing the Americans to the opposite side of the base from Camp Delta, where the hills rose steeply behind the outer fence.

Returning the binoculars to a zippered pocket in his camos, he unslung his carbine, and without a word, headed north through the scrub brush, keeping the no-man's zone fifty meters to the left. His three men fell in silently behind him.

As they approached the first guard tower, he motioned for his people to drop to the ground. They would have to continue on their bellies. Although it was the middle of the night, the U.S. Army troops here had a fearsome reputation. This place wasn't another Abu Ghraib, but not one freedom fighter or mujahideen had ever escaped. Nor did he want to run into a Cuban patrol. He took great care to make no noise, and to keep his head down until they were twenty meters past the tower, and even then he motioned for his brothers to keep low and move slow.

They had come to rescue five prisoners, not become prisoners themselves.

Several minutes later they came to a spot directly opposite the second guard tower. They were on a slight rise here, the terrain dipping down to the no-man's zone and a tall fence, before angling sharply upward to the Camp Delta bluff and inner security fences. But there was considerably more scrub brush and sea oats, providing them decent cover.

Halille, whose real name was Sharif al-Habib, raised a hand for his men to halt and drop to the ground. He checked his watch again. It was 2:37 A.M. He looked back at the others and nodded. They had reached their first objective with three minutes to spare. So far there had been no signs that their presence had been detected. The Cuban fishing boat, Nueva Cruz, that had dropped them off five kilometers southeast of the bay had not been challenged by the U.S. Coast Guard that patrolled these waters, for the simple reason that the boat was only one of a fleet of a dozen similar commercial fishermen that worked close inshore every night. In reality, the Coast Guard, like the soldiers manning the towers, and the military policemen who kept watch over the eight individual detention camps within Delta, looked inward. They were guarding against prisoners breaking out, not mujahideen breaking in.

Al-Habib took a small tripod out of a pocket, opened its legs, and attached his M8 to the base shoe. He took a prone position, and adjusted his sightline until he picked up the silhouette of the lone guard on the tower sixty meters away in his scope. His heart hammered in his chest, and all the spit had dried up in his mouth. They had gotten to this point because of good intelligence: They knew the Coast Guard patrol routes and times, they knew when the Frontier Brigade guards on the beach would be at the northern leg of their patrol, and six months ago they had been given a detailed topographic map of the U.S. facility, as well as the surrounding area on either side of the winding bay. From the maps they had spotted a weakness in Camp Delta's perimeter. A way in, and a way back out.

Now the mission depended on how accurate al-Habib's aim was.

"There is a possibility of failure at every step of your journey, Sharif," Osama bin Laden had warned him six months ago on the Pakistani side of the mountains outside Drosh. "I do not want you or the others to die for the cause yet. This is very important."

"Insh'allah," al-Habib had replied. He had been fighting Jews for more than twenty years, since he was a boy on the West Bank. He'd only been six the first time he went with his brothers to throw stones at Israeli APCs in Nablus. Now his brothers were dead, his father was gone, and he knew of no Palestinian who hadn't lost family members. He was not afraid of dying.

"Yes, God willing, but it is the hearts and minds of men who do His work," bin Laden said gently. He nodded and smiled with such incredible warmth and sadness that all the air seemed to go out of the cave. "Your heart, Sharif. Your mind."

Al-Habib had felt love washing through his body. It was, he remembered now, as if God's own hand had caressed his heart. "I won't let you down."

"It's not for me, Sharif," bin Laden said. He took al-Habib by the arm and they went outside into the cool mountain evening. They had the ephemeris of every Western spy satellite. None were in position overhead at this moment. "Your struggle is for the *jihad*. For our people. For Allah."

Bin Laden was a legend among Islamic militants everywhere because of his service in Afghanistan. He had brought only his construction equipment, his money, and his brilliance up against the might of the entire Russian army. And he had won. By doing so he'd inspired an entire generation of mujahideen to take up the fight; to be bold, to have initiative, and best of all, to have heart. If you will believe in God, He will believe in you. And al-Habib truly believed in God, in the struggle, and most of all, in bin Laden.

Sixty meters away, the tower guard disappeared. Al-Habib's heart lurched, and he looked up from the scope. Everything hinged on taking the guard down without raising an alarm, so that they could approach the fence where a drainage tunnel was located, cut through the screen, climb the bluff up to the camp, take out the two guards outside Echo, retrieve the five prisoners waiting for them, and then make their way back to the *Nueva Cruz*.

"*Men fadlak*," he whispered under his breath. *Please*. The diversion would begin at any moment. He could feel the tension of his men behind him.

A zephyr of a breeze caressed his cheek, bringing with it the hint of soft music playing from a great distance. A radio perhaps. He leaned forward into the sniper scope, steadying his aim so that the backlit reticle was centered on the tower's west observation port.

"This mission is important, Sharif," bin Laden had said. "The brothers you will rescue have an inestimable value. Do you understand?"

"We will not fail."

A mock-up of a portion of Camp Delta had been built in the desert outside Damascus where al-Habib and his people had trained. It had been cleverly constructed in disconnected sections so that the satellites would see this installation as nothing more than another base for Islamic militants. Such places were common in Syria. Bin Laden had come to the camp at great personal risk to speak to al-Habib before he left for Cuba. It had been such a huge honor that al-Habib's stature among the Syrians had immediately risen to astronomical heights.

"I do not want you to needlessly sacrifice your life for this mission, but the brothers you will rescue are even more important than you. You must free them and bring them back here unharmed."

It was night and they stood beneath an awning to conceal them from an American Keyhole satellite. Bin Laden was a full head taller than al-Habib, but he had to use the battered Kalashnikov rifle he'd carried since Afghanistan as a cane. Their eyes met and al-Habib was struck by three things: the man's patience, his great intellect, and a sadness that lay heavy around him, as if he were carrying the weight of the world on his shoulders.

"What if we run into resistance, Imam?" al-Habib asked respectfully. During the last three months of their training they'd all been struck by how fragile a mission this was. So many things could go wrong.

Bin Laden laid a gentle hand on al-Habib's shoulder. "If it becomes clear that you will not succeed, you must kill them. Under no circumstances must they fall back into American hands."

If the prisoners were so important, al-Habib wanted to know, why would they be held in the minimum-security Camp Echo? But he didn't ask the question. There were some things better left unsaid. Now, he wondered if he'd been wise, or if he'd simply been dazzled by bin Laden's presence.

The guard came into sight. Al-Habib's gut instantly tightened. He thumbed the safety selector lever to the off, single-fire position, and with his free hand, motioned for his people to make ready. It was time now. Any second—

A bright flash blossomed in the hills several kilometers to the north, directly behind the base. Before the sharp boom of the explosion arrived, the tower guard started to turn toward the light, his head in profile at the exact moment al-Habib squeezed off one shot.

With a muzzle velocity in excess of 2,850 feet per second, the 5.56-by-45mm NATO round covered the sixty meters in less than one second, the noise from the supersonic round all but lost in the confusion. The guard's head was shoved violently forward, al-Habib could see the impact of the bullet before the American was down.

The sound of the initial flash-bang mortar shell rolled across the base, followed immediately by a lot of small-arms fire, all concentrated to the northeast.

A siren sounded somewhere inland to the west, probably at base head-quarters, and lights started coming on all over the place.

Al-Habib looked up from the scope and held his breath. The next part was crucial if their mission had any hope of succeeding. The diversion had to temporarily lead the American defenses away from this end of the base. The window did not have to be a big one, because Camp Echo was less than two hundred meters from this spot. But they needed at least seven minutes to get in, free the five prisoners, and get back out.

Another flash-bang mortar round went off in the distance, and the small-arms fire intensified, mostly Kalashnikovs, but al-Habib could hear machine-gun fire, possibly the U.S.-made M60s that the Cuban military used.

Nothing moved in the tower, nor had the local alarm sounded, which meant that the guard had gone down without hitting the Panic button. No one was coming to the rescue. Yet.

Al-Habib detached his weapon from its tripod and, keeping low, scram-bled down the shallow slope to the two-meter-wide drainage ditch that paralleled the fence. An oval, corrugated metal drainage pipe, just wide enough for one man at a time to enter, crossed beneath the fence to a sim-ilar drainage ditch on the inside of the camp. The opening was covered by a thick metal grate.

He dropped to one knee and trained his scope on the nearest tower one hundred meters to the north as Abu Bukhari slung his weapon and started on the grate with bolt cutters.

The distant tower guard was gone, and when he raised his scope, he could see no activity on the bluff.

In less than thirty seconds Bukhari had the grate off, and without a word climbed into the twenty-meter-long tunnel and disappeared in the darkness. Ibin Kamal and Omar Sufyan, good West Bank boys, followed, leaving al-Habib alone for just a moment in the middle of a mission for which all of his self-confidence had disappeared. Once they were inside the perimeter, the Americans would shoot to kill.

Al-Habib touched the fingers of his left hand to his chest to feel for the one-kilo block of Semtex plastic explosive taped to his body. It had been his idea. Bin Laden didn't want any of the prisoners they'd come to rescue to be recaptured. Neither would he or his men be taken alive. For just an instant he had a vision of his father's tear-stained face, and he shook his head.

What is writ by the hand of God cannot be put asunder by the mere will of man.

The *jihad* was right and just. "Writ by the hand of God," al-Habib mumbled. "No question."

He ducked into the tunnel and crawled on his hands and knees to the other side, reaching the opening just as Sufyan was pulling himself out. He didn't suffer from claustrophobia, nevertheless he was glad to be back out in the open air, even though he was getting the increasingly uncomfortable feeling that he had come to the end of his life.

The action to the north was heating up as American forces began returning fire. There would be nothing in Cuban or U.S. newspapers about the routine probe, but a U.S. military report would mention the incident, the greater-than-usual quantity of ordinance expended, and the fact that no casualties were sustained. Nothing would be mentioned about the prison break, or the casualties here.

The four of them crossed the no-man's zone and started up the steep slope, clawing at the loose sand and crumbling rock, trying to hurry as fast as they could while making the minimum of noise.

At the crest of the bluff, they held up. Camp Delta, behind its own razor-wire-topped fence, consisted of several dozen concrete block detention units, each with its own inner fence and security station manned by MPs.

Kamal pointed two fingers at his own eyes and then pointed them in the direction of a low, concrete block building just outside the main detention area, which housed Camp Echo.

Al-Habib rose up over the edge for just a moment and immediately spotted two American Military Police guards outside the tall, razor-wire-topped fence that surrounded the building. They'd stepped around from the guard shack, their weapons slung over their shoulders, and were facing north toward the noise and flashes of the Cuban probe.

No other activity was in sight. No movement, no other soldiers. The Camp Delta inner perimeter fence was across a dirt road and a barren field of low brown grass and gravel.

Al-Habib motioned that he would take out the MP to the left, and for Sufyan to take the other.

"Let it begin now," al-Habib told himself. "Let my hand be steady and my heart be strong." He nodded. "*Insh'allah*," he whispered.

"*Insh'allah*," Sufyan replied.

They both rose at the same moment. Al-Habib centered his reticle on the back of the guard's head and squeezed off his shot at almost the exact moment as Sufyan's. Both American MPs collapsed to the ground.

A tall, nicely proportioned, young black woman stepped out of her room in Gitmo's BOQ near base headquarters and padded on bare feet down the short corridor and outside to an awning-covered patio used as a smoking area. She was dressed only in an brief bra and panties, the white material almost fluorescing against her dark skin. The sounds of the attack had awakened her, and although she wasn't particularly concerned for the moment, she was curious. The big siren in front of Gitmo's HQ was blaring, and spotlights along the northeastern perimeter were trained on the hills behind the base. She walked to the edge of the patio to get a better look, but all she could make out from here was an occasional flash in the distance, and the sharp sounds of assault rifles and perhaps a machine gun.

She'd been down here on special assignment for the CIA for ten days now, and this was the third Cuban probe on their defenses. But this morning the firing seemed more intense than it had the other times.

She flinched when another mortar round landed with a big flash of light somewhere in the hills behind the base, and she got the notion that the Cubans weren't shooting at us, they were just making a lot of noise for some reason.

To draw our defenses away. From what?

"What the hell are you doing out there?" someone called to her from the door of the BOQ.

Gloria Ibenez glanced back and smiled. "Can't sleep with all this racket." Her eyes were wide and dark, and her black hair fell in cascades around her high cheeks, full lips, and narrow, finely sculpted nose. She was a beautiful thirty-two-year-old Cuban-born woman, and she turned heads whenever she walked into a room.

"Come on, Ibenez, put some clothes on before you start a riot," her partner, CIA field officer Robert Talarico, said. He was bare-chested, but he'd pulled on a pair of jeans. He came out to the patio where she stood, and offered her a cigarette.

She shook her head as another flash-bang rolled across the base, followed by a fresh crackle of small-arms fire.

"It's a big one tonight," Talarico said. His father had been a tunnel rat in 'Nam, and like his father he was short, slightly built, and moved in tiny swift steps like a bird. He was two years older than Ibenez, but she was the senior partner, a fact he did not resent. He had a lot of respect for her tradecraft and her intelligence.

Gloria turned and stared toward the distant firefight as a pair of APCs roared up Main Street and headed northeast in a big hurry. "Too big, maybe."

"They've hit us before. Nobody gets hurt, they're just letting us know that we're pissing them off by being here. No big deal."

"This time's different," Gloria said. "It's already lasted longer than before. And it's more intense. Could be a diversion."

Talarico straightened up. "Okay, you've got my attention. This maybe has something to do with us?" He gave her a sidelong glance. "With you specifically?"

"Probably not."

Gloria's father, Air Force General Ernesto Marti, who'd been Castro's chief of air operations, had defected to the United States when Gloria was thirteen. Pretending that he was experiencing engine trouble, he'd landed his Cessna 182 in downtown Havana on the Avenida San Antonio Chiquito in front of the Necrópolis de Colón, where his wife was waiting with their only child. Before anyone could do a thing, he'd taken off and headed northeast toward Key West. Who was going to question the chief of air operations?

But the airplane had developed an actual engine problem, and they'd crashed five miles short of the island. Gloria's father pulled her out of the wreckage, but she could never forget the look of helpless surprise on her mother's face as the airplane sank just outside the reef in five hundred feet of water.

General Marti went to work as a special adviser on Cuban affairs to the CIA, and after law school and a brief stint in the Navy's JAG, Gloria had followed in his footsteps. They were both very high on the Cuban Intelligence Services most wanted list.

"What time is it?" Gloria asked.

Talarico checked his watch. "Quarter to three."

Gloria and Talarico worked in the Special Projects Division for the deputy director of operations. For the most part their recent assignments had not involved the use of legends—cover stories. Most recently they'd been in Afghanistan, interrogating every peasant and mujahideen they could get their hands on, to come up with some hint of where bin Laden might be holed up. Last week they'd been assigned to Gitmo to see what information they could get from the Afghani and Iraqi prisoners. But it had turned into a dicey operation. The guys working for naval intelligence, which handled most of the interrogations, resented the CIA sticking its nose into their territory, and Amnesty International had been sniffing around lately, looking for another Abu Ghraib scandal.

And now these Cuban probes on Gitmo's defenses. The last two times they'd hit the perimeter just off the beach below Delta. But this morning the attack was to the north.

Well *away* from the detention camp. At three o'clock in the morning. When nearly everyone was supposed to be sleeping.

Another flash of light lit up the night sky to the north, followed several seconds later by an impressive boom.

"Get dressed," Gloria said. "We're going to take a ride." She turned and headed back to the BOQ, Talarico right on her heels.

"Where?"

"Delta."

"You think it's a prison break?"

Gloria looked at him, and shrugged. "I don't like coincidences," she told him. "The Cubans are up to something."

"That'd mean they were cooperating with al-Quaida," Talarico said.

"Now there's a thought," Gloria replied at the door to her room. "But we *are* the common enemy."

"Ain't it the truth."

"Bring your pistol."

Kamal and Sufyan dragged the bodies of the two MPs out of sight in a shallow depression in the sand and gravel next to the road, while Bukhari figured out the control that released the gate lock. Al-Habib stood in the shadow cast by the guard shack, his attention toward the Delta outer fence about thirty meters away, every sense alert for any sign that their incursion had been detected.

But there was no movement, no sirens, no guards coming across on the run. All the noise and activity was directed to the perimeter fence five klicks to the north.

"No keys," Bukhari whispered urgently.

"What about the gate?"

"It's electric, I found the switch."

"Do it," al-Habib whispered. So far as they knew, opening the gate at this hour of the morning would not trigger an automatic alarm. But no intelligence report was ever one hundred percent certain.

A moment later the gate lock buzzed, and the three bolts snapped with an audible *pop*.

Al-Habib's hand tensed on his weapon, and he held his breath, once again listening for any indication that someone was coming for them. His nerves were jumping all over the place. But there was nothing. Their luck was holding, and for the first time since they'd come ashore he was beginning to feel that they might pull this off.

He motioned for Bukhari to come with him. Kamal and Sufyan would remain outside to cover their backs.

Al-Habib reached the steel door to the low concrete block building and stepped away for Bukhari to mold a one-hundred-gram block of Semtex around the door lock. A heavy wire mesh covered the narrow window beside the door. Someone in an orange shirt was there. Al-Habib urgently motioned for him to get back.

An air-conditioning unit at the rear of the building noisily kicked on at the same moment Bukhari inserted a slender pencil fuse into the gray putty material and cracked the acid chamber.

He and al-Habib moved to either side and turned their backs to the door. Two seconds later, the Semtex blew with a muffled crack, the sound all but lost to the noise of the air conditioner. The smoldering lock mechanism and handle landed in the dirt three meters away.

Bukhari pulled the door open, and al-Habib, his rifle up, safety off, his finger alongside the trigger guard, rolled inside, sweeping his M8 left to right.

There were five prisoners dressed for bed in orange suits in the corner farthest from the door, but no American guards.

"Musafa Bakr," al-Habib called softly.

A slightly built man with a pencil-thin mustache came forward with a heavy limp. "*Aywa*," he said. *Yes.* The other four were right behind him.

"Are you hurt?" al-Habib asked, concerned that they would have to carry him down the bluff to the fence and then to the beach. It would seriously slow them down.

"Not badly enough to cause a hindrance," ex-Iranian Navy Commander Bakr said.

"What happened—"

"We can talk later. Do you have a weapon for me?" He held out a hand.

It wasn't what al-Habib expected, though he could hardly deny the request. He took his 9mm Steyr GB pistol from a zippered pocket and gave it to the man. "Our luck is holding so far, but it won't last," he said.

Outside, al-Habib, Bukhari, and the five prisoners hurried across to the open gate. Kamal and Sufyan waited in the shadows, their attention directed toward the main entrance to Camp Delta.

"Anything?" al-Habib asked.

"Nothing," Sufyan replied.

They shut and relocked the gate, and, al-Habib in the lead, started across the field toward the edge of the bluff. The night sky to the north was lit by the occasional flash of a mortar round. The small-arms fire had not slackened, but it would not last much longer. And once the attack was over, someone might start to wonder what was going on. If a check was made of the guard posts, the game would be up.

They had to be down on the beach before that happened if they were going to have any chance of getting away.

Al-Habib glanced back at Bakr right behind him. If something did go wrong, and the prisoners had to be killed, doing so would be more difficult because one of them was armed.

A military vehicle crested the road that came up from the main part of the base, and headed directly toward Camp Delta, the headlights briefly sweeping across the field where al-Habib and the others crouched.

"*Yalla!*" al-Habib whispered, his heart in his throat. *Let's go!*

.   .   .

"What the hell is that?" Talarico demanded urgently. They had just reached the top of the hill and were heading toward Camp Delta's main gate. Gloria was behind the wheel of a Humvee from the base motor pool.

"What was what?" Gloria turned to him. He was pointing off toward the edge of the hill that plunged down to sea level.

"Four or five people, maybe more," he said. "Black outfits, but at least three were wearing orange." There was the hint of amazement in his voice. "You were right, it's a prison break."

"Goddammit to hell," Gloria said. She hauled the all-terrain vehicle off the road in the direction Talarico had pointed, and pulled up short, in a hail of dust and loose rocks. Nothing showed up in the headlights except for the open field that dropped off about thirty meters away. "Are you sure, Bob?"

Talarico grabbed a flashlight off its bracket on the hump and jumped out of the vehicle. "I saw something out there," he called back through the open door. He directed the narrow beam across the field, on either side of the swath cast by the Humvee's headlights, then slowly followed it back toward the Camp Echo facility.

"There!" he shouted. He pulled out his pistol and headed in a dead run around the front of the Humvee back to the ditch beside the road directly in front of Echo, where two figures lay facedown.

Gloria jumped out of the Humvee and yanked the walkie-talkie from her belt clip with one hand, and her 0.45in. ACP MK 23 (SOCOM) pistol from the quick-draw holster at the small of her back, her attention directed across the field.

"They're dead!" Talarico shouted.

Gloria glanced at him. He was hunched over the two bodies. "Our guys?"

"MPs," Talarico said, straightening up. "I'm guessing Echo guards. They've been shot in the head."

Gloria motioned toward the drop-off across the field and she headed out. She keyed the walkie-talkie. "TAC One, TAC One, this is a Red Release. I repeat, a Red Release, looks like from Echo. They're already over the hill."

Talarico had started after her, keeping a few meters to the left. He'd switched off the flashlight.

"Who's on this channel?" the on-duty Security Ops officer came back. He sounded harried with all that was happening along the northeastern perimeter.

"Ibenez. I'm with Talarico. We're on your special ops duty roster," she radioed back. The Cubans probably monitored all the non-secure channels, but it would take time for someone to figure out she was on their hit list. "You have two friendlies down outside Echo right now. About two minutes ago we spotted two or more figures in black, going over the crest of the hill to the east, with three or more guys in orange pj's. Copy?"

"Roger, copy that," the OD radioed back. "What's your ten-twenty?"

"We're in pursuit about twenty-five meters out," Gloria responded. "Standby one." She motioned for Talarico to hold up just before the edge of the drop-off. She didn't want either of them to get shot by a rear guard waiting for them to show themselves.

She dropped to her hands and knees and crawled the rest of the way to the edge, where she got on her belly. For a second or two she couldn't see any movement. A guard tower about sixty or seventy meters directly below was dark, as were the towers to the north, and the one to the south just above the beach.

But then she spotted several figures, maybe half of them in black, and the other half in orange, scurrying across the no-man's zone where they disappeared one at a time into a tunnel under the fence. She keyed the walkie-talkie.

"TAC One, I count at least four POWs and four bad guys just going through a tunnel under the east perimeter fence, a few hundred meters off the beach."

"The guy in the tower's got to be asleep," Talarico said.

"Or dead," Gloria replied. She spotted a movement on the other side of the fence, and she keyed her walkie-talkie. "TAC One, they're out."

"Roger that," the OD replied. He sounded disgusted. "It's not our problem now. If they reach the beach the Coasties will be on them. I have people coming your way. Stand by."

"Bullshit," Gloria radioed.

"They're in Cuba!" the OD came back. "We can't do diddly."

Gloria jumped to her feet and started down the steep slope, Talarico right behind her. "We're going after them," she radioed. "Tell your tower guards we're on our way. And warm up a chopper, we might need a quick extraction."

"The beach will be crawling with Frontier Brigade—"

"Negative. I'm betting that they're all on the northeast perimeter."

Gloria clipped the walkie-talkie to her belt, and at the bottom she and Talarico crossed the no-man's zone to the drainage culvert. She motioned for him to hold up, as she cautiously peered into the tunnel. It was possible that the POWs and whoever had sprung them knew they were being pursued, and had stationed someone at the other end.

"You sure we want to do this?" Talarico whispered urgently.

The tunnel was empty. Gloria could see a circle of dim light on the other side. She looked up at her partner. "Why'd they go through the trouble to stage a jail break from Echo when most of those guys are scheduled for release anyway? Unless someone didn't want us to talk to them."

He immediately saw her point. "What are we waiting for?"

Gloria nodded. He was a good man; smart, talented, and she had a lot of respect for him. He had a couple of kids and a successful marriage, which was something of a rarity for a field officer. She envied his wife. She ducked into the tunnel and scurried through to the other side, holding up once again at the opening to make sure she wasn't leading them into an ambush.

The night on this side of the base was quiet. During a momentary lull in the small-arms fire to the north, Gloria was certain she heard something out ahead to the south; someone running through loose gravel.

Talarico was at her shoulder. He'd heard it too. "They're heading for the beach."

Gloria grabbed the walkie-talkie and called the OD. "TAC One, this is Ibenez. They're trying for the beach. We're going after them, but you'd better give the Coast Guard the heads-up."

"Stand down, Ibenez, that's an order direct from Commander Weiss. He's en route your position."

"Negative, negative," Gloria radioed back. "I want a chopper standing by, ASAP." She switched off the radio, crawled out of the tunnel, and headed south along the perimeter fence, keeping her pistol at her side, the muzzle pointed slightly away from her leg.

The timing of the breakout bothered her almost as much as the professionalism. They'd known the exact route to Camp Echo, which meant there had to be prisoners they wanted out before the CIA could get to them. It was driving her nuts to think that not only were the Cubans cooperating with al-Quaida, but that there might be someone inside Gitmo on the payroll as well.

Talarico fanned out to the left, slightly behind her, his pistol in hand.

They moved quickly, and as noiselessly as possible, stopping every few dozen meters to listen.

One hundred meters from the drainage tunnel, Gloria spotted the silhouettes of a small group of figures moving south, at the same moment one of them, dressed in black, turned around. She pulled up short and motioned for Talarico to stop.

For several seconds the main body of the escaping prisoners continued toward the beach, while the one figure remained where he stood, thirty or forty meters out. He dropped to one knee and raised something in front of him.

All of a sudden Gloria realized that the son of a bitch was armed and was about to shoot at them. "Down!" she shouted to her partner.

The black-clad figure opened fire with what sounded to Gloria like a small-caliber suppressed carbine of some sort.

She squatted to a shooter's stance, brought her pistol up, thumbed the safety catch to the off position, and started firing.

The range was all but impossible under the conditions, but the noise from her unsilenced pistol was impressive. A lot of people on both sides of the fence had just been put on notice that the battle had shifted here from the northeastern perimeter.

Talarico opened fire, as several other black-clad figures turned and returned fire.

She dropped to the ground, and continued firing, until her weapon went dry. Talarico suddenly cried out and went down. But there was no time to help him. This was her fault, because she had been stupid; she hadn't counted on them being so heavily armed. She ejected the spent magazine, pulled the spare from her back pocket, and rammed it home. The returning fire was starting to concentrate on her now, rock chips flying all over the place from near misses.

She rolled left as she continued to fire.

A helicopter swooped down from the crest of the Camp Delta hill with a deep-throated clatter of its rotors, its spotlight cutting a broad swath down the slope, across the fence, and along the no-man's zone. Gloria and Talarico were briefly illuminated, but then the knot of black-clad shooters and prisoners dressed in orange was lit like day.

Spotlights in the guard towers all along the perimeter fence came on and a lot of sirens started blaring up and down the line.

The Boeing MH-6J chopper peeled off to the east, firing a spray of 7.62mm rounds from both of its miniguns, bracketing the escaping prisoners.

At least one of them raised his weapon and fired at the helicopter, but the rest of them concentrated their fire on Gloria.

Something blunt hit her hard, like a baseball bat, in the left hip, and her leg went instantly numb. She squeezed off two more shots, and one of the POWs in orange went down.

The chopper was coming around for a second pass when two of the black-clad figures suddenly turned and started shooting the POWs.

Gloria propped herself up with her good leg so she could get a better look. It made no sense that they would kill one another.

The helicopter pulled up short in a hover twenty or thirty meters away, its spotlight illuminating the scene like day. All of the POWs were down. One of the black-clad figures looked up, shook his fist at the chopper, and suddenly disappeared in a bright flash-bang, the noise hammering off the side of the hill.

Gloria's mouth dropped open. He'd killed the POWs he'd come to rescue, rather than let them be recaptured, and then had committed suicide.

She pulled out her walkie-talkie to warn the chopper pilot to stay back, when the other three black-clad figures disappeared like the first in flash-bangs, blowing themselves up.

Moments later the chopper came back and set down hard ten meters from where Gloria was up on one knee. Two armed men in Marine Corps BDUs sitting in the starboard doorway jumped out and raced back to her.

"We're going to have company real soon, ma'am," one of them said, hauling Gloria to her feet. His sewn name tag read JONES.

The other marine had dropped beside Talarico, who lay facedown in the sand. He looked up and shook his head.

"Okay, we're outta here—now," Jones said urgently.

"We're not leaving Bob," Gloria said, pulling away.

"We've got a Frontier Brigade patrol just about on top of us, and we're not allowed to shoot at them—"

"We're not leaving my partner!" Gloria shouted.

Jones slung his weapon, hustled Gloria over to where Talarico lay, and between him and his partner dragged the body back to the chopper. They stuffed it unceremoniously inside, then helped Gloria up onto the sill.

The instant the marines were aboard, the chopper pilot hauled the machine airborne and immediately peeled to the west, just clearing the razor wire atop the perimeter fence, before climbing steeply to the crest of the Delta hill.

Gloria held tightly to Talarico's lifeless body, his half-open eyes staring up at her, his face unnaturally white. She had killed him as surely as if she had shot him herself. Her heart was sick just thinking what she would have to tell his wife. It was a part of the business they were in; some of her friends had bought it in Afghanistan and Iraq. And her own husband had been tortured to death in a Cuban Intelligence Service prison outside Havana. She knew about loss.

But this time she had been the one in charge; this time the responsibility had rested on her shoulders.

PART
ONE

ONE

☐

CABIMAS, VENEZUELA

No one looked twice at the Russian sea captain as he got out of his cab in front of the Cabimas Hotel Internacional, paid the fare, and headed toward the lobby. Nor did any of the smartly uniformed bellmen stationed at the front doors offer to help with his battered leather satchel and matching garment bag. He smiled inwardly. He was used to such treatment, he didn't have the look of a successful man. And this was a busy town of important oil executives, heavy hitters, big money.

He had the typical broad shoulders and barrel chest of a Great Russian, but his face was surprisingly round, with a delicate nose and soft, almost dreamy eyes under short dark hair that made him look like a poet-soldier. He carried his five-feet-ten like a man long accustomed to being at sea; on the balls of his feet, as if he were constantly working to keep a perfect balance.

The captain entered the deluxe hotel, and crossed the busy lobby to stand in line at the registration desk. He'd never stayed here before, but the woman at GAC-Vensport had booked a suite for him. Nothing but first class for the new captain of the Panamax oil tanker *Apurto Devlán*. In the morning he would be helicoptered out to his ship, currently loading crude, but this evening he would live in the lap of luxury and enjoy it.

When it was the captain's turn, one of the clerks, a haughty young man in a crisply tailored blue blazer, motioned him up to the desk. "Do you have reservations?"

"Yes," the captain said. He smiled faintly. Aboard his crude carrier he would be the undisputed lord and master, but the moment he stepped ashore and interacted with civilians he became a nobody. His wife, Tania, back in St. Petersburg, bought him expensive clothes in Helsinki and Paris, but on him even designer labels looked shabby.

He handed over his Russian passport, which identified him as Grigoriy Ivanovich Slavin.

The clerk handled the passport as if he thought his hands would get dirty. He glanced at the photograph and looked up at Slavin. All of a sudden something apparently dawned on him, because his face fell. He laid the passport down and quickly typed something into his computer. He looked up again, a broad smile plastered across his stricken features. "Captain Slavin, we were not expecting you so early."

"Well, I'm here," Slavin said. "Is my room ready, or will I have to wait?"

"Of course not, sir. Your *suite* is at your immediate disposal." The clerk laid a registration card on the counter and handed Slavin a pen. "If you will sign in, sir, I'll have your bags taken up and personally escort you."

"Not necessary," Slavin said curtly. He signed the card and laid the pen on the counter. He preferred being a nobody ashore, because he didn't like being fawned over. Aboard ship he gave orders and his officers and crew followed them. No questions, no bargaining, no diplomacy. It was the discipline he enjoyed.

The clerk handed back his passport, and motioned for a young, handsome bellman, who scurried over from the bell station near the front doors. The clerk passed him a plastic key card. "Take *Capitano* Slavin's bags to the Bolívar Suite."

"It's not necessary," Slavin growled.

The clerk was suddenly nervous. "Sir, it's hotel policy for all VIP guests. GAC-Vensport expects no less from us." His rigid smile broadened. The company was responsible for all of Venezuela's oil shipping, which was the major source of the nation's income. It was big.

Slavin remembered one of the old Russian proverbs his *babushka* used to use when the family was poor. *We're all related, the same sun dries our rags.* He nodded. "*Da.*"

The clerk gave him a relieved look and he came around from behind the counter as the bellman disappeared with Slavin's bags. "Just this way, sir," he said, and he escorted the captain across the soaring atrium lobby to a bank of elevators.

"A helicopter is coming for me at oh-eight-hundred."

"Yes, sir, we'll let you know when it's twenty minutes out," the clerk said. The hotel provided helicopter service with Maracaibo's La Chinita

Airport eight minutes away, and to the ships loading at fueling platforms out in the lake.

Slavin was impressed despite himself. In the Russian navy such perks were reserved for flag officers, and during his eleven-year career in the merchant marine he'd never had the privilege of such treatment. At 275 meters on the waterline with a beam of nearly forty-four meters, his new command, the *Apurto Devlán*, was the largest crude carrier that could transit the Panama Canal, and the largest and most important vessel he'd ever been given responsibility for. He'd transited the canal ten times before aboard smaller ships, three times as skipper of container vessels, but being helicoptered out to a ship of his own would be a first. He decided that he would try to loosen up and savor the moment. It was the other thing Tania had tried to change in him; he didn't know how to relax.

When they reached the top floor, the clerk held the elevator door for Slavin, and then led the way to the suite at the end of the plushly carpeted corridor, where he opened the door. "I believe that you will find these rooms to your liking, Captain."

Slavin suppressed a grin. "This will do," he said.

The suite's sitting room was very large, furnished luxuriously with long leather couches, massive chairs, and dining-table-sized coffee tables facing an electronic media complex that featured a huge plasma television hanging on the richly paneled wall. The opposite side of the room was equipped with a wet bar, a dining area for eight, and a home office corner. Recessed lighting softly illuminated the artwork on the walls and on display tables here and there. A sweeping staircase led upstairs.

The clerk went across the room, touched a button, and heavy drapes that covered the entire rear wall opened, revealing a stunning view of Lake Maracaibo through floor-to-ceiling windows. "At night when an electrical storm crosses the lake, it's quite spectacular from this vantage point," he said breezily.

"What's upstairs?"

"The master bedroom, his and hers bathrooms and dressing rooms, an exercise area, a balcony, and, of course, a Jacuzzi."

The bellman arrived with Slavin's bags. "Shall I unpack for you, sir?" he asked.

"No need, I'm only staying the night. Put them on the bed."

"Very well, sir," the bellman said, and he took the bags upstairs.

The clerk crossed the room to the wet bar, where a bottle of Dom Pérignon was cooling in a bucket of ice. He opened the champagne, poured a glass, and brought it to Slavin. "Compliments of the hotel, Captain," he said.

The wine was sour to Slavin's taste, but he said nothing. The clerk was watching him closely for a reaction. In the old days, to be caught reacting in the wrong way or doing something that was socially inept was to be *nekulturny*. He'd never forgotten his lessons in humility at the Frunze Military Academy, where on the first evening in the dining room he'd been taught the proper use of the linen napkin and numerous utensils.

Once a word is out of your mouth, his grandmother used to say, you can't swallow it again. He'd learned the hard way.

The bellman came downstairs. Slavin set his wineglass aside, and reached for his wallet, but the clerk shook his head. "That will not be necessary, sir. Vensport is taking care of everything."

"I didn't know," Slavin said to cover his mild embarrassment. Tomorrow would not come soon enough.

The clerk handed over the plastic card key. "I hope that you enjoy your brief stay with us, Captain. My name is Mr. Angarita. If there is anything that you need don't hesitate to call me."

"Thank you," Slavin said.

"Our La Terraza restaurant by the pool is first-class. Shall I make reservations for you?"

"I'll decide later."

"As you wish, sir."

When the clerk was gone, Slavin took his champagne back to the wet bar and emptied it into the small sink. He found a bottle of Stolichnaya and a glass, and poured a stiff measure of the Russian vodka. He knocked it back, poured another, and then, jamming the bottle in his coat pocket, headed upstairs while loosening his tie with one hand.

The master bedroom was just as grand as the sitting room, with a huge circular bed facing large floor-to-ceiling sliding-glass doors that opened to the balcony. It was midafternoon and the late-afternoon sun was low behind the hotel, casting a beautiful gold light across the lake. At this point the west shore was fifty kilometers away, lost in the mist, but the view was spectacular. The two-hundred-kilometer-long lake was studded with oil drilling platforms, waste gas burning in long, wind-driven jets of fire from many of them; broad loading platforms where tankers bound for refineries all over the world loaded Venezuelan sweet light crude; and the ships themselves, outbound for the Golfo de Venezuela and the open Caribbean, or inbound under the five-mile General Rafael Urdaneta high bridge at the neck of the lake to take on their cargoes.

"*Yob tvoyu mat*," Slavin swore softly. *Fuck your mother.* He raised a toast. Tania had computed that he had been at sea for twenty-one and a half of the twenty-four years they'd been married. She never complained, in part because the money was very good. But just lately she'd started to ask him about an early retirement. Not to quit the sea, rather she wanted to travel with him to some of the places he'd told her about, as civilians, as tourists, as lovers.

God help him, he did love it. And maybe he would do what she asked, retire before he turned fifty. But not to give up the sea, just to voyage differently. It was an intriguing thought.

He poured another drink and went into the whorehouse of a bathroom, where he found the Jacuzzi controls and started the jets.

Slavin was slightly drunk. Lying in the Jacuzzi, he'd finished the first bottle of vodka, and then, dripping wet, had padded downstairs to fetch a second bottle from the bar. That had been two hours ago, and that bottle was nearly empty. He was finally beginning to relax after the long air trip from Moscow to Paris with Tania, and from there across the Atlantic to Caracas, and finally the short hop up to Maracaibo.

Air travel was fast, relatively safe, and cheap these days, but no aluminum tube with wings, into which a couple hundred passengers were crammed like sardines for endless hours, could ever replace an oceangoing vessel in which a man had more room than even in his apartment ashore.

It was starting to get dark out on the lake. The waste gas flames, combined with the oil derricks and platform lights, and the lights on the ships, made a kaleidoscope of ever-changing colors and patterns that was comforting. Like watching waves coming ashore, or burning logs in a fireplace.

Someone came into the bathroom. Slavin saw the reflection in the window glass and turned.

For a moment he thought it was the idiot clerk again. A man of moderate height, dressed in a dark jacket and open-necked shirt, stood in the doorway, longish blond hair around his ears, with a round face and dark glasses hiding his eyes. The intruder wore latex surgical gloves, and it began to dawn on Slavin that something was very wrong.

"Who are you—?"

The man brought a small-caliber silenced pistol from where he'd concealed it behind his back, raised it, and fired one shot. Something like a hammer struck Slavin in his head, and a billion stars burst inside his brain.

TWO

□

CABIMAS HOTEL INTERNACIONAL

The assassin, Rupert Graham, stood for a long moment gazing wistfully out the tall windows at the light show on the lake. Soon he would be at sea again, where he belonged. The *Apurto Devlán* was in the last stages of her loading, ready for sailing in the morning, her crew missing only the captain. So far as he had been able to determine, none of them had ever sailed with Slavin before. The only trouble would come if there was a last-minute replacement who knew the Russian.

But he would deal with that problem if and when it arose.

Graham looked at Captain Slavin's body. The force of the .22 suppressed long rifle round had been enough to throw the man's head back against the side of the Jacuzzi, before the body slid underwater. Only the face, its sightless eyes staring at the ceiling, remained above the furiously bubbling surface. An angry red and black hole in the Russian's forehead, a few centimeters to the right of the nose, had bled very little. And there was no exit wound; the fragmentation round had broken up inside the skull, destroying a massive amount of brain tissue. Death had been nearly instantaneous.

It had been too easy, Graham thought with some regret. He laid his pistol on the toilet seat, removed his rubber gloves, and cocked an ear to listen. The suite was utterly quiet except for the noise of the Jacuzzi's pumps and the swirling water.

Walking on the balls of his feet, exactly as he'd watched the Russian doing it downstairs in the lobby, Graham approached the Jacuzzi and turned off the jets. He touched two fingers to the side of Slavin's neck, the water very warm, but, as he expected, there was no pulse. Nonetheless for a man in his profession it paid to be methodical. His life often depended on the care he took with his actions.

He had the entire evening to make his preparations, but he wanted to be finished in time to make a little test of his new persona by ordering room service. Captain Slavin had checked in this early afternoon, interacting with a desk clerk and a bellman, and later this evening he would interact with a room service waiter.

Continuity. A Russian checked in, a Russian ordered dinner, and a Russian checked out. The same Russian.

He took his pistol and gloves back into the bedroom where he stripped off all of his clothing, laying his things on the bed next to the Russian's leather satchel and garment bag. He was nearly two inches shorter than Slavin, but with the same general build. It had taken him two months to find a ship captain whom he could impersonate. And another two months studying the man's mannerisms and habits before he was certain he could fool everyone, except someone who'd sailed with the real Slavin before. And finally, the necessary strings had been pulled with GAC to have Slavin assigned to the right ship.

That had been the easy part for bin Laden. GAC, which was responsible for carrying all of Venezuela's oil around the world, maintained its international headquarters in Dubai, United Arab Emirates, and brothers in Dar al Islam did each other favors, no questions asked. It was the symmetry of the thing that Graham most admired.

Back in the bathroom, Graham grabbed hold of the Russian's elbows and heaved him up over the side and onto the tiled floor like a landed fish. It was difficult because the body was slippery, and out of the water it was more than eighty kilos of deadweight. He rolled the corpse over and dried it with a bath towel, making certain that it was leaking no fluids that could stain the carpeting downstairs in the sitting room.

He rolled it over again on its back, and grasping it under the armpits, dragged it out into the bedroom and then down the curving staircase, where he left it across from the dining table.

Slavin's right eye had rolled up into its socket, only the bloodshot white showing, while his other eye had turned inward, making it appear as if he was staring at the tip of his nose. No one looked dignified in death, at least not the ones Graham had assassinated, and he idly wondered how he would appear to his killer when the time came.

He'd checked into the hotel yesterday afternoon with two ripstop nylon sports bags. Last night he'd smuggled an aluminum footlocker into the hotel and up to his room, making absolutely certain that no one had seen him. He'd brought all three items with him to Slavin's room, taking the chance that someone might see him, in which case he would have had to kill them. But his luck had held. He'd used a universal key card to open the door, and again luck was with him. The Russian had not latched the security chain, nor had he been right there in the sitting room.

"You will need to depend upon a certain amount of Allah's good fortune," Osama bin Laden had told him eleven months ago in Karachi when they'd first hatched the canal mission.

Graham had met with bin Laden and four of the man's top advisers in the M. A. Jinnah building in the heart of downtown to work out the details. Afterwards, bin Laden had taken him aside for a private talk.

"They don't understand," bin Laden said. "Luck has played a very important role in what we've accomplished, what we will do together."

"Luck is what we make of it," Graham had said. As a submarine commander in the British navy he'd had a career blessed with plenty of luck because he'd been the best. But in his personal life the opposite had been true, right up to the time his wife had died of cancer while he was out on a ninety-day patrol beyond recall.

After that he'd had no use for luck. It was as if he were a cat that had used up eight of its lives, and was recklessly speeding toward its own final destruction. He no longer cared.

"And you've done well at it these last two and a half years, but you are not expendable," bin Laden had replied seriously. "Your life is mine. Do not forget it."

Graham smiled bitterly. His life was his own. Bin Laden and al-Quaida only provided him the means to hit back at the kinds of bastards who'd allowed Jillian to die alone and in pain.

He brought the aluminum footlocker across to the Russian's body and opened the combination lock. The lid came up stiffly because of its thick rubber hermetic seals. It wouldn't do for any odors to be released at the wrong time. Even a corpse-sniffing dog would smell nothing.

Graham hoisted Slavin's body with great effort and stuffed it facedown inside the footlocker. Only its head and torso fit. Its arms and legs from the knees down stuck out. Jamming a foot against the body's back, Graham pulled one of the arms backwards until the shoulder joint broke free of its ligaments with an audible pop, and suddenly it was loose and folded neatly inside the trunk over Slavin's neck. He did the same with the other arm. The Russian's hip joints were much stronger than his shoulders, and it took every bit of Graham's strength to dislocate them in such a fashion that they could be folded over the body, and the lid closed and locked.

When he was finished, he dragged the heavy footlocker across the room next to the entry hall table. In the morning he would check the case with the bellman for storage until he was scheduled to return in three weeks. It was his master's library, which he wouldn't need on this trip. Reference books, for the most part, all of them dreadfully heavy. He didn't think anyone would ask where it came from. He was a VIP.

He carefully examined the beige carpeting where he'd laid the body, and the carpeting up the stairs into the bedroom, for any signs of blood or other stains. But there was nothing.

He took the smaller of his two nylon bags into one of the twin bathrooms, where he laid out hair clippers, dark hair dye, soft brown contacts, and a makeup kit with the ingredients to thicken and darken his eyebrows, soften the lines in his face, and tone down his skin color several shades.

First he cut his hair so that it was the same length as the Russian's, and then worked in the hair dye, making sure that he didn't miss a spot. Slavin was forty-six, but he had no gray hair. Possibly he dyed it, but whatever the case, it made Graham's transformation all the easier if he didn't have to add gray to his coloring job.

The instructions on the hair-coloring kit required a forty-five-minute wait until the dye could be rinsed out and a conditioner applied. He used the time to flush the hair clippings down the toilet and make sure that the bathroom was devoid of any trace of what he'd done so far. Then he padded on bare feet downstairs where he turned on some music, poured a glass of Dom Pérignon—which was quite good, he thought—and went back upstairs where he stared out the windows at the lake until it was time.

When his hair was finished, he worked on his eyebrows and skin tone, put the contacts in his eyes, and got dressed in Slavin's clothes. He'd brought lift shoes with him, which he slipped into, giving him an extra two inches to match the Russian's height.

He found Slavin's passport, which he took into the bathroom where he compared his appearance in the mirror with that of the photo. No customs officer in the world would question his identity.

Finally, he transferred his two nylon bags and their contents into Slavin's luggage; it was a tight fit, but not impossible.

Downstairs, he poured another glass of champagne and then called room service. He hadn't eaten since breakfast, and maybe some blinis and caviar with iced vodka would make a nice start.

"*Poshol nakhuy.*" He was hungry.

LAGO DE MARACAIBO

Lake Maracaibo, which stretched nearly two hundred kilometers from the small farming town of San Antonio, Zulia, in the south to the large city of Maracaibo in the north, was studded with hundreds of oil derricks and loading platforms that stretched in many places across the entire one-hundred-kilometer width. Sixty percent of Venezuela's oil and natural gas was pumped from beneath the lake. Ships ranging in size from small crude carriers to the 275-meter Panamax tankers that were the largest ships able to transit the Panama Canal, and even some Very Large Crude Carriers capable of loading four times as much oil, arrived and departed the loading platforms and docks 24/7.

Rupert Graham, dressed in khaki trousers, a yellow Izod polo shirt, and a dark blue windbreaker with MASTER, APURTO DEVLÁN sewn over the left breast, followed a young bellman across the roof to the helipad where a Bell 230, its rotors slowly turning, was waiting to take him out to his ship. The morning was crisp and sunny, with a light breeze out of the east keeping the heavy gas and oil stench offshore.

Last night and this morning had gone smoothly, though the room service waiter had shot him an odd look when he'd given the man a generous cash tip. But he'd not been questioned about his heavy aluminum footlocker by the bellman, who'd come to collect it for storage earlier, or that large tip.

The real test, of course, would come once he stepped aboard the *Apurto Devlán* and began to interact with the crew.

The young, handsome bellman stuffed the two bags into the chopper's storage compartment aft of the open cabin door. Graham handed him a twenty-dollar bill and climbed into the helicopter.

"Thank you, sir," the bellman said, "but it is not necessary."

"*Da*," Graham replied gutturally. "It's only money."

The bellman gave him a very odd look, but Graham pulled the door closed, gave the helicopter pilot the thumbs-up, and put on his seat belt. Moments later the seven-passenger chopper lifted off and headed to the east, out over the lake.

The shipping lanes were busy this morning. Graham counted at least twelve tankers headed north toward the narrows out to the Golfo de Venezuela, and at least as many still docked at their loading platforms strung out as far as the eye could see. This place represented Venezuela's lifeblood, just as the Panama Canal represented the lifeblood of nearly half the planet.

He was the only passenger aboard the helicopter, and he closed his eyes for a moment to compose himself. He'd been tempted to get roaring drunk last night, like he'd done in the old days before he'd been kicked out of the Royal Navy. But he'd finished the bottle of Dom Pérignon and had left it at that. He was going to need his wits about him for the next few days, all of his wits.

But when it was over he would get drunk and stay drunk until the next mission. It was the only way he could live with his memories. If only she hadn't died, if only she'd been strong enough for him.

THREE

□

GUANTANAMO BAY

Nine pale green, ghostly figures emerged from the drainage pipe at tower two east, hesitated for a moment as if they were expecting an ambush, and then headed south. They kept to the brush above and parallel to the no-man's zone. Four of them were armed with what looked like Heckler & Koch carbines that the tower-mounted low-lux closed-circuit cameras picked up in reasonably good detail.

Lieutenant Commander T. Thomas Weiss looked up from the surreal images on his computer monitor and shook his head. No one in Ops had picked up on the break. There would be some serious shit coming down from above, of course, but it would be nothing he couldn't take care of.

The CO, Brigadier General Lazlo Maddox, had already jumped his ass this morning, wanting to know, "What the hell in Christ was going on with security?" And he was just the first. The director of the Office of Naval Intelligence was sending down a hit squad to find out how Weiss had managed to screw the pooch so badly.

He turned back to his computer as Ibenez and Talarico emerged from the drainage ditch, and his jaw tightened.

"The CIA has no business here," he'd told them ten days ago. "We've got the press snooping around, and if that isn't enough of a headache, Amnesty International has inspected us three times in the past five weeks. Now you."

"You're naval intel, Commander, which means we're supposed to work together," Ibenez had said sweetly. "And as long as you can refrain from the obvious shit like they pulled at Abu Ghraib, and keep a lid on your people if something does go down, we'll all be okay."

"Don't tell me how to do my job," Weiss had shot back, his anger spiking. His boss had sent the woman's jacket down last week, to give him a heads up, and it had chapped his ass that not even the Pentagon could stop the CIA from sending people to stick their noses into navy business. Not only that, they'd sent a woman who thought she was hot shit.

At thirty-two, Weiss was still in superb physical condition; he worked out nearly every day not only to keep the same edge he'd maintained lettering in football three years at Annapolis, but to keep his same physique that he knew women found attractive. He was six-two, at two hundred pounds; his face was craggy, what an old girlfriend had once said made him look stalwart. Along with snow-white hair and wide, coal-black eyes, he cut a dignified figure. It was an image he'd carefully cultivated since high school when he first realized that he was good-looking.

Weiss turned back to the digital images on his computer monitor, these now from the rescue helicopter's nose camera, as the mujahideen incursion team opened fire on the prisoners they'd broken out from Echo.

As the helicopter came around for another pass, the first of the mujahideen committed suicide in a bright flash. "At least one kilo of plastic," the chopper pilot reported. "I saw the same thing in Iraq."

Weiss could not tear his eyes away from the screen.

In addition to the five prisoners and four intruders, three MPs were down, and the bitch's partner had taken a round in the head. This was truly a cluster fuck, and a lot of heads were going to roll.

It was the navy way.

And so was covering your own ass. He was damned if he was going to take any heat because the CIA had come down here and fucked up.

Gloria Ibenez lay propped up in bed at the hospital while she talked via encrypted satellite phone to her boss, Otto Rencke, at Langley. He was in charge of Special Projects under the DDO. She'd been working for him nearly three years, and every minute of that time had been nothing short of amazing. And at times like these she felt close to him, as if he were her uncle, or a very longtime dear friend. She had a lot of respect for him.

"It wasn't your fault, ya know," Rencke said. "You were doing your job. Anyway, it could have been you taking the bullet. Would you have liked that better?"

Rencke was the most brilliant man she'd ever met. He was also the strangest, and at times, the sweetest person. He'd designed the CIA's entire computer system from the ground up, but he seldom dressed in anything fancier than old blue jeans, torn and dirty sweatshirts, and battered sneakers that never seemed to be tied. Most of the time he came across as an aloof genius, his head in the clouds, his brain processing some esoteric mathematical equations, when suddenly he would come out of his daze, hop back and forth from one foot to the other with a big grin on his face, and tell you what a fine person you were.

"I was in charge, and I went against a direct order not to follow the prisoners outside the fence," Gloria said. Her drug-induced dreams from the painkillers she'd been given last night had been like watching a sci-fi movie. She was inside Bob's head when the bullet exploded in his brain. She'd seen a billion stars, but there'd been no pain. She hoped there had been none for Bob, but she couldn't be sure and it was driving her nuts.

"Adkins got a call from General Maddox complaining about you," Rencke said. Adkins was Director of Central Intelligence. "You must have struck a nerve."

Gloria's husband Roman Ibenez had been a good man, with a sweet face and a disposition to match. He'd fancied himself an opera singer and he did have a wonderful voice. But he was also a fine intelligence officer, and they'd made a great pair working together in Havana. Until the evening Cuban Intelligence Service operatives had stormed their apartment, and dragged him away. Gloria had gone around the corner to get a bottle of wine for their late supper and she'd stepped back into the shadows as Roman was being dragged down the stairs. She'd been close enough to see the look of resignation on his face. He was as good as dead; he'd known it and so had Gloria.

She'd been as helpless then as she had been last night, unable to prevent the death of someone she cared deeply for. And she didn't know how many more times she could go down this path.

"Apparently I did," she told Rencke. "But the prison break was a setup by someone inside who had the cooperation of the Cubans." She'd already come to that conclusion last night, and yet she had led Bob under the fence. For what? Her ego?

"Okay, Gloria, what do you want to do about it? Stay down there and create some waves? See what shakes out?"

Gloria's jaw tightened. "I have a few ideas."

"I'll see what I can do, but Adkins is getting pressure to pull you out of there ASAP," Rencke said. "Might be for the best if you came home to file your field report. If you're right, it could give the bad guys a false sense of security after you've left. They might screw up, ya know."

"You have a point."

"But, how're you doing?" Rencke asked. "You were wounded."

"I took one in my hip, but it didn't break the bone," Gloria told him. "The doc says I'm going to be sore as hell for a couple of weeks and I'll probably have a limp for a few months, but I'll live." She closed her eyes, and she could see Bob's slack death mask when she held him in her arms in the chopper. "I was lucky."

"Yeah," Rencke said quietly. "When do you get out?"

"Sometime this morning, I think."

"Okay, sit tight, I'll get back to you."

Gloria broke the connection, laid the phone on the bedside table, and looked out the window toward the bay and the ferry landing. One of her senior instructors at the Farm had told the small graduating class that sooner or later every field officer comes to the point in their career when they question their validity. The good ones keep asking, "Am I making a difference?" but the bad ones stop caring. In reality, the really bad ones sold out—like Aldrich Ames had to the Russians for nearly five million dollars. Or they ate the bullet. Suicide was more of an occupational hazard in the intelligence community than death at the hands of your enemy. Bob had been one of the exceptions.

The CIA had been on a quiet but intense worldwide hunt for Osama bin Laden for sixteen months, ever since Don Hamel had been appointed the new director of National Intelligence. Bin Laden's capture or assassination would serve as a showpiece for the supposedly overhauled U.S. intelligence system. All fifteen intel agencies, including Homeland Security, the FBI, and the military units, were in on the hunt. But the CIA had taken the lead.

There were more than one thousand al-Quaida fighters in U.S. custody, some of them in Afghanistan and Iraq, but many of them here in Camp Delta. Gloria and Talarico had been sent down to chase a few leads they'd unearthed last month in Afghanistan. Three al-Quaida messengers, who might have clues to bin Laden's whereabouts, had supposedly been arrested last year, and were being held here. But the three had come in as Unidentified Alien Combatants along with several hundred other UACs.

Gloria had a hunch that they'd somehow been tipped off that the CIA was closing in on them, their transfer to Echo along with two others had been arranged, and an al-Quaida incursion squad had been sent to get them out or kill them.

It was a pretty morning outside. Just across the bay, past the airfield, the western fence separated this base from her homeland. There were times when she missed her childhood with her mother and father. She'd been an only child, and doted upon. But that was dead and buried forever. There was no peace here now. The tropical sun was shining, the trade wind breezes were blowing just as they had yesterday, only this morning her partner was dead, and his blood was on her hands.

She closed her eyes and began to cry silently, something she hadn't done since her mother's death.

In addition to the five hundred prisoners, nearly three thousand military personnel, dependents, and civilian contractors were housed on the base. The navy hospital, which served them, was very much like a small county general medical center, taking care of everything from sprained ankles to birthing babies. It was noisy around the clock; nurses checking on their patients, televisions and radios playing, and announcements coming over the PA system.

A few minutes after eleven, Lieutenant Commander Weiss, looking sharp in his summer undress whites, showed up at Gloria's door, his hat in hand. He was angry. "Nice night of work, Ms. Ibenez. The body count was sure as hell impressive."

"I think you guys call operations like that a cluster fuck," Gloria said. She was done crying for now. But there'd be more when she spoke to Bob's widow, Toni, and saw the kids.

"That's about what General Maddox said to me this morning," Weiss said. He came the rest of the way in the room and closed the door, but didn't come closer than the end of the bed. He didn't want to get contaminated. "What were you thinking?"

"We stumbled into the middle of a prison break, I called it in, and we went after them," Gloria said. "Anyway, who were those guys?"

"Suspected al-Quaida," Weiss replied tightly. It was obvious he was holding his temper in check.

"Was that why they were being held in Echo?" Gloria shot back. She knew why Weiss had come to see her, and it wasn't to find out how she was faring.

"That's none of your business."

"That's exactly my business, Commander."

"Cuban television is all over this deal of yours like stink on shit," Weiss said. "They're reporting that our people opened fire on nine unarmed prisoners. They're calling it a massacre, and *The New York Times, The Washington Post*, and just about every other fucking news organization in the world has shown up in San Juan wanting permission to come here."

"They must have had help," Gloria said.

Weiss's eyes narrowed. "What are you talking about?"

"They knew that the Frontier Brigade would be on the opposite side of the base making a racket, which gave them a clear shot at coming ashore, which means at the very least they had the Cubans on their side. But how'd they get past the tower guard?"

"They took him out. One shot to the head."

"No one heard anything?"

"There was a lot of noise," Weiss replied, his lips compressed.

Gloria felt a bit of compassion for him. Although the Army MPs ran

Delta and the other detention centers, the overall security and intelligence mission belonged to the Office of Naval Intelligence, and Weiss was the officer in charge. Last night's fiasco had definitely landed on his lap, and he'd already felt a lot of heat, with a whole bunch more to come. "I'm sorry, Commander, but I didn't make last night happen. Bob and I just stumbled into it."

"And you got him killed, Ibenez," Weiss said. "What the hell were you doing up there at that hour of the night? There weren't any interrogations on the schedule."

Gloria refused to look away, even though her innards were roiling, and she kept seeing Bob's face in death. "I had a hunch."

"About what?"

"The Cuban probe on the perimeter went on longer than normal, it was way up north, well away from Delta, and it was happening in the middle of the night."

Weiss was looking at her as if he was watching a lunatic who was babbling nonsense and didn't know any better.

"I think that Bob and I might have been made, our mission compromised."

Weiss nodded as if he'd come to a conclusion. "One of the prisoners realized that you were CIA, made a quick phone call to bin Laden himself, and in just ten days arranged an attack on the base so that you and your partner could get in the middle of it and be taken out." He smiled. "Have I covered everything?"

"Don't be an asshole," Gloria flared. "You know goddamned well that there've been unauthorized sat phone emissions out of here."

"Not for the last ninety days."

She reached for her satellite phone on the nightstand. "Maybe you missed one."

"No," Weiss said flatly. "We picked up your encrypted transmission a couple hours ago. I just came over to tell you that you'll be leaving on the first available transport."

"You don't have that authority."

"General Maddox does," Weiss said. "I'll talk to your doctor about releasing you this morning. Short of that I can arrange a medevac back to Washington. But you're out of here today. Get back to the BOQ, pack your things, and go home, and let us do our job."

Weiss turned to go, but Gloria sat up. "Why those specific prisoners? And why were they killed?"

"I don't know yet, but we're looking into it," Weiss said. He shrugged. "Who the fuck knows what those people are thinking?" He gave her a baleful look. "While you're at it, you'd best pack Talarico's things as well. His widow will probably want them."

After Weiss left, Gloria telephoned Rencke again, to tell him that she would be ordered out of Gitmo sometime today.

"Adkins thinks it's for the best," Rencke agreed. "I'm going to take a quick peek into ONI's system to see what shakes loose."

"See if you can find out who the five prisoners were in Echo, and why they'd been transferred out of Delta, if that's where they came from. Al-Quaida was concerned enough to spring them, and yet they didn't want those guys recaptured."

"Interesting question."

"Yeah," Gloria said. "Maybe we were closer than we thought."

FOUR

□

APURTO DEVLÁN, MARACAIBO VENSPORT PETROLEUM LOADING FACILITY 39A

Graham stepped down from the helicopter onto the loading deck amidships well forward of the aft superstructure. This was the only place anywhere aboard ship that was clear of the maze of cargo transfer and management piping for a helicopter to land. A young Filipino AB in dark blue coveralls was standing by to help with the captain's luggage. He handed Graham a hard hat, which everyone wore on deck while in port.

As the crewman was pulling Graham's things from the storage compartment, a slightly built man, his head shaved, his features dark, came out of the superstructure and quickly made his way forward. He was dressed in a short-sleeved white shirt and blue jeans.

"Mr. Slavin?" he shouted over the noise of the helicopter's rotors. His Hispanic accent, which Graham could not place, was very strong.

"That's correct."

"I'm Jaime Vasquez, I'm your first officer." They shook hands. "Welcome aboard, sir."

The crewman headed aft with the bags, and Graham led Vasquez away from the helicopter, which immediately took off with a loud roar and strong downdraft. Graham had to hold on to his hard hat so it wouldn't blow away.

"Where is your hard hat, Mr. Vasquez?" he asked in neutral tone once the helicopter was gone.

"We finished our loading procedures last night, and the ship is ready for sea, sir. I didn't think it was necessary."

"The AB who came to get my luggage brought me a hard hat. Apparently he's more mindful of company regulations than you are." Graham's Russian accent was credible. He'd practiced for the past few months with a mujahideen from Tajikistan, and he could speak a few phrases. But the lingua franca aboard was English, because the Apurto Devlán, like most ocean-going cargo ships, employed many different nationalities. As long as there were no real Russians among the officers or crewmen he'd have to interact with, he would pass.

"Would you like me to return to my quarters to get mine, sir?" Vasquez asked. He was wary, but the corners of his narrow mouth wanted to turn up in a smile, as if he thought the new captain might be pulling his leg.

Graham fixed him with a penetrating gaze for several beats, but then shook his head. "In the future I expect my officers to set an example for the rest of the crew. At all times. Do I make myself clear?"

"Perfectly. Won't happen again."

"See that it does not," Graham said. He glanced at his watch. It was just eight thirty. "I'll have my things stowed in twenty minutes. I want you and my officers, including my chief engineer, in my sitting room at oh-eight-fifty. I'll brief you and then we'll make an inspection tour. I would like to be under way at ten hundred hours. Precisely. Vy pahnemayeteh myenyah? Do you understand me?"

"Yes, sir," Vasquez said. "May I show you to your quarters?"

"*Nyet*, it's not necessary," Graham said. "Oh, and bring the crew's personnel records, if you please. *All* the records, including yours."

The *Apurto Devlán* was 900 feet long at the loaded waterline with a beam of 110 feet. She was rated Panamax, the largest class of ships that could transit the Panama Canal, the limiting factor in her case being her width. Under extreme circumstances, her highly automated systems would allow her to be maneuvered by as few as five seamen plus the skipper. Normally her complement was twenty-four officers and crew, but for this trip she was shorthanded with nineteen crew and officers, which included a cook, a cook's assistant, and two female stewards, plus the captain.

All the way aft was the superstructure, which rose sixty feet above the main deck, and housed the crew's living quarters and recreation dayroom, the galley, mess, and pantries, and the small first-aid station. The uppermost decks housed the quarters for the ship's first, second, and third officers, the chief engineer and his assistant, and the officers' combined mess and wardroom. The uppermost deck contained the bridge; wing lookouts; a combined chart room and radio room, which contained the ship's gyros and repeaters for all the electronic instruments used for navigation; and the captain's relatively luxurious quarters, which consisted of a bedroom, a large bathroom, and separate sitting room. Just behind the bridge were the captain's sea quarters where he bunked in emergencies when his presence was required around the clock, and which doubled as the ship's office when customs and immigration officials came to inspect the ship's papers and issue sailing clearances.

Directly below the superstructure were the engineering spaces where the ship's two gas turbine engines were housed. The *Apurto Devlán* was less than five years old. She had been constructed in Cherbourg, France, and outfitted with the latest machinery and electronics, which not only took up less space, leaving more room for product, but which allowed the ship to make very fast, very safe transits with less crew, thus maximizing profit for GAC.

"My engines are in top form," Chief Engineer Hiboshi Kiosawa told Graham. He was a very small, slightly built man, dressed this morning in spotless white coveralls, a very large smile on his narrow face. The ship's gas turbines had been built by Mitsubishi, the first marine engines the Japanese corporation had ever designed, and Kiosawa was justifiably proud. Most oil tankers were powered by single slow-turning diesels.

Vasquez had brought the personnel files, which he laid on the table in Graham's sitting room, and then had introduced the chief engineer; First Engineering Officer Peter Weizenegger; Second Officer William Sozansky; and Third Officer George Novak.

"Gentlemen, I expect a quick, trouble-free passage," Graham said. "What about our product load?"

"We have aboard fifty-two thousand long tons as of midnight that gives us a draft of thirty-seven feet, maximum for the canal," Kiosawa said. His assistant engineer doubled as loadmaster while in port, but the ultimate responsibility lay with the chief engineer, who answered directly to the captain.

"Fire suppression?"

"All tanks have been topped and capped."

They were carrying light sweet crude that constantly evaporated a host of complex hydrocarbons, all of which were extremely flammable or even explosive. Once the product had been loaded into the ship's twelve separate cargo oil tanks, inert nitrogen gas was pumped in to replace the air in any free spaces, and the compartments were sealed. Even if a blowtorch were to be lit inside one of the tanks, nothing would happen. There was no oxygen to support a fire or explosion.

"All notices to mariners have been noted and logged?"

"Yes, sir," Sozansky said. His primary duty was navigation officer.

"Diagnostics have been conducted on all our electronic equipment, including radar?"

"Yes, sir," Kiosawa said. "We are ready in all respects for sea."

"Very well," Graham said. Oil tankers were infinitely less complex than the Trafalgar Class nuclear-powered submarines he had commanded in the Royal Navy. And with a crew of only nineteen aboard versus seven times as many to operate a submarine, personnel problems would be infinitely less complex.

In any event, before the Apurto Devlán left the second Gatun lock she would be a ghost ship, with a dead crew and no skipper. The ultimate solution to insubordination and dissention.

Graham smiled, and his officers visibly relaxed. "I would like to see my ship."

"Yes, sir," Vasquez said. "Would you like to start with the product spaces, or the engines?"

"First I want to meet the rest of my crew, and inspect their quarters and workstations."

"Sir?"

"Without them, Mr. Vasquez, we'd never leave the dock," Graham said. He glanced at his chief engineer and other officers. "The heart of any ship is her people, not her engines, don't you agree?"

"Naturally," Vasquez agreed.

"Very well, everyone but Mr. Vasquez will return to work, we get under way at ten hundred."

His officers nodded and left.

Starting three decks down, Vasquez led Graham on a quick tour of the crew's quarters and mess. None of the twelve men and two women would be off duty now until they got under way, and started ship's-at-sea routine of six hours on, four hours off, six hours on, and eight hours off.

In addition to the five officers, there were fourteen in the crew: three in engineering under Kiosawa, and the rest, seven able-bodied seamen, the cook and his assistant, and two stewards under Vasquez. Their sleeping quarters were grouped together down the main athwartships alleyway on B deck, with direct access to the stairways and the port and starboard deck hatches. They were unoccupied for the moment, but Graham insisted on inspecting each.

One deck down he was introduced to Bjorn Rassmussen, their cook from Oslo. He was a giant of a man with an infectious smile, a massive belly, a filthy bloodstained apron, and long blond hair covered by a hairnet. "Son of a bitch, Captain," he boomed. "You're going to like my cooking for sure."

Graham considered for a moment reprimanding the man, and ordering him to cut his hair and get a clean apron before they got under way, but it didn't matter. One hundred hours from the time they slipped their loading dock lines, they would arrive at the Panama Canal. It would not be long before the cook would be dead, the blood on his apron his own.

A woman came up behind them and said something in Russian that Graham could not understand. He turned around.

"Irina Karpov, assistant steward," Vasquez said.

Graham stared at her for a long moment. "The language aboard this vessel is English, Ms. Karpov," he said sharply. "Is that clear to you?"

She nodded uncertainly. "Yes, sir. I'm sorry—"

Graham held up a hand to silence her. She knew something was wrong, he could see it in her eyes. But she wasn't sure. She couldn't be sure. But if need be she would have an unfortunate accident.

"She was just trying to be pleasant," Vasquez said on the way down to the engine room.

Graham stopped and fixed his first officer with a hard look. "I'm not master of this vessel to be made pleasant with. I'm here to see that the product we have loaded transits the Panama Canal and makes a smart run to Long Beach, takes on ballast, and returns. So long as you and the rest of my officers and crew understand these simple facts, we will get along fine." Graham stepped closer. "I'm not your friend, Mr. Vasquez. Nor do I wish to be. I'll be pleased if you pass the word."

"As you wish, Mr. Slavin."

In the fifteen minutes before the *Apurto Devlán* was to slip her lines, Graham had returned to his quarters to quickly scan the personnel folders of his four officers, beginning with Vasquez. Standing now on the bridge, the ship's engines spooled up, line handlers aboard and on the loading dock ready, an AB at the helm, his second officer ready to radio the exact time of their departure to Harbor Control in Maracaibo, and his first officer standing by for orders, Graham hesitated.

Conning a 280-foot submarine away from a dock was different than directing a fully loaded Panamax tanker away from her loading facility in the middle of a lake. Completely different.

His officers were looking at him.

"I understand that this is Mr. Vasquez's last trip as first officer aboard a GAC vessel," Graham said.

A cautious flash of pleasure crossed the first officer's face, but then was gone. Like everyone else aboard he wasn't sure about the new master.

"He'll be given command of his own ship."

"Yes, sir."

Graham handed him the walkie-talkie used to communicate with the line handlers. "Take us out to sea, Mr. Vasquez. I want to see how you do."

FIVE

□

CIA HEADQUARTERS

"They shot the men they came to rescue, and then blew themselves up," Gloria Ibenez told Otto Rencke. They were on their way up to the DCI's office on the seventh floor and Gloria was walking with a cane. The wound in her hip throbbed, but it wasn't impossible.

Rencke held the elevator door for her. "I'm surprised they didn't wait for the chopper to drop in on them. Could've bagged some of our guys."

"I don't think they were on a suicide mission. They just didn't want to get recaptured."

Just off the elevator they were subjected to a body scan with electronic wands, something that everyone visiting the DCI had to go through. Sometimes it felt like all of Washington had been on lockdown since 9/11 with no real end in sight. It was a couple minutes after 10:00 A.M., and the director had just finished his morning briefing via video link with Donald Hamel, the director of National Intelligence, and the heads of the other fifteen intelligence services. He had a few minutes for them, and in fact had specifically asked Rencke to bring her up when she got back from Guantanamo Bay. The incident at Gitmo was gaining momentum in the world press, and the White House was already beginning to feel the heat.

Down the plushly carpeted corridor, they entered the DCI's office through glass doors etched with the CIA's shield and eagle. The director's secretary, Dhalia Swanson, a stern and proper white-haired older woman, looked up and smiled warmly. She'd been secretary to four DCIs now, and was practically a permanent fixture in the Company.

"My poor dear, how are we doing this morning?"

"It's not bad, Ms. Swanson," Gloria said, unable to stop from smiling, even though she couldn't get Talarico's death image out of her head. "Really."

"Were you able to speak with Toni this morning?"

Gloria closed her eyes for a moment and nodded. "Yes." It had been all the more horrible because Talarico's widow had not blamed her for Bob's death. Her husband had made her understand from day one that such a thing was ultimately possible.

Ms. Swanson picked up the phone. "Mr. Rencke and Ms. Ibenez are here." She looked up. "Yes, sir." She hung up and motioned them in.

The director of Central Intelligence, Dick Adkins, was sitting at his large desk in front of bulletproof floor-to-ceiling windows that looked out over the Annex building, beyond which were the lush green rolling Virginia hills that ran down to the Potomac a mile to the east. He was a slightly built man with thinning sandy hair, and a slight stoop from back problems. He'd been deputy director of the CIA under Roland Murphy and then Kirk McGarvey after a twenty-year career during which he had steadily risen through the ranks. When McGarvey had resigned last year, Adkins had taken over as acting DCI until his overwhelming confirmation in the Senate. His was a steady, if unimaginative, hand on the helm; a nearly perfect fit as a subordinate to Don Hamel.

Across from him were the Company's General Counsel Carleton Patterson, and Rencke's boss, Deputy Director of Operations Howard McCann. Patterson had been a lawyer with a prestigious New York law firm before coming to work, temporarily, for the CIA. That had been ten years ago, but he still dressed for work every day in British-tailored three-piece suits, with an old-world manner to match, and talked about returning to New York. McCann, on the other hand, looked and acted like a factory worker. Before McGarvey had resigned he'd suggested that the old DDO, David Whittaker, be bumped upstairs as deputy director of Central Intelligence, working directly for Adkins, and that McCann, a former standout field officer, director of the Eastern European Desk, and chief clandestine operations adviser to the Company training facility near Williamsburg, be appointed to run operations.

Adkins got to his feet when Gloria and Rencke walked in. "Here they are," he said. "How are you feeling, Ms. Ibenez?"

"Sore, but I'll live," Gloria said. She and the director shook hands.

"I don't know if you've met our general counsel, Carleton Patterson."

"No, sir," Gloria said.

Patterson got to his feet and they shook hands. "My condolences on your partner's death," he said. "But you've created quite a firestorm."

Gloria tried to gauge the mood of the others, especially Adkins, but no one seemed to be gunning for her. With any luck she might not be the main course for lunch, after all, something she'd worried about on the flight up from Gitmo yesterday afternoon. She'd disobeyed a direct order not to go under the fence, she had violated Cuban territory, thus putting herself at high risk for capture and interrogation, and she had caused the death of her partner. She'd thought that a firing squad might not be too extreme a punishment.

"Yes, sir, I guess I have," she said. "But I wasn't going to let them get away. It was just too much of a coincidence to my way of thinking."

Adkins exchanged a look with the others. "That's the whole point," he said. He motioned for Gloria and Otto to have a seat. "Coffee?"

"No, sir," Gloria said, and Rencke shook his head.

"Bob's funeral will be sometime next week, we'll let you know," Adkins said. He shook his head. "It's a bad business."

Gloria lowered her eyes. She would not cry. Not here. Not now. "Yes, sir."

"Have you seen the *Post* this morning?" Patterson asked.

"They're calling it a massacre," Gloria said. "It's the same on TV. We're not giving any answers, so the media are having a field day. It's going to get as bad as Abu Ghraib. Maybe even worse."

"That's because we *can't* give them anything," Adkins said. "You were right all along, it wasn't a coincidence." He turned to Rencke. "Have you briefed her?"

"I was in the middle of a couple of search programs when she came in, and I wanted to see where they'd take me," Rencke said. He had folded his legs under himself on the chair and sat on his heels, fidgeting like a kid in church. "It's gone pink, ya know, and it's gonna get worse."

Rencke had devised a mathematical system, using tensor calculus to work out the highly complex relationships in any given set of circumstances—between hundreds, even thousands of people spread around the globe; between governments and intelligence organizations; law enforcement and military agencies; the weather; sea conditions; satellite and electronic intel; the historical record—to come to some predictions about what might be coming our way. He'd been able to reduce the mathematics to colors: Tan was safe, while lavender meant something very bad was looming on the horizon. Pink was a heads-up that something was going on that needed attention before it got out of hand.

Everyone who knew Rencke had a healthy respect for his abilities. He was a genius, and without him the CIA would practically cease to function as a viable intelligence agency. Under McGarvey's quiet suggestion to Adkins last year, the Company was currently on an all-out manhunt for Rencke's understudy, against the day he'd step down or have to be replaced.

"What have you come up with?" McCann asked. He was fairly new to the DDO's desk, and he still hadn't made his peace with Rencke. He didn't understand the man.

"Well, first off, they knew the Frontier Brigade's patrol schedule and they knew when the probe would start, which means they had Cuban help. And then they went to the weakest point in the perimeter at just the right time." Rencke's head bobbed back and forth as if it were on springs, his features animated.

"Do you think they had help from *inside?*" Gloria asked.

Rencke shrugged. "It's starting to look that way, especially with what I came up with this morning just before you got here."

"Whose system did you hack this time?" McCann asked, but Adkins held him off.

"You have our attention, Otto," the DCI prompted.

"The five guys they sprung had been transferred from the main prison population in Delta to minimum security outside the fence at Echo that morning," Rencke said.

"Whoever signed the order is our man," McCann said.

"It ain't that easy, kimo sabe." Rencke shook his head. "Those guys weren't al-Quaida, at least they weren't directly fighting our troops in Afghanistan. They were Iranians that a Marine patrol ran into just across the border a few klicks inside Afghanistan. Way south, near the Pakistani border. They said they were lost."

"It's no secret that the Iranians sent people to help the Taliban," McCann said.

"Navy officers?" Rencke asked. "Four hundred miles from the Gulf of Oman?"

All of a sudden it was beginning to make sense to Gloria. The Cuban help, the Gitmo contact, the transfer of prisoners. Even what they'd been doing inside Afghanistan, but very near to Pakistan.

"What the hell were they doing there?" McCann demanded.

Gloria interrupted. "Which way were they headed?"

"Northwest," Rencke said.

"I'll tell you what they were doing there," Gloria told them. "Trying to get back to Iran after meeting with bin Laden."

McCann and the others had skeptical looks on their faces, but Rencke was beaming, practically bouncing off the chair.

"Continue," Adkins said.

"Either bin Laden called them across to parley, or the Iranians offered, but it was just plain bad luck on their part that they were caught," Gloria said. "They were so important that al-Quaida was willing to risk its assets in Gitmo to get them out. But if something went wrong they had to be killed."

It dawned on everyone else what she and Rencke were getting at.

"Are you trying to say that the bastards want to hit us by sea?" McCann asked.

"It's something we gotta think about," Rencke replied. "They could hijack a container ship after it's cleared its outbound port."

"That's not out of the realm of possibility," Adkins said. "It's happened before." He looked at the others. "We all remember the incident under the Golden Gate Bridge two years before 9/11."

Al-Quaida had smuggled a small Russian-built nuclear demolitions device aboard a cargo ship bound for San Francisco. It had been set to explode while the presidential motorcade was crossing the bridge ahead of more than one thousand Special Olympians participating in a half-marathon.

"If it hadn't have been for Mac, the president and a whole lot of people would have lost their lives."

"There's a lot tighter port security just about everywhere these days," McCann said.

Rencke shrugged. "Okay, so maybe they could rendezvous with a private yacht somewhere offshore and load just about anything imaginable. From there they'd be virtually unstoppable."

"We know the shipping lanes, we could watch them by satellite," McCann argued.

"We know the shipping lanes, but they know our technical means schedules," Rencke countered. "We can't watch every piece of ocean 24/7. It just ain't possible."

Gloria's gut was twisted into a knot. She'd been stationed at the UN, and was at her desk in the American Delegation's headquarters across the street when the first airliner struck the World Trade Center. She'd been within a block of ground zero, helping with rescue operations when the first tower had collapsed. The following days and weeks had been made more surreal by the fact that she and a lot of other people had known that something big was on the wind.

They'd been so damned helpless. There was so much data coming in that it was impossible to process and evaluate even a small percentage of it in a timely manner. And in those days there hadn't been nearly enough communication between the CIA and most of the other intel agencies.

"They could sail into New York Harbor and let it blow," Rencke said. "A weekday, rush hour. They would kill a whole bunch more than twenty-seven hundred people, not to mention how badly another strike on Manhattan would demoralize the entire country."

"How about something to cheer us up," Patterson said to fill the heavy silence.

"Finding bin Laden is still the key," Gloria said. "There're still the three al-Quaida mujahideen hiding somewhere in Delta who might know where he's hiding."

"That, and finding a crew," Rencke said. "Especially a freelance captain willing to work for al-Quaida. Those kinds of guys gotta be in short supply."

"Have you come up with any names?" McCann asked.

"I'm working on it," Rencke said. "But you know that Gloria is right, we have to find bin Laden this time and nail him. No shit, Sherlock. It's gotta be done."

"We're working the problem," McCann said. "We'll go back to Guantanamo Bay as soon as the dust settles—"

"Now," Rencke said. "And we're going to need some outside help."

"Do you think he'll go for it?" Adkins asked. "And does anybody even know where he is?"

"I know," Rencke said. "And all we can do is put it to him. He's never said no before."

"Will you go?" Adkins asked.

Rencke nodded. "I'll leave this afternoon."

"Who?" Gloria asked.

Rencke smiled at her. "Mac," he said. "Kirk McGarvey."

SIX

☐

APURTO DEVLÁN, LOS MONJES ISLANDS

On the bridge a course-change alarm sounded on the main navigation systems coordinator. It was 0818 Greenwich mean time, 0318 local, under mostly cloudy skies, with an eighteen-knot breeze off the starboard beam, and confused two-meter seas.

"We're coming on our mark, sir," the AB at the electronic helm station called out softly.

Vasquez, who'd gone off duty at ten, had come back up to the bridge, not because he mistrusted their second officer, Bill Sozansky, but because this was the critical course change to clear Punta Gallinas, the northernmost tip of South America, and take them safely out into the open Caribbean for the run southwest to the canal.

He set his coffee down, and walked over to the starboard combined radar-course plotter display. The AB who had been looking at the radar returns stepped aside. Their current position was plotted on an electronic chart that was overlaid with a real-time image of what their radar was picking up.

"Have I missed anything?" Sozansky asked.

"Not a thing, Bill," Vasquez said. "It's your bridge, but it's my ass if something goes wrong. I don't think our new captain likes me."

Sozansky chuckled. "I don't think he likes any of us."

Two large ships, probably tankers, were more than ten miles behind them and slightly to starboard, and one other was twenty-five miles ahead and already turning northeast out to sea, just passing the tiny Los Monjes island group.

The South American headland, fifteen miles to the west, appeared as a low green line that sloped from southeast to northwest across the radar screen.

Vasquez got a pair of binoculars from a rack and went out on the port-wing lookout. South America's final outpost, the tiny town of Puerto Estrella, only a small dim glow on the indistinct horizon, was falling aft, leaving nothing but darkness ahead.

The evening was warm, nevertheless Vasquez shivered. His *abuela* would say that someone had just walked over his grave. He had a lot of respect for his grandmother, who had raised him from birth, and thinking about her now, dead for eight years, sent a chill of darkness into his heart. But he didn't know why.

Back inside the bridge that was dimly lit in red to save their night vision, Vasquez checked both combined radars, but nothing was amiss. They were exactly where they were supposed to be, there were no hazards to navigation ahead, no other shipping on intercept courses, and yet he felt uneasy.

"What is it, Jaime?" Sozansky asked. "You're getting on my nerves. Something wrong?"

Vasquez looked up, and slowly shook his head. "Not that I can see." He'd been born in the slums of San Juan, Puerto Rico. His mother had died giving birth to him and he'd never known his father. If it hadn't been for the strong hand of his grandmother, he would have turned out to be just another street kid. But she had made him finish school, and she had made him join the U.S. Merchant Marine, where after two years as an ordinary seaman he was offered a berth at the Merchant Marine Academy in Kings Point, New York, because he was bright and dedicated, and the service needed men of his caliber.

He'd graduated number three in his class, and since then his promotions had been very rapid. His superiors said that he was an officer with good instincts.

"If you're going to act like our new captain and prowl around in the middle of the night when you get your own ship, you're going to give your crew the crazies."

"He was up here?" Vasquez asked.

"Twice."

"What did he want?"

"The same thing as you," Sozansky said. "Do me a favor, Jaime, go back to bed, let the computer run the ship, and let me do the babysitting."

"Did he say anything?"

Sozansky laughed. "Not a word. Not one bloody word."

Something about the captain wasn't adding up in Vasquez's mind, but for the life of him he couldn't figure what it might be. He'd worked under a lot of sour, even angry masters before; men who were mad at the world. And they had the same smell about them, the same look. But with Slavin it was somehow different. Maybe because he was a Russian.

"I'm going to bed."

"Oh, the last time he was here he took the watch schedule with him," Sozansky said. "I thought you might want to know."

"I gave him a copy this afternoon."

Sozansky shrugged. "Maybe he's going to change it. Captain's prerogative."

"Yeah," Vasquez said. He left the bridge and went down one deck to officers' territory. Just at his cabin door, he hesitated for a moment. If their new captain was prowling the ship, maybe he was looking for something; maybe the man's instincts were telling him that something was wrong.

No one was out and about at this hour of the morning. The bridge was manned and the engine room would have someone on duty to watch over the machinery, and he supposed the cook and his assistant might be stirring by now, prepping for breakfast. But most of the crew and officers were in bed, asleep, as he should be.

He let himself into his cabin, careful to make as little noise as possible, so as not to wake up his girlfriend, Alicia Mora. She was one of the stewards, and she'd have to get up in a couple of hours to help set up the officers' wardroom for breakfast.

None of them had gotten much sleep in the past few days, trying to make the ship as presentable as possible for their new master. Last night when she'd come to him, she'd been tired and a little cranky. After they'd had a couple of glasses of wine and made love, she'd fallen asleep and had not awoken when Vasquez got out of bed, got dressed, and went up to the bridge.

"Jaime," she called softly.

"Go back to sleep," Vasquez said. He got undressed, hanging his clothes over his desk chair.

"What time is it?" Alicia asked sleepily. "Is something wrong?"

"Nothing's wrong," he told her. "Now, go back to sleep, you've got a couple hours."

The bedside light came on. Alicia was sitting up in bed, her short dark hair standing on end in spikes. The covers had fallen away exposing her tiny, milk-white breasts. "British girls don't get tans," she'd explained to him. "We just burn and peel."

"Something's wrong," she said. "I can see it on your face."

He kissed her, and got into bed beside her, propping up his pillow so that he could lie back against the bulkhead. She came into his arms, and he held her against his chest. When they were first getting to know each other, they had sat up in bed talking like this sometimes the entire night. He was taking her with him aboard his new ship, and after their first cruise he was going to ask her to marry him. They were lovers, but even more important they were friends. She had become his sounding board.

"It's our new captain," he said.

"What about him?"

"I don't trust him," Vasquez said. "I don't know what it is, but something's not quite right with the man." He looked down into Alicia's large brown eyes. "He's been turning up all over the place at all hours of the day. Like he's looking for something."

"It's a new ship for him," Alicia suggested. "Maybe he's trying to get the feel for her, and for his crew."

"The son of a bitch is waiting for us to fuck up," Vasquez told her, all of a sudden understanding what had been bothering him. "He's waiting for *me* to fuck up so he can take away my new command even before I get it. He had me take the ship out. He said he wanted to see how I did." Vasquez shook his head. "He *wanted* me to fuck up."

"So don't screw up," Alicia said. "You're a good officer, otherwise the company wouldn't have promoted you."

"I don't trust him."

"Neither do I."

Something cold stabbed at Vasquez's heart. "Has he tried to hit on you?" he demanded.

Alicia shook her head. "I almost wish he had," she said. "When he looks at me, there's nothing in his eyes. It's like he was dead. Nobody's home." She laughed a little at herself. "Gives me the creeps."

Graham held up in the starboard stairwell at the officers' deck. Vasquez had returned to his quarters from the bridge five minutes ago, and it was likely that he was settling in for the rest of the night. It was also likely that the steward who'd come to his cabin around ten would be staying.

He listened to the sounds of his ship; the oddly pitched engine vibrations of the gas turbines, the air coming from the ventilators, perhaps a radio or stereo playing what sounded like American country and western, but from a long ways off, below, perhaps in the crew's galley. The cook's assistant was from Chicago, or someplace like that, and he'd been playing hillbilly music when Graham had passed the galley after dinner last night. He'd be up now, prepping for breakfast.

Timing would be everything. If his actions were to be discovered too soon, and an alarm raised, his mission could disintegrate.

Around midnight, less than twelve hours from now, conditions throughout the ship would be essentially the same as they were this morning. It would be the third officer and two ABs on the bridge. He would kill them first, and then send his message.

When he'd received confirmation that the rendezvous was set, he would immediately go to the engine room where he would kill the two or three men on duty.

If he could clear those two spaces without detection, he would return to the officers' deck where he would kill the chief engineer, and the two remaining deck officers—Vasquez and Sozansky—and the first officer's woman if she were with him.

He would reload then, and descend one deck to the crews' quarters where he would work his way down the main alleyway, starboard to port, opening doors and killing everyone in their beds.

He had made up a new crew schedule, so that he would know where every single soul aboard would be located. But it was important that he maintain a running tally of the body count. He did not want to miss anyone who could reach the bridge and radio a Mayday.

It came down to timing and accuracy.

He was wearing a dark blue windbreaker with his name and the name of the ship stenciled on the left breast. In his left pocket was a stopwatch, and in his right a spare flashlight battery, which represented the eighteen-round spare magazine he would carry.

Stuffed in his belt beneath his jacket was a long, three-battery flashlight, which represented the 9mm Steyr GB pistol and silencer he would be using.

Graham turned and went back up to the bridge deck, his non-skid, rubber-soled sneakers whisper silent. He moved like a ghost, an avenging angel, but he felt no emotion other than a sharp desire to do the job right so that he could survive to strike the next blow. And the next.

Sozansky looked up in surprise as Graham came through the hatch. "Good morning, sir," he said. "Didn't expect to see you again so soon."

Graham managed a tight smile. "First night out aboard a new ship."

Sozansky nodded. "I understand," he said. He glanced at the integrated display, which showed the ship's course and speed. "We just finished our first turn to northwest, round Point Gallinas."

"Right on schedule, are we?"

"Yes, sir."

Graham went over to the port-wing lookout, put his hand in his left pocket, and started the stopwatch. He turned back to Sozansky and hesitated a moment to simulate pulling the pistol from his belt.

Bang. The officer was down. The two ABs would be startled. They would start to turn. Bang, one of them would go down. Bang, the second would fall.

"Sir, is everything okay?" Sozansky asked.

"Just fine," Graham said. *He would move to the short-range VHF radio, careful not to step in any of the blood that would be pooling on the deck, and send the message.*

"Yes, sir," Sozansky said uncertainly.

The second officer was confused and a little irritated; it showed on his face. But by midnight the only look on his face would be one of death.

He would wait for the reply, which should come immediately.

"I'll get out of your hair now," Graham said, and he left the bridge.

The short alleyway to his cabin was empty, as was the starboard stairwell, which he took all the way down to the gallery one level up from the main deck, which housed the turbines and control panel in its separate space behind a plate-glass window. The noise was deafening.

Two men, including First Engineering Officer Peter Weizenegger, were seated in the control room, their backs to the main floor. One engineering AB, next to a tool cart pulled up to an electrical distribution panel directly below where Graham stood, was taking a measurement with a multimeter. He wore sound-suppression earmuffs.

Graham moved along the gallery catwalk to the center ladder, which he took down to the main deck between the two turbines. From here he could not be seen by anyone in the control room.

He stepped around the end of the turbine where it angled down through the deck. He was a couple of meters behind the AB.

Bang. The AB would fall. He was number four out of nineteen.

Keeping a neutral expression on his face, he walked across to the control room, and went inside.

Weizenegger and the AB looked up, startled. "Captain," the engineering officer said.

"Is there something wrong with our electrical system?" Graham asked. *Bang, the officer was dead. Number five.*

Weizenegger glanced toward the AB on the main deck. "No, sir. Chiang is doing a scheduled P.M. routine."

"Very well," Graham said. He looked at the AB. *Bang, the man fell. Number six.* "Carry on."

"Yes, sir," Weizenegger said.

Graham headed topside toward the officers' quarters, but he heard the music again coming from the galley. At midnight the cook might not be in the galley, but it was likely that his assistant and perhaps some of the crew coming off duty might be in the mess.

This morning it was Rassmussen, the cook, mixing pancake batter and frying bacon. He looked up when Graham appeared at the doorway. "Ah, Captain, can't sleep? Son of a bitch I know how it is. Coffee?"

"No, I'm on my way to bed," Graham said. *Bang, the cook or whoever was in the galley would be down. Number seven.* "Everything okay down here?"

The cook nodded effusively. "In my son of a bitch kitchen, it's always okay."

"Very well," Graham said. He went back into the mess.

Four steel tables with six stainless steel stools were bolted to the deck. No one was here at this hour, but he had to count on at least some crewmen eating a midnight meal. Say three of them? *Bang, the crewman at the coffee urn fell. Number eight. The two at their table were rising in alarm. Bang, number nine. Bang, number ten of nineteen.*

Graham hurried up to the officers' deck where he stopped at the chief engineer's door. *Bang, number eleven.* He moved to Vasquez's cabin where he and his girlfriend would be in each other's arms. *Twelve and thirteen.*

Down one deck, he stopped at the doors of the remaining six crew members. *Fourteen, fifteen, sixteen, seventeen, eighteen, nineteen.*

The Apurto Devlán had become a ghost ship.

Graham headed topside to his quarters. He took the stopwatch from his pocket and clicked the Stop button. Nine minutes and fifty-eight seconds had elapsed, and the ship was his.

SEVEN

MARINA JACK, SARASOTA, FLORIDA

Kirk Cullough McGarvey raised the air horn and blew one long and one short, the signal requesting the tender to stop traffic and open the New Pass Bridge. It was a few minutes after noon, the spring Saturday beautiful. Although traffic was heavy the bridge tender immediately sent back the long and short, that the bridge would be opened as requested.

A part of him was reluctant to return to the real world after fourteen days of vacation, while another part of him was resigned. Something was out there. Someone was coming for him.

Four days ago at the Faro Blanco Marina in the Keys, the dockmaster had come out to where the Island Packet 31 sloop, which McGarvey and his wife Katy had chartered, was tied up. He said that he'd forgotten to get the Florida registration number on the bow. But that was a lie.

McGarvey had followed him back to the office, and watched from a window as the man tossed the slip of paper on which he'd jotted down the registration number into a trash can, then made a telephone call. It was a pre-coms; someone was sniffing along his trail.

Yesterday, anchored just outside the Intracoastal Waterway channel near Cabbage Key, they'd been overflown twice around dusk by a civilian helicopter. He was certain that the passenger had looked them over through a pair of binoculars.

He'd said nothing to Katy about his suspicions, but that evening while she was having a drink in the cockpit, he'd gone below for his 9mm Walther PPK that had been safely tucked away since the start of the cruise. He checked the action, and loaded a magazine of ammunition into the handle, racking a round into the firing chamber.

When he turned around, Katy had been looking at him from the cockpit hatch. "Gremlins?" she'd asked.

"I'm not sure," McGarvey said. "But somebody seems to be interested in us."

Katy shook her head, disappointment on her pretty face. "I thought it was over."

"Me too."

McGarvey was a tall man, fiftyish, with a sturdy build and a good wind because of a daily regimen of exercise that he had not abandoned last year after he'd resigned his position as director of the Central Intelligence Agency. Although there was no longer anyone to oversee his workouts, he went out to the Company's training facility near Williamsburg as often as he could to run the confidence course and spend an hour or two on the firing range. Just to keep his hand in, and to see how his daughter Elizabeth and her husband, Todd, were doing. They were instructors.

He had quit the CIA after twenty-five years of service—first as a field officer, and then for a number of years as a freelancer, working black operations, before he came back to Langley to run the Directorate of Operations, and finally the entire Agency—because he was tired of the stress.

Good times, some of them. Good people. Friends. But more bad times than he cared to remember, although he could not forget the people he'd killed in the line of duty. All of them necessary, or at least he had to tell himself that. But all of them human beings, whatever their crimes. Their deaths were on his conscience, especially in the middle of the night when he often awoke in a cold sweat.

Because of his profession his family had been put in harm's way more than once. It was another reason he'd quit.

Kathleen came up on deck, shading her blue eyes against the bright sun. "Are we there yet?" she asked, a slight Virginia softness to her voice. She was a slender woman, a few inches shorter than her husband, with short blond hair and a pretty oval face with a small nose and full lips.

"We will be if they open the bridge for us," McGarvey told her. There were several other sloops, their sails also furled, and a couple of powerboats whose antennae or outriggers were too tall to pass beneath the bridge when it was closed.

"Then what?" Kathleen asked.

"I'll give Otto a call and see if he's heard anything."

Traffic up on the bridge was coming to a halt as the road barriers were lowered.

"I meant afterwards," Kathleen pressed. She was serious. "You're taking the teaching job at New College. We're selling the house in Chevy Chase and moving down here. Permanently. Right?"

The roadway parted in the middle and the two leaves began to rise.

McGarvey pointed the bow of the Island Packet to the middle of the channel and gave the diesel a little throttle. The tide was running with them through the narrow pass into Sarasota Bay, giving them an extra three or four knots.

"Right?" Kathleen repeated.

McGarvey glanced at her and smiled. "That's the plan, sweetheart."

She shook her head and smiled ruefully. "God, you're handsome when you lie," she said. She came aft to the wheel, gave her husband a kiss on the cheek, then started pulling the dock lines and fenders from a locker.

She was wearing a bikini with a deep blue and yellow sarong tied around her middle; her feet were bare. McGarvey was dressed only in swim trunks, a baseball cap, and sunglasses. Except for the couple of nights they'd dressed for dinner ashore, they'd worn nothing else for most of the fourteen days since they'd slipped their lines at Marina Jack and headed out to the Gulf of Mexico.

They'd gunk-holed down Florida's west coast, slowly heading for Key West; anchoring early in small coves, drinks in the cockpit at dusk, power up the barbecue grill for dinner. Awake with the dawn, the water flat calm for a swim before breakfast, then pull up the anchor, and sail farther south. Sometimes they'd stop especially early so they could snorkel along the reefs just offshore, or walk the beaches, or fish, or just lie in the cockpit in the shade of the bimini to read a book.

For two weeks they never turned on the radio, saw a television set, or read a newspaper or newsmagazine. And the trip had done wonders for both of them, after the hell they'd gone through because of McGarvey's last assignment in which he'd resigned from the CIA in order to track down an al-Quaida killer. Kathleen, who'd been pregnant as a surrogate mother for their daughter Elizabeth, had very nearly lost her life in the ordeal. But Mac had saved her and the baby, who'd been born six months ago.

This trip had been exactly what the doctor had ordered. Or at least it had been until the incidents at Faro Blanco and yesterday in the Intracoastal Waterway with the helicopter. Like so many times before in his connection with the U.S. intelligence establishment he had to tell himself that the business was not finished for him. Perhaps it would never be over until he was dead, because there were a lot of people still very interested in what he knew, and any number of others who wanted to pay him back for what he'd done.

They made the broad turn south around Quick Point and the one-design sailing squadron toward the new John Ringling High Bridge. Sarasota's downtown with its glass-faced office buildings, sixteen-story condos, and the Ritz-Carlton intermingling with palms, bougainvillea, and flowering trees, looked subtropical, laid-back, even peaceful.

Kathleen was rigging the dock lines on the bow cleats. McGarvey locked the wheel, and went below for a moment to get his pistol. He stuffed it in the waistband of his trunks, then pulled on a T-shirt, and went back up to the cockpit.

Kathleen turned around as he got back behind the wheel and gave him the resigned look of hers that she knew he was carrying. She didn't like it, but she never complained now like she had in the early days, when their marriage had gone on the rocks. His abilities combined with his instincts had saved their lives more than once. She'd come to understand that when he armed himself it was almost always for a good reason.

They passed under the John Ringling High Bridge, and less than one hundred yards south, picked up the channel markers into Marina Jack where they'd chartered the boat. More than two hundred sail- and power-boats were docked on either side of the modern glass and steel restaurant that was located in its own quiet cove right on Tamiami Trail, which was much like the Quai d'Anglais along Nice's chic waterfront.

McGarvey picked up the microphone and called the dockmaster on VHF channel 16. "Marina Jack, this is *Sunday Morning.*"

"*Sunday Morning,* switch and answer seven-one."

McGarvey switched to the working channel. "Marina Jack, *Sunday Morning.* We've just passed marker eight A. Where do you want us?"

"Tie up at the fuel dock," the dockmaster radioed. "Welcome back. Have a good trip?"

"We're sorry to be back."

"I hear you," the dockmaster said. "You've got someone to see you. He's been here most of the morning."

A tall figure with frizzy red hair came out onto the dock. "Yeah, I know,"

McGarvey said. Even from one hundred yards out he could recognize Otto Rencke. "*Sunday Morning* out." He returned to channel 16.

"It's Otto," Katy called from the bow. She was relieved for the moment. She waved, and Rencke waved back.

A couple of dock boys came out as McGarvey throttled back and eased the sloop starboard side too at the fuel pumps, their speed bleeding to nothing. Kathleen tossed one of the boys the forward line, and McGarvey tossed the other a stern line.

"Hi, Otto," Kathleen said.

Rencke, dressed in tattered blue jeans and a raggedy old CIA sweatshirt with the sleeves cut off, leaned against the building, in the shade of the second-floor overhang. "Hi, Mrs. M," he said. He didn't look happy.

Lavender, McGarvey guessed, or something close to it.

They didn't have to return the boat until tomorrow morning. They'd planned on spending the afternoon packing and cleaning up. This evening they would have dinner, and tomorrow they would fly back to Washington for the closing on their Chevy Chase house on Tuesday. Later in the week they would drive back here to get their new house on Casey Key up and running.

Shutting down the engine, McGarvey had a feeling that there might be a change of plans. Or at least that Otto had come down here to make an offer.

Katy came aft. "You didn't know it would be Otto, did you?"

"No."

"He's got the look, darling. You're going to turn him down, right?"

"You need your holding tank pumped out, Mr. McGarvey?" one of the dock boys asked.

"Please, and when you've filled the diesel run her over to the slip for us, would you?"

"Sure thing, sir."

"Right?" Kathleen asked.

"He's a friend, I'm going to listen to him, Katy," McGarvey said. He went below, put his pistol away, and slipped into a pair of Topsiders.

Kathleen joined him. "What about me?" she asked.

"Otto and I are going for a walk. Why don't you get dressed and meet us at the bar? We'll have some lunch."

"I meant *us,* goddammit," Katy said, keeping her voice low.

"I don't know," McGarvey said. He tried to kiss her cheek, but she pulled away.

"We'll just be a few minutes," he promised. "It'll be okay."

"I don't think so."

McGarvey went topside, opened the lifeline gate, and stepped up onto the dock. Rencke came across to him and they shook hands.

"Oh wow, Mac, Mrs. M didn't look very happy to see me," Rencke said. "Is she okay?"

"Depends on why you're here," McGarvey said. "Was it you looking over our shoulders the past few days?"

"Yeah."

"You could have called."

"Your cell phone was out of service, and I didn't want to use the radio."

McGarvey nodded. "Let's take a walk."

They headed around the restaurant to the parking lot and the sidewalk that followed Tamiami Trail over to City Park a couple of blocks away. There were a lot of people out and about, walking, roller-blading, biking, working on their boats, having picnics, flying kites, fishing. White noise. He and Otto were anonymous here and now.

"This is about Osama bin Laden again, isn't it?" McGarvey said.

Rencke nodded. "Ultimately," he said. "We're on the hunt for him, just like you suggested, but we've stumbled on something else. Maybe even bigger than 9/11 or the suicide bombers you stopped last year."

It felt odd to McGarvey to be back on solid land after two weeks, but not odd to be talking to an old friend about the business. Katy understood him better than he did.

"Who sent you, or did you come down here on your own?"

"Adkins. But no one was sure that you'd come back, or even agree to listen to me. He thought it was worth a shot, and so did I."

They got off the path and walked down to an empty picnic table at the water's edge.

"It's nice here," McGarvey said. He looked at his friend. "I've got a job teaching Voltaire at New College, starting this fall. Did you know that?"

Rencke nodded glumly. "Good school," he said. "But you know that they'd like you to take over at the Farm. You could make a lot of difference for the kids coming in."

"I've heard the offer," McGarvey said. "Now get on with it, Otto. What'd you bring for me?"

"Nine months ago NSA began picking up references to something called Allah's Scorpion, buried in a couple of Islamic Internet sites. Nobody knew what it meant, but we started to get the idea that it might refer to another al-Quaida strike. Possibly here in the United States, possibly elsewhere."

"We've been getting those kinds of signals for a long time," McGarvey said. "But there's been no way of quantifying any of them; telling which one is real and which one is pure fantasy."

"But the chatter has been pretty consistent, Mac," Otto said. He was starting to vibrate. "Over the past few months the talk has spread to just about every Islamic Web site, sat phone, and courier network that we've got handles on. Allah's Scorpion is al-Quaida, we're pretty sure of that. And we think it'll be another sea operation. They might try to hijack a ship, take on a cargo and hit us, or our interests, somewhere in the world."

"Come on, Otto, you guys know that the real key is bin Laden," McGarvey said. When he'd been DCI he'd gone over the same argument with the White House almost on a daily basis. The president had agreed, in principle, but the Company had never been given real marching orders. *Find bin Laden, but don't make waves; we have enough on our plate in the Arab world as it is.*

Otto's head bobbed up and down. "We're looking for him, Mac. Bigtime. Honest injun. But right now we've got this problem to deal with, and we think it's become immediate."

"They'd need a crew."

"Two days ago an al-Quaida strike force broke into Camp Delta down at Gitmo, and tried to spring five Iranian prisoners," Otto said. "They didn't get out of there, in fact when they knew they were cornered, the al-Quaida guys killed the Iranians, and then blew themselves up."

"Navy?"

"Bingo," Otto said. "But they would need a captain. Someone who really knew what he was doing. And the good news is that there just ain't that many guys out there, on the loose, or buyable, who'd go to work for bin Laden."

"Have you come up with a short list?"

"As of yesterday morning, six guys," Otto said. He was excited. "But on the way down I narrowed it to one strong possibility. Guy by the name of Rupert Graham, ex–British Royal Navy, till he got kicked out over some issues stemming from his wife's death. Abuse of power. Excessive use of force. Poor judgment, leading to several international incidents that were embarrassing to the government."

"Continue."

"Until eighteen months ago we think he was pirating in the South China Sea," Otto said. "And doing a bang-up job of it. Of course that's mostly speculation, nothing could ever be proved against him." Otto got up on the tabletop and sat on his legs, something he did when he was superexcited. "He dropped almost totally out of sight, but the Brits, who've got him on a watch list, may have spotted him in Karachi eight months ago, and Islamabad two months after that."

"Bin Laden?"

"It's a thought, Mac," Otto said. "But best of all Graham might have been seen in Mexico City last week. One of our guys, spotting flights to and from Havana, shared the pictures with Gordon Guthrie, the MI6 chief of station there. Looked like a match."

"So Mr. Graham gets around," McGarvey said.

"You don't get it, Mac," Otto said. "He flew down to Maracaibo three days ago."

"Oil tankers," McGarvey said.

"Security is pretty tight in the lake. It'd be tough for an imposter to talk his way aboard a ship, and then convince the crew to sail it out of there for him. But the Venezuelan currency has taken a dump. Could be he's shopping for a crew."

"Has Venezuelan intelligence been notified?" McGarvey asked.

"On the back burner," Otto said. "They've tightened security, but that's about it. Al-Quaida isn't their fight."

How many times had he been called to arms like this? Dozens, and yet he could remember each and every incident as if it was the only one.

"You'd have limited cooperation down there from their Central Intelligence Division," Otto went on. "They made it very clear to me that they didn't want to get involved, but they won't get in your way. In fact, your passport won't even be stamped. You'll never have been there."

No coastal city on the planet would be safe. And it came down to one man—as it almost always had.

"Find him for us, Mac," Otto said. "Take him out. We've got no one else who can do the job. If a guy like Graham gets his hands on a ship, even with a minimum crew, he could get to within spitting distance of New York, Washington, Miami, anywhere, and set off a dirty nuclear weapon, or even lob a missile into the heart of downtown." Otto shrugged. "Could be done, ya know."

The difficult part would be explaining to Katy why he had to do it. Only this time he was going to finish the job once and for all. He would stop Graham, but afterwards he would find bin Laden and put a bullet in the man's brain.

EIGHT

APURTO DEVLÁN, WESTERN CARIBBEAN

Alone in his quarters Rupert Graham replaced the slide on his Steyr GB, clicking it home, and pressing the muzzle cap against its spring until it latched in place. With the pistol cleaned and reassembled, he methodically reloaded three magazines of ammunition, slid one into the handle of the gun, and the other two into the pocket of his dark jacket hanging in the closet.

"There must never be mercy for the infidel until our jihad is finished," bin Laden said to him in the beginning. "It is something you might not understand."

"But I'm an infidel," Graham had responded. Eighteen months ago he did not care if he lived or died. "Does that mean I shall be killed?"

"We all die when Allah wants us," bin Laden said indulgently. "For now you are an instrument of His Messenger."

It was a lot of bleeding bullshit, only now that he was in the middle of a mission, he didn't want to die. He wanted to continue with the fight; stick it to the bastards, and keep sticking it to them. He lowered his head and closed his eyes for a moment.

It was shortly after one in the afternoon. He had disassembled his weapons, spreading the parts out on his bed; cleaned them, reassembled them, and reloaded them, getting ready for tonight's killing.

He'd risen early, before dawn, after only a couple hours of sleep, to be on the bridge when the first morning watch under Third Officer George Novak came on duty. He had stayed up there until an hour ago, when he'd returned to his cabin, and ordered a lunch tray to be brought up from the galley.

In the past few days he had started to get worried. He could bring up a picture of bin Laden in full detail in his mind's eye. That was easy. But he was losing the details of Jillian's face. His wife had been a small woman; her features round, her dark hair usually cut short, bangs across her forehead; she'd looked like a pixie.

He knew all that intellectually, but he couldn't see her, and he was afraid that he might be losing his mind.

He opened his eyes when someone knocked at the door. He got up, flipped the bedcover over his Steyr, the .22 caliber pistol he'd used to kill Slavin, and the Heckler & Koch M8 baseline carbine, and went out to the sitting room, closing the door to his bedroom before he answered the outer door.

The Russian steward, Irina Karpov, was there with a tray. "Your lunch, Captain," she said, smiling. She was a small girl, with narrow shoulders, dark eyes, and short dark hair that framed a round, pixie face. She was dressed in dark trousers and a crisp white jacket.

For just an instant Graham was struck dumb by the similarity between this girl and his wife. He hadn't noticed the resemblance when he'd seen her for the first time yesterday. But her face was the same.

He stepped aside for her and she came in and set the tray on the small table. She took the covers off the dishes. "Cook has made borscht just for you, and some smoked salmon with creamed cheese, onions, capers, and corchinons, and toasted bagels."

"It looks good," Graham said. "Please thank Mr. Rassmussen for me."

"We didn't know if you wanted wine, beer, or mineral water, so I brought all three," Irina said. It seemed as if she were stalling, for some reason, a sly look in her wide eyes.

"Very thoughtful of you, Ms. Karpov."

"*Spassibo bolshoyeh*," she said. *Thanks very much.*

Graham suddenly understood what she was trying to do. She was suspicious of him. He let his expression darken. "I hope that I do not have to continually remind you that the language aboard this vessel is English."

She lowered her eyes. "I'm sorry, sir."

"If it happens again, I'll leave you ashore at Long Beach and hire another steward."

"Yes, sir."

"Do you understand this perfectly?"

She nodded. "I just wanted to thank you for your compliment, sir."

And test my Russian. "I know," Graham said. "Now return to your duties."

"Sir," she said, and she went past him to the door.

"Ms. Karpov," Graham said, before she went out.

She turned back. "Sir?"

"*Pazhaluystah,*" he told her. *You're welcome.*

She was startled. It wasn't what she'd expected. She said something else in rapid-fire Russian that Graham didn't catch, then nodded. "Yes, sir," she said. She gave him a final, searching look and left.

Graham's jaw tightened. It'd been a mistake to speak Russian to her. Even one word. He'd seen the immediate understanding on her face that she knew he was an imposter. He turned away from the door, his mind in a dark turmoil. He wanted to lash out; strike something; destroy someone; shatter them, drive them to their knees, kill the bastards who were responsible.

He slowly came back from the brink, unclenching his fists, willing his muscles to relax.

The stupid bitch had no proof. And in twelve hours she and the others would be dead.

No one was using the officers' mess this noon, but Irina stopped by to make sure that the coffee and tea service was clean and filled. She busied herself loading the few dirty cups, glasses, spoons, and tea bags and wrappers onto a tray, and replacing the stale lemon wedges with fresh ones from the small refrigerator under the counter.

She didn't want to think too hard about the captain, because that would lead her into places she did not want to go. But for the life of her she couldn't understand why Captain Slavin was pretending to be a Russian, when clearly he was not.

Ever since she was a child in Moscow, her father, who had been a brilliant physicist, encouraged her to be an independent thinker. "Do not be shy," he would say. Her mother, on the other hand, was a typical Russian who loved to quote proverbs to get her messages across. Her favorite for

Irina was that once a word was out of your mouth, you couldn't swallow it again. And another was, all the brave men and women were in prison. Her father wanted her to speak up, while her mother wanted her to keep her mouth shut. She'd been torn between the two all her life.

Only a couple of stragglers lingered in the crew's mess room when she brought the tray of dirty cups and glasses to the galley. She rinsed them off and loaded them onto the dishwasher belt. She was confused.

Rassmussen was busy rolling out piecrusts for this evening's dessert. He looked up, a sloppy grin on his broad Norwegian face. He always seemed to be in a jovial mood. "Son of a bitch, what'd the captain say about my borscht?" he boomed.

Irina was startled. She spun around. "What?"

"My borscht. What'd the captain say?"

"He said thank you."

"Thank you!" Rassmussen shouted. His grin widened. "Son of a bitch, wait'll he has my pumpkin pie tonight."

"Russians don't eat pumpkin pie," Irina said absently.

"This one does, he asked for it. Son of a bitch."

Irina turned back to work, rinsing the rest of the lunch dishes, loading them onto the belt, and starting the dishwasher. The galley was clean, as were all but one table in the mess room. Alicia had tided up before going off duty.

"I'm going to my cabin for a couple hours," she told the cook.

Rassmussen nodded. "Be back at four. I'm roasting turkeys with all the trimmings. You'll serve the wardroom."

"Yes, sir," Irina said tiredly. She dried her hands and went up one deck to her cabin in crew territory. She'd been up since four thirty to help with the morning meal for the change of watch standers, and she wanted to rest for an hour or so. Sleep. Shut her mind down. But she couldn't stop from thinking about the captain. The man was pretending to be a Russian, and she could make no sense of it.

Alicia had just gotten out of the shower, and she was in her robe in front of the mirror drying her spiky hair. She looked around when Irina came in. "Hi, sweetie," she said, smiling. But then she lowered the hairdryer. "You looked bushed. Are you okay?"

Irina took off her jacket and tossed it on her bed. "I'm just a little tired, is all."

"Nope," Alicia said. She put down the hair-dryer and came out to Irina. "What's the matter?" she asked, concerned. "Is George hitting on you again?" The third officer had been trying for three months to have Vasquez talk Alicia into setting him up. He wanted the same arrangement with Irina that Vasquez had with Alicia.

"No," Irina said. "It's the captain, he's an imposter."

Alicia was surprised. She shook her head and laughed. "That's rich," she said. "Would you mind telling me how you came to such a brilliant conclusion?"

"His name is Grigoriy Slavin. He comes from St. Petersburg."

Alicia laughed again. "Don't Moscow girls get along with guys from St. Petersburg?"

"He doesn't speak Russian," Irina blurted. "When I tried to talk to him yesterday, and just now when I brought his lunch tray to his cabin, he told me that we had to speak English."

"It's a sensible rule," Alicia said. "We must have ten different nationalities aboard."

"But I thanked him in Russian, and he said, 'You're welcome,' in Russian."

"Okay, so he was being nice."

Irina shook her head. "But his accent was all wrong. Sounded like he was from Tajikistan or someplace like that. But that's not right either. It's driving me crazy."

"Come on, kiddo, you're just tired and you're imagining things."

"Just before I left his cabin, I said something else to him in Russian. If he'd understood he would have fired me on the spot."

Alicia shrugged. "What'd you say?"

"*Yob tvoyu mat . . .*"

"In English."

"I said, 'Fuck your mother, but I think you're a prick,'" Irina said.

⊓I⊓ᛂ

□

MARACAIBO, VENEZUELA

McGarvey, carrying only an overnight bag, emerged from the American Airlines jetway at La Chinita Airport a few minutes after four in the afternoon. Katy had driven him over to Miami's International Airport, where she made him promise to take care of himself.

"I'm not going to try to talk you out of this," she'd said. "It's what you do, and there doesn't seem to be anyone else with the guts to step up to the plate. They're all hiding behind their bureaucracies, and whatever the politically correct flavor of the month happens to be." She was bitter.

He'd taken her in his arms outside the security check-in area. "It's not all that bad, Katy. There are some good people doing the best they can under the laws they have to deal with."

"It never stopped you."

"No," McGarvey said heavily. Following the letter of the law, and especially political correctness, had never exactly been one of his priorities. He'd always done whatever was needed to be done at the time it needed doing, and damn the consequences. Depending upon whatever administration was in charge he'd either been admired or reviled all his career.

But no matter the administration, he'd always been called into action whenever his particular expertise was needed. He was an assassin; the means of last resort to reach a political goal, especially one in which a war could be avoided.

Lawrence Danielle, an old friend in McGarvey's early days with the CIA, had told him that had we known in the mid-thirties what we know today, we would have been more than justified in sending an assassin to kill Adolf Hitler. "Eliminating that one man might have spared us World War Two," Danielle said.

But there'd been some unintended consequences, what in the intel business were called blowbacks, to some of his missions. Instead of killing bin Laden he'd tried to negotiate with the man to give up a suitcase-size nuclear demolitions device. That al-Quaida mission to strike the United States failed, because of McGarvey's intervention. But the ultimate consequence was 9/11.

There'd been other smaller blowbacks, none as spectacular as the attacks on the World Trade Center and the Pentagon, but McGarvey remembered each of them in full detail; they were etched into his brain, like acid designs were etched into glass.

"Take care of yourself, darling," Kathleen told him. "I'll be watching for you to come up the driveway."

Her words had stuck with him on the three-hour flight, but once they'd touched down, he'd put all of his thoughts about her into another, safe compartment in his mind, freeing his total concentration for the job at hand. Anything less could be fatal.

McGarvey followed the other passengers down a long, filthy corridor and around the corner to passport control where two lines formed, one for Venezuelans and the other for everyone else. The afternoon was much hotter and more humid than in Florida.

A slender, handsome man with long black hair, intense coal-black eyes, and a swarthy complexion that reminded McGarvey of the actor Antonio Banderas was waiting to one side. Like McGarvey he was dressed in an open-collar shirt and a light sport coat. He looked like a cop.

"Mr. McGarvey," he said in good English.

"I am if you're Juan Gallegos."

"At your service, señor," Gallegos said. Otto had assured McGarvey that Gallegos was a friend of the CIA, and although what help he would be allowed to give was limited, he would not tie Mac's hands. But he seemed a little nervous.

"I sent a small package under diplomatic seal as checked baggage," McGarvey said.

"Si," Gallegos said. He eyed McGarvey's single carry-on bag. "Do you have any other luggage?"

"No."

"Then if you'll come with me, we'll retrieve your package and go to the hotel. We can talk on the way into town."

McGarvey followed the intelligence officer around passport control, a few of the passengers glancing at them curiously, then down another filthy corridor to a large hall where luggage from the Miami flight was already showing up on the carousel. An airport employee in dark coveralls came from the back and handed a small leather bag to Gallegos, who had to sign for it.

When he was gone, Gallegos handed the bag to McGarvey and they headed toward the customs counters beyond which were the doors out to the Departing Passengers exit, where several buses and taxis were waiting.

"I assume this contains your pistol," Gallegos said. "If you fire it on Venezuelan soil, and especially if you injure or kill someone, there will be a very thorough investigation with possibly harsh consequences. Be very certain that your reasons are compelling and necessary."

"I don't think it'll come to that," McGarvey said, which was a lie. If he found Graham and if he could tie the man to an al-Quaida mission, he was going to take him out.

Gallegos stopped and gave McGarvey a harsh look. "Then why are you here?"

"To find a man."

"And if you find him?"

McGarvey shrugged. "We'll have to see."

Gallegos nodded. "Yes, we'll have to see."

None of the three customs officers even looked up as McGarvey followed the CID agent out of the terminal to a waiting Toyota SUV with big off-road tires and splattered, mud-caked fenders and doors. A fair amount of traffic had built up from a couple of earlier flights.

"I spent the last week in the north outside of Paraguaipoa, in the rain," Gallegos explained. "It's on the border with Colombia."

"Drugs?" McGarvey asked, tossing his bags in the back, and climbing up into the passenger seat.

Gallegos gave him another less-than-friendly look. "The U.S. market is never-ending and the money is very good. It's a powerful aphrodisiac for poor farmers and fishermen. They can make a year's wages for one night of work."

"Maybe we should legalize drugs, and regulate them like we do alcohol," McGarvey said.

Gallegos laughed, and pulled away from the curb ahead of a bus heading into town. The day was very hot and humid, and the air stank of crude oil, natural gas, and other petrochemicals. Oil pumped out from beneath the lake was a major contributor to Venezuela's economy, and the people along the lake paid for it with lousy air.

"Otto sent me a file, which included a couple of decent photographs of the man you're looking for," Gallegos said. "If he came here within the past thirty days it had to be under a false passport, and possibly in disguise. The name Rupert Graham doesn't show up on any list—immigration, customs, or hotel registrations. I had one of the photographs distributed to every port of entry official in the entire country, not just here in Maracaibo, but so far I've received no hits."

"Thanks for the effort, but I don't think he's traveling under his real name. He's on Interpol's most wanted list—"

"Yes, we know this," Gallegos said impatiently. "But what Otto failed to tell me was why he believes Graham came here. The man's wanted for piracy. He couldn't be planning on hijacking an oil tanker, unless he's incredibly stupid. Vensport security is airtight."

The Autopista 1 highway from the airport was in reasonable condition, although traffic was heavy, and trash seemed to be everywhere; garbage, the rusted-out hulks of old cars, a dead horse; and halfway into the sprawling city of more than one million people, a weed-choked field was covered with abandoned cargo ship containers. Windows had been cut into the sides of most of them, and half-naked children played in the muddy lanes between the rows. People were living here.

"Venezuela is in a depression," McGarvey said. "The bolívar is down, oil exports are sagging, the World Bank is pressing for some of the hundred-billion-plus debt, and unemployment is right around thirty percent."

Gallegos scowled, but he nodded. "Which makes the drug trade all the more appealing." He looked at McGarvey. "And not just to poor fishermen and farmers along the border. What does that have to do with Graham?"

"Unemployment among sailors is just as high or higher than your national average. He might be here looking for crew."

Gallegos shrugged. "Nothing wrong with that. Caracas would give him a medal if it were true."

"He works for bin Laden."

"That's not our fight," Gallegos said sharply.

"It will be if al-Quaida uses a crew of Venezuelans for its next strike," McGarvey said.

. . .

They were set up in adjoining rooms at the Hotel Del Lago right on the lake with a fantastic view of the oil derricks, loading platforms, and heavy shipping traffic that never ceased 24/7. Gallegos was heading off to an old boy meeting at the Girasol Restaurant in the Hotel El Paseo with the chief of federal police for Stato Zulia, to see if a quiet APB could be issued. Graham had violated no Venezuelan laws, but it wouldn't hurt to keep an eye out for him, in case he did something wrong.

"For the moment my government and yours are not on the most friendly terms," Gallegos told McGarvey. They were in the hotel's lobby bar. It was busy, but they were out of earshot of anyone. "I don't suppose you'll stay in the hotel until I get back later tonight."

"I thought I might poke around," McGarvey said. He knew exactly what he wanted to find out, and exactly where to find it. Having a Venezuelan CID officer tagging along wouldn't help.

Gallegos nodded. "I'm sure you do," he said. "But try to stay out of trouble, Mr. McGarvey. No gunfights, if you please."

"When will you be back?"

It was already eight o'clock. "Not until late. We often don't eat dinner out until midnight. So unless you need to speak to me tonight, I'll see you in the morning."

"Fair enough," McGarvey said.

Gallegos gave him a last look and then got up and left the bar.

A couple of minutes later, McGarvey finished his beer, signed for the tab, and went back up to his room to change into jeans and a dark short-sleeved pullover. He stuffed his pistol in the quick-draw holster under his shirt at the small of his back, and outside took a cab down to the commercial waterfront district.

If Graham had come to Maracaibo to raise a crew, he had a four-day head start, which meant he'd have made some waves, ripples in a pond into which a rock had been dropped. There'd be someone who had been interviewed but hadn't been hired who'd be willing to talk to an American paying cash.

The cabbie dropped him off at the head of a seedy-looking district that stretched for several blocks two streets up from the main drag along the commercial wharves. The area was ablaze with colored lights, bars or *chinganas* with open doors, and half-naked prostitutes sitting in the open second-floor windows of their *burdeles*. It was early on a Saturday night but the district was already crammed. It reminded McGarvey of Bourbon Street during Mardi Gras.

He bought a cold beer from a street vendor and headed into the district, trying to think like an ex–British naval officer looking for a crew. Unless Graham spoke gutter Spanish he wouldn't get along with the average seaman down here; only the whores would listen to him because he would have money. Another possibility was finding an out-of-work, disgruntled Venezuelan merchant marine officer. If Graham had been able to make contact with such a man, hiring a crew would be taken care of in one stroke.

McGarvey's problem of picking up Graham's trail was solved in the first *chingana* he walked into. The girls from the *burdel* upstairs worked the long marble bar and the tables in the tightly packed saloon for marks.

The instant he sat down at a free table near the door, a small, narrow-hipped woman, with a tiny, round face, large dark eyes, and short hair came over with a big smile, and sat on his lap. She was wearing a nearly transparent white blouse that showed her large, dark nipples, and a black miniskirt so short that the fact she wore no panties was obvious.

"Hey, gringo, what are you doing here?" she asked in English. "Do you want to fuck me?"

"I'm looking for someone," McGarvey said.

"It's your lucky day. Here I am!"

A scantily clad, horse-faced waitress came over. McGarvey held up the beer from the street vendor. "A pink champagne cocktail for your friend?" she asked.

McGarvey nodded and the waitress went back to the bar to get another beer for him and the ten-dollar cocktail made of a few drops of Angostura bitters in a glass of seltzer water with a paper umbrella.

"You a horny gringo?" the girl whispered in McGarvey's ear. "Around the world, fifty dollars." She parted her thighs a little wider.

The going rate for an AB would be around ten or fifteen dollars. But all Americans and Western Europeans had plenty of money.

"What would I get for a hundred dollars?" McGarvey asked.

The girl pulled back to look into his eyes to see if he was kidding around. Her face lit up in a broad grin, two of her teeth missing. "Anything you want, baby!"

McGarvey took out the picture of Graham and held it up so that she could see it in the dim light. For a moment or two she didn't seem to comprehend what was going on, but suddenly her face contorted, and she snatched the photograph from McGarvey's hand.

"¡Qué hijo de puta!" she screeched. *What a son of a bitch!*

The waitress with their drinks at the bar looked up.

"You've seen this man?" McGarvey asked.

The whore jumped off McGarvey's lap and screeched something else in Spanish at the top of her lungs, while brandishing Graham's photograph over her head.

Some of the other customers were beginning to take notice, and the waitress was saying something to a very large, bald-headed man behind the bar.

"Two days ago, *puta!*" the whore shouted in his face. "Are you his friend?"

"I came here to kill him," McGarvey said, just loudly enough for the girl to hear. He took a one-hundred-dollar bill from his pocket and laid it on the table. "Where is he?"

A crafty look came into the girl's eyes, and she reached for the money, but McGarvey batted her hand away.

"What was he doing here?" McGarvey said. "If you're lying, I'll know."

The bald-headed bouncer started across from the bar. He carried a baseball bat. Several of the patrons had gotten to their feet and blocked McGarvey's path to the door.

"If there's a fight, you won't get the money," McGarvey said.

The whore understood the situation. "Cabimas," she told McGarvey. "He said he was shipping out. He was going to Cabimas to get his ship. If he's still in Venezuela he'll be there, across the lake."

"Was anyone with him?"

"No."

McGarvey got to his feet as the bouncer reached him. The girl snatched the money and got out of the way. A crowd was gathering inside the bar and outside on the street. Sailors loved a good fight. But once it started it would become nearly impossible to get away before the police arrived.

He'd gotten an answer, although it wasn't the one he'd expected. The girl had said Graham had come for a ship; he'd not mentioned anything about a crew. Either he'd been indiscreet or he had been covering his tracks.

The girl said he'd been here two days ago. But if Cabimas had been his target, why had he spent his first two days on this side of the lake, in this kind of a neighborhood? And why had he bothered to get a whore mad at him?

The bouncer planted himself a couple feet away from McGarvey, a fierce grin on his broad face. He knocked the baseball bat into the palm of his left hand with a flat slap. He was at least six-five and three hundred pounds, most of which was not fat.

McGarvey spread his hands and stepped away from the table. "No trouble," he said. He wasn't going to pull his pistol for fear someone innocent would get hurt, but he wanted to get back to the hotel, find Gallegos, and get over to Cabimas as soon as possible.

The bouncer poked the bat into McGarvey's chest. "I don't like gringos," he said in good English. "Loud-mouthed bastards who come here with their money to buy the little *Maracuchos*."

He poked the bat in McGarvey's chest again.

"I don't want any trouble," McGarvey tried one last time.

"¡*Bastardo!*" he said. "You're leaving feet first."

The bouncer cocked the bat as if he were preparing to hit a home run. McGarvey stepped inside the man's swing, and hit his Adam's apple with a short, very sharp chop.

The bouncer reeled backwards, suddenly off-balance, unable to catch his breath through his badly bruised trachea. The horse-faced waitress came to his side as he dropped the bat and slumped to one knee.

A hush had come over the crowd, and they parted to make a path for McGarvey as he left the bar. "Bad attitude," he said to one of the sailors outside. "I don't think he liked me."

TEN

□

APURTO DEVLÁN, WESTERN CARIBBEAN

It was midnight local when Graham held up at the door to the bridge. He'd managed to get a couple hours of rest in his cabin after dinner with his officers, but he'd not been able to sleep because of the recurrent nightmare about his wife, and he was very tired now. He would see her somewhere, usually downtown London in the workday crowds. He called her name, but she never heard him. When he tried to run to her, his legs were encased in mud.

Helplessly he watched her step out into the street into the path of a police car, its lights flashing, weaving in and out of traffic, and she was struck and killed instantly.

It was his fault that he wasn't able to get to her in time. And now it was even worse because he could not see her face in his mind's eye. Instead, he saw her likeness everywhere; the attendant on the Aeromexico flight to Maracaibo four days ago, the whore two days ago, and, aboard ship, the meddlesome Russian steward.

He saw Jillian in all of them, and the fact that they were alive and his wife was dead filled him with a nearly uncontrollable rage. He wanted to lash out. Destroy them. Beat them into the ground. Mutilate them so that they would no longer resemble her.

For a second or two longer, he stood at the door, swaying on the balls of his feet, a thin bead of sweat on his upper lip. This afternoon on the bridge and again earlier this evening in the officers' wardroom his first officer, Jaime Vasquez, had given him odd looks, as if the man was searching for something, as if he were suspicious.

It was the Russian steward who'd probably said something to Vasquez's girlfriend, who in turn had gone to her lover. Nattering bitches just like some other women he'd known; unable to keep their noses out of people's business. In that, at least, Islam had it right; women needed to be kept silent behind their veils.

Graham took the pistol out of his pocket, checked to make certain that the silencer was tight, and slowly racked the slide back.

If Vasquez had become suspicious, as he had every right to be, he should have done something about it, Graham thought. At the very least call the company in Dubai to confirm Slavin's background and description. Why couldn't a Russian from St. Petersburg speak proper Russian? Had the tables been reversed it's what he would have done.

He held the gun out of sight behind his back, squared his shoulders, and entered the bridge, closing the door behind him.

Third Officer Novak stood leaning against the chart table by the back bulkhead, several navigational charts, manuals, and plotting tools laid out. He was young and ambitious enough to study for his second officer's test at every available opportunity. He'd confided that he had a fiancée in Detroit whom he would marry as soon as he made first officer. "An admirable plan," Graham had told him.

Only one AB was on the bridge, at the starboard radar display.

Novak looked up, mild surprise on his face. "Captain."

"Where is your other crewman?" Graham demanded.

"I sent him below for some coffee," Novak said. "He should be back any minute."

The AB, a young Pole, looked up. "Sir, I'm painting a small vessel about eight miles off our starboard bow. She's coming right at us. Very slowly."

"Damn fool," Novak said, starting for the radar display.

Graham brought the pistol from behind his back and fired one shot, hitting Novak in the back of the skull, driving him forward facedown on the deck. The front of his head exploded, spewing blood and brain tissue across the instrument panels and the side of the AB's face.

Graham switched aim and fired a second shot, hitting the AB high in the chest, staggering him backwards against the radar display. He was still alive. He raised his hand, as if to ward off another blow, his eyes wide, unable to believe what was happening. Graham steadied his aim and fired a third shot, this one hitting the AB in the forehead, killing him instantly. His body slumped to the deck.

Keeping an eye on the door for the second AB, who would soon be returning with coffee for his dead shipmates, Graham went to the VHF radio, switched to channel 67, and took down the mike.

"Ready one," he said. "Ready one."

"Ready two. Ready two." The reply came immediately.

The door opened and the AB who'd gone for coffee came in, carrying a tray laden with two thermos pitchers and a plate of sandwiches from the galley. He spotted the mess in front of the starboard radar display, and pulled up short.

Graham calmly replaced the mike on its hook and raised the pistol as he turned toward the young crewman.

The AB dropped the tray and frantically scrambled back through the door as Graham fired one shot, hitting the crewman high in the left shoulder, and staggering him to his knees.

Graham calmly walked to the door. The AB, his blue eyes wide, his mouth open in shock, blood splattered on his long blond hair, held out a hand in supplication.

No one had heard the tray clattering to the deck, nor had the crewman cried out for help.

Graham fired one shot at point-blank range into the boy's forehead, flinging him backwards onto the deck. Careful not to step in the gore, he dragged the body back onto the bridge so that it would be out of the way when the mission crew came aboard. The little messes throughout the ship would have to be cleaned up, of course, and the bodies either dumped in the bilges, or stuffed in the frozen food lockers. But all that would be accomplished long before the sun rose this morning.

The rendezvous was set for two hours from now but Graham needed most of that time to get the ship slowed down so that everyone could safely get aboard. First he needed to finish the job of eliminating the crew.

He had already fired five times, which left thirteen rounds still in the pistol, plus a full magazine of eighteen. More than sufficient.

Graham shifted his attention to the ship's multifunction display. They were on the proper course at the proper rate of speed, there were no incoming messages from the company waiting for a response, and the AB at the helm hadn't had time to push the Automatic Distress Signal button.

Everything was as it should be.

He closed his eyes for a moment, but he could not bring Jillian's face to his mind's eye. This time his rage was replaced with a sense of calm; he supposed that he was going crazy finally, but it was of no import. He was willing to take refuge in his insanity, just as bin Laden had done. It was plain by the expression in the man's eyes, and Graham was sure that he too had the same intense, yet disconnected look.

Graham glanced at his watch. He was running a couple of minutes late, but he wasn't seriously behind schedule. He took one last look at the multifunction display above the helm then went out into the corridor to the starboard stairway. He would begin with the engine room, just as he'd planned.

He started down, but something out of the corner of his eye made him stop and look back. For a second he didn't know what had attracted his attention. But then he understood. A light shone from beneath his cabin door behind the bridge. But when he'd left a half hour ago he'd turned out his lights. He was sure of it.

His first thought was that the Russian steward had come to search his room. But she wouldn't have the courage to do something like that on her own. She'd probably convinced Vasquez and his girlfriend to help her.

It was just as well, Graham thought as he walked back to his cabin door, his sneakers whisper-soft on the steel deck. If all three were there he'd kill them first, no matter what they had found.

Concealing the pistol behind his back as he'd done earlier, he opened his door and took one step inside. The situation was worse than he'd feared.

Vasquez, a 9mm Beretta pistol from the ship's emergency locker in hand, was positioned at the doorway to the bedroom, obviously standing guard. He looked up, startled. "He's here," he said, and he brought his pistol to bear before Graham could do a thing.

Beyond him, Irina and Alicia had found his two leather bags, opened them, and spread everything out on the bed: Slavin's clothing, as well as the Heckler & Koch M8 compact carbine with four magazines of ammunition, six one-kilo bricks of Semtex with a small metal box of detonators, leather gloves, a wire garrote, a stiletto and sheath, and an encrypted satellite phone/walkie-talkie.

"Good evening, Mr. Vasquez," Graham said, weighing his options, measuring the angles. Vasquez was a seaman, not a cop or a trained killer. He would be slow to fire at a man he assumed was unarmed.

"What's all this shit, Captain Slavin, if that's really your name?" Vasquez demanded. He was nervous. It was obvious that he'd never held a gun on a man before.

"My personal property for starts," Graham answered mildly. "What made you think that you could break into my quarters and rifle through my things?"

Irina came to the bedroom door, and said something to him in rapid-fire Russian.

"That's not necessary," he said pleasantly. He nodded toward the weapons laid out on the bed. "It's obvious that I'm an imposter. Thing is, what are you going to do about it?"

"Call the company for one, to find out where the real Captain Slavin is," Vasquez said.

"I killed him," Graham said conversationally. "In Cabimas."

Vasquez was visibly shaken. "In that case we're going to arrest you and hold you for the authorities when we reach Colón in the morning."

Graham shrugged, and held up his left hand as if he were giving up. "I guess I can't argue with a man who's holding a gun on me," he said.

Vasquez started to say something when Graham stepped backwards into the corridor and slid away from the open door.

"Shit!" Vasquez shouted. A second later he appeared in the doorway, a frightened look on his face. Too late he saw Graham standing right there and he tried to rear back.

Graham fired one shot into the first officer's left temple. The man's eyes suddenly turned blood-red, his head bounced against the door frame, and he crumpled to the deck half in and half out of the captain's cabin.

The women started to scream.

Graham hurriedly stepped over the first officer's body, dragged it the rest of the way into the sitting room, kicked his gun aside, and closed the door lest someone hear the racket and come to investigate.

Alicia had come into the sitting room. Her hands were clutched to her breast, and she was wailing Vasquez's name. But Irina had grabbed the M8 carbine from the bed, and was fumbling with a magazine of ammunition, trying to load the weapon.

"You should have minded your own business," Graham told Alicia, and he shot her in the face, the bullet striking her at the bridge of her nose, killing her instantly.

Irina was frantically trying to get the magazine into its slot in front of the trigger guard, but in her haste she was forcing it in at the wrong angle.

Graham walked across the sitting room, careful not to step in Alicia's blood.

Irina looked up at him, her face screwed up in a mask of absolute terror.

"You'll never get it loaded that way, my dear," Graham said. He smiled.

"You're the devil!" she cried.

"Da," he said in Russian, and he shot her in the forehead from a range of ten feet.

Her body bounced off the bulkhead and crumpled to the deck, leaving a bloody streak on the white wall beside the large square window. But no blood got on the bedcovers, which for some reason Graham found pleasing. He'd always liked to think of himself as a tidy man, and the sooner he could get his operators aboard the sooner the ship could be cleaned up.

Graham let himself out of his quarters, and headed down one deck. He had changed his plans. Now that the first and third officers were dead, it left only Sozansky and Chief Engineer Kiosawa alive, probably in their quarters. He meant to kill them first before sweeping through the galley and the crew quarters.

At the end he would descend to the engine room, kill the crew, and slow the big computer-controlled turbines to idle.

Nothing would get in his way. In less than ten minutes he would be the only one alive on the *Apurto Devlán.*

A few minutes after two, the oil tanker was making less than one knot through nearly flat seas, under an overcast, pitch-black sky. Graham stood on the main deck amidships on the starboard side. The forty-eight-foot Feadship motor yacht *Nueva Cruz* out of Santiago de Cuba, showing no lights, was directly below, its pilot matching speeds perfectly.

Ali Ramati came out on the yacht's aft sundeck, and waved. He was a slightly built man who'd shaved his beard and his head to make him look very much like Vasquez. He was from the West Bank town of Ramallah, and he was a little crazy, but he was dedicated and bright. He had trained as Graham's first officer for this mission, and, like the others, he was prepared to commit suicide for the cause without hesitation.

The rest of the crew, fifteen of them men, most from the Philippines, plus the two women from Cairo, would remain out of sight until the boarding ladder was safely secured to the tanker, and they were given the all clear.

Everything at this point was being done by hand signals. Although they'd detected no other ships out to fifty miles, well beyond the range of a walkie-talkie, Graham wanted to take no chances.

He waved back.

Ramati opened a large locker, took out a coiled, one-quarter-inch messenger line, and tossed it up to Graham, who caught it as it came over the rail.

The line was attached to a boarding ladder, which came up out of the locker as Graham hauled it in hand-over-hand. In five minutes he had the ladder attached to a pair of big deck cleats, and Ramati begin sending up the crew.

As soon as they were all aboard, the *Nueva Cruz* would immediately head toward Costa Rica a little more than four hundred miles to the southwest, where the four supposedly wealthy French-Muslim businessmen who had chartered the yacht would fish for blue marlin. They would be directly off the Panama Canal tomorrow evening.

First aboard was Mohammed Hijazi, one of their Syrian-trained explosives experts. He had dark eyes, a serious five o'clock shadow, thick shoulders and arms, but the delicate fingers of a piano player. As he came over the rail he smiled.

"*Ahlan wa sahlan,*" he said formally. *Hello.* He was from Nablus, but for the past half-dozen years he'd operated out of the Damascus al-Quaida organization. He had fought in Bosnia, Afghanistan, and Iraq, with a lot of bridges, police stations, schools, and hospitals to his credit.

"As soon as everyone is aboard, get them started in the engine room, but watch out for the blood, I don't want it tracked through the ship," Graham told him.

Hijazi glanced up at the aft superstructure. "They're all dead?"

"Yes," Graham said impatiently. He didn't have time for twenty questions. "I want to be back to cruising speed within the hour, and I want this ship cleaned up before sunrise." There was a possibility, however remote, that one of the satellites GAC regularly bought time on to watch out for its interests, had taken notice that the *Apurto Devlán* had stopped in the mid-Caribbean for some reason and the company would call to find out why.

A second crewman came over the rail, with three behind him on the ladder.

"As soon as Ali is aboard send him up to me on the bridge."

"*Aywa*," Hijazi said. *Yes.*

"English," Graham barked and headed aft.

He had a plausible story about a propeller shaft vibration, but someone had to be on the bridge in case a call from Dubai came.

ELEVEN

□

MARACAIBO

Gallegos wasn't at the restaurant in the Hotel El Paseo when McGarvey showed up, nor was the maître d' inclined to help out even when McGarvey flashed a one-hundred-dollar bill in front of him. There was nothing left for him but to return to the del Lago, and see if Gallegos had come back yet.

He stopped at the noisy lobby bar, got a couple bottles of Red Stripe beer, and brought them upstairs in his own room. He took off his jacket, laid his pistol on the desk, opened one of the beers, and telephoned Gallegos, but there was no answer. Next, he telephoned Otto Rencke on the secure satellite phone.

"Oh wow, Mac," Otto answered on the first ring. He'd been expecting McGarvey's call. "Have you come up with anything?"

"He's here all right, or at least he was as of two days ago."

It was coming up on ten in the evening, and a deep-throated ship's whistle sounded somewhere out on the lake, but very close. It reminded McGarvey of how much he didn't know about Graham, and the situation here and over in Cabimas, and the fact that Graham had a two-day head start.

"All the normal al-Quaida Web sites have gone real quiet in the past twenty-four hours," Otto said. "Just the usual CDLR shit out of London, and the IALHP in Prague. But it's just background noise." The CDLR or

Committee for the Defense of Legitimate Rights, and the IALHP or the Islamic Army for the Liberation of Holy Places, had stepped up their fundraising activities ever since 9/11 had galvanized the Muslim world. Even the elections in Afghanistan and Iraq hadn't stopped the influx of money to bin Laden—much of it from Saudi Arabia, but incredibly a lot of it from the United States.

"How about Louise?" Louise Horn was Otto's wife. She ran the National Security Agency's Satellite Photo Interpretation shop over at Fort Meade.

"Nada, kimo sabe," Otto said. He sounded tired and a little depressed. "If they're not talking on their Web sites or by phone, they have to be communicating via courier, but our Jupiter constellation is picking up almost nothing in infrared."

The National Reconnaissance Office's Jupiter satellite system had originally been put up to watch the India-Pakistan nuclear situation. But since 9/11 it had been pressed into service to also watch the border between Pakistan and Afghanistan where bin Laden was supposed to be hiding.

"Maybe they don't need to talk to each other," McGarvey said. "The mission has started and they're keeping their heads down until it happens."

"That's the conclusion we came to," Otto said. "But what have you come up with? Has Graham been trying to recruit a crew?"

"Apparently not," McGarvey said. "Or at least not here in Maracaibo. But he made a big impression on one of the whores. When I showed her Graham's picture she went ballistic. Claims he told her that he'd come down here to pick up a ship in Cabimas."

"Shit," Otto said. "What is Juan saying?"

"He's at a meeting with the local chief of police. He promised to try for an APB, but the mood down here isn't very good. In fact, if Graham did come down here to recruit a crew the government would probably help him. But Gallegos doesn't think hijacking a ship is possible. He told me that Vensport security is tight."

"Yeah, right," Otto said. "And I've got some water-view property three hundred miles east of here I want to sell you. But he didn't fly to Venezuela for his health. If he's not recruiting a crew then he has to be hijacking a ship, no matter what Juan thinks."

"That's what I figured. I'm going to try to get to Cabimas tonight, but in the meantime I want you to find out what ships have sailed in the past forty-eight hours and their destinations."

"I'll get on it right away, Mac," Otto said. "But why would a guy like Graham blab his guts out to a whore? Seems kinda sloppy to me."

"He might have figured that someone was right behind him and he threw up a smokescreen. Make us think he was going to Cabimas when in fact he was staying right here. Or maybe he's arrogant, and thinks he's bulletproof."

"Or maybe he's nuts," Otto said. "He was kicked out of the navy for some reason. Could be anything."

"Do you have anything new on him?"

"Nothing other than the Interpol package that you've seen. But a friend at MI6 has promised to send over his Royal Navy personnel file. I should have it by morning. If I don't, I'll hack their mainframe and get it."

There was no computer security system in the world that Rencke couldn't break if he put his considerable talents to the job. But for him hacking wasn't just getting into a system and raiding its files. It was getting in and out without being detected.

Three years ago, when McGarvey was still the DCI, he'd invited the top computer experts from all fifteen U.S. intelligence services, plus the top U.S. law enforcement agencies and a dozen key U.S. corporations such as Boeing that did considerable classified business with the government, to a one-day seminar at CIA headquarters. Rencke had come up with a foolproof way of hacking into the latest Quantum effects encryption algorithms, and McGarvey felt that the CIA ought to issue a warning.

One hundred and fifteen enthused computer division supervisors had entered the first-floor briefing auditorium at nine in the morning, and by four that afternoon only a handful of them went away with any understanding of what Otto had told them. The rest of what Otto called the geek squad left Langley wondering if perhaps they should change professions.

"For the moment at least I've got to go with the Cabimas lead, it's the only thing I have, unless you come up with something new from his navy file," McGarvey said.

"He had a four-day head start," Otto said. "Why'd he blow two days of it staying there in Maracaibo to piss off a whore?"

Another possibility suddenly came to McGarvey. On the way in from the airport Gallegos had given him some background on Maracaibo. It was Venezuela's second-largest city with a metro-area population of more than one million. "What's the population of Cabimas?"

"Just a sec," Otto said. A moment later he came back. "A hundred twenty thou."

"Anonymity," McGarvey said. "Maracaibo is ten times the size of Cabimas. He got down here too early, and it's easier to hide out in a big city than in a small town."

"He was waiting for something," Otto said. "A ship."

"A specific ship," McGarvey said.

"I'm on it," Otto said. "Give me an hour and I'll have the name and crew complements of every ship out of Cabimas in the past forty-eight hours."

"They'll have a specific target, and whatever it is, it will be big."

"He's most likely after an oil tanker, which would probably head for the California refineries. If they blew it up at the unloading dock, it could hurt us pretty badly. The gas shortages would all but cripple us until a new refinery came on line. And that could be years."

"You'd better give the Bureau a heads-up."

"We're supposed to go through Don Hamel's office—" Otto said, but McGarvey cut him off.

"Say hello to Fred Rudolph for me," McGarvey said. Rudolph had risen to head the FBI's Counter-Terrorism Division. He was the one man over at the J. Edgar Hoover Building for whom McGarvey had total trust and respect.

"Will do," Otto said. "I'll get back to you within the hour."

"Do that," McGarvey said. He telephoned the front desk and asked that Gallegos call as soon as he arrived.

"Señor Gallegos has just walked in the door," the front desk clerk said. "Un momento."

Gallegos came on a house phone in the lobby. "He refused, and I can't blame him. Graham has broken no Venezuelan laws."

"Never mind that," McGarvey said. "How far is it to Cabimas?"

"Forty-five minutes," Gallegos said. "Is that where he went?"

"I think so. I'll meet you out front, we'll drive down there now."

"What have you learned?" the intelligence officer asked, his tone guarded.

"I'll tell you on the way."

"First thing in the morning," Gallegos said. "We won't do any good down there this time of night."

McGarvey figured the man was right, but it was frustrating to spend the night doing nothing. "I think he's here to hijack one of your ships."

"Impossible," Gallegos said. "I've already told you that Vensport security is airtight."

"There's no such thing," McGarvey said. "But I'll have the names of some possibilities for you within the hour. You can at least alert security down there to be on the lookout."

"Look, Señor McGarvey, this is Venezuela. My service has agreed to offer you whatever help it can. But believe me when I tell you that our shipping security is the best in the world. It has to be, because oil is our lifeblood. If anything were to happen to that industry we would be in more trouble than you can imagine. Do you understand this?"

"If Graham's not after a crew, he came to hijack a ship."

"Sí, you've already said that."

"He evidently figured out a way to do it, otherwise he would not have wasted his time coming here."

"Then he's in for a surprise, because his picture has been sent to Vensport Security."

"When?"

"This morning," Gallegos said. "Get some sleep. We will drive to Cabimas after breakfast, and you will see."

The call from Otto came a few minutes after eleven. In the past forty-eight hours, twenty-seven ships had departed the various oil-loading facilities along the lake, bound for ports from Salvador, Rio de Janeiro, and Montevideo in the south, to St. Croix and New York in the north, and seven transiting the Panama Canal for ports in the Pacific, three of which were in California. Another eleven ships were due to head out over the next twenty-four hours, six of which were bound for U.S. ports.

"There's been no trouble reported from any of the ships already at sea," Otto said. "And the Vensport Lake Terminal Security net has been quiet. If Graham went to Cabimas he's kept his head down."

"Fax the list to the hotel," McGarvey said.

"No need, Mac. While we were talking I downloaded the entire list to your sat phone. Just key your address book."

"Good," McGarvey said. "In the meantime give Homeland Security the heads-up on all the U.S. ports on the list. My bet would be the California refineries."

"Me too, I think," Otto said, somewhat distantly. "But we've got a little time. The *Apurto Devlán*, which is the first ship on the list, isn't due at Long Beach for another ten days."

"Keep me informed, Otto," McGarvey said.

"Will do."

TWELVE

□

APURTO DEVLÁN, LIMÓN BAY HOLDING BASIN

Thirty minutes after they dropped their hook in the holding basin off Colón, a small ex–U.S. Coast Guard gig flying the Panama Canal Transit Authority pennant came alongside and tied up at the lowered boarding ladder. Immediately four men and two small dogs on leashes started up.

It was a few minutes after seven in the morning, and a soft warm breeze came from the southeast, bringing with it the pleasant, damp earthy odors of the rain forest that made the operation of the canal possible. The *Apurto Devlán* flew the tricolor Venezuelan flag from her stern, and the Panamanian courtesy flag and yellow quarantine pennant from her starboard spreader atop the superstructure.

Graham and his second officer, Mohammed Hijazi, watched from the port bridge wing as the boarding party was met by Ali Ramati, who was presenting himself as First Officer Vasquez.

"Why the dogs?" Hijazi asked.

"I expect they're looking for explosives," Graham said. Seeing the dogs and their handlers coming on deck, he'd had a momentary stab of fear that somehow this mission had been blown. But if that were the case, he reasoned, the ship would never have been allowed to come this far. They would have been stopped by a U.S. Navy warship while they were still well at sea.

Hijazi laughed disparagingly. "They should have brought trained fish."

There was something about the two men with the dogs that was bothersome, however. They were taller than the other two, and they weren't wearing uniforms, just dark jackets and dark baseball caps. One of them turned and looked up. Graham involuntarily stepped back. Emblazoned on the front of his cap were the initials FBI.

Hijazi spotted the cap at the same time. "Is it a trap?" he asked, his hand going to the pistol beneath his light jacket.

Graham touched his elbow. "I don't think so," he said. "The Panamanians have probably asked the Americans for security help. They're afraid for their canal."

The four on deck headed aft to the superstructure.

"I'll deal with the paperwork myself," Graham said. "But the FBI agents will want to let their dogs sniff around the ship. I want you to personally escort them. Take them to the product tanks, anywhere they want to go except for my cabin. They won't find anything."

Hijazi was clearly nervous. "We're not ready," he said. "If something goes wrong now we won't be able to destroy the ship."

"Nothing will go wrong," Graham said. A possibility existed, however slight, that the FBI did, in fact, suspect something, and were here to take a preliminary look. If it came to that he'd order the four men and their dogs killed. The ship could be prepared to explode within a half hour. Within that time the *Apurto Devlán* could be driven to the middle of the narrow entrance to the Gatun approaches. If she sank there, it could take months before the canal could be put back into operation.

His crew would die the martyrs' deaths they wanted, so that their families would be paid fifty thousand in U.S. dollars, and he would make his escape using the Transit Authority boat.

But first things first. There was no need to shed blood. Yet.

"Have Ali show the transit people to my sea cabin," Graham said. "And keep your head around those FBI agents."

Hijazi nodded uncertainly. He went back into the deserted bridge and headed downstairs.

Graham took a moment longer to study the eighteen or twenty other ships in the holding basin. All of them were either Panamax oil tankers like the *Apurto Devlán* or container ships. No U.S. warships were anywhere in sight. Nor did anything seem out of order, although at the moment no ships were entering or leaving the cut to the locks.

He contemplated that single fact. Was it a momentary lull in traffic, or had the canal been closed in the face of a terror alert?

A single piece of evidence could never be the basis for a conclusion. Yet something was happening. He could feel it in his bones. Ever since Perisher school he had learned to trust his instincts, and they were telling him loud and clear that someone was coming, sniffing down his trail, and he'd better be ready for them.

He walked back to his sea cabin directly behind the bridge. Leaving the door open, he sat down behind his small desk on which was stacked the crew's passports. Since no one would be going ashore in Panama, health certificates would not have to be presented.

He got to his feet and smiled faintly as Ramati and two men came up the stairs and crossed to his cabin. One of them was in the dark blue uniform of the Panama Transit Authority, but the other much older and heavier man wore a dark business suit, white shirt, and conservative tie.

Ramati's eyes were narrowed, his lips compressed, as if he was trying to warn Graham about something.

"*Dobroyeh ootroh*," Graham said, extending his hand to the uniformed officer. *Good morning.*

"Good morning, Captain, I'm Pedro Ercilla, your canal boarding official," he said, shaking hands. "And of course you must know Señor Almagro."

Ramati's eyebrows rose. He'd stepped aside and his right hand went into his jacket pocket.

"No, I'm afraid that I do not," Graham said, shaking the man's hand. "Should I?"

Almagro smiled pleasantly. "Actually not," he said. "I'm the GAC agent for our ships transiting the canal." He turned to the CBO. "This is Captain Slavin's first voyage with the company. But I'm sure that his name will be quite familiar to us very soon. Isn't that so, Captain?"

"I'm sure of it," Graham said. "May I assume that our transit paperwork is in order?"

"Yes, Captain," the CBO replied.

"I have the crew's passports—"

"Were there any crew replacements at Maracaibo?" Ercilla asked.

"Other than myself, no," Graham said.

"Then I need only see your passport," the CBO said.

"Of course," Graham said. He got his passport from the top of the stack and handed it to the transit official. This would be the first real test of his disguise.

Ercilla glanced briefly at the photo, but then took out a small notebook and jotted down Graham's name, place and date of birth, and the passport number. He handed the passport back. "Thank you," he said.

"I came out because I wanted to meet you," Almagro said. "But also to bring you good news. Instead of the usual forty-eight hours' waiting time, you'll actually be able to begin your transit at midnight. In less than eighteen hours."

"That is good news," Graham said. They could not retrieve the explosive charges, put them in place, and prepare the product tanks when it was light outside. The shortened waiting time would make a difficult job nearly impossible. But they would make do.

"You may expect your pilot at eleven," Ercilla said. "Please have your ship and crew ready, we have a busy transit schedule this evening."

"Of course," Graham nodded pleasantly. But then he hardened his expression. "Now tell me why you brought two American FBI agents and their animals aboard this ship without my permission." He turned to Almagro. "I do not like dogs. I have an allergy."

"I'm sorry, Captain, but you should have been informed before you left port," the company agent apologized. "It's new policy."

"Since when?"

"It was instituted last week," Ercilla said. "My government asked for help. In the present, shall we say, mood of certain international organizations, combined with the sensitivity of canal operations—"

Graham let surprise and relief show on his face. "They're looking for explosives," he said. "Well, very good. I'll sleep better when they're done."

Ercilla smiled and nodded. "So will we, Captain. Believe me."

"If a ship like mine were to suddenly explode in the middle of one of the locks it could conceivably close the canal for months," Graham said.

"No, Captain Slavin," the transit official said. "It would close the canal for years."

"The effect on the world economy would be devastating," Almagro added.

"I expect it would," Graham agreed wholeheartedly. "Now, may I offer you gentlemen coffee or tea while we wait for the FBI to complete its inspection?"

THIRTEEN

□

CABIMAS

"I'm sorry, señor, but we have reached a dead end, as I warned you we would," Juan Gallegos said. He poured another glass of wine and sat back.

It was just nightfall, and he and McGarvey were having an early supper at a small but fashionable *cafetería* on the waterfront, but well away from the commercial district. Traffic had not yet picked up for the evening, and from somewhere they could hear someone playing a guitar, the melody coming to them over a gentle breeze.

They were missing something, just out of reach at the back of McGarvey's head. It had been a frustrating day of running down the shipping agents for each of the twenty-seven tankers that had left port in the past forty-eight hours, plus the eleven scheduled to depart in the next twenty-four hours, showing them Graham's photograph, and trying to get them to look beyond the simple black-and-white image, and imagine that man in a disguise.

Next they had talked to all the hiring agencies to find out if someone might have been trying to recruit a crew. But no one had seen a man who even closely resembled Graham.

All this late afternoon they'd talked to the clerks in several hotels where Graham might have stayed: taxi drivers, on the remote chance that they might run into someone who'd had Graham as a fare; restaurant waiters who might have served him a meal; and with ferry operators who might have taken a man matching Graham's description out to one of the ships. All without luck.

"Will you be returning to the States in the morning?" Gallegos asked. He was polite now that he had done what he could for the gringo and had been proven correct. "I can make sure that you get a first-class seat on the Miami flight. They're usually full."

A waiter came to clear away their plates. McGarvey had scarcely touched his *churrasco* steak that had been cut into thin *criollo* strips, marinated, and then grilled. "Is there something wrong with your food, señor?" the young pock-faced man asked. His attitude was arrogant. He didn't like North Americans.

McGarvey looked up out of his thoughts. "It was fine. I'm just not hungry."

When the waiter was gone, Gallegos asked again if McGarvey would be leaving in the morning.

"We're missing something," McGarvey said. "Graham was in Maracaibo two days ago, and according to the whore he was coming here to meet his ship."

"If you can believe her."

"Graham might have lied to her, but she was telling the truth. Still it doesn't matter. If he came to Venezuela to board a ship he could have done it just as easily from Maracaibo as here."

"Easier," Gallegos said. "There're more water taxis out of Maracaibo than here."

"Why did he come here?"

Gallegos shook his head, frustrated. "It's a moot point. If he wasn't here to raise a crew, and if he didn't bring men with him, how could he expect to hijack one of our ships? One man alone could not do it. You can see that, can't you?"

McGarvey nodded. "Maybe he wasn't planning on hijacking a ship."

Gallegos threw up his hands. "What are you talking about now?"

All at once it came to McGarvey. He motioned their waiter for the check. "Graham came here because he was after a specific ship. One that was being assigned a new officer, probably the captain."

"If he stayed at a hotel his passport would have been checked."

"He probably killed the captain, got rid of the body, and either switched photos in the passport or altered his appearance." The waiter brought the bill and McGarvey laid down a twenty, which more than covered it and a good tip. "If a new captain was here to meet his ship, where would he stay?"

"The Internacional," Gallegos said. "But we were there this afternoon."

"We only talked to the desk clerk," McGarvey said. "This time we're going to talk to the rest of the staff, starting with the bell captain. Someone may have carried the real captain's bags into the hotel, and Graham's bags back out. Room service may have brought him a meal. The chambermaid cleaning his room may have seen him. Someone might have noticed something."

The hotel was less than a block away. They drove over and parked under the canopy in front of the main entrance. "Leave it here, we'll be just a minute," Gallegos told the valet.

Inside, they approached the bell station where a young, good-looking man in the blue uniform of a bell captain was reading a newspaper. He looked up with interest, folded the newspaper, and put it away. "Good evening," he said. "Are you gentlemen checking in?"

"*Buenas noches*," McGarvey said. He handed the bell captain Graham's photograph with a twenty-dollar bill. "Have you seen this man?"

Sudden understanding dawned on the bell captain's face. "You were here this afternoon, speaking with Mr. Angarita," he said. He pocketed the money. He looked at the photo and shook his head. "I'm sorry, this man is unfamiliar to me. But if you would care to leave the photo I can ask my staff."

"That would be helpful," Gallegos said.

"Do many ship's officers stay here at the hotel?" McGarvey asked.

"Of course," the bell captain said. "Often."

"Any in the past two days?"

The bell captain nodded. "*Sí.*"

"A captain or a senior officer, maybe?" McGarvey asked. "Someone who stayed the night, and then left for his ship in the morning?"

The bell captain thought for a moment, and then nodded. "There was one."

"But not this man," McGarvey said. "Not even a man who might have looked like him, even faintly. Perhaps his shoulders. Maybe his eyes, or the way he walked. Or his manner: pleasant, indifferent, arrogant."

The bell captain studied the photo again.

"Perhaps there was something different about him," McGarvey pressed. "Maybe when he checked in he was relaxed, but when he left he was in a hurry, maybe anxious."

"The Russian captain," the bell captain said hesitantly. "Something was odd about him, I think."

McGarvey kept a poker face. He shrugged. "Odd?" he asked. "What do you mean?"

"He was a GAC guest of the hotel two days ago. Stayed only the night. In the morning the Vensport ferry service took him out to his ship by helicopter."

"Continue," McGarvey prompted.

"I personally handle most of our VIP guests, so I took his bags up to his suite when he arrived. He tried to tip me, but Mr. Angarita who'd come up with him explained that GAC would take care of everything."

"Is that common practice?"

"Yes, sir," the bell captain said. "But Captain Slavin seemed a little embarrassed."

"So?"

The bell captain looked at the photo again. "In the morning, Manuel took his bags to the helipad on the roof. He said that the captain tipped him and insisted he take it. It was odd, after his embarrassment the evening before."

"Do you know the name of the ship?" McGarvey asked.

"No, but I can find out," the bell captain said. He turned to his computer behind the desk and brought up the hotel folio for Slavin's stay, which included the destination and charge for the helicopter ferry service. "It's the *Apurto Devlán*," he said, looking up. "But Captain Slavin, or whoever he is, will be back."

"How do you know that?" Gallegos asked, in English for McGarvey's benefit.

"He checked a large aluminum trunk with us," the bell captain said.

"Where is it?" McGarvey demanded.

"Right here, in guest storage," the bell captain said. He opened a door to a small room behind his bell station. Various boxes and pieces of tagged luggage were stacked on metal shelves. An aluminum trunk about the size of a footlocker sat in a corner.

"Evacuate the hotel," McGarvey ordered.

"What—?" the bell captain sputtered.

"I wouldn't put it past Graham to leave a little surprise for us," McGarvey told Gallegos. "If he thought someone might be on his trail it would cover his tracks."

Gallegos showed the bell captain his CID credentials, and said something to him in rapid-fire Spanish, but the young man backed up and shook his head.

"Get a bomb squad over here on the double," McGarvey said. He walked back to the main entrance, where he'd spotted a fire alarm. He broke the glass with the little hinged hammer and pulled the lever. Alarms began to blare all through the hotel.

.   .   .

McGarvey and Gallegos stood outside under the canopy, while the police held the majority of the hotel guests and staff behind barriers half a block away. Police units, fire trucks, and ambulances were parked all over the place, their emergency lights flashing. A military bomb disposal squad had been choppered across the lake from Maracaibo within twenty minutes of Gallego's call to the Zulia State barracks. They'd been inside for nearly a half hour, before the supervisor emerged from the lobby. His Lexan face shield was in the raised position.

He came over to where McGarvey and Gallegos were waiting. His complexion under the harsh entry lights was pale, and his face was shiny with sweat. He looked as if he was about to be sick.

He said something in Spanish to Gallegos, who shot back a rapid-fire response. The bomb disposal supervisor glanced at McGarvey, nodded, and headed across to his truck.

"I think it was Graham," Gallegos told McGarvey. "The body of a man, who will probably turn out to be the Russian ship captain, was stuffed into the aluminum trunk."

The news was more frustrating than surprising to McGarvey. "Was anything else packed with the body?"

"We won't know until the medical examiner gets here," Gallegos said. "But you were right all along. I'm sure that my government will ask your navy for help. If some maniac has actually gotten control of one of our tankers there's no telling what will happen."

"We're already on it," McGarvey told him. "The target's probably one of our oil refineries in California, which means we have time to do something."

"How can I help?" Gallegos asked earnestly. He'd been wrong, but he was sharp enough not to hold any grudges.

"I'm probably going to need some fast transportation out of here," McGarvey said.

"I'll have Air Force on standby for you. Whatever you need."

McGarvey walked a few feet away and made a sat phone call to Rencke, who was still at Langley. "It's the *Apurto Devlán*. Graham probably killed the captain ashore here in Cabimas and took his identity. What can you tell me about the ship?"

"She's a Panamax oil carrier, nine hundred feet on the waterline, beam of one hundred and ten feet. Twelve separate tanks, carrying fifty-thousand-plus tons of light sweet crude."

"What about the crew?"

"Normal complement of a master and twenty-three officers and crew, but she's been running shorthanded. Nineteen and the captain."

McGarvey put himself in Graham's shoes. He'd apparently come up with enough information about the ship and her officers to feel confident that he could get away with posing as the captain. Once aboard, and at sea, he would have to eliminate the entire crew and probably stop at some rendezvous point to pick up their replacements.

"Where's the ship right now?"

"I'm just bringing it up now," Otto said. He sounded excited.

McGarvey could see him in his pigsty of an office; empty classified files, NRO satellite photos, top secret Company memos, and empty Twinkie wrappers would be scattered all over the floor, on the desk and chairs, while Otto, probably dressed in ragged jeans and a dirty sweatshirt, would be working a half-dozen computer monitors and keyboards like a concert organist manipulating several registers.

"Oh wow, Mac, she's in the Limón holding basin," Otto said. "Scheduled to start her transit in a few hours. Midnight."

"Have the canal authorities already cleared her?" McGarvey asked.

"Yes, but she'll stay anchored until the pilot comes aboard," Otto said. "But I just had another thought. What if Graham isn't targeting the Long Beach refineries? What if he's after the canal?"

McGarvey had kicked the same idea around in his head all afternoon as they'd worked their way through the shipping and hiring agencies. The only mistakes that Graham had made were telling the whore he was meeting a ship and then making her mad enough to remember him out of all her johns. He was professional enough to have eluded capture for the past several years even though he was a hunted man worldwide, which meant he had a very definite plan, one which he believed would not fail. He would be professional enough to realize that time was against him. The moment he'd killed the Russian captain, the countdown had begun. Sooner or later the body that he'd stuffed in the footlocker would be discovered; sooner or later someone would come looking for him.

Once the *Apurto Devlán* cleared the Panama Canal it would take nearly ten days to reach California. *Too many bad things could happen in such a long time.*

"I think you're right," he told Rencke. "Where would he blow up the ship to do the most damage?"

"The Gatun locks, on the Caribbean side," Otto said without hesitation. "I already worked it out. If he could take those out it would be a very long time before the canal could be made operational again. It's even possible that it'd never get done. The whole thing is way too small for most modern ships. If it were going to be rebuilt, it'd be better to start from scratch. Make it fit the ships out there delivering cargo, not the other way around. But nobody's got that kind of do-re-me these days."

"Okay, hang on a minute, Otto," McGarvey said, and he walked back to where Gallegos was smoking a cigarette and watching the police activity inside the lobby. They'd dragged the aluminum footlocker out of the storage room, and a photographer was taking pictures. The other officers were keeping their distance because of the smell. "Is your offer still open for a quick ride out of here?"

"Sí. Where do you want to go?"

"The Panama Canal," McGarvey said. "Probably the international airport at Panama City."

"How soon?"

"Right now," McGarvey said.

"Give me five minutes," Gallegos said, and he took out his cell phone.

McGarvey turned back to Otto. "Do we still have an Emergency Response Team in the Canal Zone?"

"Yes. They're based in Panama City."

"Alert them to what's coming their way. But make it damn clear that they wait until I get there, they'll have to chopper me up to Colón. Graham will have his own crew aboard, and they'll be willing to go up in flames for the cause if they're pressed."

"They might have their own threat-response orders," Rencke warned.

"If need be call Dennis Berndt at the White House, he's got muscle." Berndt was the president's national security adviser.

"You're going to have to hustle, Mac," Rencke said. "We're running out of time if Gatun is the target."

"Juan is working on it for me," McGarvey said, a tight smile on his lips. "I have a couple of things that I'd like to discuss with Mr. Graham tonight. I think he'll find what I have to say interesting."

FOURTEEN

□

APURTO DEVLÁN, LIMÓN BAY HOLDING BASIN

It was approaching eleven o'clock. The transit pilot would be coming aboard in a little more than a half hour, yet the job wasn't finished. Graham hesitated for just a moment on the open deck just forward of the superstructure to catch his breath in the clean air. The night sky was pitch-black, but they were surrounded by the lights of dozens of ships, large and small, most of them at anchor, although in the past two hours, three ships had headed into the narrow cut that led to the Gatun locks.

Spread out along the eastern shore of the bay, the city of Colón's sky-scrapers and business district looked like diamonds, rubies, and emeralds against a black velvet backdrop. The place reminded him in some ways of Singapore's skyline at night. He'd looked at it through a search periscope from well offshore. But that was another time and place that he didn't want to remember now.

Hijazi had taken charge of the engine room, along with one of the other operators, and they'd just finished packing enough Semtex around the rudder shaft to permanently disable the ship if something drastic went wrong. In the worst-case scenario they would jam the rudder, set the ship's engines All Ahead Full, and ram the first lock gate. It wouldn't do the same damage as exploding the ship inside the middle lock, but it would do enough to close the canal for months, perhaps even years.

The access hatch to the six starboard stairwells was open and a dim red light shone from below. The narrow stairs descended eighty feet to the bottom of the ship between the hull and the wall of the farthest aft product tank on the starboard side. Access hatches and stairs for each of the twelve oil tanks, plus the two slop tanks and six pairs of ballast tanks for when the ship was running light, ran left and right.

Graham took a last look around topside. A helicopter low in the sky was heading northwest, the sounds of its rotors against the other harbor and city noises faint on the light evening breeze. No threat there. And what was probably a commercial jetliner was coming in from the north for a landing at Panama City thirty-five miles across the isthmus.

Although the timing was uncomfortably tight, everything was going according to plan. After nightfall, they had retrieved the explosives and their weapons from the four streamlined trunks attached by powerful magnets to the hull five feet below the waterline. Fifty miles out they had attached them to the stern of the ship, where the water flow was the least disturbed, and none of them had been lost.

They faced no immediate threats to the operation. Everything was going according to plan. Yet Graham could feel that someone was coming. It was as if he were game, being stalked by a jungle cat he could not see but knew was there.

As soon as he stepped through the hatch and started down the stairs he was aware of a deep-throated hissing sound, as if he were hearing a powerful waterfall from a long distance, or compressed air being let out of a submarine's ballast tanks. It was the inert nitrogen being vented out of the tank. They had to do it slowly so that no one in the harbor would hear what was being done and come to investigate. Once the nitrogen was gone, the air spaces at the top of the product tanks would fill with an explosive mixture of gases that continuously evaporated from crude oil.

When that happened, the entire tanker would become a time bomb waiting for a simple spark, or the explosion of a few kilograms of Semtex, to blow sky-high, destroying the entire ship and anything or anyone in its vicinity.

The steel plating of the hull was cool and dry to the touch, but the wall of the product tank was greasy with condensation, and the air stank so badly of crude oil gases that it was practically unbreathable.

Ramati was crouched at the bottom of the stairs, molding a four-kilo brick of plastic explosive to the base of the tank, while Faruq al-Tashkiri, who'd been an electrical rating aboard an Egyptian destroyer, held a red light.

The noise of the venting nitrogen was very strong down here, but it suddenly stopped and Ramati and al-Tashkiri looked up, their eyes wide as if they were deer caught in headlights.

"We're almost done here," Ramati said. "And this is the last tank."

"Good," Graham said. "The pilot is due aboard in thirty minutes, and you have to clean up, change into the first's clothes, and be at the rail to greet him and bring him up to the bridge."

"Give me one minute, Captain, and I'll have the receiver wired to the detonator," Ramati said. "But for Allah's sake make sure that your transmitter is in the safe mode." He managed a thin, pale smile in the red light. "After all this work I don't want to go to Paradise empty-handed, with no infidel souls blown to hell."

Graham took the transmitter out of his pocket and held it up. "No battery yet," he said. The transmitter looked like an ordinary cell phone. But he'd not taken the battery out; he would only have to enter 9 # 11 and the *Apurto Devlán* would light up like the interior of the sun in the blink of an eye.

No one aboard would feel a thing. One minute they would be alive, and in the next there would be nothingness.

For just a moment Graham toyed with the idea of entering the code right now. End it once and for all. Maybe most of the rest of the world was right and he was wrong; maybe there was a god after all. Maybe by pushing the buttons now he could be with Jillian just as the Anglican priest at her funeral had promised.

Ramati read something of this from Graham's expression. "Captain?" he said.

Graham managed a tight smile, and put the transmitter back in his pocket. There were times like these when he thought he might be insane. But it didn't matter. He was what he was, a product of the world he lived in. "I want you both on deck in twenty minutes."

Al-Tashkiri was looking at him with a religious light in his face.

Graham nodded. "Only four hours now," he said.

The young Egyptian compressed his lips as if he was afraid to speak, but he nodded vigorously.

"See you on the bridge," Graham told them, and he headed back up on deck.

It wasn't he who was insane, it was Ramati and al-Tashkiri and the other bastards who were willing to blow themselves up for the cause. Even if there were a god, He, She, or It wouldn't require suicide bombings to kill someone who didn't believe in the right things. That was the face of insanity.

Maybe it wasn't the people who were insane, maybe it was the gods.

Topside in the fresh air, he used his walkie-talkie to call Hijazi in the engine room. "Are you ready to answer ship's bells?"

"*Aywa*," Hijazi came back at once.

"English," Graham radioed.

"Yes, everything is in order here," Hijazi said.

Graham could hear the excitement in the man's voice. He was just like the others; they thought they were going to be in Paradise in a few hours. The younger ones had written suicide notes to their families, which would be posted from Karachi when the operation was completed. The older freedom fighters like Hijazi hadn't bothered. "It's enough to know that we hurt the bastards," he'd told the others during training.

"Then stand by," Graham said. "We should be getting under way within the hour."

The channel was silent for a few moments. Graham was about to pocket the walkie-talkie when Hijazi came back, his voice subdued.

"God be with you," he said.

Religious mumbo jumbo, Graham thought. The engine room would be Hijazi's final resting place and the man knew it. He was simply trying to say his goodbyes. Graham keyed his walkie-talkie. "Insh'allah," he said.

Pocketing the walkie-talkie he headed up to the bridge. Mumbo jumbo or not, he needed Hijazi and the others for just a few more hours. And if it took mumbling blessings, then so be it.

FIFTEEN

☐

EN ROUTE TO PANAMA CITY

McGarvey was flown across the lake to the military area of Maracaibo's La Chinita Airport aboard a Venezuelan Navy Sea King helicopter. He was met on the tarmac by a dark-skinned air force captain who introduced himself as Ernesto Rubio.

"I have a Gulfstream standing by for you, sir," the captain said. "It's the vice president's, so I think you'll find the accommodations pleasant enough."

The only activity at this hour was on the civilian side. A 747 was taxiing out for takeoff, the last flight of the evening, the one McGarvey should have been on. Gallegos had escorted him to the helicopter, which had landed in a parking lot near the commercial docks, but he had not come along for the ride. He'd been ordered back to Caracas to brief the chief of Venezuelan intelligence on the situation. It had the potential of becoming a major international embarrassment. Zulia State Security had allowed a Vensport ship to be so easily hijacked that the CIA had to intervene. If the *Apurto Devlán* actually made it to California and destroyed a refinery, the consequences for Venezuela's already ailing economy would be nothing short of devastating. McGarvey was to be given all the help he wanted, while Gallegos briefed his boss on worst-case scenarios; one of which was that the ship had not been hijacked. If U.S. forces boarded her and found the legitimate captain and crew going about their lawful business, relations between Caracas and Washington would become worse than they already were.

McGarvey followed the air force officer fifty yards across the tarmac to a sleek bizjet with civilian markings already warming up inside a hangar. Its hatch was open and a young attractive woman in an air force uniform stood at the foot of the boarding stairs.

"We just got clearance to transit Colombian airspace," Rubio said as they climbed aboard. "We can head straight across to Cartagena and from there, follow the coast southwest. Should be touching down at Panama City in under two hours."

"I'll need to use my satellite phone once we're in the air," McGarvey said. " Is that going to cause a problem?"

"No, sir," Rubio told him. He said something in Spanish to the flight attendant, who smiled and nodded. Then he turned back to McGarvey. "Sergeant Contreras speaks excellent English. If you need anything just ask her. We'll be taking off immediately."

Rubio went forward to the cockpit while the attendant brought up the stairs, closed and dogged the hatch, and then stowed McGarvey's overnight bag. They were out of the hangar and taxiing rapidly across to an active runway as McGarvey strapped into one of the very large, leather upholstered swivel chairs on the starboard side. Within less than two minutes they were accelerating down the runway, and then lifting off into the night, on their way to what could very well turn into a bloodbath before morning.

The attendant came back to him from the galley. "Would you care for a drink, sir?" she asked. Her hair was very dark, and her eyes were wide and warm. She seemed to be genuinely interested in serving him.

"A cognac if you have it," McGarvey said. "Neat."

"Certainly, sir," she said.

He pulled out his sat phone and called Rencke, who answered on the first ring.

"Oh wow, Mac, the pilot is already on his way out to the ship," Otto gushed. "We picked up the Transit Authority's coms channels. Means they'll lift anchor within the hour. Probably sooner."

"How long will it take them to get into the locks?"

"An hour, once they get under way, maybe less, to make it to the first lock, and then an hour and a half or two at the most to make it through all three."

"If you were going to do it, where would it be?"

"The middle lock," Otto said without hesitation. "With any luck you'd take out all three, plus the control house, pumps, and electrical switches."

Sergeant Contreras set his drink on the low table at his elbow then returned to the galley. She was trained to make herself scarce when a VIP guest was on the phone.

"That's where it'll happen," McGarvey said. "What about the Rapid Response Team? Have they been briefed?"

"Yes, and you're going to run into a buzz saw," Otto said. "The on-duty squad is a SEAL fire team. Gung ho. The team leader is Lieutenant Ron Herring. I looked up his record; he's a good man, one of the best. Kosovo, Afghanistan, and northern Iraq. Same team. He wasn't going to back down even for Berndt, once he was briefed."

"What does he want to do?"

"Take the ship right now," Otto said. "In the holding basin, before she raises anchor."

"They might pull the pin the moment someone sets foot aboard," McGarvey warned. But even as he said it, he wasn't sure. Graham's crewmen were probably Muslim fanatics, al-Quaida-trained mujahideen. They'd sacrifice themselves. But Graham had a long record of terrorist attacks against Western interests. Just like bin Laden, Graham was one of the generals who led other men to die for him. He wasn't planning on killing himself just to prove a point. He had an escape plan; one that he considered foolproof.

"Herring knows that you're on the way. He's going to sit tight for the moment, but he's waiting for your call. He wants to talk."

"Good, I want to talk to him," McGarvey said. "What's his phone number?"

"Just a sec," Otto said. "Okay, I just sent it to you. Hit phone book, his number will come up first, then press Send."

McGarvey smiled and shook his head. "Has anyone ever told you that you're scary?"

Otto laughed. "Oh, boy. Not lately and not by you. Thanks, Mac." He took it as a compliment. "Good luck."

Lieutenant Herring was waiting for the call. He answered on the first ring. "Mr. McGarvey, I presume." He sounded young, but no-nonsense.

"That's right. I'm aboard a Venezuelan air force Gulfstream, and we'll be touching down in Panama City in less than two hours. What's your present situation?"

"My team is standing by on the ramp," Herring said.

"What's your plan?" McGarvey asked tersely.

"Save lives first, and the canal second," Herring shot back. "If I'm allowed to do my job without civilian interference."

"Look, Lieutenant, the ship's real crew has probably been murdered, and the ship rigged to explode—"

"It's my intention to prevent just that," Herring said. "Before the ship gets into the canal."

"You'd better be quick and accurate," McGarvey said. "The moment they find out your people are aboard they'll push the button and the *Apurto Devlán* will light up like a Roman candle. Anything nearby will be destroyed as well."

"They may blow the bottom out, and the ship might sink, spilling its oil into the bay, but aside from an ecological disaster the damage won't be as widespread as it would if the same thing happened inside one of the locks. My engineers tell me that the hydraulic shock of a substantial underwater explosion could put the lock doors out of commission."

"Did your engineers tell you what would happen if the nitrogen gas in the oil tanks was bled off first?" McGarvey asked.

Herring hesitated for just a beat. "Someone at anchor in the holding basin would have heard it. From what I'm told the operation is noisy."

"Not if it was done slowly, over the past half-dozen hours or so," McGarvey countered.

"I'll concede the point, Mr. McGarvey. But it's all the more reason to hit the ship before she enters the locks."

"Except for one thing," McGarvey said. "Everyone aboard is a Muslim fanatic. Willing to die for the cause. Everyone except for the captain, who is ex–British Royal Navy. He won't push the button unless there is no way out for him."

"Continue," Herring said.

"He has an escape plan."

"How do you know that?"

"Men like him always do," McGarvey said. He'd been going up against Graham's type for more than twenty years. The names and some of the methods changed, but the mindset was pretty much the same; they were willing to kill for their twisted reasons, but none of them were quite as willing to die for their cause. "And I know this guy, do you?"

"No," Herring admitted. "So what do you want to do, McGarvey?"

"He means to get into the second Gatun lock before he pushes the button," McGarvey said. "I want to let him do exactly that."

"Whose side are you on?" Herring shouted.

"The explosives will be on a remote detonator, which only Graham will have," McGarvey explained. "All we have to do is throw a monkey wrench in his plan to get off the ship before he pushes the button. But without him knowing about it."

"How in hell are you going to do that?" Herring demanded.

"Meet me at the airport and I'll tell you," McGarvey said. "In the meantime don't alert the Panamanian authorities, I don't want to start a panic."

SIXTEEN

□

APURTO DEVLÁN, LIMÓN BAY HOLDING BASIN

Graham lowered his binoculars and turned around from where he'd been studying the entry to the Gatun locks as Ramati came aboard the bridge with the Panama Transit Authority pilot. The dark-skinned, substantially built man wore dark slacks and a light blue short-sleeved shirt with his name and position, PILOTO, sewn above the left pocket. He carried a small leather satchel.

"Captain Slavin, our pilot has arrived," Ramati said.

Graham laid the binoculars aside. "Welcome aboard, Mr. Sanchez," he said, reading the name tag.

The pilot shook hands with Graham, but he had an odd expression on his face. "I don't remember you, sir," he said.

Graham shrugged. "I don't believe that we've met."

Sanchez shook his head. "No. But I was sure that the name was familiar."

Graham considered the unexpected problem for just an instant, and then he smiled. "My cousin Dimitri is employed by GAC. You probably worked with him. We could be brothers."

Sanchez was skeptical, but he shrugged. He walked past Graham, set his satchel down beside the helm station, took out a pair of binoculars, and looked through the windows at the foredeck. "Are your engines ready to answer the bells?"

"Of course," Graham said. "We're anxious to get started."

Sanchez lowered the binoculars and turned around. His gaze lingered for just a moment on al-Tashkiri who would be standing by at the helm, then to Ramati who would relay the pilot's orders to the deck crew, and finally to Graham. "Why are your line handlers not on deck?" he asked mildly, no hint of rebuke in his tone of voice.

He was just doing his job, but Graham felt sure that the man was suspicious that everything was not as it should be here. "I was waiting for your arrival, Mr. Sanchez," Graham said evenly. "No need to have my people standing by in this heat and humidity until they're required."

"They're required now, Mr. Slavin, if you please," Sanchez said. "When they are in position, you may raise anchor and we shall proceed."

"As you wish," Graham said. He nodded for Ramati, who keyed his walkie-talkie. Just for an instant Graham had the terrible thought that his number one was going to speak in Arabic, in which case the game would be up, the pilot would have to be killed, and they would probably not make it to the locks.

His own escape was assured. If he had to abandon the plan out here in the bay, he would activate a small homing beacon, don a life jacket, and slip over the side. Within minutes the *Nueva Cruz*, which had followed them from the rendezvous yesterday, would pick him up. When they were far enough out, he would detonate the explosives and then head northwest to Costa Rica where he would be put ashore near Puerto Limón. From there he would make his way overland to the international airport at San José and then Mexico City.

On the other hand, if they did make it all the way into the second lock, he would simply step over the side in the shadows while the ship was at the height of the lift and the deck was nearly at the same level as the lip of the canal chamber. From there he would make his way out of the damage zone, push the 9 # 11, and in the confusion get back to the head of Limón Bay where a small boat would be standing by to take him out to the Nueva Cruz.

One man, moving alone and fast in the night, always had the advantage over a superior force. Osama had proved that for five years. But the thought of coming so far and failing ground at his nerves.

Ramati keyed the walkie-talkie. "Mr. Sozansky, send out the line handlers, please."

"Roger," one of the mujahideen responded in a reasonably good English accent.

All Panamax ships were guided through the locks by electric locomotives called mules, which ran along tracks on both sides of the canal. Leader lines were tossed down to the ship, which would be used by the line handlers to pull heavy cables down on deck that would be attached to cleats starboard and port, bows and stern. The ships would move in and out of the locks under their own power, but would be guided and held in place by the mules.

Graham picked up the ship's phone and called Hijazi. "Mr. Kiosawa, stand by to raise anchor, please."

"The pilot is here?" Hijazi asked.

Graham glanced at Sanchez, who had pulled a handheld VHF radio out of his satchel. "Yes. We'll be getting under way shortly."

"Insh'allah."

"Yes, indeed," Graham said, careful to keep the anger out of his voice. Hijazi was assuming that the pilot could not hear what he was saying. But he'd taken an unnecessary risk for the sake of his religious sensibilities.

Ramati stepped across to the starboard wing so that he could see astern as well as forward. He spoke into his walkie-talkie then came back onto the bridge and crossed to the port wing, where he spoke again into his walkie-talkie, then came back.

"Our line handlers are in position," he told Graham.

"Very well," Sanchez said, without waiting for Graham to confirm the report. He keyed his VHF radio. "Gatun Control, this is the *Apurto Devlán* with pilot ready for upbound transit."

"Roger, *Apurto Devlán*, you are cleared for transit."

Sanchez turned to Graham. "Mr. Slavin, you may raise anchor, and get under way. Course one-seven-four, speed two knots."

Graham called Hijazi. "Raise the anchor, and prepare to give me two knots."

"Roger," Hijazi said, subdued now that they were actually getting under way. In a few hours everyone aboard ship would be incinerated, and it had finally gotten to him.

Graham replaced the phone. Hijazi and the others would finally get the answer they'd spent their lives seeking. *They would probably be disappointed.*

SEVENTEEN

□

PANAMA CITY INTERNATIONAL AIRPORT

The lights of Panama City had sparkled from a distance as the Gulfstream carrying Kirk McGarvey flew across the isthmus straight down the cut between the mountain peaks through which the canal had been blasted. When the VIP jet's hatch was opened and the stairs lowered, a blast of hot, humid air, even worse than at Maracaibo, filled the cabin, bringing with it a combination of smells: burned kerojet, wet jungle, and big city garbage dumps.

Two sturdy-looking men, dressed in Navy SEAL night fighter uniforms, leaned nonchalantly against a camouflaged Humvee on the ramp as McGarvey came to the hatch.

Sergeant Contreras gave him a warm smile. "I hope your flight with us was pleasant, sir, and that good luck rides with you."

"Thank you," he told her. "I think I'll need it."

The captain opened the door to the flight deck. "I've not been authorized to wait for you," he said.

"It's not necessary," McGarvey said. "Thanks for the lift."

Sergeant Contreras handed him his overnight bag, and he stepped down from the airplane and crossed the tarmac to the waiting SEALs, who straightened up at his approach. They were young, probably in their twenties, McGarvey figured, and they looked impatient. He stuck out his hand.

"Lieutenant Herring, I'm Kirk McGarvey."

Herring shook hands. He was a little shorter than McGarvey, and his grip was anything but hard, as if he didn't have to prove anything. But he had the look: He'd been there, done that, and he wore his self-confidence like a politician wears his charisma. "We've been waiting for you," he said. "This is my assistant fire team leader, Ensign Tom Kulbacki."

McGarvey shook hands with the taller, leaner man, but turned back to Herring. "I assume that you have a chopper standing by."

"It's under cover," Herring said.

The Venezuelan air force jet had turned and was trundling back down the ramp toward the active runway. McGarvey glanced back at it. "You don't trust them very much, do you?"

"The tanker is one of theirs, for all I know the crew is Venezuelan too."

"They got me here with no questions asked," McGarvey said.

"Yeah, just what we need tonight, a civilian," Kulbacki muttered, but loudly enough for McGarvey to hear.

"I don't trust anybody, Mr. McGarvey," Herring said.

"That include CIA?"

Herring nodded tightly. "Anyone who has to use the big dogs to throw his weight around." He gave McGarvey a very hard look. "Like I told you on the phone, we don't need civilian interference. Just get the hell out of our way, and let us do the job we've been trained for."

"Lieutenant, I assume that the *Apurto Devlán* is already under way."

"She pulled up anchor ninety minutes ago," Herring shot back. He glanced at Kulbacki. "We could have resolved the situation by now."

"In that case we're running out of time," McGarvey said. "As much as I'd like to continue our pleasant little chat, I suggest that we get started. I'll brief you on the way down."

Herring was clearly frustrated, but he nodded. "Get in," he said. He turned, climbed behind the wheel of the Humvee, and immediately took off, not bothering to see if McGarvey or Kulbacki had gotten aboard.

He drove with a vengeance a hundred yards along a line of hangars, making a sharp right behind what might have been some sort of an administration headquarters, closed at this hour of the night. An H-60 Seahawk, no lights other than a dim red glow from the cockpit, was parked beneath camouflage netting, in the shadows behind the building.

Several men in black were lounging beside the chopper. Even before Herring pulled up, they scrambled inside the machine, and the rotors began to turn.

McGarvey was dressed in jeans, a dark, short-sleeved polo shirt, and boat shoes. He grabbed his bag and followed Herring and Kulbacki across to the chopper, where they climbed aboard. Herring went forward to talk to the pilot while the assistant fire team leader helped McGarvey strap in. The other six operators, all dressed in black, and equipped with night vision goggles and a variety of weapons ranging from Beretta auto-loading pistols with silencers in chest holsters, Ithaca Model 37 short-barreled semiautomatic shotguns, and Heckler & Koch M8 carbines, were strapped in and ready to go.

"We've got a set of camos for you, and a Colt Commando if you need them!" Kulbacki shouted over the rising noise.

"No thanks," McGarvey said. He took his 9mm Walther PPK out of his bag, checked the load, and stuffed the weapon in his belt. Next he took out a spare magazine of ammunition and put it in his trousers pocket. No one cracked a smile, but they all watched him. "What's our flying time to the locks?"

"Fifteen minutes!" Kulbacki shouted.

Herring came back and strapped in beside McGarvey as the helicopter accelerated from beneath the netting. As soon as her tail rotor was clear, she lumbered into the air, swinging toward the north, but keeping low.

"The *Apurto Devlán* has already made it to the first lock!" he shouted to McGarvey. "So now you have my undivided attention. What do you want to do?"

"Are we carrying a gun crew?" McGarvey asked.

"Yes. The chopper's equipped with a pair of 7.62 machine guns."

"It's my guess that Graham killed the original crew and replaced them somewhere between here and Maracaibo."

"Your guess," Herring said pointedly.

"That's right," McGarvey shot back. "But I'm not guessing when I tell you that Graham will not become a suicide bomber unless he's given no other options. He'll get off the ship, and once he's clear he'll detonate the explosives. The ship, the locks, and everyone close will be destroyed."

"They're all nuts."

"From our point of view, you're probably right," McGarvey said. "But get one thing straight: They might be nuts, but they're not stupid. Graham was a trained Royal Navy officer, he's operated as a pirate in the South China Sea, and since 9/11 has been working for bin Laden. Interpol and every intelligence service in the world have been looking for him for more than five years. From what I've learned this is the nearest anyone's gotten."

"Well, he made a big mistake this time," Herring said. "We're going to take him down." He glanced at his operators. "My people will not let him get away. No chance in hell. Guaranteed."

McGarvey was beginning to lose his patience. "Graham won't be impressed by a stealth operation."

"I think he will be," Herring said. He grinned. "We'll disarm the explosives before he gets a chance to pull the trigger."

"As long as we can keep him aboard in the meantime," McGarvey said. "If he gets clear he'll push the button."

Kulbacki was following the conversation. He leaned closer to McGarvey. "Won't matter, sir. We can block his radio signal. Most of them use a simple garage door opener code. We've got a high-power transmitter that blankets their signals."

"We learned that the hard way in Iraq," Herring said.

"I hope you're right," McGarvey said. "But if at all possible I want to take the man alive."

"We're going to be pretty busy," Herring said. "I can't guarantee that we'll have the time to take prisoners."

"I only care about Graham. Once we show up he's going to jump ship. I want to take him before then."

"I'm listening," Herring said.

"We go in fast and noisy," McGarvey said. "But there'll be a civilian pilot on the bridge. So everyone has to be careful. I don't want any civilian casualties. And the same goes for workmen ashore. No collateral damage."

"We'll do our best—"

"You'll do better than that, Lieutenant," McGarvey said. Before Herring could object, McGarvey cut him off. "I don't want to come on strong. We're on the same side; fighting the bad guys for the same reasons. But I'm here and I'm not going away. And that's a fact."

Herring held himself in check with a visible effort. "Go ahead, sir, I'm listening."

"Assuming you can either find and disarm every explosive package they've set in place, and/or block the remote detonator signal, there are still two worst-case scenarios concerning Graham. One, he gets away. If that happens he'll be even more strongly motivated to hit us, maybe with another 9/11. Maybe something worse."

"What's the second?" Kulbacki asked.

"That somebody kills him."

"What's wrong with that?"

"If we can take him alive, I think he might be the key to finding bin Laden," McGarvey said. "And that's one man I'd very much like to get close to again."

Herring exchanged a glance with Kulbacki. "Okay, Mr. McGarvey, you have my attention now. How do you propose we handle this?"

"Graham's not going to be impressed by anything we do, but his crew will react to a shock-and-awe strike, which is exactly what I want your people to give him."

"And what happens if you're wrong?" Herring asked. "What happens if Graham isn't aboard, and we start shooting at innocent Venezuelans?"

"I'm not wrong," McGarvey said. "The real captain's body was stuffed in an aluminum trunk and left in a hotel storage room."

"I see."

"I want the chopper gun crew to stand by to make sure Graham doesn't jump ship."

EIGHTEEN

□

APURTO DEVLÁN, GATUN LOCKS

The *Apurto Devlán* eased slowly into the middle lock leading to Lake Gatun fifteen minutes before one in the morning, slightly ahead of schedule. A second Panamax vessel, this one a cruise ship, was in the lock ahead of them and more than twenty-five feet higher and rising.

She was a Carnival ship, out of Miami, which gave Graham a particular pleasure. When he pressed the detonator code, not only would the *Apurto Devlán* go up in a ball of flame, completely destroying the Gatun locks, but the cruise ship would also be wiped out, killing Americans. Probably even more than died in the World Trade Center attacks.

"Engines Back All Slow," Sanchez told al-Tashkiri.

"Back All Slow." Al-Tashkiri acknowledged the order, just as he had been taught to do.

Ramati was starting to become agitated. Graham glanced over and slowly shook his head. His first officer acknowledged the warning with a nod. The ship would never leave this lock, and everyone aboard except for the Panamanian pilot knew it.

The ship's engines responded to the order, and her forward momentum bled off as her bows approached the forward gate, and the stern mules took up the slack, keeping her centered.

"Stop All Engines," Sanchez ordered softly.

"All Engines Stop," al-Tahskiri responded. He was sweating, his face dripping, his khaki shirt soaked at the armpits and across the back.

The pilot looked at him, then went to the port wing to check their clearance aft.

"Get a hold of yourself," Graham whispered urgently to al-Tashkiri.

When the pilot came back, he keyed his walkie-talkie. "Gatun Control, *Apurto Devlán* ready for number-two closure." He held the walkie-talkie to his ear momentarily to hear the response then keyed the Talk button. "Roger," he said. He looked pointedly at al-Tashkiri, and then Ramati. It was obvious he sensed that something was wrong.

From the moment they'd raised anchor and slowly made their way north up the seven-mile channel past docks, shipyards, and fueling stations, the pilot had been edgy. He'd not engaged in any conversation, other than to issue orders, and from time to time he gave them odd, searching looks.

"Are we in position, Mr. Sanchez?" Graham asked to distract the man. They only needed a few more minutes in case Gatun Control had something else to speak to Sanchez about.

"Yes," the pilot said. "Mr. Sozansky, are you feeling well?"

It took a moment for al-Tashkiri to realize that the pilot was addressing him. He turned and nodded. "Yes, sir. Just fine."

"Is this your first transit?"

Graham reached for his pistol.

"No, sir," al-Tashkiri said. "I've been here before."

Graham motioned for Ramati to move out of the line of fire.

The pilot pointed to the sweat stains on al-Tashkiri's shirt. "You seem a little nervous to me."

Graham's hand tightened on the pistol in his pocket.

Al-Tashkiri choked out a strangled laugh. "Yes, sir. I'm always nervous. I've been this way since I was a little boy in . . . Poland."

Sanchez shot a look at Graham as if to say it was the captain's fault if a crewman was so nervous he was drenched in sweat at the helm. But then the massive steel gates began to close astern, and the pilot went again to the port wing to check clearances.

Graham snatched the ship's phone from its cradle and called the engine room. "We're done with the engines. It will happen very soon."

"*Insh'allah*," Hijazi said softly, and with great respect.

"Yes, God willing," Graham told him. He hung up just as Sanchez came back.

The pilot laid his walkie-talkie on the shelf beneath the center windshield, took a thermos of coffee from his pack beside the helmsman, and poured a cup. He did not offer some to Graham or the others.

As soon as the gates behind them were closed, sealing off this lock, massive valves would be opened and water from Gatun Lake would rush into the chamber, rising the ship to the center level, more than fifty feet above the Caribbean, in about fifteen minutes.

At that point the lead gates would open, the cruise ship, which would be twenty-five feet higher, would be disconnected from the mules and would sail out into Gatun Lake, leaving the chamber to be filled for the *Apurto Devlán*. Before that happened Graham wanted to be off the ship and well enough away to trigger the explosives.

The timing was tight, but manageable. He would make it so. He smiled.

"Mr. Slavin, I've been thinking," the pilot said.

Not for long, Graham thought. "Yes, Mr. Sanchez."

"I don't remember your cousin. But I'm sure that I remember the name: Grigoriy Slavin."

"I'm flattered," Graham said. "There must be thousands of vessels through here each year."

"More than fourteen thousand," Sanchez said. He was looking at Graham over the rim of his coffee mug. "A figure that as a Panamax master you should know."

Graham glanced behind him through the port windows. They were slowly rising. The valves had been opened. He smiled. "I've never been one for someone else's exact numbers," he said.

The pilot shook his head. "You're not Grigoriy Slavin," he said. "You're an imposter."

"Yes, I am," Graham said. He took out his pistol, and before Sanchez could move or even speak, shot the man in the middle of the forehead, blood splashing across the port radar set.

The pilot's head was flung backwards. He dropped his cup, which shattered on the steel deck, and his body bounced against the forward bulkhead as he fell on his side, dead.

Al-Tashkiri closed his eyes and began to rapidly mutter something. Graham figured he was praying, preparing his soul for Paradise.

Ramati, on the other hand, was highly animated, flinging his arms outstretched as if he simply could not contain himself. Graham had to briefly wonder if it had been like this for the crazy bastards in the last minutes of the flights that hit the World Trade Center.

Graham switched aim and fired at Ramati, the shot catching his number two in the middle of the chest.

Ramati staggered backwards, but he was still alive. He desperately clawed for his pistol in his pocket, when Graham fired again, hitting him in the right eye, the back of his skull disintegrating.

Graham turned and fired almost at point-blank range into the side of al-Tashkiri's head as the kid opened his eyes and started to step away.

For several long seconds Graham listened to the sudden silence, as the *Apurto Devlán* continued to rise. But then he got his cell phone and hit a speed-dial button. When the call went through to the operative standing by on the *Nueva Cruz*, it was answered on the first ring.

"*Sí.*"

"*¡Ahora!*" Graham said. Now! "*¡Ahora!*"

"*Sí,*" the man responded, and the connection was broken. Within minutes a small speedboat would be launched from the mother ship and come ashore.

Graham pocketed his cell phone and pistol, and went to the port wing as the ship continued to rise to the level of the mule tracks. The only people around were the canal operators in the control room, the mule drivers, and the canal workers who handled the lines.

No one would notice a lone man stepping ashore and disappearing into the darkness. And even if they did, by the time they reacted the ship would be gone in a brilliant flash of searing heat, and they would be dead.

NINETEEN

RAPID RESPONSE TEAM BAKER

McGarvey and Herring had donned headsets so they could communicate with the flight crew. They'd flown low and fast straight south along the route of the canal, coming across Gatun Lake no more than twenty-five feet above the water, in excess of 140 knots. They were at hover two hundred meters out from the locks.

The side hatch was wide open, and Herring's operators were ready to deploy. Two chopper crewmen manned the 7.62mm machine guns. There was no way Graham or anyone else was getting off the ship alive.

A cruise ship, all her lights ablaze, was in the forward lock, the *Apurto Devlán* right behind her in the middle lock.

"Do you see any activity on deck?" McGarvey radioed the pilot. The flight crew was wearing night-vision equipment.

"Two bad guys on deck, at the bow," the pilot radioed back. "Look like line handlers."

"What are they doing?"

"One of them is on his knees," the pilot came back. He hesitated. "Almost looks as if he's praying."

"He is," McGarvey told Herring. "It means they're ready to pull the trigger. We have to take them down now."

Herring motioned for his operators to lock and load. He radioed the pilot. "Take out the two bad guys on the bow as we pass over them. Set us down in front of the superstructure. Soon as we're feet dry, I want you to dust off and stand by off the starboard midships. Anybody tries to jump ship, take them down. But watch out for the canal workmen ashore."

"Wilco," the pilot responded crisply.

Kulbacki had produced a ship's diagram of the *Apurto Devlán*, and on the short flight down from Panama City he'd gone over the deployment orders with the team. The drill was a standard one that they'd practiced countless times on ship mock-ups in San Diego.

It was assumed that the Panamanian pilot would be topside on the bridge, so everyone on deck would be considered hostile and would be taken down.

A three-man team would head to the engine room, taking out anyone they encountered; their objective was to secure the engineering spaces from any kind of sabotage, including disabling the engines and/or the steering controls, before they swept the rest of the ship for terrorists.

Kulbacki would lead his team of three operators on a lightning-fast sweep, first to the twelve oil tanks to find and disable any explosive devices, and then into the bilges to look for kickers that might have been placed to take out the ship's bottom and sink her in the middle of the lock. Their orders were to take down any and all hostiles they might encounter.

Herring would accompany McGarvey up to the bridge, taking down any bad guys they ran into, securing the Panamanian pilot, and subduing Graham without killing him, if at all possible.

"The knees, hips, shoulders, elbows, or wrists," McGarvey said. "Anywhere but the head or torso."

"That'll be tough if he's shooting at us," Herring said. "You sure you don't want to wear a vest? We brought one for you."

McGarvey shook his head. "When he shoots it'll be a headshot."

The big helicopter suddenly banked hard to the left, the open hatch on the low side, and roared along the length of the cruise ship, the tips of its rotors clearing the ship's gigs by less than ten meters.

Kulbacki and another man positioned in the hatch would be the first to hit the deck.

There were passengers on the promenade deck of the cruise ship. Some of them waved as the helicopter passed.

"Take out the two on the bow," Herring radioed to the gun crew.

"Wilco," someone responded.

A second later the pilot swung the tail around so that the nose gun was pointing at the men on the *Apurto Devlán*'s bow, and started to sideslip along the length of the open deck. Both machine guns opened fire at the same moment, and stopped almost immediately.

"Scratch two," one of the gunners radioed.

The operator crouching next to Kulbacki in the open door suddenly lurched backwards.

"Incoming fire," Kulbacki shouted, and he sprayed a deck hatch that was open amidships.

The helicopter set down hard just forward of the superstructure and immediately came under intense small-arms fire from somewhere aft. Small-caliber bullets pinged into the fuselage, and ricocheted off the ship's deck.

Herring and another of the operators shoved McGarvey aside and hauled the downed man to his feet, as Kulbacki and the other SEALs exploded from the open hatch and laid down a heavy line of fire toward the port and starboard passageways.

The operator who'd taken a round in his chest armor would have a hell of a bruise by morning, but otherwise he was still good to go.

"Clear!" Kulbacki shouted.

McGarvey was next out of the chopper, rolling to the right so that he would be out of the way and in the shadows of the towering seven-story superstructure. He noticed out of the corner of his eye that the mule driver on the starboard bow had jumped out of his locomotive and was heading across the access road in a dead run.

Herring and the last operator jumped down on deck, and as soon as they were clear, the helicopter lifted off with a tremendous roar, banked almost over on its side, its rotors barely clearing the deck, and accelerated over the mule, while turning its nose gun back toward the ship.

Camera flashes were coming in a nearly continuous stream from the stern of the cruise ship twenty-five feet above them.

"Marchetti, go." Herring pumped his left fist, and the three operators who would take care of the engineering spaces headed aft. They would leapfrog along the portside passageway, and thence into the ship and down the ladder, clearing the way ahead with flash-bang grenades, and then shooting anything that moved.

Kulbacki and his three men had already started forward to the product tank access hatches, to find and disarm the explosive charges. Each of them would take one tank, and with any luck they would run into light or no resistance and the job could be done in a few minutes.

If they did have to fire they would need even more luck that they wouldn't inadvertently touch off an explosion in one of the tanks, which would set the others off like a string of firecrackers.

But, as Kulbacki had explained with a sardonic grin on the way down here, "That's the chance we signed on for when we put on the uniform, sir."

At that moment a light breeze sprang up, blowing the sounds of the chopper's exhaust and rotor noise away, and the *Apurto Devlán* became as quiet as a ghost ship. The hairs at the nape of McGarvey's neck stood on end.

It wasn't this simple. They were forgetting something. He was forgetting something. Something in Graham's file that the Brits had not yet sent to Otto. Something they were hiding?

"The next part is your show, Mr. McGarvey!" Herring shouted.

"Right," McGarvey said. "The bridge." He sprinted to the portside passageway, then aft to the first doorway. The hatch was open.

Two men dressed in dark blue coveralls, APURTO DEVLÁN stenciled on the backs, were down with headshots, blood spreading on the steel deck. Marchetti and the other SEALs heading down to the engine room had taken them down.

McGarvey hesitated only a moment to make sure they were dead. He didn't want some fanatic filled with religious zeal coming up from behind. A tight-lipped Herring nodded his approval.

A stairway led six decks up to the bridge. McGarvey stopped at the first turn and motioned for Herring to hold up. He cocked an ear to listen for sounds from above. For a moment the ship was silent, but then he thought he heard someone talking.

Herring heard it too.

"Radio," McGarvey mouthed the word. Probably from the bridge, which meant the door up there was open.

Herring nodded again, and McGarvey continued up, pausing for a moment at each turn, until they reached the third deck where someone from above opened fire, bullets ricocheting off the bulkheads, shrapnel flying everywhere.

McGarvey fell back and fired three shots up the stairs, aiming for the door frame to carom his shots off the steel plating into the corridor.

Someone cried out, and fired another burst from what sounded like an M8.

"Stay here," McGarvey whispered to Herring. "I'm going to take the passageway one deck down across to the starboard side and see if I can get behind whoever's shooting at us."

"We don't have much time," Herring whispered.

"Keep them busy," McGarvey said, and he turned and hurried down to the next deck, while above, Herring opened fire again.

TWENTY

APURTO DEVLÁN, ON THE BRIDGE

The gunfire was coming from two decks below.

The big helicopter had come as a total surprise. But from the moment it had appeared from the north, Graham had known it was just a matter of minutes before he'd be cornered up here with nowhere to run. There was no time to be angry, or to try to reason how the authorities had uncovered the plan. There was only time to act.

He'd seriously considered punching the 9 # 11 detonator code on his cell phone, and ending everything in one brilliant flash of light. There would be absolutely no pain, and the deep ache inside his soul for Jillian would finally come to an end.

But there was more to be done. More blood to be shed, not for the cause the nutcases who surrounded bin Laden believed in, but for the pure sweet joy of the battle. Revenge by any other name became tactics. Outwit your enemy, kill him on the battlefield, and live to fight another day.

The helicopter had American navy markings. It hovered on station just across the road, waiting for someone to try to get off the ship.

The troops that had deployed were dressed all in black and apparently knew what they were doing. By now they would be finding and disabling the explosives, though there was still time to enter the code. If only one of the tanks went up, the rest would explode too.

But how had the Americans found out so soon? No one at the Syrian training camp knew the target, nor had any of his crew been told until they were already en route. Which left only a handful of bin Laden's inner circle who knew all the details.

The first glimmerings of rage began to fill him with the determination to get out of here alive, so that he could make it back to Karachi and take his revenge on whoever had sold them out.

He wouldn't be able to shoot his way out, and even if he was successful, and managed to slip over the side, the helicopter was standing by, probably with orders to kill anything that moved.

Nor could he hide aboard for very long. If this were his operation he'd order a thorough search of the ship for just that possibility.

The VHF radio was alive with chatter, most of it in Spanish, from Gatun Control, demanding to know what was going on. Graham caught the pilot's name, and the solution came to him all at once. The Americans were going to give him a ride to the hospital, and from there, freedom.

Hurrying now lest he get caught, Graham put down his weapon and cell phone, and stripped the shirt and trousers from the pilot's body.

There was a sudden burst of pistol fire one deck down, and someone cried out in Arabic.

Graham pulled off his shirt and trousers, and hurriedly put them on the dead pilot's body, getting blood all over himself in the process.

"Now," someone called softly. In English.

Graham donned the pilot's trousers, which were slightly too small for him, and the light blue shirt, the front of which was covered in blood.

Someone was coming up the stairs, he could hear their footfalls.

Moving swiftly but silently, he laid his cell phone next to the pilot, then placed his pistol in the dead man's hand.

Whoever was coming was just outside the door now.

Graham smeared blood all over his neck and face and in his mouth, then staggered back across the bridge where he fell to one knee next to the helm station and al-Tashkiri's body. He was unarmed, and he no longer had the means to trigger the explosives. But as his operators would say, Insh'allah. If God wills it.

A tall, stocky man dressed in civilian clothes appeared in the doorway. He was armed with a pistol, which he swung left to right, centering on Graham.

"No, por favor, señor," Graham shouted, holding up a hand as if in supplication.

The civilian moved aside, his pistol never wavering, to allow a much younger man dressed all in black, a black bandana on his head, a Heckler & Koch M8 in his hands, and a pistol strapped to his chest, to enter the bridge.

Graham didn't know about the civilian, but the other man was definitely a U.S. Navy SEAL, almost certainly part of the Americans' Rapid Response presence here in the Canal Zone. They were almost as good as the British Special Air Service paratroopers; highly trained to take down any force they encountered with a very high degree of accuracy and lightning speed.

"Por favor, señor. ¡Ayúdame!"

"Do you speak English?" Herring asked.

"Sí," Graham said. "I mean, yes."

McGarvey had moved over to the dead pilot, and keeping one eye on Graham, kicked the pistol away, then bent down to check for a pulse in the man's neck. He glanced at Herring and shook his head.

"What happened here?" Herring asked.

"The crazy bastardos killed each other!" Graham shouted desperately. "They tried to kill me, but this one interfered. They have bombs."

Herring said something into the small mike at his lapel.

McGarvey checked for a pulse in Ramati's body and then came to where Graham was kneeling and checked for al-Tashkiri's pulse.

"What's your name?" he asked Graham.

"Sanchez. I am the *piloto*, the pilot." He looked up into McGarvey's gray-green eyes and he could see wariness and skepticism. But the SEAL had lowered his weapon.

"The ship is secure," Herring told McGarvey. "I've called the chopper back, they'll take Mr. Sanchez to the hospital."

"*Por favor*, we have to leave now," Graham pleaded. "The dynamite will kill us all."

"It's all right, sir," Herring said. "They didn't use dynamite, and my people have disarmed the charges."

"Can you walk?" McGarvey asked.

"I think so," Graham said weakly. He held up a hand, but McGarvey stepped back, his pistol still pointed more or less in Graham's direction.

Herring slung his carbine, came over, and helped Graham to his feet. "Where are you shot?"

"I don't know. They hit me on the head, and then there was a lot of shooting."

Herring keyed his radio. "This is Baker leader, we're coming out."

"Have your people found any of the real crew?" McGarvey asked.

"Fifteen of them so far," Herring said, grim-lipped. "All shot to death."

"We'll need a new crew then," McGarvey said. He went back to the body, dressed in the captain's clothing. Something was wrong.

"Not until we make damned sure that none of the bastards is holed up somewhere," Herring said.

McGarvey picked up the cell phone and removed its battery. "I'm taking this with me. It's probably the detonator, and there might be some numbers in its memory."

The helicopter came into view in the bridge's windows with a tremendous roar and settled on the deck just forward of the superstructure.

"Whatever you want," Herring said. "I'm going to take the pilot down to the chopper. Are you staying here?"

"I'll be right behind you," McGarvey said.

It was obvious to Graham that something was bothering the civilian; the man knew that everything wasn't as it seemed to be.

McGarvey used the cell phone's battery cover to scoop up some of the dead man's blood, and then replaced the cover on back of the phone.

Herring stopped and looked at him.

McGarvey glanced up. "I want his DNA."

"Good idea," Herring said. He held on to Graham. "We'll take it nice and easy," he said.

Graham thought that the young man's death would be eminently satisfying. But the civilian's death would be more important.

TWENTY-ONE

□

APURTO DEVLÁN, ON THE BRIDGE

McGarvey pocketed the cell phone and battery, and holstered his pistol as he followed Herring and the Panamanian pilot from the bridge. He stopped for a moment one deck down and looked back the way he'd come, his gray-green eyes narrowed in thought.

Maybe he was getting old, but he knew damn well that something hadn't been right up there. Some little thing had been out of place. But for the life of him he couldn't put his finger on what was bothering him.

Besides the two terrorists he'd taken down on deck four, and the two just inside the companionway on deck one, there would be bodies scattered throughout the ship. The ones he'd seen so far were dressed either in deck crew coveralls, or in civilian clothes that most merchant marine officers wore.

Nothing unusual. The terrorists had either come aboard dressed as crew or officers, or, after they'd killed the real crew and officers, had switched clothes.

Herring pulled up short at the hatch to the open deck, and keyed his lapel mike. "Baker leader at the hatch." He waited a moment, then helped the wounded pilot out of the superstructure.

McGarvey stopped again for a moment to listen to the sounds of the ship, although it was difficult to hear much of anything over the roar of the helicopter's engines and rotors. But he could feel in the soles of his shoes that the *Apurto Devlán*'s engines were not running. There was no vibration in the deck plating that was always present when a large vessel's power plant was up and running.

The terrorists had meant for the ship never to leave this lock. The explosion of the twelve oil tanks would have taken out not only all the locks, but probably would have destroyed the cruise ship in the front lock, with a major loss of life.

It would have been another 9/11; a spectacular blow not only against the United States, but this time against the entire world.

Again he looked up the stairs he'd just come down. Graham's plan was to destroy this ship and the Gatun locks. But he'd not been the kind of man to commit suicide for the cause. According to Otto's research, the ex–British Royal Navy officer had had plenty of opportunities to do so over the past years. This time was to have unfolded in the same way for Graham as had so many of his other operations; he would walk away moments before the killing and destruction so that he could live to fight another day.

What had happened in the last moments up on the bridge? Why had the terrorists apparently gone berserk and shot one another to death?

He could think of any number of possible reasons—maybe Graham had a last-minute change of heart, maybe one of his people somehow found out that Graham had no intention of staying aboard—but none of them struck the right note for McGarvey. His intuition was telling him that there was another explanation.

He stepped outside. The main deck was awash in lights from the ship as well as from stanchions along either side of the lock.

Marchetti and the other SEALs who'd helped secure the engineering spaces and sweep the ship were on deck, but Kulbacki and his team that had disarmed the explosives had apparently shifted their search to the bilges.

Herring was leading the wounded pilot across to the helicopter, which had touched down one-third of the way forward from the superstructure.

McGarvey's eyes were momentarily drawn to the stern of the cruise ship looming twenty-five feet above the bow of the *Apurto Devlán*. It was moving away. Camera flashes were still coming almost continuously. None of the passengers, however, could realize how close they had come to being incinerated.

Herring had reached the helicopter. A crewman jumped down from the open hatch and helped the canal pilot up into the machine. They didn't have a medic aboard, though all the Rapid Response Team operators, including the helicopter crew, were trained in battlefield first aid. But it would be only a matter of a few minutes before the pilot reached the hospital in nearby Colón.

The man had been understandably confused on the bridge. He'd nearly lost his life, he knew that much, but it might be until tomorrow before he came out of shock and could talk about what happened.

The pilot had walked awkwardly. Probably because he was hurting.

Climbing up into the helicopter he'd moved stiffly, almost as if his trousers were too tight, restricting his movements.

McGarvey stared at him.

The ship's engines had been shut down. Graham had been finished with them because the *Apurto Devlán* wasn't supposed to move out of the center lock. Then why hadn't he killed the pilot, whose services were no longer needed?

Herring said something to the crewman, then stepped back. A moment later the helicopter roared into the sky, banked to the right, and took off toward the northwest to Colón.

The answer was up on the bridge. Rupert Graham's body.

McGarvey ducked back through the hatch and sprinted up the stairs, careful to avoid the pools of blood where the terrorists had gone down. The SEALs were mopping up the last of the terrorists as well as searching for and disarming any other explosives. The ship was all but secure. Nevertheless McGarvey had his pistol out, the safety catch off. He did not want to be caught flat-footed by one of the bad guys who might have been hiding.

On the top deck he held up at the door to the bridge and listened for several seconds. Now that the helicopter was gone, the ship was ultra-quiet.

He looked over his shoulder, the way he had come up, then slipped through the door, sweeping his pistol left to right.

Nothing had changed. The three bodies lay where they had fallen.

Once again he was struck by an odd feeling between his shoulder blades, as if someone were aiming a laser sight on his back.

Rupert Graham's trousers were too long.

McGarvey holstered his pistol and carefully eased the body over on its back. The man's eyes were dark, as was his hair and his complexion.

But Graham was an Englishman. Not dark.

There was a look of surprise and perhaps fear on his features. He hadn't been expecting this to happen to him.

When the U.S. Navy helicopter had suddenly roared over the *Apurto*

Devlán's bows it must have been a shock. But Graham was a professional killer. He'd known the risks. He would have known how to instantly improvise when something went wrong in mid-mission.

It suddenly came together.

The man lying on the deck was the canal pilot, and Rupert Graham was making his escape off the ship courtesy of the SEAL team that had come to arrest or kill him.

McGarvey pulled out his pistol and went to the door, where he held up for a brief moment, then raced to the end of the corridor and took the stairs two at a time down to the main deck, where he held up again at the hatch.

"McGarvey at the main hatch!" he shouted.

"Come," one of Herring's men replied from a few feet around the corner.

McGarvey stepped outside.

The SEAL had his M8 at the ready, the butt just above his right shoulder, his shooting finger along the trigger guard. He hesitated for just a split second to make certain that he'd correctly ID'd McGarvey, then lowered the carbine. "We wondered where you went, sir."

"Where's Herring? We need to warn the chopper crew."

"The boss is on his way to the engine room," the SEAL said. "Warn the crew about what?"

"That wasn't the canal pilot. It was the terrorist leader."

"Are you sure, sir?" the SEAL asked.

"Just do it," McGarvey told the young man, but it was probably too late already.

As the SEAL spoke into his lapel mike, McGarvey turned and looked in the direction the helicopter had gone. They hadn't even thought to search the imposter.

This attack had been stopped. But there would be others if Graham and bin Laden were allowed to live.

This time, McGarvey vowed, he would finish the job.

TWENTY-TWO

□

CIA HEADQUARTERS

Riding over to the White House from Langley in his limousine, Dick Adkins decided that he didn't like being the director of Central Intelligence. In fact, he'd never liked the Washington power-broker game in which each White House administration wanted only the intel to support its agendas, and nothing else.

But ever since the creation of the director of National Intelligence, who was supposed to oversee all intelligence activities, the game had shifted into high gear. It was what the Company's general counsel Carleton Patterson called the "9/11 syndrome." No one wanted to be wrong, which meant that facts were bent and sometimes altered to fit the prevailing opinion.

Nuclear weapons in Iraq had been one of the prime examples. Another had come last year when McGarvey had been forced to resign from the CIA when he and the president had a falling out. McGarvey had wanted to go after a wealthy Saudi playboy who he thought was a top bin Laden killer. The administration wanted to protect its oil relationship with the Saudis, so the president would not believe McGarvey.

As it turned out, Mac and the president had both been right, after a fashion, but by then Mac was no longer welcome at Langley, or anywhere else in or around Washington. Going against a sitting president was not the thing to do and still expect to be welcome at the table.

And now this morning Adkins was bringing the president news that once again McGarvey had saved their asses. Coming down Constitution Avenue to 17th Street and the Ellipse, minutes away from the White House, he girded himself for what he expected would be a confrontational briefing.

Telling the truth, no matter how unpopular it was in Washington, was an ethic that Mac had instilled at the CIA.

For better or worse, tell it like it is. But whatever you do, don't blow smoke up my ass. Don't lie to me.

Those were McGarvey's words, practically etched in marble over at the Building in Langley. And, for better or worse, Adkins had decided that he would tell the president the truth; the whole, unvarnished truth.

His limo was passed through the West Gate, and after he signed in and his attaché case was scanned, the president's chief of staff Calvin Beckett was there to bring him over to the Oval Office. The former CEO of IBM seemed tense.

"He's going to ask why you didn't hand this to Hamel—whatever it is—instead of bringing it directly here."

"It's a little delicate," Adkins said. "I didn't want anything lost in the translation."

Beckett smiled nervously. "You want to take the heat yourself," he said. "Admirable, but your timing stinks. The man's in a bad mood. He just got off the phone with Crown Prince Abdullah. The Saudis are cutting production by three percent. Oil prices are sagging, and OPEC is raising hell."

"Four bucks a gallon for regular in L.A., and prices are sagging?"

"The United States should get in line with the rest of the world, where gas prices have always been four or five dollars a gallon," Beckett said. "You know how it is. We're one year out from Senate elections, and this time it's going to be tough to hold the majority."

"Yeah," Adkins replied, he did know how the game was played. The Democrats were going to love this latest move by the Saudis. "He's going to like what I'm going to tell him even less."

"I was afraid of that."

President Lawrence Haynes, his jacket off, his tie loose, and his shirt-sleeves rolled up, stood looking out the thick Lexan windows at the Rose Garden in full bloom when Beckett rapped on the door frame. He was alone in the Oval Office, and it seemed to Adkins that he was a man with the weight of the world on his shoulders, and even though he could have been a lineman for the Green Bay Packers, the burden seemed too heavy.

"Mr. President, Dick is here."

Haynes turned, and smiled the famous Haynes smile that had won him every office he'd ever campaigned for. "Good morning, Dick. I'm a little surprised to see you here this morning."

"I'm sorry, Mr. President, but I felt that the issue was too important and the timing too tight to pass it through Don Hamel's shop," Adkins said. "And too delicate."

"I see," Haynes said. He motioned for Beckett to close the door, then called his secretary to ask Dennis Berndt, his national security adviser, to join them. "Coffee?" he asked Adkins.

"No, sir. My initial brief won't take long, but I've brought over the book, which gives more details. It's al-Quaida again."

The president's expression immediately darkened. "Christ," he said softly. "Is there anything new in the search for bin Laden?"

"Nothing yet, sir," Adkins said. "But we've committed considerable resources to the job." He laid his attaché case on the coffee table, took the leatherette-bound briefing book out, and handed it across the desk to Haynes.

"What is it this time?" Beckett asked.

"They're calling it Allah's Scorpion—" Adkins said as Dennis Berndt walked in.

"Who are the they?" Berndt asked. He was a rumpled, tweedy man with a kind face. For the last year he had been trying to get back to academia to teach history, but the president wouldn't let him go.

"Al-Quaida," Adkins said. He handed a second briefing book to the national security adviser.

Like the president, Berndt's mood instantly darkened. "Has Don Hamel seen this yet?"

"No."

"Why?"

"He was just getting to that," Beckett said.

None of them had taken a seat, nor did the president motion for them to do so. "You have my attention," Haynes said. "Give me the highlights."

"Al-Quaida has planned another big attack. This time by sea again, what they called Allah's Scorpion."

"Called?" Berndt asked. "As in past tense?"

Adkins nodded. "For the moment. But we're confident it's not over. They'll try again, in part because the kingpin of the attack we stopped managed to get away."

The morning was nice: clear blue sky, very little haze, but the sunlight didn't seem able to penetrate into the Oval Office.

"Continue," Haynes prompted.

"We started getting indications several months ago on a number of al-Quaida Web sites that something big might be in the works. Homeland Security took us to orange in mid-April, as you remember. But after ten days when nothing happened, we dropped back to normal."

"The American public is sick of holding its breath," Beckett said.

"Yeah, but then in the past couple of weeks the chatter started again, and earlier this week there was an attempted prison break at Guantanamo Bay."

"I saw the report," Haynes said. "It was incredible. They committed suicide rather than allow themselves to be recaptured. But there is no concrete proof that the Cubans were helping them."

"No, sir," Adkins said. "But the five men who broke out were all Iranian naval ratings. Which got us to thinking that al-Quaida was trying to raise a ship's crew. And if that were the case, they would need to hire a captain, someone to run the ship. So we went looking for just such a man."

Berndt and the president exchanged a look. "And?" Berndt asked.

"We got lucky," Adkins replied. "The guy is a former British naval officer by the name of Rupert Graham. He was kicked out of the service five years ago, and for a couple of years he operated as a pirate in the South China Sea. And a damned good one from what we've learned. About two years ago he apparently came to the attention of bin Laden and he may have started working for al-Quaida, funneling money and material into the cause."

"Why?" Berndt asked.

"I'm not sure of all the details, but apparently his wife died while he was at sea and the navy never notified him." Adkins shrugged. "The man is nursing a grudge."

"What about him?" the president asked.

"Three days ago he hijacked a fully ladened oil tanker in Maracaibo, Venezuela. He killed the entire crew, apparently took on a new crew somewhere in the western Caribbean, and this morning, less than six hours ago, he managed to get the ship as far as the center lock at Gatun, where he'd planned on blowing it up."

Berndt whistled softly. "Would have shut down the canal for years," he said.

"The engineers we talked to thought there would have been a good chance that the canal might never have reopened."

The president nodded with satisfaction. "The Rapid Response Teams we put down there did the job," he said, a glimmering of his smile returning. "Well done."

"There's more, Mr. President," Adkins said. "Four days ago we'd traced Graham to Caracas, but then lost him. We— I— felt that the man was enough of a credible threat that we needed to go after him to find out what he was up to. But quietly because of our . . . somewhat strained relations with the Venezuelan government."

The president, Berndt, and Beckett all had the same expectant look on their faces.

"Let me guess," Berndt said. "You recruited Kirk McGarvey, and he did the job for us."

Adkins nodded, his eyes never leaving the president's. "We have assets in Caracas, but they're under deep cover at the embassy. It would have been next to impossible to get one of them up to Maracaibo in time."

"Where is he now?" Haynes asked quietly.

"On his way back here."

Haynes nodded. "I thought that he and his wife were moving to Florida. He was taking a teaching position."

"Yes, sir," Adkins said. This would be the tough part. "But there's more. Graham managed to escape in the confusion, while the explosive devices on the ship were found and disconnected. He's still out there, and our analysts think that al-Quaida will try again. They still have their very capable and extremely motivated captain."

"What is the CIA recommending?" Haynes asked, point-blank.

"I want to hire McGarvey to find Graham before he mounts another operation against us."

"Yes?" Haynes said.

"Then I want to send McGarvey to find bin Laden."

"And?"

"Mac's brief will be to assassinate both men as soon as possible," Adkins said. He pursed his lips. "Let's end this once and for all, Mr. President. For this kind of operation McGarvey is our best asset—"

"Our *only* asset," the president said. He was troubled. He turned away and looked out at the Rose Garden again. "After I'd won the first election, but before my inauguration, I came here so that the president could brief me. Just the two of us, in this room, discussing things and options that only the president is allowed to know. Frightening things. Impossible things. Unreasonable things. Enough so that I had to seriously doubt my sanity for ever wanting this job." His shoulders seemed to slump. "It's the moment of truth for every incoming president." He shook his head. "You can see it in their eyes. They're one person going into the meeting, full of confidence and expectations, and another completely different person coming out, worried, stunned."

The president turned back to Adkins, hesitated for just a moment, but then nodded. "I don't see that I have any other choice."

"No, sir," Adkins said, relieved. He gathered up his attaché case.

"Will he go for it?" Berndt asked.

Adkins shook his head. "I honestly don't know, Dennis. One part of me thinks that he'll tell me to go to hell when I ask him, while another part of me thinks nothing I say or do would stop him from doing it." He smiled. "You know Mac well enough to know that when he has the bit in his teeth nothing can stop him."

"He's a one-man killing machine," Beckett said.

"That he is," Adkins agreed.

"Dick," the president said.

"Sir?"

"Tell him Godspeed for me."

TWENTY-THREE

□

SAN JOSÉ, COSTA RICA

Graham stood at the ninth-floor window of his suite in the downtown Tryp Corobici Hotel, waiting for his satellite phone call to go through. It was night, and the lights of the city spread out below him were beautiful. But he was seething with barely controlled rage because he had failed.

He could not get rid of the image of the U.S. Navy helicopter suddenly appearing as if out of nowhere at the bow of his ship, gunning down two of his crewmen. For the first time in his career he'd given serious thought to his own mortality.

The encrypted connection was made, and bin Laden came on the line. "There was nothing in this morning's news broadcasts."

"That's because it never happened," Graham said. It took every ounce of his resolve to keep from screaming obscenities at the stupid son of a bitch. Obviously there'd been a leak somewhere between Panama and Karachi.

"Where are you calling from?"

"The hotel in San José. I was the only one left alive, a Navy SEAL team was waiting for us at the locks." Graham closed his eyes. He had to calm down. Taking a crewman's sidearm and forcing the Seahawk pilot to set down in an industrial park in the opposite direction from the beach had been easy. They weren't prepared for the hijacking or for their deaths when he shot them at point-blank range.

He'd radioed the *Nueva Cruz* from the helicopter, and before dawn had hitched a ride in a farmer's truck back to Limón Bay, while overhead several aircraft, among them two helicopters, crisscrossed the night sky, presumably looking for the missing chopper and wounded canal pilot.

"You must have attracted some attention in Maracaibo," bin Laden said, his tone maddeningly reasonable. "Or one of the ship's crew may have suspected something and radioed a warning."

The image of the whore screeching at him flashed through his head. "It wasn't me," he said. "There is a leak somewhere in your organization. It cost the lives of fourteen of my crewmen, and nearly got me killed."

The sat phone was silent for several beats. Graham opened his eyes and looked out at the city. He could imagine bin Laden sitting on a prayer rug in his dayroom. It was a few minutes after seven in the morning in Pakistan, and the man was an early riser.

"Why didn't you blow up the ship when you had the chance?"

Graham laughed. "I'm a mercenary for the cause, not a martyr, I thought we'd already got that straight, chum."

"I want to know everything, beginning with your arrival in Caracas," bin Laden said. "It's certainly not out of the realm of possibility that you were spotted and identified for who you are at the airport. The CIA has a presence there."

"If I had been made, they would never have allowed me to board the ship. Vensport Security controls all the ferry operators on the lake."

If he had sown the seeds of his own failure it would have been with the Russian steward who had spotted him as an imposter and reported her suspicion to the first officer. But they had only gotten to the point of searching his room when he'd walked in on them. They wouldn't have had the time to make a call.

"Very well," bin Laden said. "You got aboard and sailed out of there. What happened next?"

"I killed the crew, made the rendezvous, and picked up my people without a hitch. Then in Limón Bay we picked up the canal pilot and headed into the Gatun lock."

The pilot had come to the realization that Graham was an imposter, but he'd not had a chance to radio for help.

"The explosives were set?" bin Laden asked.

"Yes, and we even made it to the middle lock, but before I could get ashore and press the button the U.S. SEAL team was on top of us."

Bin Laden said something in Arabic that Graham didn't catch. "How did you know that it was a U.S. strike team? Perhaps they were Panamanian."

"They came in a Seahawk helicopter with U.S. Navy markings, and they spoke English," Graham said. "The point is, what's next? This operation is dead—"

"Only this operation," bin Laden interrupted. "How was it you escaped, if as you say, your ship was taken over by the American military?"

Graham told him everything, including the parts about hijacking the helicopter, killing the crew, and making his rendezvous with the Nueva Cruz.

"That was inventive," bin Laden said. "But then you are a clever man."

"Only the civilian seemed to be suspicious. I have a hunch he was CIA, which is what's bothering me the most. How did they get involved unless your organization has an informer?"

"What about the civilian?" bin Laden demanded sharply. "What made you think he was a CIA officer?"

"He was in charge, he was armed, and he knew what he was doing," Graham said. *It was the expression in the man's gray-green eyes. He'd seen things, done things.* "He was a pro."

"What did this professional look like? Describe him."

"Taller than me, husky, athletic-looking. Green eyes—"

"What?" bin Laden demanded sharply.

"Green eyes."

"Did he speak with an accent?"

Graham was confused. "I'm not a bloody expert on American accents," he said. "Southern, maybe. I don't know. Oklahoma?"

Bin Laden was silent again for several seconds. When he came back his tone of voice was different, as if he'd received some bad news. "If the civilian is who I think he is, you may consider yourself lucky to be alive. How good a look did he get of you?"

"Very good, but I was in disguise," Graham said. He decided not to tell bin Laden about the cell phone detonator. "Who is he?"

"A man I know very well," bin Laden replied. "Now it will be necessary to kill him, no matter the cost, because he'll not stop hunting until he finds you."

"He's just another CIA operator. They're a penny a pound."

"Not this one," bin Laden said. "I want you back here as soon as possible, I have a new mission for you. Something much better, something more suitable to your training."

"What mission?" Graham asked, his interest piqued and his rage subsiding for the moment.

"It's called Allah's Scorpion," bin Laden said. "Come here and I'll explain everything to you."

TWENTY-FOUR

CHEVY CHASE

McGarvey stopped for a moment at the head of the stairs, as his six-month-old granddaughter, Audrey, giggled in the kitchen. It was nine thirty, well past her normal bedtime, but Elizabeth and Todd hadn't been able to come over until past seven, and Katy wouldn't have allowed them through the front door if they hadn't brought the baby.

When he'd gotten home a little before one this afternoon, Katy had searched his face to find out if he was done. What she'd seen hadn't pleased her. She knew without asking that her husband's return from the field was temporary; he was on the hunt. He had the old look: lean, hungry, determined.

But they'd made the best of the afternoon because the kids were coming for a late dinner and they were bringing the baby, and she was the joy in their lives that they'd all desperately needed for a long time.

Adkins had called around four, wanting McGarvey to come to the Building first thing in the morning. He hadn't pressed for any details, but he'd broadly hinted that the operation was far from over.

"Someone will have to go after Graham," McGarvey had agreed. "I don't think he's a man who quits easily."

"There's more," Adkins had said.

McGarvey had chuckled. "There always is."

The house was in complete disarray. Boxes were stacked everywhere, waiting for the movers who were supposed to come on Thursday. Furniture was tagged, paintings, pictures, and mirrors were off the walls and crated, and his study had been completely disassembled.

They'd bought this house ten years ago for $350,000, just before he and Katy had split up and he'd run to Switzerland. They'd put it on the market two months ago, and it had sold in two days for $1.9 million— $200,000 more than they were asking.

Coming downstairs, he was suddenly struck by his history here. It was from this place that he and Katy had ended their marriage, and it had been here that they'd reunited.

But there had also been bad things. His wife and daughter had been placed in harm's way, more than once. And just outside across the street his bodyguard and friend, Dick Yemm, had been assassinated.

Time to head for sunnier climes. Time to get back to teaching, and back to the book on Voltaire that he'd been writing for several years.

But first there was one remaining task, other than Graham. Something he should have done in 2000 when he'd had the opportunity. In many respects the failure to stop 9/11 was as much his fault as it was anyone else's.

This time he would not stop until he had personally put a bullet in Osama bin Laden's brain.

He went down the stair hall and into the kitchen, where Audrey in her high chair had been pulled up to the counter and was eating her dinner. She had strained beets in her hair, her ears, her eyes, and in the creases of her neck.

Katy looked up. "Did you find the camera?"

McGarvey shook his head. "It's in one of the boxes. I couldn't find it."

"Don't worry, Mother, Audie does this with every meal," Elizabeth said. "We'll send pictures."

"Your granddaughter is a slob, Mrs. M," Todd said.

Katy smiled. "So was your wife."

"She still is," Todd added.

Liz shot a playful slap at him when the telephone rang.

Katy answered it, and her smile faded. "Of course," she said, and hung up. She looked at Mac. "Otto's just pulling into our driveway. Says it's urgent."

It had to be about Graham. Rencke had been working the problem around the clock ever since he'd come down to Sarasota to ask Mac to take the job.

"I'll try to make it short," McGarvey told his wife, then went to the front door to let the CIA's director of Special Projects in.

Rencke had brought a young, good-looking woman with him. "Gloria Ibenez," he introduced her. "She's one of our field officers working the bin Laden search. And, oh boy, you just gotta hear what she came up with."

She shook hands with McGarvey. "It's a pleasure to finally meet you, sir." She glanced at the boxes stacked in the stair hall. "You're leaving?"

"In a few days," McGarvey said. He ushered them into his study, where the walls and shelves had been stripped bare, and shut the door. All the chairs had been boxed, so there was nowhere to sit.

"It's not over, Mac," Otto gushed. He hopped from one foot to the other, his face animated. "It fact it's just starting. The canal gig was bonus time; it wasn't the real Allah's Scorpion."

"What are you talking about?" McGarvey asked. He'd had the feeling from the moment he knew Graham's target was the canal and not someplace in the United States that there would be more.

"I finally got Graham's navy file. The full file. His wife died while he was at sea on patrol, and his boss never notified him. Pissed him off and he went all to hell. Drinking, making really bad decisions that put his crew's lives in jeopardy, that kinda shit."

"We figured as much," McGarvey said.

"But here's the kicker, Mac, and, honest injun, this is the big one. Guess what Graham's job was in the navy. Just guess."

"What?"

"He was a Perisher graduate," Otto gushed. "Top of his class."

"Submarines," McGarvey said in wonder.

"Bingo!" Otto cried. "He was a sub driver, and a damned good one from his early fitreps." He glanced at Gloria. "But it's even better than that."

"I was in Guantanamo Bay last week, interrogating prisoners," she said. "My partner and I stumbled into the middle of a prison break. We think it was al-Quaida trying to spring five guys. Iranians. When they were cornered they killed themselves rather than risk being recaptured."

"Her partner was killed too," Otto said gently.

"The five guys they were trying to grab were all ex-Iranian navy," Gloria said. "And for some reason, which no one down there wanted to talk about, they weren't in Camp Delta. They were in the minimum-security lockup for prisoners ready to be released back to their home countries."

"Al-Quaida is planning to grab a sub somewhere, and hit us hard," Otto said. "They've got the captain, and they're searching for a crew."

McGarvey had been watching Gloria's eyes. There was a sadness there, and something else. "Sorry about your partner," he said. "But are you trying to tell me that al-Quaida had help down there? Someone on our side?"

"I think so," Gloria said. "It would mean that someone in the organization has a direct pipeline to the camp. I want to go back and find out. It could very well lead us to bin Laden himself."

"I'm going with you," McGarvey said. Gitmo would probably be difficult, he thought, but nowhere near as difficult as it was going to be when he told Katy.

"Yes, sir," Gloria said, obviously impressed and pleased.

"I'll come out to the Building first thing in the morning," McGarvey told Otto. "See if you can come up with the names of any other of the prisoners who might have navy backgrounds."

"Will do."

"And put together everything you got not only on Graham, but on bin Laden."

"Oh, boy," Otto said, hopping from one foot to the other, and clapping his hands. "The bad guys are going down."

PART
TWO

TWENTY-FIVE

□

KARACHI, PAKISTAN

Rupert Graham reached Karachi's Jinnah International Airport via Paris around eight in the evening aboard a battered Pakistan International Airlines 727 that had to have been thirty years old. As they came in for the landing, most of the Muslim passengers aboard took out their prayer beads and closed their eyes. A good many of them believed that their prayers were all that kept PIA's aging fleet in the air.

Except for security concerns, Graham had been all but mindless of his surroundings since he'd left San José yesterday morning. He was seething inside because of his failure, and now arriving in Pakistan he was beginning to feel like a junior ensign being called before the skipper for a Captain's Mast disciplinary action.

Yet something of what bin Laden had said during their brief telephone conversation kept repeating in his head, booming like a drum calling him to battle. *Allah's Scorpion. Something much better, something more suitable to your training.*

Graham, dressed in a charcoal-gray business suit, his hair and eyebrows light again, the soft brown contacts gone, the lift shoes discarded, shuffled down the corridor with the other passengers to immigration, where he showed his Australian passport, which identified him as forty-one-year-old Talbot Barry, from Sydney, here to write a piece for a travel magazine.

He was passed through without question, but when he retrieved his single hanging bag and presented it at customs, two armed officers and a drug-sniffing dog conducted a thorough search not only of the bag, but of his body. Through it all he kept his composure, cooperating completely, and even smiling.

Pakistan had been granted the most favored nation status by the United

States and was getting a lot of aid. As a result, Islamabad was doing every-thing in its power to keep up the illusion that it was actively seeking out terrorists, especially the remnants of the Taliban, as well as al-Quaida and specifically bin Laden, who was supposedly hiding out in the mountains of the far northwest.

When his bag was finally stamped and he was given an entry pass, he marched through the busy terminal and outside, where a dark Mercedes S500 with tinted windows pulled up to the curb. Graham got into the backseat and the driver, a bulky dark-complected man in a business suit, pulled smoothly out into traffic and without a word headed into the city.

"Were you followed?" the driver asked, in English, his voice low, men-acing. He was one of bin Laden's chief bodyguards and gofers.

It was an extremely rude question, but one that Graham could philo-sophically understand because of his failure in Panama. "I was not."

It was a weekday and the traffic volume was heavy the nearer they got to downtown, especially in the broad band of slums they had to pass through. But Graham was again lost in thought, only subliminally notic-ing his surroundings.

He'd been born and raised in the Collyhurst slum of Manchester, his father a collier and his mother a laundress. Early on he'd learned to defend himself from the other boys, because he was small for his age.

There was never enough money, and yet he showed an early promise in grammar school, so on the advice of the schoolmaster, and a scholar-ship, they managed to scrape together enough money to let him finish through college prep.

Of course college was completely out of the question, financially, so Graham had joined the Royal Navy and was sent to Dounreay in Scotland to learn nuclear engineering, graduating number five in his class of fifty.

From there he received his primary submarine officer's training, grad-uating first in his class, and was sent out into the fleet.

A century ago, he reflected. A completely different lifetime, because in those days he'd had legitimacy, a pride in what he was doing. There had been more schooling, more promotions, new ships, new mates, new ad-ventures.

And throughout it all, almost from the beginning had been Jillian; dear, sweet, pixie-faced Jillian whom he had loved with every fiber of his being.

He closed his eyes, a frown crossing his features. There had been two incidents during Perisher before he'd been given command of his own sub, in which the old man had taken him aside for a word in private.

Jillian had been admitted to the base hospital twice in three months; the first with cracked ribs and a lot of bruising on her arms and chest, and the second with a fractured left arm and three teeth knocked out. In both incidents she'd told the emergency room doctors that she was clumsy and had fallen down the cellar stairs.

But it wasn't true, and although no one had believed her stories, nothing could be done. The old man had counseled Graham on anger management during times of extreme stress.

"You'll need your wits about you if you should suddenly find yourself in a dicey situation a dozen miles off some Russian peninsula in the Barents Sea. Can't be losing your head. Your men will be watching your every move."

The thing was, he could no longer remember the incidents in any great detail, nor could he bring up an image of Jillian's face in his mind. It frightened him.

But what was permanently etched in his brain was the fact that the same man who had counseled him on anger management had not sent the recall message so that Graham could get back from sea in time to be at Jillian's side when she died.

Afterwards he'd demanded that the staff judge advocate's office investigate. But his request had been denied. Admiral Woodrow S. B. Holmes had acted well within the responsibilities of his office by not recalling a nuclear submarine on patrol for the sake of a personal problem, no matter how high-ranking the officer was, nor how serious the problem was. The needs of the Royal Navy had to come first.

In the heart of the city's business and banking district the Mercedes turned onto M. R. Kayani Road and two blocks later entered a secured underground parking garage that served the forty-eight-story M. A. Jinnah Commercial Centre.

Graham had only been here twice before, and he thought that it was a great irony that bin Laden had been hiding out in Pakistan's largest city all along, when the entire world, especially the American CIA, believed he was somewhere in the mountains on the border with Afghanistan.

Five levels down the driver pulled up at an elevator, but he didn't get out to open the car door for Graham. "You may go directly up. He is expecting you."

"Will you wait for me?" Graham asked. The driver was looking at him in the rearview mirror.

"That will be up to him."

"Very well," Graham said. He let himself out of the car, got his bag, and walked across to the elevator, which automatically started up. A closed-circuit camera mounted near the ceiling was trained on him. Security in this building was very tight because of all the wealthy business tenants. No one who didn't belong here got in or out. Ever.

But an even more delicious irony was that a small international investments company on the tenth floor that handled money transactions for the Afghanistan heroin trade was, in fact, a front for a CIA special mission station. Only a very few people in Pakistan's secret intelligence service knew about it, or its purpose, which was to find and eliminate Afghanistan's drug overlords as well as the handlers along the pipeline to the United States.

The elevator came to a halt on the twenty-fifth floor and Graham stepped out into a plushly carpeted entry hall, across which was a single door. An old man in Western dress was there.

"Good evening, Captain Graham," the old man said. He was one of bin Laden's inner circle, though Graham had never been told his name.

"Will I be staying here tonight, or have hotel arrangements been made for me?"

"You will remain here, with us, for the time being," the old man said. He was frail and his voice was pleasantly soft, but there was no warmth in his eyes or his manner. "Come with me."

Graham followed the old man into the suite of offices and living spaces, down a long corridor to a small room in approximately the center of the building. Furnished only with an Oriental rug and a small television set on a tiny round table, the space was lit by a single small-wattage bulb that hung from the ceiling. There were no woven hangings, pictures, or any other adornments on the walls, nor were there windows. This was the inner sanctum, where bin Laden prayed five times per day, where he watched CNN, once in the morning and once each evening, and where he held the most secret of his meetings.

"Wait here," the old man said, and he withdrew.

Graham dropped his garment bag in the corner, slipped off his shoes, and sat cross-legged on the edge of the rug.

Both times he'd been called to this place he'd met with bin Laden in this room, but never before had he stayed in the building for more than an hour. All of his other planning sessions with the man had been conducted via encrypted e-mail or encrypted satellite phone or, once in person, at the training camp in the Syrian Desert.

And at each meeting bin Laden had greeted him like an old friend, a long-lost brother. Graham suspected that this time it would be different. The mission had failed and he knew that he would be blamed, though he strongly suspected that the leak had come from someone here in Pakistan, or more likely someone from the Syrian training camp.

There was a twenty-five-million-dollar bounty on bin Laden's head, but no one who knew the man's real location would ever reveal it. He would not live to collect the money, let alone spend it. But feeding the American authorities information about al-Quaida missions was becoming a high-stakes cottage industry. In practical terms it meant that only a very select few men were allowed to know the whole picture of any mission.

Graham decided that if nothing else happened he would find the traitor and personally slit his throat.

A clean-shaven bin Laden, dressed in khaki slacks and a white long-sleeved shirt, entered the room. Graham started to get to his feet, but bin Laden waved him back. "It is good that you have returned unharmed. You may consider yourself lucky."

"Who was he?"

Bin Laden sat down on the rug and faced Graham. "His name is Kirk McGarvey."

Graham allowed a look of wonder to cross his face. "He was the director of the CIA."

"Yes, but more than that he is an assassin."

"The Americans no longer do that sort of thing. . . ."

"You're a submarine commander, not an intelligence officer, so your error is understandable," bin Laden said mildly. "And now you are the second man to come to me a failure against McGarvey."

"Where is the other?"

"He tried again and died," bin Laden said.

"I'm not so easy to kill," Graham said, irritated.

"I sincerely hope not. But McGarvey is not your problem. You will remain here until he is eliminated."

Graham's anger spiked. He sat forward. "I want him," he said sharply.

Bin Laden was unmoved. "If he sees you again he will kill you," he said. "I don't want that to happen. I have another use for you."

"What?"

"In due time, my friend. Do not let your anger and impatience get the better of you. Not if you wish to continue your *jihad* against the godless men who abused your trust so harshly."

"You said it was a mission more suited to my training," Graham said. "Can you at least tell me if it involves a submarine?"

Bin Laden looked at him for a long time, before he finally nodded, the gesture so slight it was almost unnoticeable.

A thrill coursed through Graham like a hit of cocaine to a desperate man. All of his training had been for one purpose, and one purpose alone; to command an underwater warship. To train a crew and lead his men into battle. All other considerations were secondary: pain, fear, conscience, ego. Even love.

"Until the mission preparation fully develops you will remain here at my side."

"I should be involved in the planning," Graham said. "For God's sake, I'm a trained sub driver. I have the knowledge."

"Yes, which is exactly why you will not be allowed to leave this place until the time is correct," bin Laden said. "You are too valuable an asset to risk."

"Then why was I sent on the canal strike?" Graham demanded.

"Because I wasn't sure that we could get a boat," bin Laden said.

"My God, you've done it? You've got a sub?"

"In due time," bin Laden said. "Now leave me, I wish to be alone. Salaam will show you to your quarters."

Graham got up, retrieved his bag and shoes, and left the room without another word. His mind was alive with the possibilities that another command would give him. The entire world would be his, and he meant to take it.

By the time he was finished, the damage would be incalculable.

TWENTY-SIX

GUANTANAMO BAY

Across the bay from Leeward Point Field, which served as Gitmo's airport, the U.S. Navy Station senior personnel were housed in base headquarters, which was also home to the U.S. Army's senior Detainee Ops personnel.

The navy ran the station, but the army was in charge of the prisoners—mostly al-Quaida and Taliban, and the mujahideen who fought for them.

The navy's ONI handled most of the prisoner interrogations after the backlash against the army's methods at Abu Ghraib, but Army MPs were still in charge of security at all six camps.

It was an odd melding of the services, but it seemed to work, despite pressures from Amnesty International, the ACLU, and the international media to close the place.

This morning McGarvey and Gloria Ibenez had flown down aboard a Navy C-20D, which was a Gulfstream III used to transport VIPs. They were seated at a conference table at base headquarters across from Brigadier General Lazlo Maddox, who was the CO of detainee operations, his chief of intelligence operations, Lieutenant Colonel Daniel Higgins, and Lieutenant Commander T. Thomas Weiss, the one Gloria had warned McGarvey about. He was the senior ONI officer at Delta.

"I was asked by the secretary of defense to cooperate with you," General Maddox said. "And that's what we'll do. But I don't like it." He was a tall, rangy man in his early fifties, with salt-and-pepper hair cut short in the Depression-era style with no sideburns. He was dressed in camouflage BDUs.

"We appreciate it, General," McGarvey said pleasantly, and he glanced over at Weiss, who had an angry scowl on his face. "We'll try to cause as little disruption as possible, and get out of here as soon as we can."

"There will not be a repeat of last week's incident in which three of my people were KIA, do I make myself clear?"

Gloria stepped in before McGarvey could speak. "Excuse me, General, but my partner and I did not start it." She was hot, but on the way down she'd promised to control herself. "Your three people were already dead by the time we stumbled onto the prison break."

McGarvey sat back. They had not made a decision to play bad-cop, good-cop, and it wouldn't work with Maddox anyway. He'd seen the general's jacket. As a young captain during the first Gulf War he had been awarded every decoration except the Medal of Honor. His nickname was "Icewater." But with Weiss it could be different. The man was in love with himself.

"If you had stayed out of it, your partner wouldn't have been shot to death," Weiss jumped in angrily. He was in crisp summer undress whites. "And most likely the Coast Guard would have recovered all five prisoners, and the strike force that hit us, before they got five miles offshore."

"They could have been halfway back to Iran before anybody knew they were gone," Gloria shot back. "Bob was just doing his job, something you apparently don't understand."

McGarvey held up a hand. "Can we get back on track here?"

Weiss started to say something, but Maddox held him off. "Amnesty International will be here in two days to make sure we're no longer using Biscuit teams." Psychiatrist M.D.s had been used in units called Behavioral Sciences Consultation Teams, Biscuit teams for short, to help interrogators increase the stress levels of prisoners. It made questioning of them a lot easier. But there had been ethical issues and the White House had ordered the practice be stopped. "You will be gone from this base before they arrive. Is that also clear?"

"I expect we'll be done by then," McGarvey said.

Maddox turned to Weiss and then Gloria. "And the fireworks between you two will cease and desist right now."

Weiss wanted to protest, but he nodded darkly.

Gloria smiled. "Sorry, General, just trying to do my job."

"Very well," Maddox said. "What brings a former CIA director here, or is your mission so secret we can't be told?"

"Not at all," McGarvey replied pleasantly. He watched Weiss's eyes. "Al-Quaida has hired an ex–British Royal Navy submarine captain, and we think the organization is trying to raise a crew for him. The five men who were broken out last week were all ex–Iranian navy."

Weiss didn't blink.

"We didn't know that," Lieutenant Colonel Higgins said. He was a West Point graduate who had never seen battle. He'd gotten his law degree and had spent a large portion of his career at the Pentagon. He was a mild-mannered–looking man, with thin brown hair and wire-rimmed glasses. Like Maddox, he was dressed in BDUs.

"Not ex-navy," Weiss put in. "We think they were on active duty when they were rounded up on the Iranian border. We were working on confirming it, in which case they would have been released."

"Why wasn't I told?" Higgins demanded.

"Dan, we just weren't sure," Weiss said. "And we still aren't." He glanced at Gloria. "If we could have recaptured them alive we might have found out."

"There've been no IDs on the bodies of the strike force they sent against us," Higgins told McGarvey. "We think they were al-Quaida, but in light of this they could just as likely have been Iranian special forces here to rescue their people."

"With the cooperation of the Cubans—" Gloria said, but McGarvey held her off with a gesture.

"That's purely speculation," Higgins replied calmly. Unlike Weiss, who was posturing, he was in control; a lawyer discussing the dry facts of a civil case. "They probe our perimeter at least once a week, and that's been going on for months now."

Gloria wanted to protest, but McGarvey held her off again. "Our people are working on that aspect."

"I'm sure they are," Maddox said. "Which brings us back to the question at hand. What are you doing here?"

"We have the names of four additional prisoners we believe might have navy backgrounds. We'd like to interview them. If al-Quaida is trying to raise a crew the word will have gotten out. They may have heard something."

"There've been no unauthorized communications to or from this camp," Weiss said, and he looked to Higgins for confirmation, but the colonel merely cocked his head as he looked at McGarvey.

"Right," McGarvey replied dryly. "They've got themselves a sub captain, now if they can come up with a crew they could hit us harder than 9/11."

"Isn't the CIA forgetting something?" Weiss wanted to know. "Captains and crews don't mean much if they don't have a boat. Or are you saying they managed to snatch someone's submarine."

"We're working on it."

"I'll bet you are. In the meantime, the prisoners belong to me."

McGarvey held his silence. If Weiss was on someone's payroll, he was either very dull, or bright enough to hide behind what was almost too obvious a show of stupidity.

Weiss again looked to Higgins for support, but again the colonel said nothing. "Give me your names, and I'll check them against our database," he told McGarvey. "If I come up with something, I'll arrange for the interviews. Supervised interviews."

McGarvey nodded. "We'll need a translator who speaks Farsi as well as Arabic."

"We have them," Weiss said. "And I'll be looking over your shoulder."

Otto had come up with the four names, out of the three-hundred-plus prisoners being held here. But he had no solid evidence linking any of them with the Iranian navy, only speculation derived from the transcripts of the interviews of more than two thousand detainees since the start of the war against the Taliban in Afghanistan. The only real information he'd come up with was on the five prisoners who had been broken out last week. McGarvey didn't think they would learn much from these four, but he wanted to see what Weiss's reaction would be. If the navy spook was the conduit, breaking him could give them a path that might stretch all the way back to Pakistan.

"I have no objections to that, provided you promise not to interfere, and that you'll give us a decent translator," McGarvey said.

"We can have one of ours flown down by this afternoon," Gloria suggested on cue.

"I have some good people on staff," Weiss said, not asking the obvious: Why hadn't they brought their own translator in the first place?

But Higgins got it, and he managed to hide a slight smile behind his hand.

"Very well," McGarvey said.

Gloria took four thin files from her attaché case and handed them across the conference table to Weiss. "Assa al-Haq, Yohanan Qurayza, Zia Warrag, and Ali bin Ramdi," she said. "We know that they're here, but not much else."

Weiss briefly glanced at the material, then nodded smugly. He'd managed to push his weight around. "Go over to the BOQ, get settled, and grab a late lunch over at the O Club. As soon as I come up with something, I'll send a runner for you."

"Make this happen, Commander," General Maddox said. "Without trouble, so our guests will get what they came for, and leave on schedule."

"You can count on it, sir," Weiss said. He got to his feet, nodded to Higgins, and left.

"We're in a delicate situation here, Ms. Ibenez," Maddox said. "Is there any chance that Cuban intelligence knows that you've returned?"

"I honestly don't know, General," she said. "It might depend on if there's a leak here on base."

The general's expression darkened. "Do your job and get out of here." He gave McGarvey a bleak look, then got up and left the conference room.

Colonel Higgins stayed behind. "Do you need transportation?"

"Just get us a vehicle, we won't need a driver," McGarvey said. "What's the problem with Weiss?"

Higgins managed a slight grin. "Tom takes some getting used to. His friends love him, but everyone else has trouble with him. But he's got a tough job to do, and he's under a microscope that stretches all the way back to Washington. Your being here doesn't help."

"Does he have any friends?" Gloria asked.

Higgins shook his head. "None that I know of."

TWENTY-SEVEN

□

CIA HEADQUARTERS

Adkins and the others stood up as his secretary, Dhalia Swanson, ushered Bob Talarico's widow, Toni, and her two children, Robert Jr. and Hillary, into the DCI's office.

It was nearly two o'clock and he'd not had the time to have lunch, for which he was grateful now, because his stomach did a slow roll. Toni

Talarico was a small woman, scarcely five feet tall—Bob had called her his pocket Tintoretto—but this afternoon it seemed as if she had sunk inside herself. Her ten-year-old son was as tall as she, and her eight-year-old daughter came to her mother's shoulders.

She wore a black dress and a small pillbox hat, and the children, one on each hand, were dressed in black as well.

They looked shell-shocked. It was the first impression that came into Adkins's mind. They weren't so much sad as they were dazed, especially Toni. It was as if they'd been in a fierce battle, but that they expected Bob to be here in the DCI's office waiting for them. They wanted someone to tell them that everything would be okay.

But it wouldn't be. Because Bob was dead, and Adkins thought back to when his wife had died. He hadn't really accepted that fact as reality until six months later when he woke in the middle of the night in a cold sweat. He'd turned on every light in the house and had gone searching for her, convinced that she had been hiding from him. That morning, he'd finally come to terms with his loss, and had finally begun the process of grieving and healing.

He sincerely hoped that Toni would recover faster than he had; for her children's sake, if not for her own.

Her husband's boss, Howard McCann, gave her and the girl a hug, and shook Robert Jr.'s hand. "I'm sorry, Toni," he said, choking on the words.

She smiled up at him and patted his arm. "He knew the risks when he took the oath. I just want to know that what he gave his life for was worth it."

"Every bit," Adkins said. "What he and his partner did might have saved us from another 9/11, or at least pointed us in that direction."

Toni looked at the others—the DDCI David Whittaker and the Company General Counsel Carleton Patterson. "Where is she?"

"We can't tell—" McCann started.

"She's back in Cuba following up," Adkins said. "She has Kirk McGarvey with her. But that can't leave this room."

Toni actually smiled, which nearly tore Adkins's heart out. "Bob always said that he was the best man to ever work here. And don't worry, Mr. Director, we're a CIA family. We know how to keep a secret."

"Dad taught us," Robert Jr. said, trying very hard to be brave.

Adkins caught his secretary's eye. She was at the door, tears streaming down her wrinkled cheeks. She started to leave, but he motioned her back. "You may stay," he said.

She closed the door and came to stand just behind Toni and the children.

Whittaker handed Adkins a long narrow hinged box, and a leather-bound citation folder. "You must also understand that this cannot be made public."

Toni's lips compressed, and she nodded. "But the children and I will know. That would have been enough for Bob. He wasn't looking for hero status."

"But he was just that, Mrs. Talarico," Patterson told her. "An American hero."

Adkins opened the silk-lined box that contained an impressive-looking medal attached to a ribbon and brass clasp, and he and everyone else in the room straightened up.

"The United States of America, the Central Intelligence Agency, and a grateful nation, bestow posthumously the Distinguished Service medal to Senior Field Officer Robert Benjamin Talarico, for service far beyond the call of duty," Adkins began solemnly. "Although the details of the mission in which Robert gave his life cannot be disclosed at this time, be assured that the operation was of extreme importance and absolutely vital to U.S. interests here and abroad, as well as the safety of all Americans everywhere.

"Be also assured that witnesses on scene, including his partner, Senior Field Officer Gloria Ibenez, report that to the very end Robert did not hesitate to perform his duty, even though he was under direct fire from a hostile force superior in numbers and armament."

Adkins looked into Toni's eyes, momentarily at a loss for words. But then he handed her the medal and the citation folder. "He did good," he said softly. "Really good."

"Thank you, Mr. Director."

Adkins gave her a hug. "If you need anything, day or night, call me," he said in her ear. "And my name is Dick."

TWENTY-EIGHT

□

CAMP DELTA

By six in the evening McGarvey was getting the impression that just about all the prisoners knew something big was on the verge of happening. Al-Quaida was preparing to strike another deadly blow at the infidel West, and very soon. It seemed to be an article of faith at least as strong as their belief in the Qur'an. As the MP bringing in the last of the four prisoners for interrogation commented, "They're happy." It was ominous.

Weiss had sent a runner over to the Officers' Club around two thirty to bring McGarvey and Gloria up the hill to the interrogation center inside Camp Delta. All four of the men on Otto's list had been located, and had been brought over to one of the holding rooms.

Weiss had also brought a translator, Chief Petty Officer First Class Sayyid Deyhim, who'd been born in Tehran, but who'd been raised and educated in the United States since he was thirteen. He was a short, slightly built man with dark skin, thick black hair, and deep-set eyes.

"Do you also speak Arabic?" McGarvey had asked when they were introduced.

"Yes, but I do not like it," Deyhim shot back. "Iranians are Persians, not Arabs. There's a big difference." He was angry. Weiss had probably warned him not to cooperate with the CIA.

"Not these days," McGarvey had told him. "Anyway, I thought that you were an American."

They had gathered in one of the interrogation rooms, furnished only with a low wooden bench that was bolted to the bare concrete floor. A water hose was connected to a spigot at the back of the small room, and there was a drain in the floor beneath the bench. There were no windows, but the room was brightly lit by recessed bulbs in the ceiling, protected by steel mesh.

. Deyhim glanced at Weiss, who just shrugged.

"We don't have to be friends," McGarvey said, his voice cold. "But we will be taping the interviews, so I suggest that your translations be accurate."

"I have nothing to hide."

"Sir," McGarvey said.

Deyhim had glanced again at Weiss. "Yes, sir," he said.

That had been three interviews ago, during which time the man had apparently done his job well; providing simultaneous translations of McGarvey's and Gloria's questions into Farsi, and the Iranian prisoners' answers into English.

The MP ushered the round-faced prisoner into the interrogation room, where he was directed to have a seat on the bench. He was dressed in orange coveralls, white slippers on his feet. His hair had been closely cut, and his wrists were bound by a plastic restraint, which the MP cut loose before he left the room.

"This one is a Saudi," Weiss said. "Ali bin Ramdi. He was arrested in early November oh-three, in Qandahar, Afghanistan, along with eighteen other so-called freedom fighters. He follows the rules, but to this point he's given us no useful intel."

The prisoner looked from Weiss, who was leaning against the wall near the door, to Gloria, who was standing next to Deyhim. He seemed calm, sure of himself, and just like the others, even a little excited, maybe happy.

McGarvey sat down astraddle the opposite end of the bench, and smiled. "How soon before Saudi women get the vote?" he asked.

Deyhim hesitated for just a moment, but then translated the question into Arabic.

A smirk crossed the prisoner's face. " 'Never,' he said," Deyhim translated. " 'We are not Kuwait or Iran.' "

"Where do you get your news, Ali?" McGarvey asked pleasantly. Kuwaiti women had not been given the right to vote until after bin Ramdi's arrest. Supposedly prisoners here were not given access to newspapers, radios, or televisions.

" 'One hears things,' " Deyhim translated.

"I'm sure they do," McGarvey agreed. "It's too bad about your brothers last week."

Bin Ramdi shrugged, but said nothing.

"Their deaths were meaningless. They served no purpose. They were not martyrs." McGarvey shook his head. "No Paradise for them."

" 'Paradise awaits all who serve the *jihad*.' "

"Yes, but not like the brothers who died hitting New York and

Washington," McGarvey said. "They truly died martyrs. Allah had to be pleased. Whereas with you and the others . . ."

Bin Ramdi's eyes narrowed.

"Palestinian women are willing to die for the cause, why not Saudi women?"

Deyhim looked over at Weiss and then McGarvey. "I don't understand this line of questioning, sir."

"It's not necessary for you to understand," McGarvey said. He didn't take his eyes from the prisoner's. "Just translate, please."

Deyhim translated the question, and bin Ramdi's thick lips twisted in a smirk. " 'Our women play a more important role than to be wasted thus.' "

McGarvey smiled and slapped his knee. "I couldn't agree more," he said. "It's the same for American women. They even work for the FBI and CIA. Some of them serve in our military forces."

Bin Ramdi shook his head. " 'That is not allowed for Saudi women.' "

"Not even in your navy?" McGarvey asked, as if he were surprised. "They could be trained to serve on something like one of the gunboats you crewed."

" 'I was on a destroyer—' " bin Ramdi said, but he immediately realized his mistake and stopped.

"Destroyer?" McGarvey said. He turned to Weiss. "Commander, let me see this man's file."

Weiss had an odd, thoughtful expression on his face that was hard to read; it was as if he'd been caught by an unpleasant surprise. He hesitated for a moment, but then brought the file over.

McGarvey opened it, and pretended to read. He looked up. "This says you were a gunner's mate aboard a patrol boat. Have we been wrong about you?"

Deyhim translated, but bin Ramdi knew that he had walked into a trap, and he kept silent.

"Look, straighten us out, if you will," McGarvey said. "If you were a gunner's mate who we think went over to al-Quaida, that's one thing. We'll keep you here for as long as we want." McGarvey looked to Gloria after Deyhim finished translating. "Tell him."

"If you follow Uncle Osama you are a pig and deserve to die," she said harshly.

"We're not going in that direction," Weiss broke in before Deyhim could translate.

"Why?" McGarvey said, keeping direct eye contact with bin Ramdi.

"We're not allowed to humiliate them."

"But they're allowed to crash airplanes, killing innocent people?" McGarvey shot back, without raising his voice. "Get your head out of your ass, Weiss, I may be on to something here."

"Amnesty International would love to get its hands on something like this," Weiss said. "Your interviews are over. I'll talk to the general, but you two are definitely out of here. If not tonight then first thing in the morning."

"What the fuck are you hiding?" Gloria asked.

"What's that supposed to mean?" Weiss demanded.

"Are you protecting this bastard, or just covering your own ass?"

Bin Ramdi was paying close attention to the exchange. It seemed to McGarvey that the man probably understood more English than he'd let on. It was in his eyes, a tightening at the corners when Gloria had challenged Weiss. The son of a bitch knew what was going on.

"The commander is right," McGarvey said, getting to his feet. "We're about done here."

Gloria gave him a searching look.

"We lost one of our people, and we were to blame," McGarvey told Weiss. "Sorry if we came on strong, but we wanted to make it right."

Weiss was only partially mollified. "We don't want another Abu Ghraib here," he said. "And Ms. Ibenez is right, I am covering my ass, and everyone else's working for me."

McGarvey looked at bin Ramdi and when he had the man's complete attention, he winked. Neither Deyhim nor Weiss caught it, but Gloria had. He turned back. "Will you join us for dinner at the O Club, Commander?"

"No," Weiss replied tersely.

"Very well," McGarvey said, and he and Gloria left the interrogation center.

Outside, they got in the Humvee, Gloria behind the wheel, and headed back to the BOQ. "What was all that about?"

"What do you mean?" McGarvey asked absently. The first three prisoners knew nothing of any value. If they'd been in the Iranian navy, as Otto thought was possible, they had to have been very low ranking; certainly they were not officers. They had come across as dullards, probably not the sort of crew a man such as Graham would be looking for. But the Saudi had been different. There'd been intelligence and shrewdness in his eyes. His only mistake had been rising to McGarvey's bait about being a crewman aboard a gunboat.

"You winked at him," Gloria said.

The shift change had already been made and driving down the hill from Camp Delta the base seemed almost deserted. There was very little traffic, and not many people out and about. This was the arid side of Cuba, and it was more like a desert than a subtropical island. It was bleak here, McGarvey thought. For the guards and support personnel, as well as for the prisoners.

"I wanted to give him something to think about," he told her.

"We're going back in?"

"Tonight. Without Weiss or his translator."

TWENTY-NINE

□

CHEVY CHASE

Kamal al-Turabi raised a pair of Steiner binoculars to study the house at the end of the cul-de-sac as Imad Odeah brought the Cessna 172 through a lazy turn to the left at an altitude of 1,500 feet. An Atlas moving van was parked in the driveway, and as he watched, workmen brought furniture from the house and loaded it aboard.

It was late, after six, and it seemed as if the men were in a hurry.

He'd driven down from Laurel, Maryland, yesterday afternoon in a Capital Cleaners van, to make a quick pass. The garage door had been open, but a Mercedes convertible and a Range Rover SUV were parked in the driveway. The garage had been filled with boxes. It looked as if the Mc-Garveys were leaving town.

Now the moving van confirmed it.

"I think if we stay here much longer we will arise suspicions," Odeah warned, his dark eyes flashing. The airspace anywhere near the capital was very closely watched.

"Wait," al-Turabi said. A slender woman with short blond hair came out of the house and said something to one of the workmen. A moment later she looked up, directly at the airplane, shading her eyes with a hand. His stomach tightened.

"We must leave, Kamal," the pilot insisted.

Al-Turabi lowered the binoculars. He was a slope-shouldered man with a hawk nose. "Yes, take us back now."

Odeah turned to the northwest toward Hagerstown where they'd picked up the light plane from the club that he belonged to. Even after the post-9/11 hysteria, and the creation of Homeland Security to keep the skies safe, it had been ridiculously easy, even for a Muslim, to join a flying club.

"Every law-enforcement agency will be searching for men such as yourself," Osama bin Laden had told al-Turabi in the Afghan mountains six months after 9/11.

"I understand," al-Turabi had said.

"While in America you must blend in. Documents will be made available for you to get your license to practice dentistry, and you will open a clinic in Laurel, Maryland. You will dress as an American. You will register to vote, hold a driver's license, and have a Social Security card and a U.S. passport. You will eat pork and drink liquor like an American. And you will speak like an American—hating all Muslims, especially me."

Al-Turabi, who'd originally been a dentist in Jeddah, Saudi Arabia, had been nearly overwhelmed by what was being asked of him. But he had bowed his head in deference to the only man other than his father whom he had ever loved. He had fought alongside bin Laden in the last two years of the righteous war in Afghanistan and he knew about duty and honor.

"You will be sent recruits one or two at a time, who you will train in the ways of America," bin Laden had instructed. "This time they will hide in the open. Under the noses of the American authorities. And when the time comes your cell will be called into action. Do not fail me."

The call had come thirty-six hours ago, and al-Turabi had spent that time trying to devise a foolproof plan. The best would have been to kill McGarvey while he slept in his own bed. He no longer had a security detail assigned to him, so it would have been a relatively straightforward hit.

"It looks like they're moving away," Odeah said, breaking al-Turabi out of his thoughts. "In a big hurry."

"Yes, but there was no security detail as we feared might be down there," al-Turabi replied. "McGarvey is on his own."

"Did you see him?"

"No, only his wife."

"We can come back tonight," Odeah suggested. "But we're going to have to get someone down here before the truck leaves so we can follow it."

"It won't be necessary."

"We don't want to lose them—"

"It's not necessary, Imad, because I know precisely where McGarvey will be two days from now, and precisely what time he will be there. We'll just have to wait until then to kill him."

They were passing over the busy Beltway where I-270 split off to Rockville, and Odeah adjusted his course to skirt the city to the south. "You're talking about the funeral?"

"Four o'clock in the afternoon at Arlington. We'll get there a half hour early, and spread out. As soon as McGarvey arrives we'll hit him and everyone else with everything we've got." Al-Turabi had come across the funeral arrangements for the dead spy, Robert Talarico, on the CIA's low-security Web site. He had considered it only as an alternative, because although killing McGarvey would be fairly easy, getting away afterwards would present some problems.

Insh'allah. *Paradise awaited the fighter for the* jihad.

"Killing a grieving widow and her children is not a good thing."

Al-Turabi's anger, which had been fueled by fear ever since he had joined the struggle, suddenly spiked. "They are infidels!" he shrieked. He was seeing red spots and flashes in front of his face. He wasn't aboard an airplane over the Maryland countryside, he was in a fierce battle north of Kabul, and the incoming tracer rounds from the Russian position were flying all over the place.

"Yes, Kamal, but are they worth dying for?"

"We have to kill them all."

"McGarvey I understand, but not the others," Odeah argued. "Listen to reason. I am no suicide bomber. Neither are the others. We're willing to give our lives for the struggle, but not like some crazy kids from the West Bank."

"Or like Mohamad Atta?"

Odeah was suddenly uncomfortable. He glanced nervously at al-Turabi. "He was a great hero. When he died he took more than two thousand infidels with him. Not a handful attending a funeral."

"Pray that you die so usefully," al-Turabi replied, no longer angry.

"Do you mean to kill us then?"

"If our deaths serve the *jihad*, yes."

THIRTY

CIA HEADQUARTERS

Adkins sat behind his desk, looking out the bulletproof windows across the woods behind the Building, enjoying the rare moment when he was alone, no telephones, no one seated across from him, no secretary, no pressing commitments to a National Intelligence Estimate or Watch Report. It was a few minutes after seven in the evening and all that was done for today.

But his desk was piled high with reports that would need his attention first thing in the morning, and with letters yet to be written, others to be signed, and a brutally grinding schedule of appointments that wouldn't end until well after seven.

He'd decided that when this business was done, he was going to resign—retire, actually—like McGarvey, only his retirement was going to be permanent. He'd never been a spy, in the classical, Cold War sense, he'd been more of an administrator. He could keep the gears well oiled, the machinery moving, but he'd never had those sudden flashes of inspiration or intuition that came so naturally to men such as McGarvey. They thrived on the game, as so many of them thought of the business. For them it was a black-and-white issue, us versus the bad guys. Administration meant nothing. Neither did realpolitik.

Von Clausewitz had written something to the effect that war was a political instrument. Adkins's poli-sci professor at the University of Indiana had vehemently disagreed. Of course he was a raging knee-jerk liberal, as Adkins had been at the time. But now everything was different. Maybe the old German had been right all along, but it was a philosophy that Adkins could not bring himself to embrace.

His secretary, Dhalia Swanson, had left for the evening, as had Dave Whittaker and most of the other senior staff. The Watch down in DO was manned 24/7 as was the NRO's photo interp shop, but most of the Building was quiet.

The inner door to his office was open, and he saw Otto Rencke's reflection in the window glass. Adkins turned around as the Special Projects director came in, his long frizzy red hair flying out from beneath a baseball cap with the sword and shield logo of the old KGB. His short-sleeved sweatshirt was from Moscow State University. He figured that his outfit was a good joke here at CIA headquarters.

"I thought you'd be gone by now," Adkins said, girding himself for bad news. Rencke had the look.

"The lavender is getting really deep, Mr. Director, I had to let you know right away. Mac doesn't want me to bother him at Gitmo, and you probably gotta do some stuff before he gets back."

"Why aren't you supposed to call him?"

Rencke shrugged. "He and Gloria are probably in the middle of some serious shit, ya know."

Adkins supposed that one of the core reasons he hated this job was that lives were on the line. He'd lost some good people in Afghanistan, several in Iraq, and then Talarico last week. Gloria had been wrong; Bob's death wasn't her fault, that burden was the DCI's, who had given the orders to send people into harm's way.

"Okay, Otto, what have you come up with and what stuff do I have to do?"

"We may have caught a break, 'cause José Martinez, one of our guys in Mexico City, thought he spotted Graham, or someone close enough he could've been a clone, at the airport's international terminal two days ago."

"Why'd he wait so long to get that up to us?" Adkins demanded. His stomach was sour.

"He wasn't sure until just now," Rencke said.

"Is he one of McCann's people?"

"He's a Mexican national we burned eighteen months ago," Rencke said, sidestepping the question. "Works airport security. He was the one who spotted Graham heading down to Venezuela."

Mexico City had always been a big center for intelligence-gathering. The Soviets, and these days the Russians, fielded more intelligence officers from their embassy than from any other embassy in the world, including here in Washington. Some of the networks such as Banco del Sur and CESTA had been in continuous operation, spying not only on the United States, but on Mexico and all of Central America as well, since the early fifties.

McGarvey had come back from a delicate operation down there more than ten years ago, in which a lot of people had lost their lives, including Donald Suthland Powers, possibly the most effective DCI in the Company's history. Adkins remembered it well, because he had been a senior Watch officer under Jon Lyman Trotter, who'd turned out to be the mole that Jim Angleton had been searching for all along.

"Continue," Adkins prompted.

"Graham was moving fast and he was in disguise each time, but Martinez managed to get reasonably clear headshots. The first time he sent them up to us for the match with Graham. This time he wasn't so sure of himself, so he did the work himself."

"Graham?" Adkins asked.

"I sent his stuff over to Louise and she has a ninety-three percent confidence that both guys are Graham." Louise Horn was chief of the National Reconnaissance Office's Photographic Interpretation Center. She was almost as brilliant and as odd as Otto, and she was his wife.

"That's good enough for me," Adkins said. "He wasn't heading back to Maracaibo to try again, was he?"

"Pakistan," Rencke said.

"He's on his way to bin Laden," Adkins said, molten lead in his stomach. "Allah's Scorpion. It's really going to happen, and it wasn't the canal after all."

Rencke started to hop from one foot to the other. "Bingo," he said and he clapped his hands together.

"What about at that end?"

"I sent the package to Dave Coddington, but we were way too late," Rencke said. Coddington was chief of Karachi Station, one of the CIA's toughest postings anywhere in the world.

"He could be anywhere by now," Adkins said. If they could have picked up the man's trail he might have led them to bin Laden—the big prize. But this job had almost never been that easy.

"Yes, he could," Rencke agreed.

"Like a needle in a haystack," Adkins mumbled.

"Mac would let the president know about this," Rencke suggested. "We need to shift our assets into finding a Kilo sub, because that's what they'll probably use. The Pentagon has the resources to help us out, if they can be convinced to cooperate."

Adkins was mildly surprised. "I would've expected that you would just hack their system."

Rencke smiled. "Unfortunately not everything is loaded into a database. We might need Humint this time. Pete Gregory is a naval historian. If we could get to him, he might be able to tell us where a stray Kilo for sale might be located. I've got my own list, but I don't think Graham will go to the most obvious places."

"A submarine alone won't do them much good," Adkins pointed out. "They'll need a weapon."

"I'm working on that too." Rencke nodded. And that's probably going to be the worst of it."

"What do you mean?"

"That's the deep lavender, Mr. Director," Rencke said. "A lot of Kilos are capable of launching cruise missiles while submerged. Nuclear-tipped cruise missiles."

THE WHITE HOUSE

The president and his national security adviser, Dennis Berndt, agreed to see Adkins immediately. It was eight by the time the DCI arrived at the White House. His limousine was passed through the West Gate, he signed in with the Secret Service detail, and was brought back to the Oval Office.

Haynes was dressed in jeans and an open-collar shirt, which meant he'd already had dinner with his wife and daughter. Berndt was still dressed in a suit and tie. He'd been getting ready to leave for the night when Adkins called. He and the president seemed concerned.

"Would you like a cup of coffee, Dick?" the president asked. He was having a Bud Light. "Or a beer?"

"No, sir. I'm not going to take up much of your time tonight, but there have been some interesting developments that you need to know about," Adkins said.

"Concerning Graham and the Panama Canal incident?" Berndt asked.

"Graham was spotted in Mexico City two days ago, heading to Pakistan."

The president grinned. "That's good news—" he said, but then stopped, realizing what Adkins had just told him. "He's on his way to bin Laden?"

"Yes, sir. But we got the news too late to be waiting for him when he got to Karachi. By now he could be just about anywhere."

"I see," the president said. He exchanged a look with Berndt. "You didn't come here this evening merely to tell me that the CIA lost track of this man."

"No, sir. But we believe that the attack on the Panama Canal was a separate operation from one al-Quaida has been gearing up for possibly more than a year."

"Allah's Scorpion?" Berndt asked.

Adkins nodded. "We've since learned that Graham was trained by the British navy to be a submarine commander. Top of his class in their Perisher school."

"Good Lord," the president said softly.

"He's more dangerous than we first believed."

"Do the crazy bastards actually have a submarine?" Berndt asked.

"We don't know yet," Adkins admitted. "But they have a top-flight submarine captain, and they've been trying to recruit a crew, so we think it's a safe bet that they've already got a sub, or they'll try to get one. Otto Rencke thinks they'll try for a Russian-built Kilo Class boat. It's diesel-electric, so on batteries alone it's ultra-quiet. I'm told that it's extremely reliable, easy to operate with a minimum crew, and almost as common as the Russian Kalashnikov rifle. Half the navies in the world own one or more. Iran has three."

"Okay, assuming bin Laden recruited Graham to come at us with a submarine, why'd he take the risk trying to destroy the Panama Canal?" the president asked.

"I'll tell you why, Mr. President," Berndt broke in. "If he'd been successful we would have had our hands full, just like after 9/11. We would have been looking the other way. Which means that whatever they're planning next will have the potential of hurting us even worse than the canal."

Haynes had been standing, leaning against his desk. He put his beer down, a set expression in his eyes. "What next?"

"McGarvey went down to Guantanamo Bay to question a number of prisoners who might have navy backgrounds, on the chance they may know something," Adkins said. "His primary mission is still to find Graham and bin Laden and take them out."

"Does he know that Graham went to Pakistan?"

"Not yet, Mr. President," Adkins said. "He'll be informed when he gets back. In the meantime we'd like to ask the navy for some help tracking down the Kilo boats our satellites will probably miss."

The president nodded. "I'll call Charlie Taggart tonight." Taggart was the secretary of defense and a longtime friend of the president's.

"Thank you, sir, but there's more," Adkins said.

"There always is," Haynes said, and he nodded impatiently for Adkins to get on with it.

"A lot of the Kilo boats out there have been modified so that they can fire cruise missiles from their torpedo tubes while submerged."

"Yes?"

"Before the British navy taught Graham to command submarines, they sent him to Dounreay, where he got his degree in nuclear engineering."

Both the president and his national security adviser were struck dumb for a moment. Berndt was the first to recover.

"I would think that buying or stealing a cruise missile might be even harder than getting a submarine," Berndt said.

"Yes, it would," Adkins agreed. "We think they'll probably try for a nuclear-tipped cruise missile. Graham would certainly know how to handle such a weapon."

"He could park his boat within a few miles anywhere along our coast and fire the damn thing," Berndt said. "We would have virtually no warning whatsoever."

"If we knew where, we could intercept him and destroy his boat," the president said. "Have you told any of this to Hamel?"

"No, sir."

"Don't," Haynes said. "There're too many politicians over there. We can't let one word of this get out. It'd create a panic worse than last year's suicide bombing scare."

"No matter what happens this will be the end of them," Berndt said. "We didn't collapse after 9/11, and we toppled the Taliban in Afghanistan and Saddam Hussein in Iraq. They've got nowhere to go."

"That's what we figure, Dennis," Adkins said. "From their perspective they've got to hit us. We've left them no other choice."

THIRTY-ONE

□

CAMP DELTA

A few minutes before two in the morning Gloria drove McGarvey across the quiet base up the hill to the prison's main gate.

They'd tossed their overnight bags in the Humvee and roused the Gulfstream's crew to get the aircraft ready for an immediate departure for Washington, because after this morning McGarvey figured they'd have to get out of Dodge as soon as possible, or they might be held until Adkins could pull some strings either at the Pentagon or the White House.

"They're going to want to know what we're doing here at this hour of the morning," Gloria said as they approached the gate. "What do you want me to say?"

"I'll handle it," McGarvey told her. Last night they had spread the word that they were heading home first thing in the morning, and then had turned in early to get a few hours' sleep at the BOQ. He had no doubt that Weiss had been informed, and would have let his guard down, thinking he had won.

Gloria glanced at him. "This isn't going to work if you're wrong about bin Ramdi understanding English. There's no way in hell Deyhim will cooperate."

"I know," McGarvey said. "But we're going to call him anyway."

"Why?"

"Someone is going to notify Weiss that we've showed up, and I want him to think that he's got plenty of time because without a translator it won't matter what we do."

Gloria grinned. "Sneaky. I like it. I just hope you're right, otherwise our trip was a waste of time."

She pulled up at the main gate. The MP who came out remembered her from last week. His M8 was slung over his shoulder, muzzle down.

"Good morning, ma'am," he said. His name tag read ROBERTS. He looked past her at McGarvey. "Sir, may I help you?"

McGarvey held up his CIA identification card. "We need to ask one of the guys we interviewed just before dinner a couple of questions."

"Yes, sir. I'll call Commander Weiss for authorization."

"He's on his way," McGarvey said. "But you can get our translator out of bed. He didn't answer when we tried to call just twenty minutes ago."

"Yes, sir. If you'll just stand by—"

"Look, everybody's tired, and nobody wants to be here at this hour of the morning, not us, and especially not Weiss. So go ahead and call Dey-him, but in the meantime we want to get to the interrogation center and have the prisoner brought over. It'll save us some time, and'll probably make Weiss a little less pissed off than he already is."

The MP hesitated a moment, but then he nodded. "Yes, sir," he said. He stepped back and motioned for his partner in the guard shack to power open the inner and outer gates.

They rattled slowly open, and Gloria drove into the prison main yard and headed directly over to the expansive cement block prisoner processing facility. "Weiss is going to get all over those guys for letting us in."

"I don't think so," McGarvey said. "He'll be too busy coming after me, because I'm going to break a couple of laws tonight."

Gloria gave him a curious look. "You going to kill somebody?"

"If need be," he said. Amnesty International and a lot of congressmen, and especially a big segment of the media, had come down hard on our military for prisoner abuses here and at Abu Ghraib. Our people were accused of not being sensitive to the ethnic needs of their Muslim prisoners. But the same watchdogs had very little to say about al-Quaida's beheading of its prisoners. Or of the endless rounds of car bombs. Those acts were America's fault for trying to fight back after 9/11.

Such attitudes had never made any sense to McGarvey, but he'd been battling them ever since Vietnam had blown up in our faces. We had been the bad guys, and when Jane Fonda had gone to Hanoi she had visited antiaircraft guns that were shooting down our planes, but she never went to the Hanoi Hilton where American crewmen were being starved and beaten.

"Maddox will probably have you shot."

"That's a possibility," McGarvey said as they pulled up. "Look, you can stick it out in the dayroom, it's only going to take me a couple of minutes."

Gloria laughed. "What, are you kidding?" she asked. "I wouldn't miss this for all the world. They were the bastards who killed my partner."

The OD, a tall, very thin first lieutenant named Albritton, had been alerted by the gate guards that McGarvey and Gloria were incoming from Post One. He got up from behind his desk just inside the front door when they came in.

"I've sent a runner to find Commander Weiss," he said. "But until he gets here, I will not allow any prisoner to be interrogated. That's SOP."

"That's fine with me," McGarvey said. "We need an interpreter in any event. But in the meantime you can get the man out of bed and over here."

Gloria handed bin Ramdi's folder to the OD. "The sooner we can ask our questions, the sooner we'll be gone," she said sweetly and she smiled.

The OD was shaking his head.

"Son, I don't want to pull rank on you, but I will," McGarvey warned. "These are the same bastards who killed three of your guys last week. We're just trying to find out what's going to happen next. No one wants to go through another 9/11."

"Sir, Commander Weiss will have my ass if I let you talk to one of his prisoners."

"I hate to break this to you, Lieutenant, but these are not his prisoners," Gloria said.

McGarvey snatched the phone from the OD's desk, and held it out to the man. "Call General Maddox. He'll give you the authorization."

The lieutenant looked like he'd been hit with a cattle prod. "It's two in the morning."

"Yes, it is," McGarvey said. "Call him."

"Shit," the OD said. He took the phone and dialed a number. "This is Albritton." He opened bin Ramdi's file. "I want you to bring seven-three-nine over on the double."

The clock had just started. Whoever got here first, Weiss or bin Ramdi, would determine if their trip had been a waste of time.

"I sent a runner to look for him, he's not in his quarters," Albritton said into the phone. "Just bring the prisoner over here, if you please." He glanced at McGarvey and nodded. "I'll sign for him." He hung up. "Your man will be here shortly. We'll put him in the same interrogation room you used this afternoon."

"Thank you," McGarvey said. "We'll just go back and wait for him there."

"Be sure to let us know when you've found Commander Weiss," Gloria said.

She and McGarvey went to the end of the corridor, which opened to the common room that was equipped with tables and chairs, some vending machines, and a TV set, DVD player, and a shelf full of movies. This was where MPs sometimes took their breaks. Four interrogation rooms, their doors open, were along the back concrete block wall. The lights were on but no one was there. Each room was equipped with a one-way glass. When prisoners were being interrogated, lights in the common room were kept off.

McGarvey turned his back to the closed-circuit surveillance camera mounted near the ceiling in the corner opposite the interrogation rooms and took out his pistol. He removed the magazine, eased the slide back to eject the round in the chamber, and put the magazine back in place. He holstered the gun and pocketed the 9mm bullet.

Gloria watched, her eyes bright, but she didn't say a word.

"It might get a little dicey, but I want you to play along with whatever goes down," McGarvey told her.

She nodded.

"I want you to be absolutely clear on one thing," he said. "No one gets hurt. No matter what does or does not happen, no one gets hurt. Understood?"

Gloria nodded. "What are you trying to get from him?"

"He knows something about the five prisoners who were sprung."

"They all do."

"I think he might know why al-Quaida got them out, and killed them rather than let them be recaptured." McGarvey had been thinking about little else since he'd gotten back from Panama. He thought he knew the answers, but he had to make sure.

Lieutenant Albritton and an MP came down the corridor with bin Ramdi. The Saudi was fully awake, but he didn't seem quite as sure of himself as he had earlier.

"No questions until we can get Commander Weiss over here," Albritton warned.

"Right," McGarvey said, his eyes locked on bin Ramdi's.

The MP escorted the prisoner into one of the interrogation rooms, then stepped out. He hadn't removed the plastic wrist restraint.

The telephone down the corridor rang. "Stay here," Albritton told the MP, and he hustled back to his post.

The MP, whose name tag read LAGERMANN, glanced at the lieutenant, his attention momentarily away from bin Ramdi.

McGarvey slipped into the interrogation room, pulled out his pistol, and pointed it at bin Ramdi's head. "Al saheeh," he said. The truth.

"Holy shit!" the MP shouted.

Bin Ramdi's eyes flicked back and forth from McGarvey to the marine.

"Sir, you will stand down!" the MP shouted.

"I'm going to kill this son of a bitch unless he starts talking," McGarvey said, his voice low, his tone reasonable.

"No, sir, I can't let that happen!" the MP shouted.

Gloria was right behind him. "This is the same scum bastard who kills our people, Lagermann. So who are you going to protect? Us or them?"

"Ma'am, I'm just following my orders."

"Yeah, well so am I," Gloria said.

"The truth, do you understand me?" McGarvey asked.

Bin Ramdi was still looking for the MP to protect him.

McGarvey cocked the hammer of his pistol. "Do you understand me?"

Bin Ramdi suddenly came unglued. He backed up, and nodded vigorously. "Yes," he said. "I understand you. But do not shoot me."

"Lieutenant!" the MP shouted. "We have a situation back here!"

"The five prisoners who escaped. What did they do in the Iranian navy?"

Bin Ramdi threw up his bound hands. "I beseech you. I do not know this answer."

McGarvey stepped closer. "Tell me or I will kill you. My wife died on 9/11, and it will be so easy for me to pull this trigger that you cannot imagine."

"They were in the navy!" bin Ramdi cried.

"We know that. But what did they do?"

"Sir, Commander Weiss is coming through the front gate," Lieutenant Albritton said from the doorway. "He orders you to back off. Right now, or you will be placed under arrest."

"*Al saheeh*," McGarvey said. He took a step forward.

"Submarines," bin Ramdi whispered.

It was the answer that McGarvey had expected, but the Saudi knew more. It was in his eyes, there was a certain craftiness there, as if he felt that he had succeeded in evading something even more important than what the five escapees had done in the navy.

"What else?" McGarvey demanded harshly.

"There is nothing else."

McGarvey took another step closer, so that he was only three feet away from the prisoner, and pulled the trigger. The hammer fell on an empty firing chamber with a loud snap.

Bin Ramdi flinched so badly he almost lost his balance.

"Shit," McGarvey muttered. He cycled the ejector slide, charging the pistol, and once again pointed the muzzle directly at the Saudi's head.

Bin Ramdi pissed in his jumpsuit.

"I want the rest of it. Why were those five men broken out of here?"

"I don't know, I swear it!" bin Ramdi cried. His eyes were glued on McGarvey's trigger finger.

McGarvey started to pull.

"They were transferred to Camp Echo that night," bin Ramdi blurted, nearly incoherently. "But I don't know why, except that Osama wanted them."

It was not the answer McGarvey had expected, but it made sense if Gloria's suspicion that there was a traitor inside Camp Delta was correct.

There was a sudden commotion in the common room behind McGarvey.

"Sir, I tried to stop him," Lieutenant Albritton said.

"Shoot him," Weiss ordered.

"Sir?" the MP asked.

McGarvey held bin Ramdi's eyes for just a second longer, but there was no longer any guile, only relief.

"Shoot him!" Weiss shouted.

"It won't be necessary," McGarvey said. He lowered his pistol, decocked it, and holstered it as he turned around. "We're finished here."

The confused MP had unslung his M8 carbine, but the muzzle was pointed at the floor and his finger was alongside the trigger guard.

Weiss, dressed in blue jeans and a white T-shirt, was directly behind the MP. He shoved the young man aside and fumbled for the Beretta in his shoulder holster. He was muttering something.

Gloria moved in from his right, batted his hand away from the pistol, and grabbed it out of the holster. She stepped back a pace. "Let's all calm down here, before this shit gets out of hand," she said.

Weiss was beside himself with rage. "You bitch," he growled. He backhanded Gloria in the face, snapping her head back, and sending her bouncing off the wall, the pistol falling to the floor.

Before McGarvey could move to interfere, Weiss came after Gloria, shoving her back against the wall again. But this time she was expecting it. She rolled to the side, grabbed Weiss's right wrist, and slammed his forearm against the door frame, both bones breaking with an audible pop.

Weiss screamed and staggered away from her, trying to cradle his broken arm against his chest.

The MP was stunned.

Gloria stepped forward, slammed the heel of her right hand into Weiss's nose, breaking it, blood gushing out both nostrils, then hit his left kneecap with her right instep, dislocating the man's knee.

Weiss collapsed on the floor and Gloria was about to go after him when McGarvey was at her side.

"That's all," he said softly.

She looked at him, her nostrils flared, her eyes wild.

"Come down, Gloria, it's done. We're out of here."

Slowly she came back, and nodded.

Weiss was curled up, whimpering in pain.

"Someone call an ambulance for Mr. Weiss," McGarvey said.

Lieutenant Albritton had moved well out of range and he kept looking from Weiss to Gloria and then to McGarvey. But he didn't say anything.

McGarvey looked at bin Ramdi, who had shrunk back into a corner of the interrogation room, a mostly unreadable expression on his face. But it was obvious he was impressed by what he'd just witnessed, and extremely wary.

"You sons of bitches are going to fucking jail!" Weiss shouted.

McGarvey looked down at him and shook his head. "Didn't anyone ever teach you not to hit women?"

"Evidently not," the MP said, half under his breath. "But he sure got told this time."

THIRTY-TWO

□

EN ROUTE TO ANDREWS AIR FORCE BASE

They'd not been interfered with as they left Camp Delta and drove across base down to the ferry landing. Nor were they stopped from reaching their Gulfstream, even though it was very likely that by then General Maddox had been informed about what had happened.

In this case McGarvey thought that it was probably for the best that it wasn't a prisoner who'd been roughed up, though by the time they reached Washington he was pretty sure that McCann would try to bring Gloria up on charges.

It was morning, the sun just rising above the Atlantic horizon as they approached the U.S. East Coast. Gloria had been far too keyed-up to sleep on the fourteen-hundred-mile trip back to D.C., but she hadn't wanted to talk about what had happened.

She came forward from the head where she had splashed some water on her face, and straightened out her hair and touched up her makeup. She sat down in the big leather seat facing McGarvey, a resolute expression on her round face; she had screwed up and she was ready now to face her punishment.

"I jeopardized the mission," she said. "I'm sorry."

"He had it coming."

Gloria smiled tightly, and nodded. "I might have killed him if you hadn't stopped me."

"The paperwork would have been endless," McGarvey said. "Ask me, I know."

Without averting her gaze, Gloria began to cry silently, tears welling in her eyes and rolling down her cheeks.

McGarvey's heart suddenly went out to her. She'd had a difficult life, losing her mother and then her husband, so she was seasoned to pain. But she wasn't much older than his daughter Elizabeth. And she had the same sort of tough exterior that was a cover for a sometimes confused and frightened little girl who wasn't sure if she was ready to be an adult.

He reached out and touched her knee. "You did a good job down there. Because of you and your partner we found out what Allah's Scorpion is, and now we've got a good shot at shutting it down."

"I got Bob killed."

"It wasn't you who killed him, it was the bad guys," McGarvey told her. "You'd better understand that, otherwise you're not going to be much help to me."

Her dark eyes widened slightly. "I thought I would be pulled out of the field after this."

"Are you kidding?" McGarvey asked. "Why do you think Weiss came after you?"

Gloria's jaw tightened. "Because he's dirty, and he knows that I suspect him." She shook her head. "But I don't have any proof, and Howard'll go ballistic as soon as Weiss starts making noises."

"Which might not happen," McGarvey said. "He's gotten rid of us, and I think Maddox is going to order him to take his lumps and shut his mouth."

"I don't get it, Mac, why would somebody like Weiss work for al-Quaida? It doesn't make sense. I mean he's an asshole, but he's apparently got a good career going for him. Why would he take the risk?"

"Money. Ego. Arrogance," McGarvey said. He'd seen the same sort of thing many times before. Men, and a few women, who'd thought that they were better than everyone else. Superior. Smarter. Quicker. Or, for some of them, it was the same sort of thrill that a bungee jumper gets when he steps off the edge. It was almost a death wish. When some traitors were caught they were relieved that they no longer had to lead a double life. In many respects prison would be easier.

Weiss, if he was guilty of anything other than being a simple asshole, was not cut of the same dangerous cloth as Rupert Graham. Men like Graham, and others McGarvey had come up against, who were as brilliant as they were ruthless, were at war with the world. Whatever brought them to that point, and there was no one reason that McGarvey had ever discovered, did not interfere with their skills on the battlefield.

Carlos the Jackal had been the first of the specialist killing machines in the modern era, and Graham was just another. He would never be brought to trial, because he would simply take his war into prison. Men like him had to be killed. There was no other solution.

"Hijo de puta," Gloria said softly.

"Yeah."

CIA HEADQUARTERS

Coming back out of the field, as he had done countless times before in his career, brought back a host of memories. A good many of them were very bad: missions in which he had made kills; missions in which he had nearly lost his life; missions in which his family's lives had been placed in jeopardy. Riding into the city he remembered the face of every person he'd killed. The number wasn't legion, but over a twenty-five-year career he had a lot of blood on his conscience.

Adkins had sent a Company limo out to Andrews for them, and on the drive in McGarvey had made a quick phone call to his wife.

"Touchdown," he told her.

"You're in one piece?" she asked, and he heard the relief in her voice.

"All my fingers and toes."

"ETA?"

McGarvey glanced at his watch. It was a couple of minutes after ten. When he looked up, his eyes met Gloria's. There was an odd, hungry set to her mouth. "I should make it by lunchtime or a little later. How'd the move go?"

"Most of our worldly possessions are on the way south," Kathleen said. "How about us?"

"Soon," McGarvey promised.

"As in tomorrow or the next day?"

"Soon," McGarvey said. He felt bad, because this sort of conversation had interrupted his marriage for a lot of years. These days Katy was more pragmatic about what he did, but the uncertainty and hurt was an ever-constant pressure in her gut. He could hear it in her voice. She was afraid for him.

"We'll talk then," Kathleen said and broke the connection.

The Company had provided them with a furnished apartment not too far from their house in Chevy Chase until McGarvey was finished with this assignment. He'd wanted her to drive down to their new place in Sarasota, and Liz had volunteered to ride shotgun for her mother. But Kathleen wasn't leaving town without her husband.

"You okay?" Gloria asked.

McGarvey managed a smile. "Just trying to get retired and stay that way."

"Soon?"

He nodded. "Yeah."

Their driver radioed ahead and they were passed directly through the executive gate, and whisked to management's underground parking where the elevator was waiting for them. "Welcome back, Mr. Director," the driver said.

"I'm not back," McGarvey told him.

He and Gloria rode up to the Directorate of Operations on the third floor. He got out with her. "You don't have to come with me," she said. "I'm a big girl, I can handle Mr. McCann."

"I'm sure you can, but I'll put in a good word for you anyway," McGarvey told her. "This isn't over, and I have a feeling I may be asking for your help again."

Gloria's eyes lit up with pleasure. "Any time," she said, and she headed down the corridor to the DDO's office.

McGarvey went in the opposite direction back to Rencke's office, which a few months ago had been moved out of the mainframe room here to Operations, where he could be closer to the Watch. His big office behind glass walls had originally housed a dozen cubicles where Directorate of Intelligence analysts task-shared with DDO junior desk officers. Their offices had been scattered all over the third floor.

Rencke was standing in the middle of the room on one leg, like a flamingo, his red hair flying everywhere, while data streamed across nine computer monitors arrayed around the perimeter. The wallpaper on each of them was lavender. He was leaning up against a long conference table that was strewn with maps; high-resolution satellite photos in real light as well as infrared; stacks of file folders, many of them with orange stripes denoting top secret or above material; empty Twinkie wrappers and a half-empty bottle of heavy cream.

McGarvey knocked on the glass door and let himself in.

"Bad dog, bad dog, go away and come again another day!" Rencke shouted.

"Just me," McGarvey said.

Rencke spun around so fast he almost fell over. "Oh, wow," he cried. "Did you find the golden chalice? Did you?"

"You were right, it's a submarine operation. The five guys they sprung last week had all been submarine crew."

Rencke clapped his hands. "Uncle Osama isn't about to waste the skills of a Perisher dude. No way." He stopped suddenly, the animation leaving his face. "You found something else?"

"They were transferred to Echo the same night," McGarvey said.

"Gitmo's starting to smell like a barnyard," Rencke said. "Any ideas?"

"Guy's name is Tom Weiss. He's the ONI officer in charge of interrogations," McGarvey said. "He's either an idiot or he's on someone's payroll."

"Same one who hassled Gloria last week. He couldn't have been terribly happy to see her on his doorstep again."

McGarvey explained the confrontation they'd had this morning, and Rencke was loving it.

"Big man on campus got taken down a notch by the little lady." He laughed. "Wait'll I tell Louise. She loves that kinda shit."

"Take a peek down his track, but don't make any waves yet," McGarvey said. "If he is dirty he'll have cutouts, probably someone else there on base, unless he's set up a little nest egg account somewhere. Maybe the Caymans. But he'll have to have a line of communications."

"If it's electronic I'll find it," Rencke said. "But there might be a letter drop somewhere. Any idea how often he gets back to the States? Could be here, ya know."

"I don't know anything about the man, except that Gloria thinks he's dirty, and for now that's good enough for me."

"She's kinda like Liz, isn't she?" Rencke said.

"I thought the same thing," McGarvey said. "In the meantime, while Graham is looking for a crew, we need to find out where's he's going to get a sub and a weapon. And for some reason I don't think we've got a lot of time on this one."

"It'll probably be a Kilo boat. I'm running an inventory right now for all of them our spy birds can spot, but we'll miss all the ones either locked up in sub pens, or tucked away in some remote inlet somewhere. I was thinking about asking Pete Gregory. He's a naval historian over at the Pentagon."

"Go ahead and hack their database, but hold off on Gregory," McGarvey said. "If you don't find anything in the next twenty-four hours I've got someone else in mind who might be able to help us come up with a short list. And I know that he won't leak anything to the ONI."

THIRTY-THREE

□

CIA HEADQUARTERS

Adkins closed a file folder on his desk, and got to his feet as McGarvey walked into the DCI's seventh-floor office. The director looked worn-out, the weight of the world on his shoulders. His jacket was off, his tie loose.

"Here he is at last," he said. "From what Ms. Ibenez has been telling us, you two have probably created a firestorm for us."

Gloria was seated across from the DCI, along with Rencke's boss Howard McCann. None of them looked happy.

"He had it coming, Dick," McGarvey said, crossing the room. He pulled a side chair over and sat down next to Gloria. "And there's a good chance he's dirty. I've got Otto looking into it for us."

"Dirty or not, he could charge Ms. Ibenez with criminal assault," McCann pointed out dryly. "There were two witnesses."

"Actually there were three witnesses if you count me," McGarvey said. "Has Weiss or anyone from the ONI called or filed a complaint?"

"Not yet, but I expect it's coming." McCann glanced at Gloria with obvious distaste. "God help us if the media gets the story. We'll never hear the end of it."

"We're going to put Ms. Ibenez on the South American desk until this blows over," Adkins said. "It's a good idea that she keep a low profile for now."

"That'll have to wait. Ms. Ibenez has agreed to give me a hand."

"Oh, come on, McGarvey," McCann said. "I'll give you anyone you want. Hell, take your daughter if you need a woman on the mission for some reason. But Ms. Ibenez is going to keep her head down."

"Liz and her husband have got their hands full out at the Farm," McGarvey said. He was having second thoughts about Whittaker's recommendation for McCann to head the DO. The man was a competent administrator, but he knew nothing about the sort of people who worked for him. CIA field officers were a breed apart. And he was no spy. He'd spent nearly all his career behind a desk, writing reports rather than generating them.

"Okay, I'll give you someone else—" McCann said, but McGarvey waved him off.

"She's already up to speed. And where I'm going I might need someone to cover my back." McGarvey smiled faintly. "She's already proved that she can handle herself in a fight."

"In my book, injuring a military officer when he was doing nothing more than his job is not exactly a sterling recommendation," McCann shot back.

"Apparently she hasn't told you that Weiss was pulling out his gun to shoot me with, so she had to disarm him," McGarvey said. "That alone makes her my new partner."

"She didn't have to break his arm," Adkins suggested.

"Did she tell you that Weiss hit her first, even though she was trying to defuse a situation that was getting out of hand? Nearly knocked her unconscious." He looked at McCann. "What would you have done in that situation, Howard? Throw harsh words at the man?"

"I wouldn't have been there in the first place."

"No, you wouldn't," McGarvey said. "And if you don't mind a suggestion from someone who's held your job, ease up on your people. Don't be such an asshole."

McCann flared, and he nearly came out of his chair. "Shooting people to death or threatening them with great bodily harm is not proper tradecraft." He nodded toward Gloria. "And this woman managed to get her partner shot up with no problem."

"The bad guys shot him, Howard, and then killed themselves. They're the same sort who hit us on 9/11, and the same sort who damned near nailed the Panama Canal, and who are trying to come up with a submarine, a weapon, and a crew to hit us again." McGarvey glanced at Adkins. "I've never been politically correct, and I sure as hell am not about to start now." He turned back to McCann. "Yes, I've killed people in the line of duty. And I plan on doing it again. However many it takes for me to get to Graham and stop him, and however many more it takes for me to get to bin Laden and put a bullet in his brain."

McCann wanted to say something else, but Adkins held up a hand. "Otto thinks Graham will probably try to get his hands on a Kilo boat."

"That's what he told me," McGarvey said, though he wasn't as convinced as the Special Projects director was. It seemed too pat, too easy. Maybe they were missing something.

Adkins read some of that from McGarvey's body language. "But?"

"I don't know, Dick. But I don't think we should limit ourselves. Graham knows the business. He might have connections we know nothing about. Just like bin Laden does. Pakistan and Iran both have submarines. So do a lot of other countries."

"In the meantime Otto has got the NRO doing a complete survey of every single Kilo submarine," Adkins said. "Louise is in charge of the project, but it's big. Our best guess is in excess of fifty boats spread out from Russia to India, and from Iran to Romania. A few of them are at sea, some of them submerged. Some are in sub pens and therefore invisible, some are in breaking yards being dismantled for scrap, while most are tied up at their docks in plain sight. But it's the ones we're going to miss that worries me."

"What about bin Laden?" McGarvey asked. "Have you guys turned up any new leads yet?"

"The Pakistanis may be closing in on him in the mountains along the Afghanistan border near Drosh," McCann said.

"They've been saying the same thing since 9/11."

"It's a tough place to search," McCann countered. "They're not only fighting the terrain, but the local tribal chiefs who don't much care for Islamabad."

"We have four augmented teams on the ground with ISI right now, and another four en route," Adkins said. "If he's there we'll definitely find him this time."

"I hope so, because some of those people are going to get killed up there."

Adkins lowered his eyes, and fingered the file folder. "Did you really want this job, Mac?" he asked. "Did you ever like it?"

McGarvey knew exactly what Adkins was feeling. He'd been there himself. "No one's supposed to like it. You're just supposed to try to make a difference."

"Bob Talarico's funeral is at four this afternoon at Arlington," Adkins said. He looked up. "Will you be there?"

"Of course," McGarvey said. "I have to go over to the apartment to change clothes and see if Katy's okay. Our furniture is on its way to Florida."

A bleak look came across Adkins's face. "There's no telling how long this'll take, you know."

"Don't worry," McGarvey said, getting to his feet. "I'm in for the duration."

"What's your next step?"

"Gloria and I are going to help Otto find the Kilo boat, because when it shows up Graham will be aboard."

"Good luck," Adkins said.

"We're going to need it," McGarvey replied. "If Graham gets any wiggle room at all we'll probably lose him."

"I'm going to need Ms. Ibenez to file a Sitrep and sit for a debriefing," McCann said. "No use asking if you'll do the same."

"Later," McGarvey said.

"Go ahead," Adkins told Gloria. "I'm assigning you to temporary duty under Mr. McGarvey's direction."

"Do you think that's wise, Mr. Director?" McCann asked.

"No, but that's the way it's going to be."

"Thank you, sir," Gloria said, getting up.

"Keep us posted, would you, Mac?" Adkins asked.

"Through Otto," McGarvey promised, and he and Gloria left the office and took the elevator down to the parking garage.

"Thanks for rescuing me," she told him.

"This won't be easy," McGarvey warned. "Screw up and you could get both of us killed."

"I'll try to keep up," she said. "But why me? I thought you always worked alone."

McGarvey had to smile. She was bright as well as good-looking, but she still had a lot to learn, and the curve on this one would be steep.

"I usually do, but your boss was getting set to gang up on you. And I've never liked bullies."

She turned away. "I know what you mean." When she looked back a veil had dropped over her eyes, as if she weren't focusing. "Look, can I bum a ride to Arlington with you? I don't think I want to be alone."

"I have to go home and change first."

"My apartment's in Bethesda, on the way to where you're staying. I have to change too. You could drop me off, and then pick me up on the way to Arlington." She shrugged. "If you don't mind."

"I don't mind," McGarvey said, and there was a sudden lifting at the corners of Gloria's eyes that was mildly puzzling, but he let it go. She was under a lot of stress, and losing a partner was almost as traumatic as losing a spouse.

THIRTY-FOUR

□

KARACHI

Osama bin Laden, dressed in traditional Muslim garb, entered his inner sanctum prayer room at ten thirty in the evening, local time. He paused for a longish moment to study the faces of the four men gathered at his request, then stepped out of his sandals and took his place on the rug at the head of the room, his back to the television set that had been switched off.

"Good evening, my friends," he said, his voice soft. "May Allah's blessing be upon you. We are nearly ready to strike again at the infidel and this time we will hurt them worse than we did in Manhattan and Washington combined."

Rupert Graham, the only Westerner at the meeting, gave bin Laden a bleak look. There was a leak somewhere in al-Quaida and it could very easily be either the Sudanese, Ghassan Dahduli, or bin Laden's Saudi adviser Khalid bin Abdullah. The third man, Abdel Aziz Mysko, was from Chechnya, and Graham hadn't met him until this evening. But he was in the inner command circle, which made him a suspect.

"Is it to be Allah's Scorpion finally?" bin Abdullah asked, his eyes bright. He was a stoop-shouldered man with a dark complexion and a hawk nose; a third cousin of a minor Saudi prince, which made him royalty. He was an idiot, but he was a major money source for the cause.

"Yes, we have waited far too long since 9/11, and already the world is beginning to forget," bin Laden said. He avoided Graham's eyes.

"A wait that would have ended last week, if Captain Graham had been more thorough with his preparations," bin Abdullah said harshly. "Pray that his spirit is more steadfast this time."

"Perhaps we should find someone else to lead the mission," Dahduli suggested gently. He was a homely, round-faced man with a closely trimmed full beard and very large lips and ears. He had been with bin Laden almost from the beginning, but hadn't risen to the inner circle of advisers until many of bin Laden's top people had been killed or captured during the wars in Afghanistan and Iraq, for the simple reason he wasn't very bright. He'd been a carpet merchant in Khartoum.

"That's out of the question, my friend," bin Laden replied patiently, as if he were a father explaining something to a son. "This is a submarine operation, and Mr. Graham is a submarine captain."

Dahduli refused to look at Graham. "If that's the case, why did we send him to Panama aboard an oil tanker? If he had been killed or captured, we would have lost his expertise."

"Because the time was right to strike," bin Abdullah said. "My money sources are beginning to demand action. They want something in return for the risk they are taking. With the Panama Canal destroyed by a Venezuelan ship and crew, oil from Saudi Arabia would become even more critical to the United States than it already is. Two hundred dollars per barrel would be conceivable. And such prices would surely bring the infidel to their knees."

"As well as enrich the royal family," Dahduli commented dryly. "But the question needs answering: If Mr. Graham's skills are so important to our righteous cause, why was his life placed in danger on that mission?"

"Because we did not have a submarine or a weapon to fire or a crew to operate it," bin Laden said, his voice barely above a whisper.

Graham's breath quickened, catching in his throat. He shot a glance at the Chechen, who was the only man in the room other than bin Laden who didn't look surprised. "Son of a bitch, you got a Russian Kilo boat," he said, in wonder. "From the Pacific Fleet."

Bin Laden smiled broadly. "You'll see," he said.

"We don't have the boat yet, but it would only be a matter of days once I am given the word," Mysko said. He had been introduced to Graham this evening as a major in the Russian Special Forces. He was a hard-looking man, very compact, with a three-day growth of whiskers, deep black eyes, and narrow high cheekbones that made him look like some dark jungle cat. Very dangerous. He'd pretended to go along with the Russians, fighting against his own homeland until eight years ago, when he came down to Afghanistan and joined forces with al-Quaida and the Taliban.

Graham turned to bin Laden. "Can we count on this man's promise?"

Mysko flared. "You have never trained aboard a Kilo boat, can we count on you to know how it's done without fucking it up?"

Graham willed himself to remain calm. He knew that he could kill the man here and now, but he did not want to ruin the chance to return to sea aboard his own submarine. With a Kilo boat the world would be his, because once he submerged, no navy on earth would be able to find him.

Even bin Laden's Allah would be no match.

"My apologies, Major, I meant no disrespect," Graham said humbly, his thoughts soaring. He was beginning to see Jillian's face again.

Mysko's smile was as sudden as it was disingenuous. "Nor I, Captain. But it has taken me many months, and a considerable amount of al-Quaida's hard currencies to get to this stage. I would not like to see all of that effort go to waste."

"I understand," Graham said.

"Please tell them everything, Abdel," bin Laden prompted, still smiling gently, and it came to Graham that the man was hiding something from them. Something important.

Mysko nodded. "I have arranged for us to steal a Kilo Six-fifty Class boat from Rakushka, which is about three hundred kilometers northeast of Vladivostok."

Graham's breath caught in his throat again, and he looked at bin Laden, who nodded. Almost every Kilo Class submarine was equipped with standard 533mm tubes, which gave it the capability of firing standard high-explosive (HE) short antisubmarine torpedoes as well as the long antiship weapons. But it had been rumored that a new class had been fitted with 650mm tubes that would allow the submarine to fire the SS-N-16 nuclear-tipped missile. That's the class Kilo that Mysko was talking about.

Mysko glanced at Graham to make sure the 650 designation had been understood, and he smiled. "Security up there is normally loose, but I paid more than one million U.S. to a lieutenant general in charge of overall intelligence operations for the region, to divert the key guards for our boat during a twelve-hour window. When the time comes I will share all the details with you, for now I need only to know the target date."

Bin Laden shook his head. "The details are not as important as the results," he said. "And I will give you the date very soon."

"Very well," Mysko said. "I managed to come up with eighteen Russian crewmen, who were a lot less expensive than the one general. Eleven of them are already at Rakushka, but I will need forty-eight hours to get the rest of them up there."

"Will they be sufficient to operate the boat?" Abdullah asked.

"The Kilo normally carries a crew of sixty men and officers, but it can be sailed with as few as eighteen men, if all of them are officers," Graham said.

"All the men I recruited are officers," Mysko said. "Russian navy pay is very bad, and prices are high. Even an officer has a hard time supporting himself."

"Then what?" Graham prompted.

"Security at the weapons depot there will also be nonexistent during those twelve hours. Time enough to load two missiles."

"That will create a lot of attention," Graham said. "There'll be heavy lifting machinery and a lot of lights. Someone is bound to ask questions."

"I'm assured that won't happen. But we must be done and out of there before the twelve hours is up," Mysko said. "That means we must be at sea and submerged by then."

There had to be much more than a simple breach in security for the plan to work. At the very least, U.S. surveillance satellites would pick up the submarine's move out of the pens and then the loading of weapons. The bay emptied into the Sea of Japan, which was constantly monitored and patrolled by the U.S. Seventh and the Japanese Maritime Self Defense Force, but Graham let those considerations pass for the moment. "Where am I in all this?"

"Standing by aboard a North Korean fishing boat five hundred kilometers to the east. Within twenty-four hours the submarine will rendezvous with you and surface," Mysko said. "After that she'll be your boat."

"How long to reach Panama?" Dahduli asked.

Graham was working it out in his head. "Can't go straight there from Vladivostok, Japan's in the way," he said. "I expect we'll have to sail north along the inside passage between Sakhalin Island and the Russian mainland. That's about a thousand miles north, and another thousand south before we could head through the Kuril Islands and then southeast." He shrugged. "It's a long trip. Seventy-five hundred miles perhaps, right at the Kilo's extreme range at seven knots. I'd need a schedule of U.S. satellites so I could know when to run on the surface."

"How long?" Dahduli pressed.

"If we were lucky, it'd take a month and a half, maybe six weeks," Graham said. "And you realize that once the Russians figure out that one of their subs is missing they'll come looking for us. Just like *The Hunt for Red October*, only for real."

"Are you saying now that you are incapable of doing this?" Dahduli demanded.

"Not at all," Graham responded sharply. "But it may take much longer than six weeks if I have to spend time submerged, evading detection. It's even possible that we'll need to take on diesel fuel somewhere."

"Where would that be?" Dahduli pressed.

"At sea in the middle of the night. Probably somewhere north of the Hawaiian Islands."

"That's the U.S. Navy's Third Fleet," bin Laden said.

"Yes, it is," Graham responded. "But I know someone who could bring the fuel out to us."

"Trustworthy?" Dahduli asked, sneering.

Graham raised his left hand, a gesture very rude to an Arab. "I am beginning to tire of your lack of faith, Ghassan. Take care that you do not cross the line after which I would have to take action."

Dahduli's eyes bulged. "Infidel—" he said.

Bin Laden silenced him with a glance. "We have much to do before we can strike this blow. Get on with it."

"I'll need a timetable, and personnel files on my crew," Graham said.

"Remain here, and we will discuss your role," bin Laden said.

The other three men clearly wanted to remain, they felt that their positions as inner circle al-Quaida advisers had somehow been usurped by an infidel, but they got up and left the chamber.

"You have reservations about this plan," bin Laden said to Graham when they were alone. "Tell me."

"It's far too risky," Graham said. "Getting away in the middle of the night with a submarine from Rakushka is possible. I've actually been there, I know the waters of Vladimir Bay. But I don't care what assurances Mysko gives us, loading a pair of weapons aboard would never happen unnoticed. At the very least, we'd be spotted by an American satellite, and before we ever got out of the bay and into the Sea of Japan, we'd have a reception committee waiting for us; either a Los Angeles Class attack submarine, or maybe a Seawolf or a Virginia. We wouldn't stand a chance."

Bin Laden fell silent for several seconds. But then he nodded. "I came to the same conclusion, my friend. But we will let Mysko carry on with his plan; it may divert the Americans' attention."

"You've found another submarine?" Graham asked. The catch was back in his throat.

"Yes, and two missiles; we have friends elsewhere," bin Laden said. "In any event, the Russians have no love for us."

"Will the target still be the Panama Canal?"

"In thirty days President Haynes will give a State of the Union address to Congress. If you were to get within two hundred and fifty kilometers of Washington before you fired your missiles, there would be very little time to evacuate the building."

Graham saw it all as one piece, as if he'd been planning for something like this all his life. "I'll get us so close that they will have no time to react," he said, and smiled. "This time I cannot fail."

THIRTY-FIVE

☐

CHEVY CHASE

McGarvey thought that Katy was holding up well until he walked in the door of the CIA safe house a few minutes before one in the afternoon and saw the brittle expression on her face. There was more there than the stress of their move and her husband's being called back into the field.

She had a small bourbon, neat, ready for him at the pass-through kitchen counter, and when she came into his arms and clung to him, she was shivering. McGarvey hadn't seen her this uptight since last year just before he'd resigned as DCI.

"Have you see CNN this morning?" she asked. "They're running a story about a gunfight aboard an oil tanker in the middle of the Panama Canal."

"No, I haven't," McGarvey said, surprised.

"A Venezuelan oil tanker. Someone aboard a cruise ship just in front of the tanker had a camcorder. There you were, right in the middle of it."

"It's all right, Katy," McGarvey told her. "I'm back now."

"You don't understand, Kirk."

"What don't I understand?"

"Every crazy bastard on the planet knows that you helped stop the attack, and now they know your face."

"It doesn't matter," McGarvey tried to assure her. "I was the DCI, and just about every time I testified to a committee on the Hill I made all the networks."

"Yes, but you were supposed to be retired," Kathleen insisted. "Everyone in the world now knows that isn't true." She pulled back and looked into his eyes, an intense set to her mouth. "You've done enough," she said. "Let this be the end of it. Someone else can finish the job."

He shook his head. "I'm sorry, Katy, I can't walk away from it. Not yet. Not like this."

"Until when?" she cried. "How much longer, Kirk? Goddammit, give me a date. I need something to believe in." Her fingers were digging into his arms. "I don't want to end up alone, just another widow in Florida. I can't do this, Kirk. I can't lose you. Don't you understand?"

"I don't want that to happen either, but I have to finish it this time."

"Finish what?" she sobbed. "They'll just keep coming out of the wood-work, pulling the triggers, blowing themselves up, and killing anyone nearby. We're not safe anywhere. Not in an airplane, or on a bus or train. Even sitting in a restaurant." She was searching his eyes for some hint that she was getting through to him. "You and Elizabeth were almost killed when the bomb in front of the restaurant in Georgetown went off. That was just a few years ago. Or have you forgotten already?"

"I haven't forgotten."

"What about me?" she demanded. "What about us? When is it our turn?"

"I'm going to kill him," McGarvey said softly. "It's the only way we can think of to put an end to the attacks."

"You don't know where he is," Katy pleaded. "Please don't do this, my darling. Please walk away from it. Let's drive down to Florida right now. You stopped them at the canal. It's enough!"

"I'm sorry—" McGarvey said, and Kathleen pulled away from him. She gave him a bleak look, then turned and stormed out of the kitchen. He heard her stomp up the stairs and then slam the bedroom door.

His cell phone rang. It was his daughter Elizabeth. "Hi, Daddy, are you at the safe house?" she asked.

"I just got here," McGarvey said. "And yes, your mother saw the canal story on TV, and no, she's not taking it very well."

"I have someone on the way, should be there within the next few min-utes," Elizabeth promised. "I assume you're not finished."

"Something like that, sweetheart. I want you and Todd to keep a close watch on her. I don't want the same thing happening as last year."

"Not a chance," Elizabeth said. Her mother had been kidnapped, held, and beaten badly before McGarvey could get to her. "Todd's mother is tak-ing care of Audrey until this business is finished."

McGarvey's heart warmed. "How is she?" Audrey had just turned seven months last week.

"Noisy," Elizabeth said. "And fat, and happy, and wonderful."

McGarvey closed his eyes for a moment. It was for Audrey and untold

millions of others just like her, the innocents of the world, that he was doing what had to be done.

"Daddy?" Elizabeth prompted.

"We'll get him this time," McGarvey said.

"Mom will be fine," Elizabeth said softly. "Promise."

"Okay."

"Will we see you before you leave again?" she asked.

"That depends on what we come up with over the next day or two,"
McGarvey said. "But I expect I'll be in town until then."

"Dinner tonight?"

McGarvey glanced up the stairs at the closed bedroom door. "Give it a
couple hours, then call your mother."

"Will do."

McGarvey knocked the drink back, then girded himself to go upstairs
and face Katy again. He had to change into a dark suit, and pick up Gloria.
He wanted to get to Arlington at least a half hour before the service to personally check security. But Katy had been right about one thing; just about
every bad guy on the planet knew that the former DCI had not stayed retired.

EN ROUTE TO BETHESDA

McGarvey took Highway 355, which in D.C. was Wisconsin Avenue, up to
Bethesda. It was a pretty afternoon and traffic was fairly light. He got on
his cell phone and called Rencke.

"NRO's about halfway through the fleet with no hits yet. At least nothing missing. Louise figures we should bag all but a half-dozen by tonight."

"What about those?" McGarvey asked.

"That's anybody's guess, Mac. But they'll be Graham's most likely targets. I've got some Jupiter satellite time reserved, and an Aurora is standing by at Andrews." The Aurora was the supersecret high-flying stealth spy
plane that replaced the U2 and the SR-71 Blackbird. "We'll have to take
them one at a time. But it would be my guess we'll need some on-ground
resources at some point."

"How about weapons?" McGarvey asked. At one time the countryside
out here between the city and the Beltway was mostly open rolling hills,

woods, fields, even a couple of farms. But now there were houses, businesses, and even strip malls. In Bethesda itself were a few high-rises and a
Hilton Hotel. Americans were devouring their green spaces.

"If you're talking nukes, it's gotta be Russia, or some of the breakaway
republics. Tajikistan comes to mind right off the top of my head. Hold on
a sec."

McGarvey could hear Otto's fingers on a computer keyboard. He came
back a few moments later.

"We might have something. Pavlosk Bay, east of Vladivostok. Used to be
headquarters for the Pacific Fleet's Twenty-sixth Submarine Division. But it
was disbanded six or seven years ago. Since then it's been a dumping
ground for decommissioned subs as well as the fleet's service ships, and
weapons stores. It's near the city of Dunay, right on the Sea of Japan. Unless we were looking, they could grab a sub and a weapon and break out
of there before we could do a thing about it."

"Are there any Kilo boats there?"

"Unknown, but I'll check it out."

"Good," McGarvey said. If anyone could crack a database to find something, it was Otto. "But we need the last leg of the triangle. The target."

"The big ditch?" Rencke offered. "They might not figure we'd expect
them back so soon. Anyway it would give us a better idea of their timetable."

"How do you see that?" McGarvey asked, puzzled.

"Graham is a sub driver, right? So why was he sent to hit the canal
with an oil tanker? It was partly because all Venezuelan oil ships are run on
a contract from Vensport to the transport firm GAC. Care to guess where
GAC's headquarters are located?"

"I don't know."

"Dubai. The United Arab Emirates."

"How about that," McGarvey said, not really all that surprised. It had
become a small world.

"But they sent a sub driver 'cause they were being pressured to hit us,
but they didn't have a sub."

"Yet," McGarvey finished the thought.

"Yet," Rencke said. "Are you coming in?"

Something was tickling the back of McGarvey's consciousness. Something that he was forgetting. Something important. "No. I'm going with
Gloria to Bob Talarico's funeral. It's at four."

"Oh, gosh," Rencke said, subdued. "I spaced it. Should I come over?"

"Did you know him?"

"Not very well," Rencke admitted.

"Stay there and find that sub for me," McGarvey said. "Quickly."

"Will do," Rencke said. "Oh, I almost forgot. Gloria's buddy down at Gitmo is almost certainly dirty, unless he's got a rich uncle we don't know about. He lives in a two-million-dollar house out in Kettering, he drives a new Jag, and his uniforms are all custom-tailored. Two years ago he started spending more money than he was earning. Last year alone, three-quarters of a mil."

"I thought so," McGarvey said. He decided that it was going to give him a great deal of pleasure to bust the man. "Run the money trail, and inform someone over at the ONI. I want this guy isolated, without making it obvious to him. He could be a source back to bin Laden. Or at least lead us in the right direction."

THIRTY-SIX

□

BALTIMORE

A few minutes after 2:00 P.M. an older model E300 black Mercedes sedan in decent condition turned off Eastern Boulevard in Baltimore's south side and headed into an industrial park area that had long since seen better days. Al-Turabi was behind the wheel, and he was impatient to get started, but he had forced himself to remain well within the speed limit, for fear of attracting any attention.

The Mercedes was one of three, which whoever survived of him and his seventeen men would use for their escape from Arlington once the massacre was completed and McGarvey was dead.

Most of his men would probably die. Insh'allah. Security at the funeral might not be tight, but by all accounts McGarvey was a man to be respected. He would almost certainly be armed and he would fight back.

They'd been given nearly unlimited resources for this operation, because it had the personal blessing of bin Laden himself. In addition to the nearly perfect identity documents all eighteen of them carried, they'd been equipped with the three cars and two dark blue vans that had been re-painted with the logos of the Prince William County Sheriff's Department. Drivers would wait with the three cars at the Farragut Drive exit, while al-Turabi and the other fourteen freedom fighters would take the vans to a spot above and behind the gravesite.

As soon as McGarvey showed up, they would take him out. And for that job they'd been supplied with a variety of weapons including four RPGs, and the new Heckler & Koch M8 carbine.

Against those odds and that firepower, and with the element of sur-prise, al-Turabi knew that there was no way they could fail. In a few hours McGarvey, and anyone standing next to him, would die.

Al-Turabi bumped across railroad tracks, then turned down a narrow lane between derelict warehouses in which a community of squatters had sprung up over the past few years. The police did not bother them this far south, because they were out of the public's eye, and seldom caused any trouble. One of the members of the Baltimore cell had suggested the mis-sion be staged from here, and he'd been spot on. It's as if they were invisible.

The service door on a building marked CAPITAL CLEANERS rumbled part-way open as al-Turabi approached and he drove up the ramp and inside.

One of his mujahideen was there, an M8 slung over his shoulder, and he closed the door, as al-Turabi stopped at the rear of the building where the other two cars and the two vans were parked.

Odeah came over when al-Turabi got out of the car, and they em-braced. The others who were sitting around on packing crates and chairs, making last-minute checks of their weapons and loads, which had been laid out on a tarp, looked up. They were expectant, but they had been in other battles before, from Afghanistan and Iraq to Madrid and London, so al-Turabi knew that he could count on them.

"Are you ready?" he asked.

"Yes," Odeah said. "Everything is finished here. How did it look?"

"I didn't see anything other than the normal security. A couple of cars at the Memorial Drive gate. A couple of Park Police on patrol in pickup trucks. The marine at Kennedy's grave. And, of course, the closed-circuit television cameras here and there throughout the cemetery grounds."

"Our sheriff's department vans shouldn't attract any attention," Odeah said. "How about visitors?

"About what we've been seeing for a weekday," al-Turabi said. "Nobody suspects a thing. After all, almost everyone there is already dead."

"There'll probably just be the family and maybe a couple of officials from the Agency with their bodyguards," Odeah said. "It's just a simple funeral for one of their spies."

Al-Turabi glanced at the array of weapons, and at his men. "And Kirk McGarvey," he said. "Let's not forget him."

Odeah lowered his voice. "I still say that we should find out where McGarvey and his wife are staying, and kill them there. It would be much less risky."

Al-Turabi's temper flared. "Are you afraid of martyrdom, Imad?" he asked sharply.

"Not at all," Odeah answered matter-of-factly. "But I do not want to give my life meaninglessly."

"Nothing for the *jihad* is meaningless," al-Turabi said, just as matter-of-factly. "If we all die killing McGarvey, it will be worth the sacrifice."

"One man," Odeah said in wonder.

"Yes, but a man very special to bin Laden."

THIRTY-SEVEN

□

BETHESDA

Gloria's apartment was on the second floor of a condominium-garden apartment complex off Old Georgetown Road on the outskirts. A half-dozen buildings skirted a nine-hole executive golf course, with a lot of walking paths, the fairways defined by dense woods.

McGarvey, dressed in a dark suit, white shirt, and subdued gray tie, his 9mm Walther PPK holstered at the small of his back, parked his Range Rover in front, walked upstairs to her door, and rang the bell.

He'd not been able to calm Katy down before he'd left, and her deepening fear and premonition that something horrible was about to happen weighed heavily on him. Leaving the safe house he'd felt as if he were walking away from her again, like he'd done in the old days; abandoning her, instead of remaining by her side until he could make her understand and accept that what he was doing was vital.

"It's open," Gloria called from inside.

McGarvey let himself in. A short corridor opened on the right to a small kitchen, to the left on a bedroom, and straight ahead to the well-furnished living room with sliding-glass doors that looked out on the condo complex pool and beyond to the golf course and woods. "What if I was one of the bad guys?"

Gloria laughed from the master bedroom off the living room. "I saw you drive up," she called. "How are we doing on time?"

"We're good," McGarvey told her.

"Make yourself comfortable, I'll just be a minute," she said. She came to the bedroom door. She was dressed only in a black lace bra and matching thong panties, her dark skin glowing. A small white dressing covered the gunshot wound in her left hip. She smiled. "There's beer and wine in the fridge. Pour me a white, would you?"

She was a beautiful woman, with a fantastic body. McGarvey grinned. "I will, if you promise to put on some clothes."

She put one hand up on the door frame and struck a provocative pose. "I thought you said that we were good on time."

"Not that much time," McGarvey said. He went into the kitchen. "Get dressed," he ordered over his shoulder.

Gloria laughed throatily. "Too bad," she said.

McGarvey was flattered, despite himself. In another time, another place, when he was young and single, he would have taken her up on her offer. Gladly. Such things were not unknown in the Company. In fact it was sometimes encouraged. A couple in the field seemed to pose less of a threat than the lone officer. It was a psychological thing. Though such pairings were one of the reasons that the divorce rate was so high among CIA officers.

There wasn't much else in the fridge except for a six-pack of Michelob Ultra and an open bottle of Pinot Grigio, but she and her partner had been out of the country for a long time. He found the glasses in the cabinet over the sink and poured her some wine, then went back into the living room.

"You can come get your drink if you're decent," he called to her.

She came out of the bedroom. She hadn't put on her shoes, but she was wearing a modest black dress that came down almost to her knees. It wasn't zipped up in the back yet. "Better?" she asked.

"Better for my heart," McGarvey said.

She laughed. "That's good to know," she said. She came over, took the wine from McGarvey, and took a sip. "Thanks," she said. She looked up into his eyes. "Aren't you having anything?"

"After the funeral maybe."

She put her glass down on the coffee table and turned around. "Zip me up, please."

He reached for the zipper, but she reached around for his right hand and placed it against her breast as she turned her lips to his and kissed him.

"Nice," she said huskily.

"Very," McGarvey told her, and he kissed her again, more deeply, holding her for several long moments, before parting.

Her eyes were wide, her lips parted. "We have time," she said.

McGarvey smiled gently. "All the time we want," he told her. "But it's not going to happen."

"Later?" she said hopefully.

"You're a beautiful woman, and I'm complimented that you want to go to bed with me."

Her face fell and she shrugged. "It was worth the try," she said. "No offense?"

"None taken. It's just that I'm a man who happens to be in love with his wife."

She nodded, but didn't lower her eyes though she was clearly disappointed. "Lucky her," she said. She turned around. "Just the zipper this time. Scout's honor."

EN ROUTE TO ARLINGTON NATIONAL CEMETERY

The shortest route to the cemetery would have been through downtown, but the quickest was around the city on the Capital Beltway, then the

George Washington Memorial Parkway along the river, the city off in the distance like an ancient Rome with its monuments in white marble.

"Thank you for coming with me today," Gloria said. She'd been quiet since they'd left her apartment, embarrassed by what she'd tried. And now as they got closer to Arlington the reality of what had happened in Cuba was finally starting to sink in.

McGarvey had read all of that from her body language and her reaction on the Parkway as they passed the mileage sign to the cemetery. "It wasn't your fault," he told her.

"If I had followed orders, Bob wouldn't have gotten killed," she said, staring out the window.

"You were set up. Weiss is probably on the payroll. No matter what you did or didn't do he wasn't going to let you take your investigation any further."

She turned and looked at McGarvey, her jaw tight. "I will be there when the man is brought down," she said. Her eyes glistened, and she shook her head. "But I don't know what I'm going to say to Toni and the kids."

McGarvey never knew what to say in these kinds of situations either. "The truth," he suggested. "She deserves at least that much."

"Yeah," Gloria said, and she turned away again to stare out the window.

McGarvey had taken a look at her personnel file. Ever since her husband had been captured and killed by Cuban intelligence she had thrown herself into her work. She was a damned fine field officer, even driven, but she had to be desperately lonely. According to Internal Affairs' latest annual background investigation, she did not date. The only man currently in her life was her father, and they only occasionally saw each other. Her mother was dead, what relatives there were in Cuba who hadn't been rounded up and shot after her father had defected were out of reach, and there never had been children.

Ten minutes from the cemetery, McGarvey telephoned Rencke, who answered on the first ring.

"Pavlosk is a wash," Rencke said sharply. He sounded angry with himself. "Weapons up the ying yang, waiting for anyone to pick them up, but no Kilo boats. Just derelict nukes."

"Any possibility one of them could be activated?"

"Most of the reactors have been cut out. The others leak like hell. They'd be death traps. The crew would never make it to Panama."

"What's next?" McGarvey asked.

"Let Louise do her job with the NRO's assets, and in the meantime I'll keep looking," Rencke said. "We've at least eliminated one possibility."

"Keep on it, Otto. We have to know where he's coming up with a boat."

"He might already have one, ya know," Rencke said. "Could be he's already on his way."

"That's what worries me most," McGarvey agreed. "The boat we can't find."

THIRTY-EIGHT

□

ARLINGTON NATIONAL CEMETERY

Al-Turabi lowered his binoculars and glanced at his watch. It was precisely four o'clock as a black Cadillac limousine with government plates pulled up and parked at the head of a line of nine cars and the long hearse. He was crouched in the back of one of the PWCS vans parked one hundred meters up the gently sloping hill from the gravesite. He'd not spotted McGarvey yet and he was beginning to get worried.

The six men crowded into the van with him were all dressed in deputy uniforms, with the correct badges and identifications, so they'd not been questioned by Park Police when they'd entered at Columbia Pike. But all the planning would be for nothing if McGarvey never showed.

His men were looking at him as he turned back to the silvered window and raised his binoculars to see who got out of the limo.

Two bulky men, in dark business suits, obviously bodyguards, jumped out of the front seat, their heads on swivels as they swept the area immediately adjacent to the gravesite. One of them spotted the sheriff's van and looked directly at the silvered window behind which al-Turabi was watching him, but then, apparently satisfied there was no threat, turned away.

The second van with Odeah in charge was parked fifty meters farther away from the south gate where the three cars were waiting. Between them they would catch the mourners in a cross fire from which nobody could possibly survive.

One of the bodyguards turned his head and his lips moved. Al-Turabi realized that he was speaking into a lapel mike. The bodyguard looked up and nodded at his partner, who opened the rear door on the passenger side.

A slightly built man with sandy hair got out first, and al-Turabi instantly recognized him as Richard Adkins, the director of the CIA. He turned and helped a tiny woman, dressed in black, a veil covering her face, out of the limo. She was followed by a boy, dressed in a dark suit, and a little girl, dressed like her mother in black, but without the veil.

They would be the spy's widow and family, al-Turabi figured. Well, they couldn't begin to guess that they would soon join the man they'd come to mourn this afternoon. One happy little American family together again. It would be interesting to be at the gates of Paradise to see how Allah received them. They would get no martyr's welcome.

Adkins said something to his bodyguard, and then he took the widow's arm and they headed the few meters down the slope across the grass to where a knot of about fifteen or twenty people had gathered on folding chairs around the open grave and the flag-draped coffin. The bulk of the Pentagon loomed large in the background, and the sound of traffic on Washington Boulevard and Jefferson Davis Highway was constant.

But McGarvey was not among them, and al-Turabi was beside himself with fury. The funeral service was about to begin and their target had not shown up. How in Allah's name could he have been so wrong? What was he going to tell bin Laden? And what would Odeah, who'd been perfectly correct to suggest killing McGarvey at home, report to bin Laden?

"Where is he?" Odeah radioed from the second van. "Do you see him from your position?"

Al-Turabi wanted to scream at the bastard for breaking radio silence. It was only supposed to be for an emergency.

One of the bodyguards, who'd followed Adkins and the family down to the grave, suddenly stopped and brought his right hand up to his ear. Someone was speaking to him.

He turned and looked up the road, his eyes passing the sheriff's van. He was searching for something or someone. And it suddenly came to al-Turabi that Odeah's transmission had been monitored. The infidel bastards knew that something was about to happen.

Adkins and the family had reached the gravesite, and the mourners had all got to their feet. At that precise moment, a man in a dark suit stepped out from behind a tree thick with foliage.

Al-Turabi was struck dumb. The man was saying something to the bodyguard up the hill. Al-Turabi focused on his face. It was McGarvey. He must have gotten to the cemetery first, and had been hiding like a coward all this time.

A good-looking, dark woman had gotten to her feet with the others, and she stepped to the side. There was something about her that seemed familiar to al-Turabi. She seemed to hold herself like a cop; probably an intelligence officer.

"It's him," al-Turabi told his men. "Radio Imad, we go now!"

The hair on the back of McGarvey's neck was standing on end. Neal Julien, who had been his bodyguard when he was DCI, was trying to get Adkins's attention. It was something about an intercepted transmission.

"Here in the cemetery?" McGarvey called up to him.

"Yes, sir!" Julien shouted back.

Adkins, finally realizing that something was going on, started to turn toward his bodyguard, when the Anglican minister in his dark coat and white collar suddenly exploded in a bright flash of blood, chips of bone, and big pieces of flesh and muscle.

A split instant later a tremendous bang rolled across the gravestones and trees.

The mourners, covered in blood and carnage, with more body parts dripping from the tree branches, were slow to react, having no comprehension of what was happening.

But McGarvey knew exactly what was going on. The minister had been in a direct line from a firing position up the hill. Whoever had fired what was probably an RPG had missed their intended target, but they wouldn't stop for long to reacquire.

"Get down!" he shouted. He was at Toni Talarico's side in two steps. He scooped her and the children in his arms and bodily hurled them to the ground as a second RPG slammed into the tree he'd just stepped away from with a loud flash-bang.

Almost immediately automatic weapons fire from two positions up the slope from the gravesite tore into the mourners who had been too slow to move, tearing into their bodies.

Julien had shoved Adkins to the ground behind the coffin, shielding the DCI with his own body as bullets slammed the earth all around them.

McGarvey pulled out his pistol as he rolled over, in time to spot the shooters who were crouched behind one of the sheriff's vans that had showed up just a few minutes ago. He'd seen them pull up and figured they were part of the security arrangements. He held his fire because they were way out of effective range for pistols.

But Gloria was down on one knee, firing at the nearest van, as was Adkins's other bodyguard, who suddenly cried out and was flung backwards.

More automatic weapons fire raked the gravesite from the second van fifty meters farther down the hill, and it was clear that their principal target was McGarvey.

"Stay down," he told Toni and the children, and he jumped up and headed at an oblique angle toward the second van.

Immediately, the terrorists concentrated their fire on him, leaving what remained of the funeral party in relative safety for the moment.

McGarvey raised his pistol as he zigzagged through the trees and opened fire on the second van, emptying his magazine as quickly as he could pull the trigger.

An RPG round passed his left side with an audible whoosh and a split instant later a grave marker a few feet in front of him disintegrated with a loud bang, flying chips of marble cutting his face.

He veered left toward several large trees about twenty feet closer to the second van, ejecting the spent magazine from his pistol, pulling the spare out of his pocket, and ramming it home.

All the fire from both vans was concentrated on him now, but he could hear pistol shots from the gravesite, which meant that Gloria and Julien were still on their feet.

Something hot stitched his left shoulder, causing him to stumble and drop to one knee. One of the shooters had come out from behind the second van, and unlike the others, who had simply been shooting indiscriminately, had steadied himself against the hood, taking care with his aim.

McGarvey pulled off four snapshots, the third and fourth hitting the terrorist, and spinning him away from the van, where he collapsed in a heap.

For just a second or two all but the pistol firing stopped.

McGarvey struggled to his feet and raced the last few yards to the trees before the stunned terrorists could react.

"He's getting away," al-Turabi shouted insanely. He and his men had concentrated on McGarvey's retreating figure, which had given the DCI's bodyguard and the black woman time to advance up the hill, closer to the van, where they'd taken cover. Now they were shooting methodically, pinning him and his people behind the van.

The walkie-talkie lying on the seat in the van hissed to life. "Rashid is down," Odeah radioed excitedly.

Al-Turbai reached through the open door and grabbed the radio, no longer caring if their broadcasts were being monitored. "Where's McGarvey?" he screamed.

"Imad hit him and he went down. But then he disappeared into the woods like a ghost. We must leave now while we can!"

"Not until McGarvey is dead," al-Turabi ordered.

One of his people, who had peeked around the end of the van, suddenly fell backwards, a hole in the center of his forehead just above the bridge of his nose.

"Kill them!" al-Turabi bellowed, spittle flying everywhere. He keyed the walkie-talkie. "Blanket the woods with RPGs!" he shouted.

His people had begun to lay down heavy fire in the direction of the bodyguard and the black woman, who were well hidden behind large grave markers. But even over the heavy fire he could hear several sirens in the distance.

There was no time left, and he suddenly realized that he did not want to die here.

He keyed the walkie-talkie. "We'll come to you as quickly as we can."

Two of his people went down under the accurate fire from below the road, leaving only him and twelve others; the mujahideen in the second van, plus the three drivers waiting at the south gate.

He keyed the walkie-talkie again. "Why aren't you shooting?" he demanded.

At that moment two RPG rounds exploded in the woods down from the gravesite, and he tossed the walkie-talkie back in the van, and climbed in the back. It was time to get away from this accursed place without being killed or captured.

"Let's go!" he shouted to his people. "Now!"

THIRTY-NINE

□

ARLINGTON NATIONAL CEMETERY

Two RPG rounds, one right after the other, exploded within a few yards of where McGarvey was crouched. He'd seen the two terrorists step out from behind the sheriff's van, but before he could shoot, they'd fired the rockets.

Spears of wood and shrapnel flew everywhere, several hitting McGarvey's left side, cutting his leg and torso, and opening a fairly substantial gash in his neck. The two concussions also knocked out his hearing, leaving behind a whooshing sound as if he were inside a jet engine.

Picking himself up, he staggered across to the bole of a larger tree, from where he had a good line of sight up to the second van. He counted at least four men plus the one on the ground.

The same two who had fired the RPGs had reloaded and emerged from behind the van again.

McGarvey's vision was hazy, but he steadied his gun hand against the tree and squeezed off a shot that slammed into the hood of the van. The terrorist stepped aside, and then started to bring the RPG around.

Before he could fire, McGarvey pulled off two snapshots at the other terrorist holding an RPG, knocking him down, and then scrambled as fast as he could across an open swatch of grass to another clump of trees.

An RPG round struck a few feet behind him, spraying his back with what felt like thousands of needles or buckshot.

Aiming over his shoulder he fired two shots at the terrorist who'd launched the RPG, and the slide locked in the open position, the pistol dry.

He pulled up behind one of the trees, and laid his head against the trunk. His hearing was still bad, but he thought there were sirens somewhere in the distance.

Easing around from behind the tree, he took a quick look up the hill, then ducked back. He counted three bodies on the road, and perhaps two other terrorists crouched behind the van.

He released the slide. The Company's chief armorer had been after him for years to carry a SIG Sauer or Glock, something with more stopping power than the Walther, and one that held at least fifteen rounds. But the PPK was an old friend that had saved his life on more than one occasion.

He was light-headed from his wounds and the loss of blood, and he had done all that he could. The police would be here soon, and they could finish the job.

From here he couldn't see up to the gravesite, nor could he hear any shooting.

He looked out from behind the tree as two of the terrorists were dragging the bodies off the road. A third had gotten behind the wheel of the van and was gesturing at the others to hurry.

Dropping low, and keeping behind the trees as much as possible, McGarvey headed up the hill toward the van as fast as his legs would carry him.

Fifteen feet out, one of the terrorists looked up and spotted McGarvey charging up the hill, pistol in hand, blood streaming from a dozen wounds, and he fell back against the van, a look of abject terror on his long, narrow face.

"*Kifaya baa!*" McGarvey shouted. *That's enough!*

The second terrorist had already climbed inside the van with the driver, and he was trying to bring his M8 carbine to bear.

McGarvey reached the man by the hood, grabbed a handful of his shirt, and pulled him around to cover the open door, when the terrorist inside fired the M8, three rounds slamming into the back of his fellow mujahideen's head.

The driver slammed the van into gear and stomped on the gas pedal.

McGarvey shoved the dead terrorist aside and as the van started to pull away, its tires squealing, he reached inside, grabbed the man's arm, and pulled him out, both of them tumbling backwards off the road.

The terrorist had lost his rifle, but he pulled out a Beretta auto-loader from his belt. McGarvey snatched it out of his hand and smashed the butt of the pistol into the bridge of the man's nose, knocking him senseless.

Scrambling to his feet, McGarvey hobbled back up to the road and fired three shots at the retreating van until it finally got well out of range.

Someone was shouting his name as if from a very great distance. It sounded like a woman's voice to McGarvey.

He turned in time to see the second sheriff's van barreling up the road, practically on top of him.

McGarvey caught a glimpse of Gloria, racing on foot down the hill from the gravesite shouting his name, as he leaped backwards. The van swerved to hit him, but its front wheel dropped off the side of the road, and the driver frantically brought the van back onto the pavement.

Gloria started to fire at the retreating van, but she ran out of ammunition by the time she reached McGarvey, who had landed in a bloody heap next to the still unconscious terrorist he'd pulled from the first van.

Gloria bent over at the waist, clutching her sides as she tried to catch her breath. She had taken some shrapnel or marble chips in her head, and the wounds were oozing blood.

"You don't look so hot," McGarvey said, sitting up. "You okay?"

She nodded. "Ambulances are on the way," she said, her voice far away. "You have any serious wounds?"

"I don't think so. How about Toni and the kids?"

"They're okay, thanks to you. But we lost six people, plus Max Schneider, one of Adkins's people." She glanced over at the terrorist. "How about him?"

"He'll live," McGarvey said.

"Well, he's the only one we have, unless the Bureau or someone catches up with the others," she said, looking down the road in the direction the two vans had disappeared. She turned back to McGarvey. "They were after you."

"Yeah, I know."

She managed a slight smile. "You're not a very popular guy."

He smiled back. "Do you suppose it's my personality?"

PART
THREE

FORTY

□

PORT OF LA GOULETTE, TUNISIA

There was virtually no traffic at four in the morning, though the nine ships in port were ablaze in lights, from aboard as well as from along the north quay where most of the cargo vessels were unloaded. The night shift had left one hour ago, and the port would not be open for business again until seven. A man dressed in dark slacks and a pullover, carrying an ordinary seaman's duffel bag, walked along the quay, stopping at the gangway of a tramp steamer.

Rupert Graham looked up at the bridge windows, but only a dim red light was showing, and there didn't seem to been anyone aboard, though he could hear the distant sound of machinery running inside the hull. He knew this ship and her master almost as well as the men and pirate ships he'd commanded. Neither were much to look at, but both man and vessel were trustworthy.

She was the MV *Distal Volente*, owned by a small Greek shipping company, and registered in Liberia. Built in 1959 in the United Kingdom by Sunderland Shipbuilders, she had seen better days. Now she was considered a scrapper, which was a boat so battered, so eaten with rust that she was fit for little else other than a breaking yard where she would be cut up and sold for scrap.

At 150 meters on deck, her superstructure was amidships, leaving cargo spaces in her holds as well as on deck forward and aft. Four cargo containers were lashed to the afterdeck, and two others were secured forward. She rode low in the water, ready to leave as soon as the Tunisian pilot arrived sometime this morning.

A short, slightly built man, wearing an open-collar white shirt, stepped out of the shadows and came to the rail. "It is good to see you again, my old friend," he called down softly, his singsong Indonesian accent distinctive.

"I thought that you would be dead or in jail by now," Graham said.

"Dead someday, jail never," Captain Halim Subandrio said, chuckling. "Did anybody spot you coming here?"

"I don't think so," Graham said. He'd taken a great deal of care with his movements. Finally he was going to hit the bastards hard, and he didn't want to screw up his chances.

"Come aboard then, we need to talk before we put you in hiding."

Graham started up the gangway, aware that Subandrio was looking down the quay back toward the road. He was a tough old bastard who'd been working the South China Sea pirate trade for years before Graham had shown up. He'd survived that long because he was a cautious man.

"Never forget to always look over your shoulder, my friend," he'd told Graham early on. "In that way you will minimize nasty surprises, and live another day to share the bed of a good woman."

Graham had almost killed the man on the spot; his grief over Jillian's death was still fresh in his mind, and his hate was a bright pool of molten metal in his gut.

Subandrio had picked up a little of that from Graham's eyes. He smiled gently and laid a hand on Graham's shoulder as a father might with a son. "Also remember that the past can never be lived again. No matter how terrible or joyous, we must go on."

Graham and his crew had learned to time their hijackings to coincide with the *Distal Volente*'s sailing schedules. Within hours of boarding a hapless vessel, killing its crew and stealing its cargo, they would meet Subandrio and transfer the stolen goods. Graham's ships had been boarded three times, but always after they'd gotten rid of their cargo, so no charges had ever been brought against him.

At the top, Graham shook hands with the man. "Is my crew here?"

Subandrio nodded toward the containers lashed to the afterdeck. It was clear he wasn't happy. "They came aboard in one of those yesterday afternoon. As soon as it got dark they let themselves out and came belowdecks." He shook his head. "It's bad business, Rupert, between them and my crew. You will have to do something before the situation gets completely out of hand."

Bin Laden had arranged for eighteen crewmen, most of them Iranians, for the tough mission. But although they had a great religious zeal for the *jihad*, they were misfits who would have been better as suicide bombers in Baghdad, or mujahideen doing battle with the Americans in Afghanistan, than as a crew aboard a submarine. Graham had never met any of them, he'd only seen their dossiers, but he was convinced that by the time they got across the Atlantic they would be molded into an acceptable crew. He would kill any man who didn't cooperate, and the sooner he got that message across the sooner their training could begin.

They would have only one shot at what he planned to do, and those plans did not include committing suicide for the cause. He would let his crew have that honor.

"What exactly is the trouble?" Graham asked.

"Let's get off the deck first," Subandrio said, and led Graham across to a hatch into the superstructure.

The passageway was dimly lit in red. Now Graham could more clearly hear the sound of machinery running somewhere below. And he could hear the murmur of several voices. Whoever was talking sounded angry.

"I want them to return to the container, but they refuse my orders," Subandrio said. "You can hear them. They've been at it all night; arguing, fighting; making a very big mess of my galley and stores. My crew refuses to have anything to do with them."

"I'll take care of it," Graham promised. It was better that he established a clear understanding between them right from the start.

"The pilot is scheduled to be here in less than three hours," Subandrio said. "He sometimes comes early. If you or your crew are spotted the game will be up."

"Is there food and water in the container?"

"Yes, and light. It will only be until we clear the breakwaters and the pilot leaves," Subandrio said. "Maybe one hour longer, depending on traffic, and you may leave your little box."

Graham put down his duffel bag. He took his pistol, a 9mm Steyr GB, out of his pocket, and screwed a Vaime silencer on the end of the barrel. "Wait here, Halim, I'll go fetch them."

Subandrio nodded. "How long will you be needing my ship?"

"We'll be gone by midnight tomorrow."

"Who are these guys? What's the mission?"

"You don't want to know," Graham said. "Do you have any rolls of plastic?"

"Should be some in the dry-stores locker," Subandrio said, puzzled.

"I'll be back in a couple of minutes," Graham said, and he headed aft to the galley and crew's mess.

Subandrio ran his ship with a crew of only nine, including a cook, but all of them were out of sight this morning, keeping out of the way of the Iranians, who were holed up in the mess waiting for their own captain to arrive.

As Graham came around a corner, he heard someone say something in Arabic from an open door at the end of the narrow corridor, and several men laughed harshly. He stuffed the pistol in his belt at the small of his back, and walked to the end of the corridor, where he held up at the open door.

The strong smell of marijuana and something else pungent wafted out of the small dining area. His eighteen crewmen, all of them dressed in blue jeans or khakis and T-shirts, several days' stubble on their faces, were crowded around two long, narrow tables littered with the remains of canned fish and beef, crackers, Coca-Cola, and other items they'd raided from the ship's stores. A serving counter and service door at the back of the room opened to the galley that looked to be in a mess.

A couple of them spotted Graham in the doorway, but they just looked at him dumbly.

"Good morning," Graham said in English.

All of them turned and looked at him with some curiosity, but very little else. One of them said something in Arabic and a few of the men chuckled.

"We'll speak English from now on, if you please," Graham said. "Who is Muhamed al-Hari?"

"I am," a tall, slender man, drinking from a handleless mug, said. According to the dossier bin Laden had supplied, al-Hari had been a navigation officer aboard one of Iran's Kilo submarines, and had even attended the Prospective Officers Special Course, at Frunze Military Academy in Leningrad.

"You will be my executive officer," Graham said.

Al-Hari's eyes lit up. "Then it's true, we have a submarine?"

"We will if we can get out of Tunisia without being arrested, which will surely happen if the authorities discover your presence aboard this ship."

"I'm not going back inside that stinking box," one of them grumbled. "We'll hide in the crew's quarters. No pilot will bother looking there."

"Very well," Graham replied pleasantly. "Mr. al-Hari, there is a roll of plastic sheeting in the dry-stores locker. Bring me a piece of it, if you would, about two meters on a side, I should think. And see if you can find some tape."

Al-Hari nodded uncertainly, but he got up and went into the galley.

"What is your name and rank, please?" Graham asked the crewman who'd complained.

"I am Syed Asif," the crewman answered as if his name meant something. "I was an ordinary seaman. But I'm not going back in that box."

"You are from Pakistan?" Graham asked.

The others were paying rapt attention to the exchange. One of them said something in Arabic, and a few of them laughed again.

Al-Hari came back with the sheet of plastic, and a roll of duct tape.

"Lay it out on the deck behind Seaman Asif, please," Graham instructed.

The Pakistani was clearly nervous now, not quite comprehending what was about to happen, but beginning to realize that whatever it was might not be so good.

Al-Hari spread the plastic out behind the seaman, then stepped aside.

Graham pulled out his pistol, and, before anyone could move, fired one shot in the middle of Asif's forehead, killing him instantly, his body falling backwards off his stool and landing on the plastic sheet.

"Wrap Seaman Asif's body in the plastic and secure it with the tape," Graham told the stunned crewmen. "When you are finished with that, you will clean the mess you have made here, and meet me topside—with the body—in ten minutes. I will be joining you in our luxurious on-deck stateroom. There is much I have to tell you."

No one uttered a sound, but their eyes were locked on his. He'd gotten their attention.

"Is that clear?"

"Aye, aye, Captain," al-Hari responded crisply.

"Very well, you may carry on," Graham said, and he turned and left.

ᖴᗝᖇ丅Ꮍ−ᗝᑎᕮ

CASEY KEY, FLORIDA

McGarvey, dressed only in swimming trunks, a towel around his neck, slowed to a walk, and looked out across the Gulf of Mexico as a V formation of brown pelicans skimmed just above the water, seemingly without effort. His left shoulder, where he'd taken a bullet two weeks ago, was still sore and stiff, but each day of strenuous exercise was bringing him back to the peak of physical fitness.

He'd only spent the one night at the hospital in Bethesda, before he checked himself out and Liz had driven him and Kathleen to their new house on one of the barrier islands just south of Sarasota. The day after they'd arrived, he'd started his exercise regime, pushing his body to its limits. He was now swimming in the Gulf for a solid hour every morning at dawn, and then running five miles barefoot on the beach.

Last week he'd started shooting again at an indoor pistol range off University Parkway up in Sarasota. One of the instructors had tried to convince him to take shooting lessons and to retire the Walther in favor of something with greater stopping power, but after watching McGarvey empty one clip at rapid fire, all the shots hitting within a one-inch circle, he'd walked away, shaking his head.

His physical wounds were healing, but to this point he'd been unable to get the vision of Toni Talarico's face out of his head, when she and her children came face-to-face with the terrorist McGarvey had pulled out of the van.

He had regained consciousness and was sitting in the backseat of a police cruiser, his hands cuffed behind him.

McGarvey was being given first aid by an EMT ten feet away, when Toni and the kids had been escorted up the hill by Adkins. She'd broken away and walked over to the police cruiser to get a closer look at the man. The expression on her tiny face was of pure hatred: raw, intense, and very personal. There was no doubt in McGarvey's mind that if someone had handed her a gun at that moment she would have emptied it into the man's head.

Her children were watching her, and when she turned back to them, they both stepped away and burst into tears. They'd been frightened not by the terrorist, but by the look in their mother's eyes.

The island was very narrow here, the single road less than one hundred feet from the beach. Across the road, houses were nestled in lush tropical growth: palms, bougainvillea, sea grapes, and dozens of different flowering trees and bushes. The McGarveys' was a two-story Florida-style, with tall ceilings, large overhangs, and a veranda that wrapped completely around the second floor. When the weather was right the house could be completely opened to catch the slightest breeze off the gulf or off the Intracoastal Waterway.

Kathleen loved the place, and that was enough for him, though they had paid what he considered an obscene price.

Reaching the path up to the road, McGarvey headed to his house, his thoughts still on the attack at Arlington. There was no doubt that he had been the target, but the only reason he could come up with was that bin Laden was afraid that McGarvey might interfere with the submarine mission.

Six of the terrorists had managed to escape clean; the one driving the van McGarvey had attacked, two in the second van, and apparently the drivers of three cars they'd managed to use as escape vehicles out the south gate. The FBI forensics people had come up with plenty of physical evidence from the abandoned vans, as well as from the bodies of the seven dead terrorists and the only survivor.

So far they'd identified nine of the attackers, all of whom were on Homeland Security watch lists. No one had any idea how they'd gotten into the United States, but according to the media, which had given the attack a lot of play, the lapse was just another example of how poor a job Washington was doing to protect the country.

McGarvey had taken only one call from Adkins last week with that information, but he had stayed out of it, for Kathleen's sake, certain that if and when something important came up, Otto would let him know.

The house was set twenty yards from the entrance, and in the back, a lawn sloped gently down to a boat dock and screened gazebo that overlooked the waterway. In the evenings they sometimes sat in the gazebo, listening to the quiet.

Inside, McGarvey passed through the large, airy entrance hall and went directly back to the huge open kitchen that looked directly out on the swimming pool and beyond to the Intracoastal Waterway.

Kathleen, barefoot in a colorful sarong and white bikini top, was at the counter slicing fruit for their breakfast. She looked up, a radiant smile on her face. "How'd it go this morning?"

"Every day it's better," he said, flexing his shoulder. He came over and kissed her lightly on the cheek. "What's on the schedule for today?"

"How would you feel about driving up to Largo this morning?" Katy asked, pouring him a cup of coffee.

The business wasn't over with, not until they found Graham and the submarine, and until bin Laden was dead. But for now there was nothing for him to do. For now it was in Otto's hands. "Sure. What've you got in mind?"

"The Island Packet boatyard is up there. I was thinking we might buy a sailboat. Or at least talk to somebody about it."

McGarvey had to smile. "You've got our retirement all planned, have you?"

Kathleen shrugged. "This fall you're going back to teaching, and probably working on your Voltaire book, and I've been talking to some of the charities about going on their boards. We're going to be busy, and we'll be needing some sort of a diversion. What's wrong with sailing? We both like it. The weather here is great."

"Do I have time to take a shower and have some breakfast?"

"We have all the time in the world," she replied brightly.

McGarvey's mood instantly darkened. "For now," he said, and her face fell, but for just a moment.

"Then we'll make the best of it while we can," she told him.

"It won't last forever, Katy," he said.

She managed a weak smile. "That's what you said last time."

"It has to be done."

"I know," she said.

McGarvey went upstairs and took a shower, the water drumming against the back of his neck soothing. Since Arlington he'd concentrated on healing his body as quickly as he could because he knew that his call to action could come at any moment, and when it did he wanted to be ready. He desperately wanted the semiretirement that Katy had planned for them, but he just as desperately wanted to see an end to bin Laden's reign of terror. The United States certainly couldn't depend on the Pakistanis to do the job; they were beset with so many internal problems that President Musharraf's hands were tied. Much of his military and a significant portion of his intelligence service personnel were sympathetic to al-Quaida's cause. There'd even been attempts on his life by bin Laden's supporters.

Taking the man out had always been a one-on-one mission.

When he was drying off, the telephone in the bedroom rang. Kathleen answered it in the kitchen on the first ring. He was dressing when she came to the door.

"It's Otto," she said, and she looked resigned.

McGarvey wanted to tell her that everything would be okay, but she'd always been able to see through that particular lie of his. He picked up the phone. "Good morning. Have you found the Kilo?"

"Oh wow, not yet, Mac," Rencke gushed. "How are ya feeling? Okay? Louise wants to know."

"I'll live," McGarvey said. He glanced up, but Kathleen was gone. "What about the sub?"

"There's none missing. Honest injun, if he had grabbed a boat we'd know about it by now."

"Then he's got help from somebody," McGarvey said crossly. "Goddammit, Otto, bin Laden didn't hire a submarine captain for no reason."

"I know, and we haven't stopped looking."

McGarvey closed his eyes for a moment. He had some serious visions about nuclear weapons being lobbed at the United States from a few miles offshore, giving absolutely no response time. "Sorry," he said.

"No sweat, Mac. If he gets his hands on a Kilo boat—from no matter where—we'll bag him."

"That's not why you called."

"No. We got lucky with the guy you pulled out of the van at Arlington. The Bureau finally figured out who he is. Kamal al-Turabi, one of bin Laden's top enforcers. They lost track of him last year, but it looks as if he was right here under their noses for at least eleven months. He was posing as a dentist up in Laurel. Neighbors said he was a great guy, about as American as they come."

"Where is he right now?"

"They've got him tucked away over at Andrews."

"Has he talked to anyone, maybe an attorney?" McGarvey asked. "Are there any leaks to the media that we've got him and why?"

"I don't think so," Rencke said.

"I'm flying up there today, but in the meantime I want you to do a couple of things for me," McGarvey said. "Tell Adkins I'm on my way. I'm going to need some help, but I'll explain when I get there. Then I want al-Turabi transferred to Gitmo tonight, but with no ID. I want him classified as John Doe, an American combatant working for al-Quaida."

"Adkins will have to pull some serious strings," Rencke said.

"Tell him to make it happen, with as few people in the loop as possible, except for Commander Weiss."

Rencke was silent for just a second, but then he chuckled. "Weiss isn't going to be a happy camper, especially if you show up down there again with Gloria."

"If we get lucky I think I know how to find bin Laden," McGarvey said. "But I also need you to ask Jared Kraus for an assist." Kraus was chief of the Company's Technical Services Division. They were the people who came up with the gadgets that field officers used.

"What do you need?" Rencke asked.

McGarvey explained what he wanted from Kraus and how he was going to use it, but there would have to be limitations.

"No sweat, kimo sabe," Rencke said. "I've already seen the technical specs, so we'll be up and running by the time you get up here."

"Oh, and send someone down here to keep an eye on Katy, would you?" McGarvey said.

"Will do."

FORTY-TWO

☐

CIA HEADQUARTERS

Cabbing it out to Langley from Dulles, McGarvey felt detached. Already he was beginning to leave his home and his family, putting his love for his wife and daughter and granddaughter in a special compartment in his mind; one in which he could forget about them while he was in the field. The bane of any assassin were attachments to places, to things, and especially, to people.

Lawrence Danielle, a mentor during his early days in the CIA, had cautioned that the field officers who lasted the longest were the ones who either carried no baggage, or those who knew when to forget home and hearth. "Completely forget, Kirk, as if there was no one in your life."

It had been one of the hardest lessons for him to learn; and one that had cost him his marriage when Katy had faced him point-blank with the choice of her or the CIA.

He had been an arrogant bastard in those days, with his own set of demons, and he had just returned from a particularly nasty assignment in Santiago, Chile, in which he had assassinated an army general and the man's wife. His emotions were all over the place, so he'd turned around and walked out the door.

He'd run to Switzerland then, to hide, and it had been a very long time before he and Kathleen got back together; lost years not only for him and his wife, but for their daughter Elizabeth.

But that was then and here he was now, ready to go back into the field.

Kathleen had stoically packed for him, saying nothing as she watched him gather his weapon, a couple of spare magazines of ammunition, and his escape kit of several passports, matching, untraceable credit cards, and ten thousand dollars in various currencies to be sent ahead as a bonded Homeland Security package.

When he was done, she handed him his tan sport coat. "Any odd idea how long you'll be gone, in case I want to make dinner reservations or something for us?" she'd asked.

"Maybe ten days, not long this time."

She wanted to say something that would make him change his mind; he could see it in her eyes. "Should I circle the wagons or something?"

"Someone's coming down to ride shotgun for you. Otto will let you know."

She'd come into his arms and shivered as he held her tight. "Take care of yourself, Kirk," she said in his ear. "Come back to me."

"Count on it."

Receiving a visitor's pass at the gate, McGarvey could remember Katy's body in his arms as they kissed goodbye at the airport, but when he signed in he'd already forgotten her scent and how badly he'd missed her even before he left.

Adkins had been advised of McGarvey's arrival and was waiting at the door to his office. "Hold my calls," he told his secretary.

"Yes, sir," Dahlia Swanson said. She'd been McGarvey's private secretary when he'd been the DCI. "How are you feeling, Mr. McGarvey?" she asked.

"Much better, thank you."

She was an older woman with white hair and old-school reserved manners, but she gave him a warm smile. "I am glad."

He winked at her, then followed Adkins into the seventh-floor office.

"I managed to push through al-Turabi's transfer to Guantanamo Bay, in fact he's probably already on his way," Adkins said, going behind his desk. He motioned for McGarvey to take a seat. "But Otto didn't give me any of the details. Would you like to fill me in?"

"Al-Turabi is one of bin Laden's top executioners. Important to the cause."

"All right, I understand the reason for sending him down as a John Doe. But then what?"

"That navy commander Gloria Ibenez roughed up could be on the take. Otto is working the money trail back to the source now, but it's possible that Weiss is on al-Quaida's payroll."

Understanding began to glimmer in Adkins's eyes, and he shook his head. "Please don't tell me that you're going back down there."

"Yes, I am," McGarvey said. "And I'm taking Gloria with me, so you'll have to pull a few more strings."

Adkins sat back in his chair. "I didn't want your job, you know. So if you're doing this to get back at me, you can stop it."

"The minute al-Turabi shows up at Camp Delta someone is going to recognize him, and Weiss will get the word."

"Continue."

"Gloria and I are going to lean on him, hard, and my guess is that Weiss will arrange for him to escape."

"I don't buy it, Mac," Adkins said. "Even if Weiss is connected with al-Quaida, which would make him a traitor, why would he risk his neck with you and Gloria right there?"

"We're only going to stay for a couple hours, just long enough to put some heat on him."

"And?"

"When al-Turabi gets out of there, I'm going to follow him."

Adkins said nothing for several long moments, obviously trying to put what he was being told into some kind of perspective. "You think he'll lead you to bin Laden?"

"I think it's a possibility, Dick," McGarvey said.

"Why do you want Ms. Ibenez to go with you?"

"I want her to keep Weiss busy."

"And pissed off," Adkins said. "Because pissed-off people make mistakes."

"Yes, and this one will cost him more than a couple of bruises," McGarvey said. "But we don't want to blow the whistle until I find bin Laden."

"And finish the job," Adkins said delicately.

"Yes," McGarvey replied just as delicately. He'd come face-to-face with bin Laden in a cave in the mountains of Afghanistan. It was before 9/11, and he'd not been able to get the man's image out of his head since then. *There are no innocents in this struggle,* bin Laden had said. He had proved his point in New York.

"He knows you're coming. That's why they tried to hit you at Arlington."

"God bless the media," McGarvey quipped. The attack had hit the front page of just about every newspaper in the world.

"He won't stop, you know," Adkins said.

"I hope he doesn't," McGarvey said. "Arlington was a mistake. Who knows, maybe he'll make another."

"When do you leave?"

"Soon as I can round up Gloria."

"She's down at the Farm, finishing her debriefing," Adkins said. "Did you know?"

"No," McGarvey said. "Sounds like Howard McCann's doing."

"She'll be glad to be rescued."

McGarvey's visitor's pass would not allow him to access Technical Services' Research and Development corridor, so Jared Kraus had to come out and personally escort him inside. Kraus was a portly man in his late thirties, with a serious demeanor. Nothing was ever a joke to him. His staff claimed he had no sense of humor whatsoever.

"Good afternoon, Mr. Director," he said. "Mr. Rencke is waiting for us in the conference room."

"Were you able to come up with what I need?" McGarvey asked.

Kraus's left eyebrow rose a notch, as if the question was a personal insult. "Of course."

The doors to most of the R & D labs and testing facilities were secured with retinal print identification devices that would open only into safe boxes that acted like air locks aboard a spaceship. The inner door to the facility itself could not be opened unless the outer door was closed and locked.

The wing was a beehive of activity, but no one spoke above a whisper. This place and the people who worked here, dreaming up toys for field operations officers, had always struck McGarvey as science fiction, something out of the old *Mission Impossible*.

"Just in here, sir," Kraus said at the conference room next to his office at the end of the corridor.

Rencke was sitting cross-legged on top of a long table, fiddling with what appeared to be an ordinary satellite telephone. Beside him was a small leather case, about the size of a thick notebook.

He looked up, his eyes bright like a kid with a new toy. "Oh, wow, I just finished programming the third Keyhole, and nobody will be able to detect what I've done."

"You know that we have a serious limitation in size," McGarvey said.

"We've taken care of that for you, Mr. Director," Kraus said. "Actually we've been working on the technology for a few years now, even before you left the Company."

"What have you come up with?"

Kraus zippered open the leather case and took out one of four hypodermic syringes, each about a quarter-filled with a milky solution, and handed it to McGarvey. "It's nanotechnology."

The opening at the business end of the syringe was larger than most needles, and was covered by a plastic sheath. "What is it?"

"That's the good part. The liquid is actually a derivative of sodium thiopental—truth serum. But also contained in each syringe is the GPS transmitter you wanted, no bigger than a grain of sand."

McGarvey held the syringe up to the light, but he could not make out the device. "It can't have much range."

"That's why I programmed three satellites," Rencke said. "The Keyhole will be able to pick up the signal only if the transmitter is almost directly beneath it. It'll show up on the sat phone, but the signal will be intermittent, depending on a satellite pass."

"How do I activate the phone?" McGarvey asked.

"Four syringes, four GPS transmitters. Enter three ones and pound, and the phone will display the latitude and longitude of the first transmitter. Three twos and pound, gets you the second unit, et cetera."

"There's another downside," Kraus said. "Battery life. Best we can do is seven days, so you'll have to be quick about it. The good news is that the batteries won't go active until they've been exposed to the subject's body heat for sixty to ninety minutes."

"We're giving you four of them so Weiss won't be sure if you and Gloria came back just because of al-Turabi," Rencke said. "It's all going to depend on how quickly he can get them out of there and into the hands of Cuban intelligence. Since the last break, Gitmo has been locked up tight."

"He'll manage," McGarvey said. "Al-Turabi is just too big a catch."

WILLIAMSBURG, VIRGINIA

It was about two in the afternoon when McGarvey got down to the CIA's training facility off I-64 outside Williamsburg. Located in a remote section of Camp Peary Naval Reservation on the York River, it was where recruits were taught basic tradecraft that field operations officers needed, and it was also where old hands went to hone their skills or to pass along things they'd learned, usually the hard way.

McGarvey's daughter Elizabeth and her husband, Todd Van Buren, had taken over as camp commandants shortly after 9/11 when recruitment levels were at an all-time high. They were young enough that the recruits could relate to them, but experienced enough that the recruits had respect for them.

"Welcome back, Mr. Director," the guard at the gate said. "Mrs. Van Buren is expecting you up at the office."

"Thanks," McGarvey said, and he followed the long drive through the woods to the collection of rustic buildings that housed the camp's headquarters, classrooms, and the POW center where recruits were subjected to rigorous, sometimes even brutal, interrogations as if they were spies captured by a foreign power. The mess hall, dayrooms, and housing units were also located in the administration area.

Several cars were parked in front of the main office, and across in the parking lot a blue bus with U.S. Air Force markings had pulled up and fifteen or sixteen new recruits were piling out, to be greeted by several instructors dressed in BDUs.

Elizabeth, who was slender, with a pretty round face and short blond hair, practically a twin of her mother at that age, came out of the administration building as McGarvey pulled up. Like the instructors she was dressed in army camouflage, her boots bloused. In addition to running the camp she and Todd also taught many of the classes, including hand-to-hand combat, night field exercises in the swamp, and demolitions. She liked to blow up things as much as her husband did.

"Hi, Daddy," she said, and she and her father embraced.

"How are you, sweetheart?" McGarvey asked.

"Just peachy," she said. She linked her arm in his. "Let's go for a walk." She seemed brittle, on edge.

They headed down a dirt track behind the administration building that led eventually to the outdoor firing range, and beyond that the demolition training bunkers and urban warfare village.

"Everyone can pretty well guess why Dick Adkins called you back," she said. "We've had no luck at all finding bin Laden. You're the only one who's come face-to-face with him and lived. And the fact that they tried to hit you at Arlington pretty well proves he knows that you're gunning for him."

"That could work to my advantage, when the time comes," McGarvey said.

Elizabeth suddenly stopped and looked up into her father's eyes. "Were you aware that Gloria Ibenez is in love with you?"

It took him completely by surprise. "No."

"Well, she's been telling anyone who'll listen that she is," Elizabeth said. "So if you've come here to ask her to help you, just be careful, Daddy. She's an intelligent, beautiful woman, and I think she'd do just about anything to seduce you."

McGarvey had to smile, despite the seriousness of the situation. "Is this a subject that a daughter should be talking to her father about?"

Elizabeth wanted to argue, but after a moment she lowered her eyes and nodded. "I'm sorry."

"I'm going back to Guantanamo Bay, and I want Gloria along to put pressure on the ONI guy she's already had a run-in with," McGarvey said. "When I find out where bin Laden is hiding, I'm going after him alone. I've always worked that way."

Elizabeth looked up. "That's another part I don't like," she said. "You're getting too old for this kind of stuff."

McGarvey shook his head ruefully. "Too old for fieldwork and too old to turn the head of a pretty woman. Good thing I'm going back to teaching when this is over. And it's even better that I'm in love with your mother." He smiled. "She's practically ancient too, you know."

Elizabeth laughed lightly. "You make a good pair," she said. "A dotty old bastard and the only woman on earth who can tell him what to do."

FORTY-THREE

SS *SHEHAB*

Captain Tariq Ziyax leaned against the chart table in the control room of the aging Foxtrot diesel-electric submarine, studying the medium-scale chart of the Mediterranean Sea from the Libyan coast across to the island of Sicily. It was coming up on 2200 Greenwich mean time, which put it at midnight local, eighty-five meters above on the surface.

The *Shehab* had left her base at Ra's al Hilal three days ago on what the crew had been told was a routine patrol mission, but no other Libyan ship had accompanied them, nor since reaching their patrol station two hundred kilometers off Benghazi had they participated in any torpedo or missile drills, and the crew was getting restless. Only Ziyax and a dozen of his officers knew the real orders.

He was a small man with narrow shoulders, and a sad face that was all planes and angles, like someone out of a Goya painting. His eyes were puffed and red because he'd not slept well since he'd been handed this troubling assignment by Colonel Quaddafi himself four days ago, and his nerves were jumping all over the place, especially now that they were at their rendezvous point.

He wanted nothing more at this moment than to be home with his wife and three children, rather than here in the middle of the Mediterranean, carrying four anthrax-tipped torpedo-tube-launched cruise missiles.

To be caught out here in international waters with such weapons of mass destruction, which actually had belonged to Saddam Hussein before the war, would mean certain arrest and imprisonment. It would also go very badly for Libya if it were discovered that Quaddafi had hidden Hussein's weapons in the weeks before the Allied forces had attacked.

The secret to leading men was never to allow a subordinate to see your inner fears. Remain calm in all circumstances. Be a man of iron. It was what he had been taught by the Russians at the Frunze Military Academy.

This is especially true aboard a submarine where a man's worst fears always hovered just a few meters away at the pressure hull.

The *Shehab* was one of the last Foxtrot Class submarines that the Soviets had built in the early eighties, eight of which had been delivered to Libya. Because of shoddy maintenance practices by the Libyan navy, and because of a scarcity of spare parts since the collapse of the Soviet Union, only three of those boats were still serviceable, and the *Shehab* was most definitely on her last legs.

But, Ziyax reflected, in an effort to steady his nerves, she was still a potent warship. Under the right command, with the right crew, she was capable of dealing a sharp blow whether to a sea or land target.

At 91.5 meters on deck, *Shehab* displaced 2,600 tons submerged, and at cruising speed had a range of twenty thousand miles. She was fitted out with ten 533mm torpedo tubes; six forward and four aft. And she had been modified five years ago, two of her forward tubes modernized so that they could handle the ZM-54E1 missiles that had a range of three hundred kilometers, and could carry a variety of payloads, including normal high-explosive warheads, or air-burst canisters of anthrax. Even a small nuclear warshot with a yield of a few kilotons could be mounted to attack a ship or even a shore installation.

Ziyax shuddered to think what the outcome would be if a Libyan submarine ever made such an attack. It would be the end of their nation, and certainly the same fate that Hussein had suffered would befall Colonel Quaddafi. It was why this assignment was so vitally important.

"You will kill three birds with one stone for me, my dear Captain," Quaddafi had told him. It was early evening, and they were walking in the desert, a half-dozen bodyguards trailing twenty meters behind.

"I and my crew will do our best for you," Ziyax had promised. He had graduated with a degree in electronic engineering, with honors, from King Farouk University in Cairo, and after two years working for Libya Telecommunications Corporation, helping build an all-new telephone system for the country, he'd been drafted into the navy. He was smart, he was dedicated to his nation, and knew how to follow orders as well as give them. After four years of intensive training in Libya and in Russia, aboard a variety of submarines including Kilos and Foxtrots, he'd been appointed as executive officer aboard a sister submarine of Shehab's.

He'd also gotten married and started his family, which made him want to finally quit the sea and return to his first love, electronic engineering.

"When you have completed this assignment for me, I will release you from the navy, if that's what you still want," Colonel Quaddafi promised.

Ziyax had felt a sudden flush of pleasure. "Yes, sir, but only to return to my old position."

"You're needed there as well as here," Quaddafi said.

They walked in silence for a while, Ziyax thinking about regaining his old life. But then it occurred to ask what task he was being assigned to do. "The three birds with one stone, sir?" he prompted.

"You have read the newspapers, seen the international television broadcasts, so you know that I have promised the West to reduce our military forces in exchange for new trade agreements. The boycott against our people has been lifted."

"Yes, sir." Life in Libya, especially in the capital, Tripoli, had markedly improved over the past few years. The nearly universal sentiment held

Quaddafi in high regard, even though it had been his arrogance in the first place that had landed them in so much trouble with the West.

"You are to take your submarine into the Mediterranean, and so far as the world is concerned, scuttle her."

Ziyax's breath had caught in his throat when he understood *exactly* what Quaddafi was telling him, and the reason for telling him out here in isolation where there was no possibility of prying ears. "If I'm not to scuttle my boat, what am I to do?"

"You will make rendezvous with a civilian vessel so that your crew can be taken off and replaced by a scuttling crew, to whom you will turn over the boat."

Ziyax knew exactly whom the scuttling crew worked for, and his blood ran cold, but he didn't give voice to his thought.

"Since we have made an appeasement with the West, certain of our brothers in prayer have criticized us. This gesture will spread oil on the waters. The second bird."

Al-Quaida, the thought crystallized in Ziyax's mind. Still he held his silence.

"You may tell your officers the truth," Quaddafi instructed. "It may be that you will have to remain aboard for a few days to familiarize the new crew, though I'm told their captain is English. A graduate of their Perisher school."

Ziyax could not have been more astounded at that moment. "I'm to turn over my submarine to an infidel?"

"Precisely," Quaddafi said. "Although the West, as well as your crew, will believe that your boat was destroyed and sunk."

"We will be asked why we didn't simply dry-dock her and cut her apart for the steel."

"Because there was a dreadful, unforeseen accident," Quaddafi shot back, somewhat irritated. "But that is diplomacy, my concern. Yours is to do as you are ordered."

"Yes, sir," Ziyax replied.

"Which brings us to the third bird, what has been an anchor around the neck of Libya since oh-four. Certain weapons will be loaded aboard *Shehab*. The exact nature of those weapons will be kept from your crew."

"Am I and my officers to know?" Ziyax asked.

"There is no need, my dear Captain," Quaddafi said. "And when you return home, your reward will be greater than you can imagine."

Ziyax had replayed his surreal conversation with Quaddafi over and over in his head, each time running up against the one flaw in the plan. The crew might be kept ignorant of what had actually become of *Shehab*, but he and his officers would know. Quite possibly that could mean their death sentence, no matter how it turned out. That fact alone he had kept from his officers.

The sonar operator ducked his head around the corner. "Captain, I have a slow-moving target on the surface at our station, keeping position," he said.

Ziyax looked up out of his thoughts, catching the eye of his executive officer, Lieutenant Commander Assam al-Abbas. In addition to being a fine officer and a friend, al-Abbas served as the Purity of Islam officer aboard. Most of the men feared him.

"What is his bearing and range, Ensign Isomil?" Ziyax asked.

"Bearing two-six-five, range one hundred meters."

"What is he doing? Is he a warship? Are we being pinged?"

"No, sir, it's not a warship. I think it's a freighter. He's making less than five knots."

"Are there any other targets? Anything we should be worried about?"

"No, sir, my display is clear to ten thousand meters."

"Very well," Ziyax said. He turned back to his XO. "Turn right to two-six-five, make your speed five knots, and bring us to periscope depth. Five-degree angle on the planes. I want this to go very slowly."

"Aye, Captain," al-Abbas responded crisply and he gave the orders to the diving officer, who relayed them to the helmsman, and then turned to a series of controls at the ballast panel that blew air into a series of tanks. Immediately the submarine began rising to a depth of twenty meters.

There was nothing about this assignment that didn't worry Ziyax. At the very least he would do everything possible to prolong his life and the lives of his officers. Whatever it took. "Assam, if this is the wrong ship, I want to get out of here as quickly as possible."

"*Aywa*," al-Abbas replied. *Yes.*

"Prepare for an emergency dive to two hundred meters on my order, All Ahead Flank."

Al-Abbas repeated the order and the other crew in the control room glanced at their captain, but just for a moment, before they went back to their duties.

Ziyax stepped over to the periscope platform and, as he waited the few minutes for his boat to reach the proper depth, he examined his feelings for the untold time since they'd left base. He trained his entire career in the navy to fire warshots. But so far he'd not done so. Praise Allah. But tonight he was expected to deliver this boat and her weapons to a group he thought were madmen, little better than savages, religious zealots who had done more harm to Islam with their stupid jihad than all the holy wars through history.

"Two-zero meters," al-Abbas called out softly.

Ziyax raised the search periscope, and turned it to a bearing just forward of Shehab's starboard beam. They were slightly behind the freighter and on a parallel course.

For several long seconds he could make out little or nothing but the empty sea. Panning the periscope a few degrees left, the ship was suddenly there, very close. It showed no lights, but he could identify the silhouettes of several containers on deck, which was what he was told he would see.

He stepped up the scope's magnification and turned to the stern of the freighter. She was the Distal Volente, out of Monrovia, Liberia.

Ziyax stepped back, his heart suddenly racing. It was the ship he was to rendezvous with. He looked through the eyepiece again, but there was no movement on deck that he could discern. For all appearances, the Distal Volente could be a ghost ship.

"Rig for night operations," he said. He folded the handles and lowered the periscope as the lights through the ship turned red. "Surface the boat."

FORTY-FOUR

□

DISTAL VOLENTE

First Officer Takeo Itasaka looked up from the radar screen and shook his head. "We have arrived at the rendezvous point but there is nothing inside the ten-kilometer ring, and nothing heading in our direction."

Only he, Captain Subandrio, and Graham were on the bridge. The other three of the ship's crew plus Graham's people were out of sight belowdecks. The navigation lights had been doused sixty minutes ago, and the only lights on the bridge came from the radar screen and the few instruments clustered above the wheel. Graham had ordered even the red light over the chart table switched off.

"Stop the ship," Graham ordered, not bothering to raise his voice.

"But there's nobody here, Rupert," Subandrio replied. He had taken the helm, which he'd always done when the situation became tense. He was a wise old bird who could smell trouble even before it developed.

"There will be," Graham said. "Stop the ship, please." Graham had developed an understanding and a certain respect for the captain in the several years he'd worked with the man. It was obvious that Subandrio suspected that he and his ship might be sailing into some kind of danger.

"We're not early."

"No, we're here spot-on," Graham said. "Please stop the ship now."

Subandrio exchanged a look with his first officer, but then shrugged and rang for All Stop. Moments later, they could feel the change in the diesel's pitch through the deck plating, and the *Distal Volente* began to lose speed.

Graham walked to the window and looked out at the black sea, but there was nothing to see except for the stars above; even the horizon was lost to the darkness.

He took a walkie-talkie out of his pocket and keyed the Push-to-Talk button. "We're here," he said.

"Have they arrived?" al-Hari asked. He and eight of the Iranian crew were crouched in the passageway one deck below the crew's quarters. The remainder of Graham's submariners were dispersed throughout the ship.

"Not yet," Graham radioed. "Stand by."

"Stand by for what?" Subandrio asked.

"You'll see, old friend," Graham replied mildly. He needed the captain and crew in case the submarine never showed up. If that happened they would pay Subandrio for his trouble, and he could take them to Syria, where they could safely wait until another submarine could be enlisted.

There'd been other delays before, and Graham had learned patience very early on. Bin Laden had once called Graham a scorpion because of his stealth and because of his lethal sting. *"You will be as Allah's scorpion for me."* It was the only mumbo jumbo from any of the Muslims that Graham had ever found amusing. He smiled now. Once he took control of the Foxtrot more people than bin Laden would think of him as a scorpion. A lot more people.

Itasaka suddenly hunched over the radar screen. "Son of a bitch," he swore. He looked up.

"Where?" Graham asked.

"To port," he said excitedly. "It just showed up next to us."

Graham stepped out to the port-wing lookout, Subandrio right behind him, as the distinctively stubby fairwater and long, narrow hull of a Foxtrot Class submarine rose out of the sea one hundred meters away.

Subandrio was clearly impressed. "Who does it belong to, Rupert?"

"Me," Graham said. He took a small red-lensed flashlight out of his pocket and flashed QRV in Morse code, which meant, *Are you ready?*

Moments later the QRV flashed from a red light atop the periscope; I am ready. It was the agreed-upon signal and response.

"What have you gotten yourself into?" Subandrio asked. He was staring at the submarine. "This is a very bad business. That's not a machine for hijacking ships. It's meant only to kill."

"Indeed it is," Graham said. He brushed past the captain and went back inside. He keyed his walkie-talkie. "Now," he said. "When you're finished meet me on deck, we'll take the gig across."

"Roger," al-Hari replied crisply.

Graham pocketed the flashlight and walkie-talkie, at the same moment gunfire erupted from the crew's quarters, and elsewhere throughout the ship. He pulled out his pistol and turned around, but the port-wing lookout was empty. Subandrio had jumped overboard.

"Son of a bitch," the first officer swore behind him.

He spun around in time to see Itasaka desperately trying to get the gun locker open. Graham raised his pistol and fired three shots at the man, the second and third hitting the Japanese officer in the back of the neck and base of his skull, killing him.

The firing belowdecks intensified fivefold; then, as suddenly as it had begun, it stopped. A second later one lone pistol shot came from directly below, and then the ship was silent.

Graham went back out onto the port-wing lookout and searched the water below, but in the darkness spotting someone would be impossible. He slapped his hand against his leg in frustration. Everything had gone exactly as planned to this point, except for Subandrio jumping ship. Something at the back of his head had told him to be wary of the wily old Indonesian. The man had survived in a very risky business for a very long time because his instincts were good.

Al-Hari called on the walkie-talkie. "We're clear down here."

Graham pulled his walkie-talkie out of his pocket. "Clear up here. I'll meet you on deck."

"Roger."

Graham lingered for a few moments on the port-wing lookout, holding his breath to listen for any sounds; someone splashing in the water, perhaps. But it was a long way down, so it was possible that Subandrio had been knocked unconscious when he'd hit the water, and he'd drowned. But even if he survived the fall they were two hundred kilometers offshore, and that was a very long swim.

The captain would certainly not survive. Nonetheless, the lack of precision bothered Graham. He did not like loose ends.

SS _SHEHAB_

Approaching the Libyan submarine in Subandrio's gig, Graham almost ordered al-Hari to return to the _Distal Volente_, and immediately get under way for Syria. The warship was a piece of junk. Even in worse shape than the rust-bucket freighter they'd just left. Large off-color patches in the hull, where repairs had been made, dotted the side of the boat like a patchwork quilt. Two of the hydrophone panels on the forward edge of the fairwater were missing, and it appeared as if something—a piling or perhaps another ship—had scraped a large gouge nearly the entire length of the boat just above the waterline.

"We're submerging in this piece of shit?" al-Hari asked.

"At least it's not a nuke boat with a leaking reactor," Graham said, his hopes momentarily sinking. He had originally wanted a Kilo Class submarine, something more modern and certainly much quieter. And yet if this boat could be repaired once they got under way, it would give them the advantage of range. The Kilo would not make it across the Atlantic without refueling. It was a problem that Graham had been working on, but without a solution so far.

"We're looking at a death trap," al-Hari insisted.

"A Libyan crew brought her this far," Graham replied as they approached the submarine's starboard side just below the fairwater. Two men were waiting on deck.

"*Aywa,*" al-Hari said. *Yes.* "But those bastards are fanatics."

Graham could scarcely believe what the man had just said, and with a straight face. He almost laughed. "We'll make do. When we transfer crews bring anything you can think of to make repairs. And bring all the stores that your people haven't already eaten."

"Some of that garbage isn't fit for humans."

"I think ten days from now you'll feel differently," Graham said. He was beginning to wonder if he had picked the wrong man to be his XO. But there wasn't much to choose from.

"Are you going to tell me where we're taking this piece of dung?"

"In due time, Mr. al-Hari," Graham said. "In the meantime we have work to do."

He stood up and tossed a line to the men on deck as al-Hari throttled back and came up alongside nicely.

The shorter of the two Libyans caught the line, and Graham clambered aboard.

"I am Captain Tariq Ziyax," the taller of two men said. "And this is my executive officer, Lieutenant Commander Assam al-Abbas." He held out his hand, but Graham ignored it.

"My name is Rupert Graham, but you may call me Captain. I'm taking command as of this moment."

Al-Abbas made as if to say something, but Ziyax held him back. "This vessel is a gift to the *jihad.* We wish for you to use him well." The Foxtrot was a Russian-built boat, and Russians called their ships by the masculine pronoun.

"*Insh'allah,*" al-Hari called up from the gig, meaning it as a sarcasm that both Libyans caught.

"I will require you and your officers to remain aboard," Graham said before either of them could reply to al-Hari. "How many of your crew will need to be transferred?"

"Twenty-eight," Ziyax answered without hesitation. He'd obviously been expecting it. "There will be myself and seventeen others at your disposal for as long as need be."

"Very well, I'll let your XO see to their immediate transfer," Graham said. "I want to be under way within the hour." He turned back to al-Hari. "Get our people and supplies over here on the double. I want the Libyans in the crew's mess for their debriefing. Do you understand everything?"

Al-Hari gave him a wicked smile. "Yes, sir. Everything."

Al-Abbas tossed the painter to al-Hari, who immediately gunned the gig's engine, and headed back to the *Distal Volente*.

"Now, Captain, I would like to inspect my boat, and meet my officers and crew," Graham said.

Al-Abbas shot him an evil look, but hurried forward and disappeared down the loading hatch in the deck.

"Can you tell me your plans for my . . . for this boat?" Ziyax asked. "Colonel Quaddafi wasn't clear, except that I was ordered to assist you and the *jihad* in any way I could. But that does not include an attack on any target. Before that happens we must be allowed to leave."

"I have been led to understand that the struggle belongs to all Muslims," Graham said indifferently.

"The struggle has many forms," Ziyax responded.

Graham laughed disparagingly. "This is a warship, and that's exactly how I intend to use her."

FORTY-FIVE

SS *SHEHAB*

Standing on the bridge of the submarine with Captain Ziyax, Graham was nearly consumed with anger and impatience, though he let none of that show. It had been nearly two hours since al-Hari had returned to the *Distal Volente* to get their crew squared away, secure the transferring crew of the *Shehab*, and ferry over the repair supplies and consumables. And still the forward-loading hatch had not been closed.

Every minute they remained out here increased their risk of discovery, though the sonar and radar officers reported no targets within twenty kilometers. But there was always the risk of a chance discovery by an American or British satellite.

The interior spaces, machinery, and electrical and electronics systems aboard were only marginally better than the hull. But nearly everything worked or seemed to be repairable. The officers seemed competent; at least they appeared to know their jobs, although their resentment had become palpable the moment they'd been informed that their captain was being replaced by an infidel.

But anger was a useful tool to mold a ragged mob into a cohesive crew, Graham thought. It was a tool he'd used often.

Though not for himself. He needed to remain calm, in control, superior, the leader of men, no matter how badly he wanted to lash out at all of them; bastards who had allowed his wife to die utterly alone.

Graham keyed his walkie-talkie. "What's your situation?" he radioed tersely.

"Five minutes, Captain," al-Hari responded. He was still aboard the *Distal Volente* with two other Iranian submariners.

"Trouble?"

"*La,*" al-Hari came back. No.

Graham pocketed the walkie-talkie and picked up the boat's communicator handphone. "Sonar, bridge, has anyone taken notice of us?"

"Bridge, sonar. My display is still clear, sir."

He switched to the radar-electronic support measures officer. "ESM, bridge. What's it look like?"

"Nothing hot within one hundred kilometers," the young Iranian officer responded. He was one of Graham's. "Three minutes ago, I picked up something very briefly, but it was way east, and high. Probably Egyptian air force, and it turned away from us toward Israel."

"Keep your eyes open, Ahmad, we'll be running on the surface for most of the night," Graham ordered, then he switched to the control room which for the moment was being manned by Ziyax's XO. "Conn, bridge."

It took several moments for al-Abbas to answer, and he sounded surly. "*Aywa.*"

Graham's anger spiked, but he held himself in check. For now he wanted to get under way. He would deal with the lieutenant commander later, though not much later. "Prepare to get under way."

"Submerged?"

"Negative," Graham said. "We'll run on the surface for as long as we can. But I want the boat prepared for sea in all respects, including emergency-dive procedures."

"*Aywa.*"

Graham replaced the growler phone in its cradle beneath the coaming. Ziyax had been watching him closely.

"Assam is a good officer," he said.

"We'll see," Graham replied. Al-Hari and the last two Iranian submariners appeared out of the darkness in one of the rubber boats from the *Shehab*. The *Distal Volente*'s gig had been winched back aboard the freighter and would remain there.

He looked up. The sky had gone cloudy and the night had become even darker than it had been at midnight. But there wasn't much time until dawn, when they would have to submerge, and he was seething because of the unexpected delay. He wanted to be as far away from here as possible before daybreak.

Graham turned to Ziyax and fixed the man with a hard stare. "I suggest that you counsel him. If he or any of your officers decide they'd rather not cooperate, there will be a solution that will not be much to their liking."

"Does that include me?" Ziyax asked.

"Especially you, Captain," Graham responded.

The Libyan watched the rubber raft approaching. He nodded toward the *Distal Volente*. "What about the rest of my crew? Are they to be returned to Ra's al Hilal? It wasn't in my orders, nor was it made clear to me. I was told that you would explain where they were to be taken."

"They cannot be allowed to fall into the hands of any Western intelligence agency, or Mossad."

"Yes, I understand this," Ziyax said. It was obvious that he was beginning to suspect that something drastic might be about to happen. "Of course they can be held on base until your mission develops."

Graham said nothing, watching as al-Hari and the two crewmen reached the submarine, scrambled aboard, and deflated the rubber raft.

Al-Hari looked up and nodded before he went forward to the loading hatch, and disappeared below, closing the hatch behind him.

"They can be taken to one of your training camps in Syria," Ziyax argued. "They would be safe from capture there."

"We can't take the chance, Captain," Graham said, taking the walkie-talkie out again. "I'm told this was Colonel Quaddafi's suggestion, actually."

"Place them under arrest," Ziyax implored. "Give them a chance. They could join the jihad."

Graham switched channels, and glanced with supreme indifference at the Libyan captain. He held out the walkie-talkie. "They were your crewmen. Would you like to do it?"

"This is monstrous," Ziyax said, backing away.

Graham depressed the Push-to-Talk switch, his eyes never leaving the Libyan officer's.

The sound of a muffled bang came across the water to them, and then three others in rapid succession. The first explosive device had been placed directly beneath the mess where the Shehab's crew had been locked up. It was a bit of common decency that al-Hari had insisted upon.

"They're not our enemy."

"But they could betray us," Graham had explained, though it had been unnecessary for him to do so. Al-Hari would cooperate now, no matter the task. But sometimes it was interesting to see how far a man would go for his petty little feelings of squeamishness.

"Yes, they must die, Captain. But not by drowning," al-Hari argued. "Every submariner hates the thought of drowning more than anything else."

"As you wish," Graham had magnanimously agreed.

Now everyone aboard the Distal Volente was dead, and the ship immediately began to settle, bow down, her bottom ripped open by three explosive charges that had been placed very low in the bilges.

The growler phone squawked. "Bridge, sonar."

Graham picked it up as he watched the freighter sinking. "Bridge, aye."

"There were four small explosions close aboard, sir," the Libyan sonar operator reported excitedly.

"Insh'allah," Graham replied, and he couldn't help but chuckle as the Distal Volente disappeared.

GULF OF SIDRA

A large gray object popped to the surface a few meters from where Captain Subandrio was treading water. Other bits and pieces, the remains of his ship, appeared farther away in a widening trail of oil slick.

He could just make out the humpbacked form of the submarine one hundred meters away, and although he had been raised in a Buddhist home to have tolerance and forbearance for his enemy, he swore he would have his revenge. For that he needed to survive, and to remember exactly what he'd witnessed out here tonight, and for the past days since Tunisia.

There'd been four explosions, which he'd felt in his chest through the waterborne shock waves, and his ship had sunk in a remarkably short time.

But Graham was an expert demolitions man; as ruthless as he was handy with all forms of weapons and things that went bang. His first act on coming aboard the *Distal Volente* was to kill one of his own men, to prove a point from the beginning, Subandrio supposed, that Graham was a serious man whose orders were to be obeyed without question.

From what he'd been able to piece together over the past days, and from the sudden appearance of the submarine, Subandrio realized that the rumors about Graham working for al-Quaida were probably true. Now the fanatics had a terrible machine of war at their disposal with a highly trained submarine commander; a man who knew how to use such a warship to its greatest advantage.

The water was reasonably warm, so Subandrio did not think he would have much trouble surviving this night, and possibly all day tomorrow. But after that his life would be in the hands of the capricious gods.

He swam slowly over to the large gray object, conserving his strength, and keeping a wary eye toward the submarine in case someone came back in a rubber raft to search for him.

As he approached he could see that it was a table from the crew's mess. One end of it was blackened and twisted, while along one side was a broad streak of blood.

The cold-hearted bastards had killed his crew, and for that, if for nothing else, there would be retribution. Rupert had been a man such as others, possessed by his own devils, but he had been like a son. This now was a betrayal of trust.

There would be fishing boats out here during the day. Or, if he was lucky, perhaps a pleasure boat from Crete, maybe even a sailing vessel. He did not want to be picked up by anyone's navy, especially the Libyans. He wanted to get ashore without entanglements and, as quickly and as anonymously as possible, call the nearest U.S. Embassy or Consulate and report what had happened. Perhaps even a reward could somehow be arranged.

Subandrio gingerly pulled himself onto the table, but the balance was precarious and it tipped over, dumping him into the sea. He took a mouthful of contaminated water, and came up sputtering and coughing.

In the very dim light he could see that a man's limbs from the hips down had been snagged by a ragged edge. The man's clothing had been blown away by the force of the blast, his skin horribly blackened.

Subandrio vomited as he backed away, unable to take his eyes from the gruesome sight that he knew would stay with him for the rest of his life.

SS *SHEHAB*

"Bridge, ESMs, I have an inbound target, designated Romeo One," Ahmad Khalia reported excitedly.

Graham had been about to order them to get under way. He snatched the growler phone. "ESMs, bridge, what do you have?"

"Captain, it's low and slow, bearing one-two-five, range ninety-five miles, and closing at a rate of two-hundred-ten knots. I think it might be a Libyan patrol aircraft."

"That's exactly what it is," Ziyax said. "Someone wants to know if we're still out here."

Graham switched channels. "Conn, bridge. Prepare to dive the boat."

"Conn, aye," al-Hari responded crisply.

"Clear the bridge, Captain," Graham told Ziyax, who immediately scrambled down the hatch into the boat.

For just a moment, Graham remained on the bridge, searching the dark sea where the *Distal Volente* had gone down. There was some debris, as he expected there would be, but not as much as he had feared. His men had done a fairly good job of securing anything loose on deck, and making sure all the hatches were dogged shut before they blew the bottom out of her.

Subandrio was out there somewhere, or maybe it was his body floating in the sea. Whatever the case, there was no time to search for him.

Graham slipped through the hatch, closing and dogging it behind him, and then descended into the control room.

The boat stank of diesel oil, unwashed bodies, and what was probably a defective head that no one had bothered to repair. That, among other things, would change very quickly.

"There is pressure in the boat," al-Hari announced from his control panel near the helm station. "My board is green. We are ready in all respects to dive."

Graham went over to stand next to Captain Ziyax at the periscope pedestal. In addition to al-Hari, as the COB or Chief of Boat, the Libyan executive officer al-Abbas was temporarily acting as dive officer. Although he still had a major attitude, he seemed ready at the ballast control panel to execute Graham's orders. One of the Libyan junior officers was seated at the helm, and two of Graham's people were manning the navigation and weapons consoles. Just forward of the control room, one of his people and one of the Libyans manned the sonar displays, and just aft, Khalia manned the bank of ESMs instruments.

"Very well, dive the boat," Graham ordered.

"Dive the boat," al-Hari repeated the command.

"All Ahead Flank," Graham ordered. "Fifteen degrees down angle on the planes, make your depth—"

Al-Hari repeated the orders, and the boat accelerated as it started its dive.

Graham turned to Ziyax. "How much water do we have under our keel?"

"Thirty-five hundred meters."

"Make your depth three hundred meters," Graham ordered. He walked over to the navigation station where a chart of the Mediterranean Sea was spread out. He quickly plotted a course that would take them west, missing the island of Malta, while keeping well clear of Crete to the north and the African coast to the south.

"Come left to course two-eight-five," he ordered, and al-Hari repeated the command.

Ziyax was at Graham's elbow. "Where are you taking us?" he asked softly enough so that no one else in the control room could hear.

"Gibraltar," Graham replied indifferently. Running that bottleneck, which was more than 1,500 miles away, would be their first serious test. It gave him approximately 100 hours to mold his crew into a cohesive fighting force.

For that he would need an incident.

FORTY-SIX

□

GUANTANAMO BAY

Lieutenant Colonel Daniel Higgins was getting set to go over to the O Club for lunch when the phone on his desk rang. It was General Maddox's secretary.

"The general would like to have a word with you before you go to lunch."

"I'll be right up."

Higgins grabbed his cap, and on the way out told his ops officer in the Watch that he was seeing the general, and afterwards was going to the club. "If the Cubans come over the fence, ring me on my cell so I can go home and pack a bag," he said. It was a standing joke at Gitmo that any time the Cubans wanted to take the base back, there wouldn't be much that could be done to stop them.

Upstairs, the general's secretary told him to go straight in. Maddox was studying something out his window with a pair of binoculars. When he turned around, Higgins got the impression he was on the verge of a famous Icewater explosion.

"You wanted to see me, sir?" Higgins prompted when it seemed as if Maddox was too angry to talk.

"They just landed across the bay," the general said, his tone surprisingly mild.

"Who would that be?" Higgins asked. A little alarm bell began to jingle softly at the back of his head.

"The CIA. Same pair as last time, including the crazy bitch who beat the shit out of Tom Weiss. And we've got to cooperate one hundred percent this time." Maddox shook his head as if he'd just said something that was utterly unbelievable. "I got that personally from Newt Peyton, who got it direct from LePlante." Marine Major General Newton Peyton was boss of Gitmo, and Bob LePlante was the secretary of defense.

"What do they want this time, did they say?" Higgins asked, though he had a fair idea why the CIA was back. They'd probably gotten a positive ID on the John Doe they'd sent down here after the Arlington Cemetery attack, and they were coming to lean on him.

"They've got the names of four prisoners they want to interrogate," Maddox said. "But apparently they've promised to make it real short this time."

"Do we have the list?"

"It came in about an hour ago, but there's a potential for trouble heading our way that I want you to personally handle," Maddox said. "Whatever the hell happens, I want Tom Weiss out of sight until they're gone. The crazy bastards would probably kill him if he opened his big mouth again." Maddox handed him a message flimsy that had come from the CIA.

Higgins smiled briefly. "From what I heard he might have deserved it." The four men on the list included the John Doe, as he thought would be the case. No surprises yet.

"I don't care, Dan. I just want them in and out asap. I want you to give them anything they ask for, and I mean anything. And I want you to stick with them no matter what. I don't want them back again because they didn't get what they came for."

"I'll handle it," Higgins said. "You said something about trouble?"

"I personally don't give a flying shit how it's done, as long as Weiss and his people get results, and as long as Amnesty International keeps out of it. I won't have another Abu Ghraib. Not on my watch."

"I'm not following you, General," Higgins said, mystified.

"Drugs."

Higgins's heart skipped a beat, but he nodded. "I'll get Richardson over to do it, and we'll need a translator." Melvin Richardson was the chief medic for Delta, and had been the lead man on the Biscuit teams until they were discontinued on orders from the White House last year. If Amnesty International got wind of such a thing happening again, it would immediately go public, and a lot of heads would roll.

"You have to keep a serious lid on this, Dan," Maddox cautioned. "It could blow up and bite us all on the ass."

"Don't worry, I'll take care of it."

"Worrying is what they pay me to do," Maddox said. "Just get the job done, and get them the hell out of here."

"I hear you, General," Higgins said, and he went back down to his office, lunch forgotten for the moment. If McGarvey and the woman had just touched down, they would be at Delta within fifteen or twenty minutes.

He reached Dr. Richardson just as the doctor was leaving the hospital. One of the nurses caught up with him and told him he had a phone call.

"This is Richardson."

"Mel, I'm glad I caught you. This is Dan Higgins. I've got a rush job for you at Delta, and it's the big leagues."

"What do you need?" the M.D. asked, obviously interested.

"I'll tell you when you get over here, but I need you right now."

"Okay."

"And Mel? Bring your Biscuit bag."

There was a momentary silence on the line. "I see," Richardson said cautiously. "I'll be up in ten."

"No word to anyone."

"What, do you think I'm crazy?"

Higgins was waiting for McGarvey and Gloria in the Delta interrogation center, where one of the MPs from the main gate had escorted them the moment they'd shown up. This time there seemed to be no animosity whatsoever, and in fact McGarvey thought they were being treated too well.

Someone had passed the word down, and although he was hoping to see Lieutenant Commander Weiss, he wasn't surprised to see the chief intelligence officer instead, and a tall, slender full commander wearing medical insignia.

"Welcome to Delta, Mr. McGarvey, Ms. Ibenez," Higgins said. "Though I'm surprised you're back so soon."

"We have a job to do," McGarvey said. "If we can get to it, we'll be out of here within a couple hours."

"Where's Commander Weiss?" Gloria asked sweetly. "I hope he's okay."

Higgins studied her for a moment as if he couldn't quite figure out who or what she was. "He's on the mend. I'll tell him that you asked."

"Please do," Gloria said.

They were alone in the dayroom, and the television set was turned up high enough that it was unlikely their conversation could be picked up on tape. Nevertheless Higgins lowered his voice.

"Your four people are here, in individual rooms. We didn't know if you wanted them separated."

"That's fine," McGarvey said. "We're going to give them sodium thiopental. We just have a couple of questions for them. So like I said, Commander, we can be out of your hair within two hours."

Higgins nodded toward Richardson. "This is Mel Richardson, he used to be head of our Biscuit teams. He'll be your doc."

Richardson eyed McGarvey with obvious distaste. "I want to go on record right now that I'm dead set against this. Sodium thiopental is an anesthetic, which means it can be fatal. And it has the capability of scrambling brains. It's happened before, and it's permanent."

"About as permanent as 9/11 at the Trade Center?" Gloria asked.

"Look, Doc, I understand," McGarvey said. "Leave us some alcohol pads and we'll do it ourselves. Our Agency people said the dosage is very low, so the risks will be minimal. Contrary to what you may have been told, we don't want to screw up things here for you guys. But something very big is on the wind, and we don't have a lot of time to fool around."

"You didn't do so good preventing 9/11," Richardson shot back.

"No, we didn't," McGarvey admitted. "But we've learned a lot since then. Enough that we think we can stop them this time. Will you help?"

Richardson looked to Higgins for backup, but the intel officer merely shrugged.

McGarvey handed Richardson the small leather case. "You can give this to them now."

The doctor took out one of the needles. "This is a fucking veterinary syringe that they use on large animals. I'm not going to do this."

"Fine, we'll do it ourselves, with or without the alcohol pads, because frankly I don't give a shit what happens to the four son of a bitches we came to talk to. They're the enemy."

"They're combatants who're protected by the Geneva Convention," Richardson shot back.

"No, Doctor. They're terrorists who target innocent women and children. And whatever they're up to this time has the potential of being worse than 9/11."

"I've heard that before—"

"And you'll keep hearing it until we beat the bastards," McGarvey said, overriding him.

"Mel, nobody likes this, so the sooner we get it done the sooner our guests will leave," Higgins prompted.

Richardson looked like a man who was trapped. "I'll need some help, they're likely to object."

"I'll do it," Gloria said, and she followed the doctor into the first interrogation room, leaving the door open. Ali bin Ramdi, one of the prisoners that McGarvey had leaned on the last time, was shackled to a bench. When he saw Gloria, and then McGarvey out in the dayroom, his eyes went wide.

Chief Petty Officer Sayyid Deyhim came down the corridor in a rush, but pulled up short when he saw who was there. "Shit."

Higgins turned to him. "You will do your job, and keep your opinions to yourself. Clear on that, sailor?"

"Yes, sir," Deyhim replied. He avoided eye contact with McGarvey.

Bin Ramdi grunted something, and a few moments later Richardson and Gloria came out of the cell.

"How long before it takes effect?" McGarvey asked.

The doctor looked at him with distaste. "Just a few seconds for the drug to get to his brain. But if this is a low dose, the effect won't last long."

McGarvey entered the cell and Deyhim took up a position next to him. Higgins came to the door, but remained outside.

"*Misae el kher*," McGarvey said in reasonably passable Egyptian Arabic. *Good afternoon.* He only knew a few phrases.

Bin Ramdi mumbled something that McGarvey didn't catch.

"I didn't understand that," Deyhim said. "Do you want me to have him repeat it?"

"No," McGarvey said. "Ask him if he is a member of al-Quaida."

"Sir, we've already established—"

"Just ask the question," McGarvey said.

Deyhim asked the question in Arabic, but he had to repeat it several times before bin Ramdi gave a slurred response.

"*Aywa.*" *Yes.*

"I got it," McGarvey said. "Tell him that we know Osama bin Laden is hiding in the mountains near Drosh."

Deyhim made the translation.

"Tell him that we know this for a fact."

Deyhim translated.

"All I want is a confirmation."

Deyhim translated, but bin Ramdi was shaking his head drunkenly, and muttering something about Allah.

"Repeat all of it," McGarvey told Deyhim. "I want to make sure he understands."

Deyhim translated, but bin Ramdi only shook his head.

It was the response that McGarvey had been told to expect. Sodium thiopental reduced the subject's inhibitions, but it wasn't the truth serum of fiction. Used in conjunction with a skillful interrogator, some useful information could be gained from some subjects some of the time. But whatever was said to them would definitely place a deep-seated suggestion in their brains, one they would not soon forget.

"Sir, I think this guy is fried," Deyhim said.

"You're right," McGarvey agreed. "Let's try the next one."

As Higgins stepped away from the door, he gave McGarvey an odd, pensive look, and then glanced in at the doped-up prisoner.

Richardson and Gloria were coming out of the third cell when McGarvey and Deyhim entered the second where Kamal al-Turabi was seated, shackled to the bench. He was dressed in an orange jumpsuit, with white paper slippers on his feet. His eyes widened slightly when he saw who it was, but then it was as if a cobra's hood descended over his face.

"Good afternoon," McGarvey said in English, and Deyhim translated.

Al-Turabi was having some trouble focusing, but he did not seem as heavily sedated as bin Ramdi.

"Ask him if he works for al-Quaida," McGarvey instructed Deyhim, who translated.

An answer seemed to form on the prisoner's lips, but then he smiled and shook his head. "I am a simple dentist from Maryland," he said in English. His voice was somewhat slurred, as if he'd had several cocktails. "I've never seen you before."

Of course not, McGarvey thought. But you just made one hell of a mistake.

"We know that Uncle Osama has gone back to Somalia, where he has many friends. We would like you merely to confirm this for us."

Deyhim translated.

Al-Turabi sniggered. "*Aywa*, that's what I heard too," he replied in English. He leaned forward on the bench. "Do you know what little bird told me?"

"No, who?" McGarvey said, and he nodded for Deyhim to translate.

"It was a flock of birds," al-Turabi said. "Right here. All the hawks know. And so do the scorpions." He laughed, and his eyes drooped. "Insh'allah," he muttered.

"Shukran," McGarvey said. *Thank you.*

He and Deyhim left the cell as Richardson and Gloria were coming out of number four. "I'm finished with the first two," McGarvey said.

"Are we getting anything?" Gloria asked.

"About what we expected," McGarvey replied, and she nodded.

He and Deyhim went into the third cell where Assa al-Haq was shack-led to the bench. "Ask if he works for al-Quaida."

Deyhim translated.

The prisoner looked up sleepily and nodded. He was drooling from the corners of his mouth.

"Tell him that we know that bin Laden has run to Iran and is hiding there now."

Deyhim gave McGarvey a sharp look, but then translated.

"Tell him we merely want a confirmation," McGarvey said, and Dey-him translated. But it was obvious that al-Haq had no idea what he was being asked.

"That's enough," McGarvey said and he led Deyhim into cell four, where the Pakistani prisoner Zia Warrag was all but unconscious on the bench. "Ask the son of a bitch if he works for al-Quaida."

"Sir, I think this guy's out of it," Deyhim said.

"Ask him, goddammit!" McGarvey shouted. He felt dirty, like a voyeur peeking in a bathroom window at someone sitting on a toilet.

The prisoner looked up at the sound of McGarvey's voice, and Deyhim made the translation, but there was no response.

Higgins came to the door, but said nothing.

"Tell him that we know bin Laden is hiding in Karachi," McGarvey said. He wanted to get this over with right now, and get the hell out. "Tell him all I want is a confirmation. Yes or no."

Deyhim translated, but the prisoner just stared at him.

"Fuck it," McGarvey said. He turned and brushed past Higgins. "We're out of here."

"Did you find what you wanted, Mr. McGarvey?" the intel officer asked.

McGarvey stopped to look at the marine officer. "Yes, I did." He glanced back at the prisoner in cell four. "The poor bastards don't have a clue what they're fighting for or why. They're just killing people because some imam told them it was what Allah wanted them to do."

NAVY C-20D

"Are you okay?" Gloria asked after they'd taken off from Guantanamo Bay and headed up toward cruising altitude.

As soon as they'd boarded the Gulfstream III business jet, the steward had handed McGarvey a stiff bourbon, which he'd knocked back. He held his glass up for another, and looked at Gloria. "I'll live."

The steward came and replenished McGarvey's drink.

"It's like poking through someone's dirty laundry," Gloria said. "And I have a feeling that Weiss likes that kind of shit."

McGarvey held the cool glass against his forehead.

Gloria watched him for a long time. "Now what?" she finally asked.

"We go back to Langley and wait," he said. "Weiss will find a way to spring those four, and Otto will track them."

"To bin Laden?"

"Hopefully," McGarvey said. He wanted to take a very long, very hot shower. If this didn't work he was going to have to try all over again with a different batch of prisoners. Maybe some of them being held in Afghanistan. But no matter how long it took he wasn't going to quit.

He looked up. Gloria was staring at him, waiting for him to explain.

"Within twenty-four hours after they get out of Gitmo, they'll be leaving Cuba. Probably to Mexico City first. And unless I missed with all four guesses I suspect at least one of them will try to warn bin Laden."

Gloria understood. "When we find out which one of them is *not* running for a place to hide, we'll have the bastard."

"Something like that."

FORTY-SEVEN

☐

SS *SHEHAB*

Everyone aboard the Libyan submarine was tired. It had been eighteen hours since they had been forced to submerge north of Benghazi, and for the entire time Graham had run the crew ragged with repeated battle stations missile and battle stations torpedo.

Fifty miles from their original position he had dove the boat steep and deep; full-down angle on the planes, at flank speed in a maneuver called angles and dangles, which was meant to shake out any loose gear or problems that might crop up under actual battle conditions.

The boat, though thirty-five years old, and just about due for the breaker yards, had done its job reasonably well.

And so had the crew, Graham thought, studying the chart in the control room. He glanced up at the bulkhead-mounted clock above the nav station. It was 2200 Greenwich mean time, which put it at ten in the evening on the surface. It was fully dark topside.

The same mix of Iranian and Libyan crew was still at their duty stations in the con, and throughout the entire boat. He'd allowed no one to leave his post. Not even to eat. The cook and his assistant had distributed tea and sandwiches throughout the long day and into this evening.

The entire crew resented him, but most of all the Libyans because their captain had been forced to act as Graham's XO. But even his Iranian crew resented him because he'd demoted al-Hari to COB, which meant he and the others had to take orders from a Libyan.

Graham was doing two things: looking for weaknesses in the boat and his crew, and forcing the men to meld into a crew by giving them something to hold on to in common—hating him.

It was something that he'd learned in the Royal Navy after his wife had died, and his method, although it worked, was one of the reasons he was ultimately cashiered. There was no room aboard a warship for friendships and he'd made sure that everyone abided by that one rule.

But it always took an incident with each new crew for the men to fully understand him. An incident that he instigated.

Graham stepped around the corner to the sonar room, where one of his men plus a Libyan officer had been on duty the entire time. The compartment smelled like sweat, but there was no longer the unpleasant odor from the defective head, or of diesel fuel from the bilges. Both problems had been corrected within ninety minutes after they'd submerged.

"How's it look out there?" he asked.

Both men looked up. "Many targets," the Libyan officer said. He was a young ensign and his name was Salman Isomil. "It's busy up there tonight."

"What kind of targets?" Graham asked, holding his temper in check for the moment.

"Boats—" Isomil said with a sneer.

Graham backhanded him in the face, knocking the man's earphones off his head, and bloodying his nose. "Shall we try again?"

Al-Abbas had come around the corner. "We do not treat our officers like this," he said.

Graham looked over his shoulder at the Libyan first officer. "This is a warship, and we are on a mission. It's my intention to run on the surface for as long as possible so that we can recharge the batteries and ventilate the boat. In order to do this I need to know what's out there." Graham turned away. "That's the last time I'll explain anything to anyone aboard this stinking pile of shit that smells like unwashed rag heads, an odor that I find offensive."

The sonar operator picked his headphones off the deck and put them back on. He was no longer sneering, but his eyes were still filled with hate.

"What does it look like on the surface?" Graham asked, his voice calm.

"Sir, there are numerous surface targets, mostly cargo vessels, though earlier this evening we tracked something that was very large, and moving quite fast. Probably a cruise ship."

"Range and bearings?"

"All over the place, sir," the Libyan sonar operator said. He studied the display on the screen in front of him. "The nearest target is a small ship, bearing zero seven zero, approximately on the same course as us, range at least fifteen thousand meters."

"Are there any underwater targets?" Graham asked.

The Libyan was momentarily startled. "None that I have been able to detect, sir."

"Very well, keep alert, and let me know if anything heads our way."

Graham brushed past al-Abbas and went back into the control room.

Everyone on duty couldn't help but hear the confrontation, and some of them were looking to Ziyax to do something at last. But the Libyan captain said nothing.

Graham snatched a growler phone from its overhead cradle. "ESMs, con."

"ESMs, aye."

"We're heading up. Soon as your sensors clear the surface, I want an all-band passive search, military emissions included, especially from aircraft search radars."

"Can you tell me how long we'll be running on the surface, sir?"

"Until I order us to submerge, which may depend on you," Graham replied. "Look sharp."

"Aye, sir."

Graham replaced the growler phone. "Captain, bring us to periscope depth," he told Ziyax. He started for the periscope platform, but stopped and turned back.

Ziyax had not given the order.

"Is there a problem?" Graham demanded.

"We're too close to Malta to risk surfacing now, if that's your intention," Ziyax said. "We need to pass Isole Pelagie and Pantelleria before we're in the clear. And the men are tired. I say we let them rest."

"The batteries are low."

"Then we stop and drift to conserve power," Ziyax argued. "Or go to snorkel depth so that we can run the diesels."

This was exactly the kind of incident Graham wanted. "What are you afraid of on the surface, Captain?"

Ziyax stiffened, but did not respond to the gross insult.

"I asked a question, Captain," Graham said. "Are you a coward?"

The helmsman looked away from his instruments, his mouth open.

"Bring us to periscope depth, or I will relieve you of duty and place you under arrest," Graham ordered harshly. "Now."

Al-Abbas was suddenly right there, a compact 5.45mm PSM pistol in his hand. He placed the muzzle against the back of Graham's head. "We will be returning to base now," he said. "I am relieving you of command."

Ziyax said something in Arabic, and al-Abbas replied, but did not remove the pistol.

"You will be shot by your government as a traitor," Graham said conversationally.

"You won't be alive to see it."

"Oh?" Graham replied.

Ziyax said something again in Arabic.

Al-Abbas started to answer, when Graham suddenly stepped to the left, grabbed the officer's gun hand, and shoved the man up against the bulkhead. He pulled out his stiletto and raised it to the man's throat.

Ziyax came across the control room. "Don't do it, Captain," he said. "We need every capable man to run this boat."

"I don't want to be constantly looking over my shoulder," Graham said, looking into al-Abbas's eyes. There was nothing there now, only resignation.

"That will not be needed," Ziyax promised. He reached around Graham and took the pistol from al-Abbas's hand. "If Lieutenant Commander al-Abbas even looks as if he might try again I'll kill him myself."

The scenario had played out exactly as Graham had wanted it to do. He backed off. "Very well," he said. He sheathed his knife. "Give me his pistol."

Ziyax handed over the weapon, butt first.

Graham examined it for a moment. "Nice little gun. But I didn't know the Sovs ever exported them." He handed it to a startled al-Abbas. "Next time you'll want to release the safety if you mean to fire it." He turned his back on the Libyan. "Now, Captain, if you please, take us to periscope depth."

"Yes, Captain," Ziyax said.

GULF OF SIDRA

The sun was very high in the sky when Halim Subandrio, clinging to the precariously balanced tabletop, came out of his daze. It was hot, but he was shivering from being half-immersed in the sea for a full day and a night and now half of a second day. He was sick to his stomach from swallowing diesel-fouled seawater and his legs were cramping painfully.

For the first minute he wasn't sure where he was or how he had gotten there, or even the true nature of his predicament, or what had brought him back to consciousness. He was almost entirely focused on his thirst, which was monumental. And he couldn't understand how he could be hot and cold at the same time.

Slowly he became aware of a low rumble that he could feel in his left side in contact with the table, and heard something behind him. He thought that he could smell the exhaust from a diesel engine, and perhaps someone shouting something.

Taking great care with his movements lest he unbalance the tabletop and plunge back into the water, Subandrio turned his head toward the sound, and the shock of what he saw caused his heart to skip a beat.

A ship was at idle less than twenty-five meters away. It was painted gray and for a moment or two it seemed to Subandrio that it was carrying two very large barrels, tipped on their sides aft of a low coach house. Forward, toward the bow, was a large cannon.

It came to him all at once that it was a warship. He looked toward the stern where a plain green flag fluttered in the breeze and his spirits sagged. He was in the middle of being rescued by a Libyan navy fast-attack missile boat.

If they had come to find their submarine it could mean that his ship had been spotted by a Libyan air force patrol plane. For the first time in his life, Subandrio was truly frightened. The Libyan intelligence service was said to have learned its interrogation techniques in the seventies and eighties from the Soviets, and he was getting too old to endure such pain.

An inflatable boat was launched over the side, and two men in uniform climbed aboard, started the outboard motor, and headed across the nearly flat sea.

Subandrio tried to clear his mind so that he could work out his options before he was taken aboard the Libyan warship.

When he'd been shot he'd been enraged by Graham's betrayal, and he'd sworn to get revenge by putting a bullet in his old friend's head. But when he'd been forced to abandon his ship, and watch her sink with all of his crew, plus a dozen or more men from the submarine, his anger had deepened to something more vivid than simple rage. He vowed to remain alive so that he could be rescued, and once he was ashore he would find a way to take away the only thing that Graham ever seemed to cherish: his freedom.

But it was the Libyans with whom Graham had made a deal for the submarine, though what could have been given in exchange must have been very important to Quaddafi.

Considering the nationalities of the crew that had been brought aboard the *Distal Volente* hidden in the cargo container, Subandrio had a fair idea who was behind the exchange, if not what was exchanged other than money.

And he had more than a fair idea who would be willing to pay for such information.

First he would have to convince his rescuers that he was an innocent victim of piracy, in which his crew was murdered, his cargo stolen, and his ship sunk, and further convince them to allow him to leave the country.

The only fly in that ointment, so far as he could figure, would be if the Libyans knew what ship Graham used to transfer the crew and what its captain's name was. If that were the case, then the game might be over even before it began.

At this point there were no choices. If God so willed it, he would survive to exact his revenge and perhaps collect enough money to either retire on an island somewhere in the Java Sea, or perhaps even purchase a cargo vessel of his own.

He raised his right hand and waved as the Libyan crewmen reached his raft. "Please," he cried weakly in Bahasa, his native Indonesian language. "Help me!"

FORTY-EIGHT

□

CIA HEADQUARTERS

McGarvey's biggest challenge after he'd returned from Guantanamo Bay five days ago was facing Kathleen. She'd come up from Florida to stay at the same CIA safe house as before, over Adkins's objections. She wanted to be as close to the center of operations as possible so that when her husband returned from the field she would be there for him.

He knew that she deserved the truth about why he was going back into the field, and what he would try to do, but she'd asked no questions, offered no objections. She would stick it out in Washington until he finished whatever it was he'd set himself to do, and he felt like a heel, like he was cheating on her.

Which in a way he was, he told himself as he crossed the river and took the George Washington Parkway south. It was four in the morning and the highways were practically deserted. Otto had telephoned a half hour ago from the Building that all the pieces were en route. What they had been waiting for was finally ready to pay off.

"This is the big one!" Rencke had shouted. "The whole enchilada."

"I'm on my way," McGarvey had said, and when he'd hung up Kathleen turned on the lamp on her side of the bed and sat up, an owlish expression on her face.

"Are you leaving now?" she asked.

"No, but soon, Katy," he told her.

"Will I at least be told where you're going?"

He nodded. "As soon as I find out." He reached over and kissed her. "Go back to sleep. I'll be back later this morning."

"Shall I pack something?"

"Something dark," he'd told her, and when he'd driven off he'd glanced back at the house in his rearview mirror. The lights were on upstairs.

The riot at Guantanamo Bay three days ago had made all the newspapers and television networks, even though the military had tried to put a lid on the story. Amnesty International was saying it had been warning about just such an event because of the inhumane way in which Taliban and al-Quaida prisoners were being treated. Congress was calling for a full investigation, but the president was standing fast with the position that the White House had maintained all along. The detainees at Camp Delta, as well as at Abu Ghraib and other facilities in Iraq and Afghanistan, were combatants and therefore came under the jurisdiction of the Unified Code of Military Justice. They did not have the same rights as civilians.

What had begun in the late afternoon as a scuffle between several Delta POWs in one of the exercise yards had rapidly escalated into a full-scale riot. Windows had been broken, doors ripped off their hinges, and bedding and anything else that could burn had been piled outside the barracks and set on fire. Eight prisoners had been shot to death, twenty-seven others injured, and nine American personnel had been hurt, two seriously, before the riot had finally been put down.

So far the media had not found out how close the situation had come to being a major disaster. Before General Maddox had finally given the order for the guards to use deadly force, sections of the inner and outer fences had been torn down by the mob, and all the POWs who'd been killed had been shot to death *outside* the facility. On Cuban soil.

Nor had the media learned that four POWs were still unaccounted for. ONI's top-secret Preliminary Incident Report presumed they had drowned trying to swim out to sea. But their names had not been included, nor did the PIR mention that the four had been the same men questioned by the CIA two days before the riot.

"Curiouser and curiouser." Rencke had laughed when he'd hacked into the ONI's computer and brought the PIR up on one of his monitors.

McGarvey had been there, monitoring the four GPS signals that had moved, apparently by boat, down the coast to Santiago de Cuba, the city not far from the famous San Juan Hill. They'd remained there together until yesterday when they'd been flown up to Havana.

Now they were on the move again, and it was nearly time, he thought, for him to go back into the field and do his thing. Already his thoughts were narrowing to the mission. He was already in the process of leaving Washington and his wife and friends, placing all of that life in a safe corner of his head, so that he would be traveling without the baggage that could slow him down. More than one field officer had gotten into serious trouble because his mind had wandered back home at the wrong moment.

Rencke had called the main gate, so the guards there were expecting him. But even though they recognized him, they didn't let him pass until they'd checked his ID. Security had become very tight at the Company.

The parking lot was a third full with the night shifts in the directorates of operations and intelligence, which had gone into high gear because of the increased threat level.

The OD sent an intern down to sign McGarvey in and escort him back upstairs to the Directorate of Operations Ops Center, which was called the Watch. It was a large, windowless room in the center of the building on the third floor that was electronically and mechanically scanned 24/7 for bugs. Operators manned dozens of computer stations, most of them in cubicles, filled not only with one or more large monitors and keyboards, but desks and file cabinets piled high with files, and maps, and reference books. The worldview was on display here, in one form or another. Political situations in dozens of problem nations around the globe, current hot spots where fighting was going on or was expected to start soon, and especially ongoing or developing CIA missions were kept track of. From the information gathered in real time here, and from written reports by our assets on the ground, called Humint, for human intelligence, and by electronic and satellite information-gathering techniques, called by the broader term Elint for electronic intelligence, National Intelligence Estimates and Watch Reports were produced for the National Command Authority.

Activity in this room was never at a lull, and when McGarvey walked in most of the operators didn't bother to look up, they were too absorbed in their tasks.

Tony Mackie, the officer of the day, was waiting for him with Rencke and Gloria at a long conference table in a glass-enclosed office at the front of the room. Mackie was an ex–New York City detective who'd gone to work for the CIA after an early retirement because he had become so accustomed to being on the inside that it drove him nuts to be a mere civilian. Although he would never get to work in the field he was in his glory here, he was the perfect deskman.

McGarvey thanked the young man who'd escorted him upstairs, then went into the conference room.

"Here he is," Mackie said, looking up.

Gloria turned around and gave him a dazzling smile of triumph. "You were right, Mac," she said.

Rencke was at the head of the table, hopping from one foot to the other, and clapping his hands. "Oh boy, Mac, you hit the jackpot," he cried. He turned the large-screen laptop they'd been watching so that McGarvey could see it. "We got them all," he said. "All four."

The laptop's screen was divided into four quadrants, each of which was overlaid with a fairly small-scale map on which a small red dot moved slowly. Several lines of data scrolled across the bottom of each quadrant.

"Is this in real time?" McGarvey asked.

"Real time minus a thirty-second delay for the data from our satellites and a whole bunch of international air traffic control radars and computer systems to get here and be collated," Rencke said.

Three of the quadrants showed the same map of the eastern Mediterranean Sea from just west of Cyprus to the coasts of Syria, Lebanon, and Israel. The red dots, which were the uploaded signals from the nano-GPS units that had been injected into the four men at Guantanamo Bay, showed those three bunched on top of each other and moving directly toward Syria.

"Those three are aboard an Air Mexico jet. Once they clear Israel's northern border they'll hang a hard right, which will take them south to Damascus," Rencke said. "They're not running home to papa, they're heading to safe pastures. All-ee, all-ee, in free."

The fourth map, however, was of south-central Iran, heading eastward to Pakistan.

The data scrolling at the bottom of that quadrant showed latitude, longitude, heading, and speed. The one target was aboard a Pakistan International Airlines jet inbound to Karachi.

"Do we know which one it is?" McGarvey asked.

Rencke was grinning like a kid with a new toy. "Al-Turabi, the guy who masterminded the hit on you at Arlington."

"It could mean that bin Laden is hiding somewhere in southern Pakistan, probably Karachi," Gloria suggested. "If he was hiding up in the mountains, like ISI is telling us, al-Turabi would have flown directly up to Peshawar rather than taking a chance of being spotted switching planes."

"If he's trying to get to bin Laden," McGarvey pointed out, staring at the monitor. "He might simply be running to one of his own hideouts."

"I don't think so, and neither do you," Gloria said. "He's running home to Uncle Osama." She was grinning. "What do we do now?"

McGarvey shook his head. "*We* don't do a thing. You're staying here to help Otto backstop me."

Gloria flared. "Not a chance," she said. "I've had a partner killed and some serious guys shooting at me—including the one on his way to Karachi. I have to see this through."

McGarvey had been too distracted earlier to consider what her reaction might be. "I'm sorry, but I work alone."

"Sorry my ass!" Gloria shouted.

"If need be I'll talk to your boss, and have you pulled from the field," McGarvey told her coolly.

"I've got plenty for you to do here," Rencke said. "This op will have no official status. So far as the Watch goes, it doesn't exist. What we're doing here with Tom is nothing more than an exercise."

Gloria turned away, but not before McGarvey saw a sudden glistening in her eyes. "Goddammit," she said softly.

McGarvey could understand her frustration, but he was going up against bin Laden alone, and for more than one reason. And he wasn't going to stop to explain it to her now.

"I can get you an Aurora by the time you get home and pack," Rencke offered. The Aurora was air force. It flew nearly to the edge of space at speeds of more than mach six. Officially it did not exist. "You can be in Ramstein in a couple hours."

"I'll fly commercial," McGarvey told him.

"I can do that," Rencke said. "Which one of your work names do you want to use?"

McGarvey *had* given that bit of tradecraft a lot of thought. "I'll go in under my own name," he said.

Gloria had turned back. "He'll know that you're coming, and why," she said.

"That's right," McGarvey said. He was counting on just that.

At that moment Gloria very much reminded him of his daughter. They were both bright women, but both of them were impetuous. They didn't have the field experience they thought they had. Spying was a funny business. By the time you got it down to a fine art you were getting too old to work in the field, and too well known by the opposition. They were lessons the women had yet to learn well enough to manipulate them to their own uses.

FORTY-NINE

□

TUNIS

Noon traffic was heavy as the cab worked its way from the Hotel Cirta near the train station and post office out to the grounds of the new U.S. Embassy on Liason Nord-Sud, the Marasa Highway. The driver, spotting a break in traffic, recklessly shot around a bus that was starting to pull over to pick up several passengers, nearly hitting one of them, and just made the green light at the corner.

Halim Subandrio, seated in the back, didn't notice any of that. He was lost in thought on how best to approach the Americans. He needed to convince them of the truth of his story so that he could negotiate for a reward, while at the same time keep himself out of trouble.

It had taken him three days to convince the Libyans that he'd been hijacked and his ship sunk out from under him, but it hadn't seemed to him that they really cared very much. They were more interested in the exact spot where his ship went down than a description of the hijackers, or how he'd been stopped and boarded, and why he'd not had a chance to send a Mayday.

The Libyan doctor had treated him for a mild case of hypothermia and dehydration, and the police had even allowed him to telephone Athens to speak to Hristos Lapides, the owner of the Distal Volente, who had not been the least surprised by the news.

"Well, we made good profits from her!" he'd shouted over the phone. "I'll contact our insurance agents, so we'll make even more, eh?"

"I need a temporary passport and some money," Subandrio had told the Greek.

"Yes, of course. I'll send that by FedEx this morning. You should have it by tomorrow. But how about another ship? Will you be staying in Tripoli?"

"No, as soon as they release me I'm going back to Tunis," Subandrio said. "But listen to me, Mr. Lapides, I don't know who the hijackers were, they all wore balaclavas. They murdered my crew."

"Bastards," Lapides said, but without much feeling. "How is it that you managed to escape?"

"I saw what was happening and I jumped overboard."

"And the Libyan navy rescued you?" Lapides asked, but Subandrio had never mentioned who'd rescued him.

It suddenly came to him that he had been manipulated. The deal to use the Distal Volente to bring Graham and his crew out to meet the Libyan submarine had only been one part of an arrangement with Lapides and Macedonia Shipping. The entire deal had been to hijack the ship, kill him and his crew, as well as the Libyan crew, and sink it.

Lapides knew everything. Now Subandrio was a loose end that would have to be taken care of. But away from Libya, so that no blame could be attached to them. It wasn't a ship that would be waiting for him on the waterfront in Tunis. It would be a bullet.

"Yes, and now they're interested in the exact position where my ship went to the bottom."

"Did you tell them?" Lapides asked, his voice guarded.

"Yes, of course," Subandrio lied. "I cooperated completely."

"That was the correct decision, Captain," Lapides said. "When you get to Tunis, telephone me, and I will make arrangements for another ship for you." He laughed. "We are not finished doing business, my old friend. You'll see."

Subandrio looked up from his thoughts as they approached the sprawling twenty-one-acre complex of buildings, gardens, and fountains that had been built a few years ago, reputedly at a cost of more than forty-two million U.S. dollars. He'd gotten to Tunis by bus late last night, and checked into his hotel, but he had not telephoned Lapides, nor would he.

So far as he could figure, he had two options. He could retire right now with the money he had salted away in a Swiss bank account. It was enough to live well, though not in luxury. Or he could go to the Americans and try to sell his story.

And exact his revenge.

The cabbie turned down a side street that connected with La Goulette Road and pulled up at the main entrance. A pair of U.S. Marines stood just inside the front gate, which was guarded from the street by four concrete dolphins meant to protect the compound from a car bombing. The American flag flew from a staff above the main entrance of the embassy building that was fronted by a large fountain in the middle of well-tended gardens and olive groves. The place managed to look very modern and yet somehow traditionally Arabic.

Subandrio paid off the driver and made his way across the broad sidewalk, between the squat concrete posts. He'd purchased a Western-style business suit and shoes this morning, so that he would look presentable here, but the jacket and especially the silly tie were uncomfortable in this hot climate.

"Good morning," he said to the marine. "I'm here to see the military attaché, on a matter of some importance."

The very tall marine gave him the once-over. "May I see your identification, sir?"

Subandrio handed over his temporary passport. "My ship went down four days ago, so my papers are new."

A second marine came over and searched Subandrio's body with an electronic wand as the other marine stepped back to a call box just inside the gate and telephoned someone.

A few moments later he hung up, returned, and handed Subandrio's passport back. "The receptionist at the counter will help you, sir."

Subandrio felt the eyes of the two young soldiers on him as he passed through the gate and walked down a broad path between the trees to the main building. He had passed his first, and possibly most important, hurdle. They could just as well have denied him entry to the building.

The embassy was busy this morning, with many people coming and going. A youngish female receptionist was seated behind a low counter in the middle of a soaring atrium entrance, a computer monitor and a multiline telephone set in front of her. Two dozen people were queued down a corridor to the left, obviously applying for visas to travel to the United States.

"May I help you, sir?" the receptionist asked.

"I wish to speak to your military attaché."

"I'm terribly sorry, sir. He is currently out of the country." She smiled. "In any event, you would need to first set up an appointment, in writing."

Subandrio returned her smile. "I understand," he said pleasantly. He leaned closer so that she would be certain to hear his next words. "But you see, al-Quaida has gotten its hands on a submarine. Just four days ago. And I have the details."

The woman didn't blink. "Yes, sir. May I have your name?"

"I am Merchant Marine Captain Halim Subandrio. A citizen of Indonesia."

She picked up a telephone with an odd-looking handset and began talking. Although Subandrio was only one meter away from her he could not hear her voice. It was oddly disconcerting. He'd just stepped from one age into another, and he was no longer very sure of his decision to come here.

The receptionist hung up the phone. "It will be just a moment, sir."

A man in his mid-thirties, short, slender, mild-looking, came down the stairs from the second floor. "I'm Walt Hopper, the assistant military attaché," he said, shaking Subandrio's hand. "Why don't you come with me, and we can talk."

"Very well," Subandrio said. He followed the American back upstairs, down a short corridor, and into a room with no windows. It was furnished only with a small conference table on which was a telephone.

"You say that you have some information about an al-Quaida plot to steal a submarine, or something like that," Hopper said nonchalantly, but it was obvious that he was interested.

"I've come to sell you the information," Subandrio corrected the man. "And they're not trying to steal a submarine, they already have it. A Russian Foxtrot, I think, and crew. But what might be most interesting to you is the captain."

Hopper's eyes narrowed. "How do you know this?"

"Because I delivered the captain and some of the crew to a rendezvous with the submarine aboard my ship the *Distal Volente* four days ago."

"Can you prove this?"

"I wish to speak with your military attaché."

"He's out of the country—"

"So the young lady downstairs said. Nevertheless, I wish to speak to him. And to a representative of your CIA." Subandrio handed over his temporary passport. "My papers were lost when my crew was killed and my ship sunk from beneath me. You may check to see who I am, but with care because I believe that the owner of my ship made a deal with the Libyan government. At this moment I am supposed to be dead."

Hopper studied the passport for a long moment or two, then glanced up at a blank wall and shrugged. A few seconds later the door opened and a very tall man, with a narrow, craggy face and deep-set dark eyes under bushy eyebrows, walked in. He wore civilian clothes but his bearing was very direct.

"Captain Subandrio," the man said, coming around the table to take the passport from Hopper. He glanced at it.

"You may check my background—"

"That won't be necessary," the man said. "We know all about you. You're a smuggler, heroin sometimes, almost certainly a pirate, and therefore probably a murderer. Therefore a piece of untrustworthy shit." He tossed Subandrio's passport across the table.

"As you wish," Subandrio said, gathering his papers while hiding a little smile of triumph. He had them. He could see the excitement in their eyes, and he started to rise.

"Who is this submarine captain?" the man asked.

"Who are you?" Subandrio countered.

"Captain Russell Sterling. I'm the military attaché here."

Subandrio sat back. "I am a marked man. I will need to disappear, and that costs money."

"How much?" Hopper demanded.

Subandrio smiled. "I'll leave that to your good offices," he replied. "And those of the CIA who I think will find my story most interesting."

"The name," Sterling prompted.

"Rupert Graham, sometime captain in the British Royal Navy."

Sterling swore softly under his breath and sat down, never taking his eyes off Subandrio.

"Do you know who he is?" Hooper asked.

"Yeah," Sterling said.

"Do we have a deal?" Subandrio asked quietly.

"You're playing with fire here," Sterling said. "Al-Quaida is a hot topic for us just now. If you're lying I'm fairly certain that you'll have an accident. We might even arrange to send you to northern Pakistan. It'd be easy for you to disappear up there."

"There's no reason for me to make up such a dangerous story," Subandrio replied. "But you gentlemen must ask yourself what is a man such as Rupert Graham going to do with a submarine?"

FIFTY

□

U.S. EMBASSY, TUNIS

"Well, the man's story has merit," Sterling told CIA Chief of Tunis Station Anthony Ransom.

"He's a piece of shit, Russ," Walt Hopper observed. "You said so yourself. So why would we waste resources chasing down some cock-and-bull story?" Hopper was a CIA field officer, and worked directly for Ransom. He'd been in the Middle East for nearly five years and he was on burn-out status. Ready to go back to the CONUS.

"Because if by some odd quirk of fate he's telling the truth, even a partial truth, we could be facing a serious situation," the military attaché said. "Rupert Graham was one hell of a sub driver until he went off the deep end. Something about his wife dying in the hospital while he was out on patrol." Sterling, whose last command had been boss of a Los Angeles Class attack submarine, had a great deal of respect for men of Graham's capabilities. One submarine with a full load of nuclear warshots could start and finish a world war all by itself. Even an antiquated sub, such as the Foxtrot, could do a lot of damage with the right weapons and the right skipper.

"And that's another thing, a Westerner working for al-Quaida. I just don't see it."

"It's happened before," Sterling shot back, a little angry by what he saw as a waste of time. They didn't have enough solid information at this point to argue.

"Yeah, some pissed-off kid from Chicago who thinks he's Muhammad's son reincarnated or something."

Ransom, who had been seated quietly behind his desk, absently playing with a rubber band, looked up. "Where is the gentleman at this moment?" he asked mildly. He was in his fifties, with a nearly bald, shiny head and a red complexion. But he had deceptively warm eyes.

"I put him in the secure conference room," Hopper said.

"Is he staying in a hotel?"

"Apparently."

"Send someone to fetch his things, and then get him set up in quarters here," Ransom said. "With a babysitter, if you please, we may have him for a few days."

Hopper shifted in his chair. "You can't believe this guy. He's trying to shake us down." Ever since 9/11, selling al-Quaida stories to the CIA had practically become a cottage industry.

"We can't afford not to believe him, Walter," Ransom said.

"He's given us the position he says that he rendezvoused with the sub and his ship was sunk. We can check at least that much," Sterling said. "I'll talk to Charlie Breamer and see what his people have in the vicinity." Captain Breamer was operations officer for the Sixth Fleet based at Gaeta, Italy, which was composed of one-half a carrier battle group with about forty ships. At any given time a significant number of those ships were on maneuvers in the Mediterranean.

"It has to appear routine," the COS said. "If the Libyans are involved, as your Indonesian captain maintains, they'll be keen to keep us at arm's length. Anyway if al-Quaida has gotten their hands on a submarine, I think it's safe to assume that they'll stay in the Med. Probably hit Israel. I think I'll give Moshe the heads-up." Moshe Begin, a cousin of the former Israeli prime minister, was chief of Mossad operations in Tunisia.

"I'll give Charlie a call," Sterling said, getting up. "But you might want to consider that the Foxtrot is capable of crossing the Atlantic. Could play hell along our East Coast."

"They'd have to get past Gibraltar first," Hopper pointed out. "That's a tough nut to crack."

"Yes, it is," Sterling agreed. But not impossible for the right sub driver, he thought. It had been done before.

He walked across the hall to his own second-floor office, which looked down on one of the neatly groomed olive groves that were watered from rain catchment systems on the roofs of all the buildings, and placed an encrypted call to Sixth Fleet headquarters in Gaeta.

"Captain Breamer," the ops officer said when the circuit was secure.

"Hi, Charlie, it's Russ Sterling."

"How's the weather in Tunis?"

"Dry," Sterling said. "I have a little job for you. Might be tricky, but it could be important."

Breamer chuckled. "I didn't think you'd call on this circuit to chat about the Yankees, who, by the way, are doing shit." They were old friends with a baseball rivalry between the Yankees and the Red Sox going back to the Academy where they'd been classmates. "What do you have?"

"I want you to find and identify a shipwreck for me, off the coast of Libya. I have the approximate position, but it might not be there, the Libyans might object to our poking around, and this is pretty important but totally unofficial for the moment."

This time Breamer laughed out loud. "Why don't you give me something tough?" he asked. He said something away from the phone that Sterling did not catch, then he was back. "Okay, I can send the Simpson to take a look. She's down around the south tip of Sardinia, could be on station in about twenty-four hours." The Simpson was an Oliver Hazard Perry frigate. She carried a pair of Seahawk 60B LAMPS Mark III helicopters, and had been used for just about every mission, including drug interdiction, boardings and searches, and escort duties. She also carried underwater camera gear for sea bottom search-and-rescue missions.

"I'm not one hundred percent on my source," Sterling said.

"I can get an Orion AIP out there in under three hours to make a quick pass." The Orion P-3C land-based maritime ASW and patrol aircraft had been in service with the navy since 1969. In its latest AIP, or Aircraft Improvement Program, version delivered in 1998, the airplane had fifty-eight separate improvements, mostly electronic sensors and communications equipment. "If they find something we'll know where to direct the Simpson. If not, it'll be your call."

"Fair enough," Sterling said.

"Do you want to tell me what this is all about?"

Sterling had thought his old friend would ask that very question. Any ops officer asked to deploy resources would demand to know what they were hunting. And rightly so.

"Keep a lid on this, Charlie. But it looks as if al-Quaida might have gotten their hands on a Libyan sub."

"Son of a bitch. Is that what we're looking for?"

"We're looking for a tramp freighter sitting on the bottom. The Distal Volente, which we think the Libyans will probably try to pawn off as their sub. I need to know for sure if anything is down there, and what it is."

Breamer was silent for several moments. "I think I'll convince Nelson that it's time to run an ASW exercise in the Strait. Wouldn't do to let something like that out into the open Atlantic." Vice Admiral Kenneth Nelson was Sixth Fleet's CINC.

"No, it wouldn't," Sterling said. He liked his job at the embassy, but right now he would give his left nut to be waiting off Gibraltar to bag a Foxtrot.

ORION AIP P-3C 4457

It was a few minutes after three when the four-engine turboprop ASW aircraft reached its patrol station two hundred kilometers off the Libyan coast, north of Benghazi. Their radar and Elint equipment was painting a strong picture of three Libyan warships seventy kilometers to the south, banging away as if they were in a great rush to find something.

Lieutenant Daniel Martin pulled back on the throttle controls, as he turned the ship left and dropped to five hundred feet above the placid Mediterranean on the first leg of their search-and-identify mission.

Their preflight briefing at Gaeta had been short and to the point, exactly the way Martin liked them. A tramp freighter had apparently gone down in thirty-five hundred meters of water, and they were supposed to find it, or at least pinpoint any ferrous mass they could find at or near the latitude and longitude they had been given.

The only part Martin didn't like was the rush job. Lieutenant Commander Jerry Garcia, the squadron ops officer, wanted it done yesterday. It wasn't Martin's laid-back style to rush into things. If he'd been of that mindset he would have opted for jets out of the Academy, instead of a lumbering eighteen-wheeler prop job so slow it couldn't get out of its own way.

"We're starting our first run, Marsha," he radioed to his chief sensor operator at her ASW console in back. They were treating this as an anti-submarine-warfare mission and CPO Marsha Littlejohn had the best instincts in the fleet.

"Roger that, Skipper," she replied tersely. It was another thing Martin liked about her, she always came to the point and she never cried.

Besides the updated ASQ-114 computer system that crunched data from the ship's radar systems, the AIP Orion was equipped with infrared sensors and magnetic anomaly detectors, MAD, that could detect a mass of ferrous metal, but only along a very narrow path one thousand feet out, so it was generally ineffective for anything but pinpoint searches. She was also equipped with the blue-green laser detector, which when conditions were right, could peer down through as much as four thousand meters of seawater.

"ESMs, I want to know the minute the Libyans take an interest in us," Martin radioed.

"Aye, aye, Skipper," Petty Officer Bill Kowalski responded. "We've been briefly illuminated by at least three low-power search radars on the way in, so they know we're here. But it looks as if they're more interested in what's on the bottom than they are in us."

"That'll change once they realize we're doing the same thing."

"Roger."

"If they're looking for the same ship, one of us is in the wrong part of the pond," Lieutenant J. G Stuart Kaminski said from the right seat.

Martin glanced over at his copilot. "Let's hope our intel is better than theirs, and we find what we're looking for before they start asking questions." He keyed his helmet radio. "Talk to me, Marsha."

"All sensors are clean."

"Okay, I'm turning on our next leg," Martin said. He hauled the big airplane a hard one-eighty to the right on a new course parallel and approximately one thousand feet from their first track. Once they completed ten such legs, covering an area approximately two miles wide and five miles long, they would start a new set of tracks at ninety degrees, to form a grid. If there were anything on the bottom big enough for their sensors to detect they would find it.

All they needed was some patience and a bit of luck.

SIXTH FLEET OPERATIONS

Charles Breamer looked up from the display on his console as Sixth Fleet CINC Vice Admiral Kenneth Nelson came through the door, and he girded himself for trouble. The admiral did not look happy to be called off the golf course on his only day off in the week. He hadn't even taken the time to change into a uniform.

The P-3C that Breamer had sent out had found a large ferrous object sitting on the floor of the Mediterranean just where Sterling had said it would be. It would be up to the *Simpson* to find out exactly what was down there, but that wouldn't happen for another twenty hours or so.

The problem in Breamer's mind was that the Orion and the frigate were the only resources that the admiral had agreed to commit for the moment on what he thought would probably be nothing more than a "goddamn wild-goose chase." Nelson had been burned twice by what he had considered faulty CIA intel; once several years ago when he was chief of surface ops for the Seventh Fleet out of Yokosuka when the Agency had warned that the North Koreans had threatened to test a nuclear weapon. The CINC and vice commander were both back in the States, where it was the middle of the night. Nelson had diverted a complete carrier group from a routine training mission to make best speed possible to a point one hundred miles off the North Korean coast. The sudden rapid deployment had scared hell out of the Japanese, and although the shit had hit the fan, Nelson had ultimately been found blameless. Based on the intelligence he'd been given, his action to send a clear message to the North Koreans had been the correct one. But he'd been put through the wringer, an experience he hadn't enjoyed.

The second incident had happened just a couple of years ago, when he'd been in command of a carrier group on a mission to rescue a CIA team caught spying on Pakistan's desert nuclear testing facility. The Agency had not only convinced the White House to send an independent SEAL team—not under Nelson's command—to do the rescue, it had neglected to inform him that one of the captured CIA officers was the president's brother. He had been taken out of the loop on a mission that had had the potential to place his command in harm's way.

Nelson came directly across to Breamer's console. "I'm here, what have you got?" The admiral was a short, slightly built man, with thinning gray hair and pale, sometimes watery eyes. He looked more like a banker than a professional warrior, but he was as tough as bar steel, and his booming voice was that of a man twice his size.

Breamer got to his feet. "Sorry to bother you, sir, but the Orion found something at the position we were given," he said. He'd played football for three years at the Academy, and he towered over Nelson.

"Did they manage to find out exactly what's there?"

"No, sir. We'll have to wait for the *Simpson*, but whatever's on the bottom is approximately the same size as the tramp steamer or a Foxtrot."

"What about the Libyans?"

"We got lucky," Breamer said. "They spotted us, of course, but before they could send anyone to check us out, our guys found what they were looking for and managed to bug out."

"They're going to take a real interest when Simonetti shows up." Captain Bruce Simonetti was skipper of the *Simpson*.

Breamer risked a slight smile. "Not much they'll do about it, Admiral."

Nelson's eyes narrowed. "Don't be so sure of yourself," he warned. "It's a bad habit. Especially when you're dealing with the CIA."

"Yes, sir," Breamer said, his mood sagging. He knew what was coming next, and there wasn't a damn thing he could do about it. This was one admiral who could not be argued with, even under the best of circumstances.

"I suppose you want to deploy assets to screen the strait," Nelson said.

"I think it's wise, sir," Breamer said.

"I expect you do," Nelson replied. He was like a cobra ready to strike.

Breamer silently cursed himself for mentioning his intel for the mission had come from the CIA, but the damage had been done, and he'd be damned if he was going to roll over and play dead. "Admiral, I get paid to be your operations officer. Means I give you my best recommendations."

Nelson's mood was suddenly unreadable, but he nodded. "And they pay me to make decisions, Charlie," he said mildly. "Give me a positive ID on the wreck, and if it's not a Foxtrot, we'll seal off the strait tighter than a gnat's ass."

If it's not already too late, Breamer thought. "Yes, sir."

The admiral stepped a little closer so that no one else could hear. "You're doing a good job, I have no complaints. But you want to guard against unreliable intelligence."

FIFTY-ONE

RIYADH, SAUDI ARABIA

As the Air France Airbus from Paris turned on final for landing at Riyadh's King Khalid International Airport, McGarvey was finally able to put the last of his personal life into a safe compartment of his mind.

Actually his leavetaking from Katy hadn't been as difficult as he had feared it would be. In a large measure, he supposed, because he had told her the truth about his mission; the entire truth without hiding any of the details or the risks.

He'd always avoided such full disclosures with her, partly because what he was doing was usually classified top secret, and partly because he wanted to protect her from worry.

Although Katy hadn't demanded to know the details this time, he felt that she deserved to be told what her husband was going up against.

She had finished packing for him, and they had a few minutes for coffee in the kitchen before his cab came to take him to the airport.

"I could have driven you," she said.

McGarvey had shaken his head. "They probably know or suspect that I'm coming, and I don't want to take the chance that someone might spot you."

"They?" she said quietly, her left eyebrow rising. But then she held up her hand. "I understand."

"I'm going to assassinate Osama bin Laden."

Her breath caught in her throat and she brought a hand to her mouth, her nostrils flared, her eyes wide as if she were a wild animal caught in a hunter's crosshairs.

"We think he's hiding somewhere in Karachi, so first I'll fly to Paris, and from there to Riyadh and finally Pakistan."

"If they know you're coming, won't they set a trap for you?" Katy asked.

"I'm hoping they'll do just that," he said, his eyes never leaving his wife's. "It's the only way I'll know for sure if he's there."

She suddenly turned away. "Christ," she said softly. "And then what?" she asked. "When you find him?"

"I'll put a bullet in his brain and then get out. Depending on the circumstances I'll either run for the Indian border a hundred miles down the coast, or somehow get aboard a ship leaving the port of Karachi, or in a worst-case scenario head toward Afghanistan."

She looked back at him. "Just like that?"

He shook his head. "No, Katy, it's never *just like that*."

"Why not just put on a disguise or something and fly back home?"

"Security will be too tight," he told her. "Nor can I go to our consulate in Karachi or our embassy in Islamabad, I have to get out of the country on my own."

"Why?"

And that was the crux of the entire mission, he had thought then, talking to his wife, and now as he came in for a landing in Saudi Arabia. Plausible deniability. His mission wasn't officially sanctioned, which meant that though everyone might know the Americans had killed bin Laden, there would be no proof. Or at least none that the mission had been directed by the White House.

If he was caught by Pakistani intelligence trying to escape, he could make a convincing argument that he no longer worked for the CIA, and that he'd done this thing on his own because of the grief that bin Laden had caused him and his family over the past several years.

It was one of the reasons that he had chosen to fly commercial, out in the open, something no spook going into badland would ever do, especially one on a black mission.

"I'm on my own again," he told her.

This time she didn't look away. Her eyes filled with tears. "How much more, Kirk?" she asked. "You're going to get yourself killed one of these days, you know."

"That's always a possibility."

"Why, goddammit?"

And that was the one question that he didn't think he could answer, for the simple reason he'd never really known. Or at least he'd never been able to put it into any words that made sense, why he'd killed people for the United States over a twenty-five-year-plus career. The argument that he was a soldier simply doing his duty, striking back at his country's enemies, wouldn't wash, because on several occasions, including this one, he had no direct orders. In fact, there had been times where he'd gone directly against his orders, operating not only on his own, but illegally. There were times when he didn't give a damn about the civil rights of the men he'd gone after. He'd inflicted pain. He'd caused grief and heartache. He'd even killed a number of women.

There was seldom a night that went by when he was free of the faces of every person he'd assassinated.

A Company shrink had once glibly suggested that McGarvey had a death wish: A Hemingway complex, with the constant need to prove yourself. A constant need to gain the admiration and therefore acceptance of the people around you. And, perhaps, a latent homosexuality.

Howard Ryan had been deputy director of operations at the time, and although he and McGarvey had never gotten along, even he had sat up and taken notice, expecting that at any moment McGarvey was going to take the guy apart. Ryan's take had always been that McGarvey had become an anachronism in a world that had become too sophisticated for the blunt instrument of assassination. But of course that had been long before 9/11.

McGarvey had laughed. "I never thought of myself quite that way, but you might be right, Doc." Voltaire had written that he'd ". . . never made but one prayer to God, a very short one: 'O Lord, make my enemies ridiculous.' And God granted it."

But the man had simply been doing his job of watching out for the mental health of his flock the best he knew how. Because it was what he did.

And Katy had asked why.

"It's what I do," he'd answered, and they'd left it at that.

McGarvey had flown first class, so he was one of the first passengers to get off the airplane. His single B4 bag would be transferred to the Saudi Arabian Airlines flight to Karachi that departed in one hour, so he had no need to leave the international terminal, and therefore go through customs or passport control.

By law, alcohol could not be served in the kingdom, so there were only a few restaurants and cafeterias in the airport. McGarvey crossed the busy arrivals and departures hall to a crowded cafeteria where he ordered a tea and took it to one of the high tables. The Arab specialty had been tea for more than a millennium, so they had gotten very good at it, even better than the Brits.

Very few passengers on this side of the airport wore the traditional Muslim robes, just about everybody was in Western business suits. Saudi Arabia was where the money was, so this is where the international businessmen flocked. When the last barrel of oil was finally gone, the crowds would leave with it.

A young earnest-looking man in a dark suit with a priest's white collar came over with a glass of tea in hand. "Mind if I share your table, sir?" he asked.

"Not at all, Father," McGarvey said. "I didn't know there were any Catholics here."

"Mr. Rencke thought it was a good idea," the young man said, taking a seat. "Actually I think there might be a church in one of the burbs."

McGarvey glanced up at the television set tuned to CNN behind the bar, and let his eyes sweep the concourse without making it obvious that he was looking for someone. But it didn't seem as if anyone was taking an interest in them.

"I have a message for you, sir," the kid said. "The cock remains in its roost." He waited for a reaction. "Would you like me to repeat it?"

McGarvey shook his head. "It's not necessary." His sat phone was only good for tracking the GPS signals at short range, within fifteen or twenty miles, and wasn't encrypted, so Rencke had done the next best to get the message to him.

Before he'd left Langley they'd made sure that the position of the chip implanted in al-Turabi had not made a move toward the northern mountains that bordered Afghanistan. Rencke's message meant that al-Turabi was still in place. If he'd come to report to bin Laden, it meant the al-Quaida leader was somewhere in the city.

A lot of ifs, McGarvey thought. A lot of assumptions.

The kid looked to be in his mid-twenties at the oldest. He'd probably been trained by Liz and her husband, Todd, at the Farm. For just a moment it made McGarvey feel old. Too old?

"You're Mr. McGarvey, right sir?"

McGarvey smiled. He drank his tea, and when he was finished, he shook his head. "Nope," he said. "And I was never here."

It took a moment for the young CIA field officer to react, but then he laughed. "Yes sir, I understand," he said. He finished his tea, then slid off his stool, and started to leave. But he hesitated. "I've always wanted to use that line myself."

FIFTY-TWO

□

FFG 56 *SIMPSON*, GULF OF SIDRA

Bruce Simonetti had gone down to the Combat Information Center six hours ago when sonar had first detected what might have been air slowly leaking from a newly submerged shipwreck and he hadn't been back up to the bridge since. The noise was intermittent and very faint, almost impossible to detect even with their gas turbines spinning at dead idle, but whatever was down there was right where Sixth Fleet ops said they'd find a wreck.

"Cap'n, I've lost it again," Senior Sonar Operator CPO Donald Deutsch said.

Simonetti pulled his headset over his ears and listened to the various bottom noises, mostly biologics, that they'd been monitoring ever since they'd stumbled across what might have been a recent wreck. He pressed the expensive earphones closer, but whatever had been shedding the last of its air had gone silent.

The problem was that the Libyans had taken an interest in them the moment they'd arrived on station and started their search grid, so they'd not been able to linger over the position where they thought they'd struck gold. For most of the past six hours they had concentrated their search over a spot nearly four miles to the north, only occasionally coming back to their original find. They were on their outward track, away from the site.

His orders had been specific. Find and identify the wreck, but if possible don't let the Libyans know you've done so. Which made absolutely no sense to him, because the Libyan navy wasn't about to go up against a U.S. warship. The last time they'd done that, we'd bloodied their noses.

Simonetti took off his headset. "Okay, Donnie, secure your bottom search for now. I think we've got enough data to get us back when the coast is clear."

"Yes, sir," Deutsch said. He sat back and looked up.

"Good job," Simonetti said. He went over to Herb McCormick, his nav officer who was hunched over the electronic chart plotter. Rather than showing their position on the surface along with their course and speed, as well as other surface or subsea targets within the range of their radar and sonar, the display was now showing bottom features—those that were charted plus what their side-scan sonar was picking up.

McCormick had plotted all the contacts they'd picked up over the previous six hours. Trouble was they weren't all bunched in a neat pile as if they were coming from a specific target.

"Not much to go on," Simonetti said.

McCormick looked up from the chart. "Be my guess that we could be looking at variations in current strength, which is spreading our readings all over the place."

"Depends on what the Libyans end up doing, but we're not going to have much time on target to make a positive ID." It chapped Simonetti's ass that he couldn't just muscle his way back, and the hell with how the

Libyans reacted. These were international waters. And even if they weren't, it wouldn't make much difference to him.

"We can send down a probe on the next pass."

The ship's com buzzed. "CIC, bridge." It was Daniel Lamb, his XO. " Is the captain there?"

Simonetti picked it up. "What is it?"

"Cap'n, the Libyans are starting to get cute. You might want to come up and take a look."

Simonetti glanced over at the plotting board, which showed surface targets, and he could see exactly what Lamb was talking about. "I'm on my way," he said, and he replaced the handset in its overhead cradle. "You'll have to wing it, Herb. I want you to stand by to launch the ROV we loaded at Gaeta, and I'll need your best guess at what's down there. I expect we'll only get one pass. But I want pictures."

"Give me five minutes, Skipper."

"You've got it," Simonetti said, and he went through the forward hatch and up the half-flight of stairs to the bridge, steaming. He didn't give a damn what his orders specified, because he wasn't about to roll over and play dead, or run away with his tail between his legs.

He came from an Italian neighborhood on Chicago's South Side, where if you didn't stand up for yourself you would get slammed. He'd earned a lot of respect as a kid, because not only was he street-tough, he was smart.

The late-afternoon sun, sparkling on the nearly flat calm sea, streamed through the bridge windows on the port side. They had been bracketed on both sides by a pair of fast-attack missile boats, the Russian-built Nanuchka Class that were normally used for coastal operations. Both boats had come in very close, to less than fifty yards off, and although they were small, under two hundred feet, they carried SSM and SAM antiship missiles that could inflict severe damage on the *Simpson*, even sink her.

"Have they tried to make contact with us?" Simonetti asked.

Lamb was studying the bridge of the Libyan warship to starboard. "Not yet, Cap'n. But if they get much closer we'll be able to talk to them over the rail."

"Okay, I want them out of here now," Simonetti said.

Lamb lowered his binoculars. "We're in international waters, Bruce. They've got just as much a right to be out here as we do."

"Sound Battle Stations," Simonetti said calmly. His XO was right, but he was damned if he was going to let anyone crowd him. He grabbed a handset from the overhead as the Battle Stations Klaxon sounded throughout the ship.

"Weps, this is the captain. Spin up torpedoes one and three. I want firing point procedures as quickly as you can manage it. Targets Romeo one and two."

"This a drill, Skipper?"

"Negative, this is not a drill," Simonetti shot back. "And I want the bastard to starboard illuminated with our Phalanx radar right now."

"That'll get their attention," Lamb observed. He raised his binoculars again to study the Libyan warship to starboard.

The Simpson carried one Mark-15 Phalanx Close-in Weapons System (CIWS) gun-mounted amidships well aft. The 20mm weapon, controlled by its own targeting radar system, could fire three thousand rounds per minute. It was normally used as a last line of defense against incoming aircraft or missiles, but against smaller ships, such as the Libyan missile corvettes, it would be nothing short of devastating.

Simonetti waited a full ten seconds to make certain that the captains of both missile boats understood what was happening before he pulled the VHF mike from its bracket. "Libyan warships off my beams, turn away now, or you will be fired upon."

"Skipper," Lamb warned urgently.

Simonetti ignored his XO. "Fire one cannon shot across their bow," he ordered. He glared at his executive officer. "Now."

Lamb gave the order, and seconds later the Melara 76mm dual-purpose gun, high amidships just forward of the squat funnel, swiveled into position, and one shot was fired, splashing into the water twenty yards in front of the Libyan warship.

The effect was immediate. Both ships suddenly peeled off and accelerated as if they were scalded cats.

Simonetti grabbed the ship's phone, and called his nav officer in the CIC. "Herb, this is the captain. What's your best guess for a course and distance to the wreck?"

"One-eight-six degrees, let's say two miles to the middle of the plotted positions," McCormick replied.

"Soon as we make the turn, launch the ROV."

"Cap'n, if we make anything over five knots, the cable will break. It wasn't meant for that kind of a strain."

"Understood," Simonetti said. "Look sharp."

"Shall we stand down from battle stations?" Lamb asked when Simonetti hung up the phone.

"Negative," the captain said. "Helm, come right to new course one-eight-six, make your speed All Ahead Slow."

"Aye, sir. New course one-eight-six, All Ahead Slow."

The *Simpson* came hard right, and immediately began to slow down as her turbines were spooled back. The Perry Class ships, which were introduced to the fleet in '75, were capable of making around thirty knots, but what was impressive was the acceleration her twin gas turbines provided. If need be, she could get to where she wanted to go in a big hurry.

While they headed slowly back to the south, Simonetti took his XO aside so that the others on the bridge could not hear. "Our orders came directly from Nelson, who wants answers, not bullshit. If that means going head-to-head with the Libyans then so be it."

"Jesus, Bruce, would you have shot at them if they hadn't backed off?" Lamb asked.

"Damn straight," Simonetti said. "I want to keep a close eye on those bastards. I don't want them within ten miles of us."

"Aye, Captain," Lamb said, and he went over to the radar set to take a look at what the Libyan missile boats, already hull down on the horizon, were doing.

It took more than twenty minutes for the ROV to approach the bottom, and for the *Simpson* to reach the outermost plots for the wreck. Within three minutes McCormick was on the coms.

"Cap'n, we have a positive ID," he said.

"Go ahead."

"She's a freighter, looks fairly well intact. Name on the stern is the *Distal Volente, Monrovia, Liberia.*"

"Bingo," Simonetti said. "Take some pictures and then retrieve the ROV. When she's aboard let me know and we'll get out of here."

"Will do, Skipper."

"Good job, Herb."

U.S. EMBASSY, TUNIS

Sterling walked across the corridor to Tony Ransom's office. The CIA chief of station was getting set to leave for the day, and it didn't look as if he were in a very good mood. His number two, Walt Hopper, had been drinking a lot lately, and three nights ago he had made an ass of himself with a local cop who'd stopped him for DUI. Word had got back to Langley, and Ransom had been told point-blank to control his field personnel.

It was a reprimand on a so-far-spotless record that Ransom had hoped would carry him at least as far as DDO.

"I got a call from Charlie Breamer."

Ransom was in the act of putting on his jacket. He hesitated for a moment, then pulled it on. "Oh?" he said. "His people find something already?"

"The Orion they sent out yesterday picked up a mass of metal sitting on the bottom just where Captain Subandrio said his ship was sunk. One of Charlie's boats put down an ROV on the site. That was about an hour ago. They got a positive ID. The wreck is the *Distal Volente*."

Ransom shook his head. He looked almost bemused, as if he were having some difficulty in digesting what he'd just been told. "He was telling the truth after all."

"Looks like it," Sterling said. "I think we have to consider the possibility that he told the truth about the other thing. Al-Quaida has got a Foxtrot submarine and a first-rate captain."

"Moshe didn't seem too worried," Ransom said. "But that could have been an act."

"This should be sent to Langley," Sterling suggested.

"You're right, of course," the COS said. "First thing in the morning."

"I think you should call it in right now, Tony," Sterling said.

"Okay, assuming that the ROV took pictures, I want to see them before I do anything. This thing, if it pans out, is going to get a whole bunch of people real excited. I want to be absolutely certain that we're all on the same page." Ransom gathered his cell phone and put it in his pocket. "I'll be at home. Get me the pictures and I'll call Dave Whittaker and give him the heads-up tonight."

Sterling figured it was the best he was going to do, although he would stop by to see the ambassador. Maybe they could make an end run around the CIA. "What about Subandrio?"

"Get the pictures and we'll take care of him in the morning," Ransom said. "What's the going rate now? A hundred thousand?"

"Something like that."

"I'll talk to Dave about that as well," Ransom said.

Sterling turned and was about to leave when the COS stopped him.

"This is a CIA issue now, Russ. We'll keep it that way. If and when the ambassador needs to be told, I will be the one doing the telling. Clear?"

FIFTY-THREE

☐

KARACHI

The GPS tracker, disguised as a nonencrypted sat phone, raised no eyebrows at the customs counter in the Jinnah International terminal, for the simple reason that so many businessmen carried the phones these days they'd become commonplace. But security was tight as it had been for a long time. McGarvey's luggage was X-rayed, then hand-searched by customs officers, as was his body after he'd taken off his shoes and his jacket and turned out his pockets. His hefty Philippe Patek chronometer was examined by two different officials before he was allowed to put it back on his wrist.

It was early evening when he shouldered his bag and headed across the busy concourse to the taxi ranks out front. Ostensibly he was here, under his own name, to do freelance research for the State Department's upgrade of its Pakistan country guide blue book. He wasn't carrying a diplomatic passport, nor did he have the credentials of a journalist, so he'd been given no preferential treatment. On the other hand he'd not become the center of anyone's attention. So far.

Although he thought he could feel eyes on him, people watching his every move, he'd spotted no one obvious. But if bin Laden's people didn't know that he had arrived in the country yet, they would certainly get the heads-up when he checked into the Pearl Continental downtown where Rencke had booked him an executive suite for ten days.

For now he was a man apparently in no hurry, here in Pakistan to spend some of his government's money. Islamabad might buy the fiction, though al-Quaida would certainly not.

Bin Laden would know for certain that there was only one reason Mc-Garvey had come back. The question was how arrogant the man had become; how much of the fiction he and his people had created about his powers had he begun to believe. Enough so that he thought he was invincible? A spider that was willing to let its prey come into the web?

Just outside the automatic doors, McGarvey stepped to one side and held up well out of the steady stream of passengers who had just gotten off three flights that had arrived within minutes of one another, and from the mob of cabbies who descended upon them.

The night was warm and humid, with a mélange of smells unique to this port city; burned kerojet, the sea, diesel fumes, rotting fish and garbage, and some indefinable combination of spices and unpleasant human odors.

An older-looking, ragtag, stoop-shouldered man, wearing a dark suit coat over a dirty white shirt, baggy trousers, and flip-flops, approached from the end of the cab ranks, a green baseball cap in his left hand. "Good evening, sir. May I offer my cab into the city?" His heavily accented English was barely understandable.

"I'll wait until the crowd thins, thank you," McGarvey said.

"Yes, but my cab is clean and my rates are reasonable."

Rencke had arranged an initial contact, but this was Karachi and the messenger could have been compromised, though the man's encounter key words were correct.

"Very well," McGarvey said, and he followed the cabbie to the far end of the cab ranks and then across four lanes of the very busy departure road.

Police were directing traffic, but nobody seemed to be paying any attention to McGarvey, though the feeling that he was being watched continued to grow; as if someone were sighting a rifle on the back of his head.

He tossed his bag in the backseat of the cab, and climbed in as the driver got behind the wheel. "The Pearl Continental on Club Road."

"Yes, sir," the driver said and they headed into Karachi, merging smoothly with the rushing traffic that consisted not only of cabs and buses, but of horse-drawn carriages, human-powered rickshaws, and bicycles.

A small leather case lay on the floor behind McGarvey's feet. He picked it up and opened it. His pistol, two extra magazines of ammunition, a bulky encrypted satellite phone, an envelope containing ten thousand dollars cash, and another containing three passports—one U.S., one British, and a third French—had been sent over in a diplomatic pouch earlier today. The cabbie was a contract worker for the U.S. Consulate here.

"Good flight over, sir?" the driver asked, all traces of his Pakistani accent gone, replaced by what sounded like California to McGarvey.

"Bumpy," McGarvey said. "Thanks for my things. Do I know you?"

"I don't think so, Mr. McGarvey, but I know Todd Van Buren, your son-in-law from the Farm." The driver looked in the rearview mirror. "Name's Joe Bernstein."

"Pleasure," McGarvey said. "Anyone behind us?"

"Thought I might have spotted the same motorbike that was parked down the block from the consulate this afternoon. But it's gone now."

"How about at the airport?"

"You came in clean, unless someone was on the same flight."

"It was vetted in Riyadh," McGarvey said absently, his mind elsewhere. There should have been someone at the airport. The motorbike was a possibility, but according to Bernstein it was no longer behind them.

"Any idea how long you'll be here, sir?" Bernstein was asking.

"Couple days," McGarvey replied. They had to know he was coming.

Bernstein handed a business card over the back of the seat. "If you need anything at arm's length from the consulate, call me at the cab company. It's an answering service."

McGarvey focused on the driver. "What's your job here?"

"Just a driver with big ears," Bernstein said. "You'd be surprised what people will say in the back of a taxi. They think they're invisible."

"You speak the language?"

"Fluently. My grandmother was a Pakistani. Didn't move to the States until she was twenty-five."

"Then keep your ears open for me, Joe. I want to know if my name comes up."

"Will do, Mr. M. I'll leave a message at the hotel for you. A chalk mark on the FedEx box in the lobby."

They rode the rest of the way into the city in silence. Once they passed the Chaukhandi Tombs and got off Hospital Road into the center of downtown, traffic seemed to increase tenfold, and everyone seemed to be moving at a frantic pace, as if they needed to get off the streets as quickly as possible lest something catch up with them. Pakistan had been a nation in turmoil from its beginning in 1947.

Twenty minutes later, they pulled into the driveway of the Pearl, where a bellman came over to open the cab door for McGarvey.

"Need anything, give me a call," Bernstein said.

"Could be I'll need to get out of Dodge in a hurry."

"When?"

"I don't know yet, but if the need arises it'll be all of a sudden."

"I'll work on it," Bernstein said as the bellman opened the door.

McGarvey got out of the cab, handed the bellman his B4 bag, and carrying the small leather case with his weapon, phone, cash, and passports, entered the hotel. The lobby was moderately busy with people checking in, and others at the hotel for dinner.

He checked in at the desk with his own American Express card, but the clerk refused it.

"It's not necessary, Mr. McGarvey. Your wife has already checked in, two hours ago."

McGarvey was taken aback. He simply couldn't imagine Katy being here. It made no sense. But a sudden understanding dawned on him, and his anger spiked. "Did she leave a message?"

"Yes, sir. Mrs. McGarvey said that she would be waiting for you in the coffee shop," the clerk said. "It's just across the lobby to your left." He glanced at his computer screen. "Your dinner reservations are for eight."

"Anything else?" McGarvey asked, holding his anger in check.

"No, sir," the clerk said. "Shall I have your bag taken up?"

"Yes, please do," McGarvey said tightly, and he took the room key card from the clerk.

He handed the bellman ten dollars and made his way across the lobby past the piano player, and down two stairs to the nearly empty coffee shop. He spotted Gloria seated in a corner booth, and it was all he could do not to turn on his heel, retrieve his bag, and check into another hotel before he got her killed. She had no idea of the magnitude of her foolishness following him here. And he was disappointed in Otto for allowing this to happen, because without him he didn't think she would have made it this far.

She looked up as he approached, a big smile on her face that faded almost immediately when she saw his mood.

He didn't sit down. "Let's go, dear," he said.

The waiter came over. "May I bring you something, sir?"

"No," McGarvey said. "We're leaving." He stepped aside for Gloria to get up, then took her elbow and propelled her out of the coffee shop and across the lobby to the elevators. He knew that he was hurting her arm, but she didn't say anything, or try to pull away. They didn't speak on the way up to the tenth floor, nor did he release his grip.

No one was in the corridor when they got off the elevator. McGarvey let them into the suite, and secured the safety chain. All the lights were on, and the only sound was from a slowly moving ceiling fan, but before Gloria could say anything he motioned for her to hold her silence.

He took his pistol out of the leather case, checked to make sure that it was ready to fire, then laid the case on the hall table before he hurriedly checked out the large sitting room, huge bedroom, two palatial bathrooms, and closets. His B4 bag was laid out on the king-size bed, and Gloria's bag was hanging in one of the closets.

It was possible that since Gloria's arrival had probably been unexpected there'd been no time to plant bugs in the suite, something he'd hoped might happen. He'd planned on giving some disinformation to whoever was listening, which wasn't likely now.

He walked slowly back into the sitting room, where Gloria had remained in the entry hall. "What are you doing here?" he asked. He laid his pistol on the coffee table, and pulled off his jacket and tossed it over the back of the big sectional.

"I'm your backup in case something goes wrong," she said, coming into the sitting room. "There's beer in the minibar."

"You're leaving first thing in the morning," he said, going to the floor-to-ceiling windows that looked toward the parliament building and courthouse complex. From this vantage point it could have been any large city at night; anonymous and therefore safe.

"Otto thought me coming over was a good idea."

McGarvey looked at her reflection in the dark glass. "Otto's smart but naïve and you're a beautiful woman, you could have convinced him of anything."

"I resent that," she flared. "I'm a damned good field officer, and I don't need to use sex to get what I want."

"Perhaps not, but you do try," McGarvey said. He turned back to her. "What exactly do you think you can do for me by being here? You're not my wife, and the opposition knows that, so they'll have to guess that you're a CIA agent."

"That's right. If I can get them to watch me, you can make an end run."

"Is that what you were taught at the Farm?"

"Sleight of hand? Yes. It works."

"Not in the real world," McGarvey told her. He was tired already, and he had the rest of the night ahead of him. "I want you to stay here in the room tonight, and first thing in the morning you can take a cab out to the airport, catch the first flight out. But I don't want you to say anything to anyone here in the hotel. As far as anyone here is concerned, you're Mrs. McGarvey heading out to do some shopping."

Gloria's eyes were suddenly bright. "Are you going out tonight?"

McGarvey was having a hard time believing she wasn't a complete fool. "Yes, but you're staying put."

"I can help—"

"You'd get us both killed."

"¡Hijo de puta!" she shouted. "I want to help you."

McGarvey was across the room to her in three steps. He shoved her down on the couch, his knee between her legs, and he held her there against her struggles, his face inches from hers. "I work alone," he said harshly.

She tried to push him away, but he was too strong.

"You have no idea what I'm capable of doing. How easy it is for me to kill."

"You're a soldier—"

"No, goddammit. I'm an assassin. A thing that my own country can't acknowledge. Something my wife despises. Something that if my neighbors knew would send them running away from me in absolute terror. Something that each time I recite the Pledge of Allegiance I have to skip the words 'under God,' because I'm not a hypocrite, too. Because of me my wife has been kidnapped, beaten, tortured, and nearly killed. My daughter was nearly killed when she was pregnant. She lost that baby and can't have others. All because of me."

Gloria was looking up at him, her rage gone as quickly as it had come. "Kirk," she said softly. "I'm in love with you."

McGarvey released his hold on her and got up. "Go home."

"I love you."

"Before you get me killed like you did your partner."

FIFTY-FOUR

□

SS *SHEHAB*

It was shortly after ten in the evening on the surface when the Russian-built Foxtrot Class diesel-electric submarine, drifting slowly at a depth of one hundred meters, began to pick up a sharp increase in traffic. They had passed Europa Point, most commonly known as the Rock of Gibraltar, four hours ago and from their present position it was less than fifteen kilometers farther to the west before they would clear Cape Spartel on the African continent and finally be out into the open Atlantic.

Graham stood in the passageway around the corner from the control room from where he could look over the shoulders of his two sonar operators, and still issue orders to his fire control crew.

"Are you picking up any military traffic?" he asked the Libyan operator who was even better than the Iranian officer who'd come off the *Distal Volente*.

"It's hard to tell, sir, with all the clutter up there," Ensign Isomil answered respectfully. Ever since the incident yesterday when Graham had punished the young operator for insubordination, and had sidestepped al-Abbas's attempt at mutiny, everyone aboard the boat had sharpened up. The transformation had occurred even sooner than Graham had hoped it would. For the first time he was beginning to think that they had more than an even chance to succeed.

"I'm less interested in the ship types than I am if you're hearing any active sonar. Especially at the western end of the strait."

The Libyan officer looked up, and shook his head. "Nothing so far, Captain. Do you think they are looking for us?"

"It's a possibility," Graham said. "But once we clear Spartel we should be home free. So I want you to pay special attention to any target that might even hint at being military."

"That would mean they knew we didn't scuttle our boat, and that we're still alive," the sonar operator said.

Graham's Iranian sonar man looked up as if to say that the Libyan had no idea what they were facing, and Graham nodded.

He had his crew and now he meant to keep them sharp through the strait and all the way across the Atlantic. His Iranians knew that their chances for survival were slim, but they were fanatics for the cause, unlike the Libyans who were merely following orders. It was one of the reasons he had promoted Captain Ziyax to work as his XO rather than kill the man. It did his arrogant Iranian crew good to take orders from a Libyan, whom they considered inferior, as well as an infidel who scarcely rated any consideration.

It was Graham's intention to maintain the tension between them. Besides being a useful means to keep them on their toes, the mix would be interesting over the next ten days or so, before he was gone and they were all dead.

"The first one to find and identify a warship will become senior sonar man," Graham said.

A dark expression came over the Iranian's face, but Graham turned and stepped back around the corner into the control room.

Ziyax, who'd been studying their plot at the chart table, looked up. Like everyone else aboard he was tired. None of them had gotten any sleep in at least thirty-six hours. "We're nearing the cape. How's it look topside?"

"Busy," Graham said. "I want tubes one and two loaded with Mark fifty-sevens."

Ziyax straightened up, and al-Abbas at the ballast panel looked over his shoulder.

"What is our target?" the Libyan sub captain asked.

Graham leaned around the corner. "Are there any large civilian contacts on the way through the strait just ahead of us?"

"Yes, sir. Could be a luxury liner, I'm not sure. But she's very large. Four props. Bearing dead on our bow, on the same heading, but making twenty knots. Designate target as Sierra one-seven."

"All Ahead Flank," Graham ordered.

"Aye, Captain. All Ahead Flank," Chief of Boat al-Hari repeated the order.

"I want a firing solution on Sierra one-seven," Graham told Ziyax. "Look smartly now, if you please."

Ziyax wanted to argue, it was plain on his face, but he hesitated for only a moment. He keyed the ship's intercom. "Torpedo room, con. Load one and two with Mark five-sevens. Weapons will have the presets momentarily."

The Russian-made MK-57s were very old, free-running HE antiship warshots that under the best of circumstances couldn't possibly sink a very large modern ship, which Graham figured Sierra 17 to be. But they could inflict enough damage to create a great deal of confusion on the surface, because no one in their right mind would possibly suspect that a civilian ship had been attacked by a submarine.

"You're not trying to sink her, are you?" Ziyax asked.

"If I had the proper weapons I would," Graham replied sharply. "Hit her in the stern. I want to take out her steering pods."

Ziyax gave Graham a blank look of incomprehension.

"Unless I miss my guess she'll be the Queen Mary II," Graham explained. "No rudders, two of her four propellers are mounted on moveable pods for steering. Quite ingenious, actually. She was preparing to leave the eastern Med last week. Just our luck."

"If we miss, and put a hole in her stern, she could sink."

"More's the pity if we don't miss," Graham said sharply. The Queen was American-owned but British registry, and therefore in his mind more than fair game.

In broad strokes it was the same discussion he'd had with bin Laden two months ago. Al-Quaida had all but languished since 9/11. Western intelligence agencies were doing too good a job of rounding up or killing some key lieutenants and advisers, so that recruiting for the organization was way down. And most of the new freedom fighters were little better than ignorant thugs, in it for the glory and not for the jihad.

"The infidels have been beset by contentious elections, ongoing battles in their Congress, one scandal after the other, and best of all a plague of natural disasters," bin Laden said.

"The Old Testament in living color," Graham replied dryly. They were alone, walking on the Syrian Desert northeast of Damascus, during one of bin Laden's highly orchestrated visits to their training camps.

"I tolerate your blasphemy only because you are a good soldier for the struggle," bin Laden said conversationally.

"And I tolerate your religious mumbo jumbo only because you provide me with the means to strike back at the bloody bastards," Graham retorted. He had no fear of the al-Quaida leader, because he had no fear of dying.

"Then we are in symbiosis," bin Laden said, stopping and turning to face Graham. "For the moment."

"So long as I continue to kill the infidel for you."

"Not for me," bin Laden corrected. "But yes, so long as you continue to kill the infidel—men, women, children, there are no innocents—anywhere at any time, especially when they least suspect that death is coming for them, you will have my support and my blessing."

"Fail, and I die?"

Bin Laden shrugged, but said nothing.

Bloody well have to catch me first, Graham thought. *And that would not be such an easy task.*

"If you please, Captain," Graham told Ziyax. "We'll shoot on sonar bearings. She's too big a target even for an inept crew to miss."

Ziyax bridled at the new insult, but went over to the weapons console to see about the firing solution: the bearing, angle of elevation, and speed numbers to be dialed into the two torpedoes.

"Captain," the Libyan sonar operator called out.

Graham stepped around the corner from the control room. "What is it?"

"Distant contact, relative bearing three-five-zero, maybe fifteen kilometers, designate it Sierra one-eight." Ensign Isomil was pressing his earphones close. He looked up. "There. It's definitely a warship, sir, her sonar went active again."

Graham snatched a spare headset and plugged it in the console. At first all he could make out was the tremendous whoosh-whoosh of the QM 2's four big props, which drowned our everything around them. He was about to ask the young Libyan to filter out as much background noise as possible, when he heard the distinctive ping of a distant warship.

It was British. He was sure of it. Everyone's sonar signals were distinctive.

"I've got it," Graham said. The ship had only pinged once and then had stopped. "How often does he do that?"

"Every fifteen seconds or so," Shihabi said.

"Can you tell if his range or bearing are changing?"

"Stand by, Captain," the Libyan sonar man said.

"Captain, your weapons are preset and warm," Ziyax called from the con.

"Make the tubes ready in all respects," Graham called out. This consisted of flooding the torpedo tubes and opening the outer doors, which made a lot of noise. But with the QM 2 churning up sea, a noise like four 747s at takeoff, there was no chance that the British warship would hear a thing.

"Yes, sir," Ziyax responded crisply.

Another ping radiated from somewhere ahead, but this time it sounded much louder to Graham. "Closer?"

"Yes, sir," Isomil said. "She's heading directly for us."

Ziyax was suddenly in the corridor at Graham's shoulder. "Shall we rig for silent running?" he asked.

Graham held his temper in check. "We shall not," he said. "Are my weapons ready to fire?"

"I thought it best that we hold off," Ziyax said. He'd heard the sonar man's report.

"Why is that, Captain?" Graham asked loudly enough so that everyone in sonar and in the control room could hear him.

"There is an ASW warship out there, obviously looking for us."

"That's correct," Graham said. "What do you suppose their sonar operators are picking up?"

Ziyax opened his mouth to speak, but then glanced at the waterfall display on the Feniks sonar set tracking the QM 2. The signal was overwhelmingly solid. He turned back to Graham. "Sorry," he mumbled.

"Sorry about what, Captain?" Graham asked tightly. "Speak up, so everyone can hear you."

"I was wrong, and you were right. We are invisible behind the big passenger liner."

"You are relieved of duty, Captain," Graham ordered. "Wait for me in the wardroom, I'll be with you shortly."

Ziyax turned without another word and went aft.

"Assam!" Graham shouted.

"Yes, Captain," Assam al-Abbas replied.

"Take the con."

"Yes, sir," al-Abbas said.

Graham turned back to Isomil. "You're chief sonar man as of this moment. Don't let me down."

"No, sir," the young Libyan ensign answered crisply.

FIFTY-FIVE

□

HMS *CUMBERLAND*

Fifteen kilometers due west, the Broadsword Class British ASW frigate *Cumberland* was heading into the Strait of Gibraltar. She was on the alpha leg of her patrol station, which was meant to ensure a heads-up for anything emerging from the Mediterranean that might pose a possible threat to the United Kingdom or NATO. Her area of patrol took her endlessly back and forth through the strait fifty kilometers east of Gibraltar, then back out into the Atlantic fifty kilometers beyond Cape Spartel.

It was, the *Cumberland*'s skipper, Lieutenant Commander Willie Townsend thought, nearly as boring an assignment as he imagined being the captain of a nuclear missile submarine would be. Lying on the bottom of the ocean for weeks on end with nothing to do but play missile drills for a war that would never happen, and with no chance of getting out on deck for an occasional breath of fresh air, had to be nothing short of frustrating.

The one advantage of surface operations was the occasional sight of something really spectacular, such as the magnificent QM 2, which they had passed port-to-port with whistles a half hour ago. The luxury liner, which was two and a half times *Cumberland*'s 430 feet on deck, had been all ablaze with lights, and although it was well after 2200 hours, Townsend had been certain he'd heard music and laughter coming from the grand lady. She had finished her Mediterranean cruise and was heading back to Liverpool to take on passengers for her Atlantic crossing to New York.

"Bridge, sonar."

Townsend answered the ship's intercom. "This is the captain."

"I'm picking up a definite bogey, sir. Computer says it's probably a Foxtrot."

Earlier this evening when they'd first started their inbound track, sonar thought it may have picked up a very weak target on passive coming out of the strait, and Townsend had authorized an active sonar search. By then however the *Queen* was making so much racket that finding anything was impossible, and they'd secured the search. Once they were past and in clean water, they'd deployed their very sensitive Plessy COMTASS towed array.

"Who the hell is patrolling Foxtrots these days?" Townsend asked his XO, Lieutenant Howard Granger.

"The Libyans, I'd suspect," Granger replied. He was the intellectual among the officers. The crew wanted him to try out for the American television show *Jeopardy!* "They still have four of the boats in service."

"What's he doing?" Townsend asked the sonar officer.

"He's turned southwest, Captain, and it sounds as if he's putting his foot in it."

"Very well, he's not our problem. But I want you to keep track of him for as long as possible. If he turns north, I want to know."

"Yes, sir."

"Should we call this one in?" Granger asked.

"We'd best do it," Townsend said. "Heaven's only knows what the Libyans are doing so far from home. But it's probably not good."

SIXTH FLEET HEADQUARTERS

Charlie Breamer was just getting set to turn in for the night after a long, contentious day, when his bedside telephone rang. He'd gotten the ROV pictures of the *Distal Volente* lying on the bottom where the Foxtrot should have been from Bruce Simonetti before dinner, but he'd had to sit on them. The admiral had left for the day, and his instructions had been explicit: He was not to be disturbed for anything other than an all-out emergency. And God help the son of a bitch whose idea of what constituted an emergency was different than the admiral's.

"Breamer," he answered, and his wife stirred but didn't awaken. He glanced at the nightstand clock. It was one minute after midnight.

"Tony Parker, here. Sorry to disturb you at such a filthy hour." Commander Parker was chief of operations for the British arm of NATO's STANAVFORLANT—Standing Naval Forces Atlantic. He and Breamer were old friends, having participated in numerous NATO exercises all through the Cold War years.

"Good evening, Tony, what's keeping you up so late?" Breamer asked. He was sure that whatever the reason for Parker's call, it wasn't social.

"I think we've found that wreck your people were banging around north of Benghazi looking for."

"What boat's that?"

"The Foxtrot that the Libyans are claiming they scuttled."

"I hadn't heard that one," Breamer said. In fact, he'd gotten that bit of information from Russell Sterling in Tunis who'd gotten it from the CIA a full hour before the same message had arrived on his desk.

"I understand that you have to protect your sources and all that, especially the way your boss thinks about Langley. But listen, Charlie, one of our frigates spotted a submerged Foxtrot sneaking out of the strait into the open Atlantic not more than an hour ago."

Breamer's grip on the phone tightened. "Are you guys tracking her?"

"Out of our AO. Once she cleared the cape, she headed southwest apparently in a big hurry." Parker hesitated. "We have no idea what the Libyans are doing out of the Med, but since they're heading to your side of the pond we thought you'd like the heads-up."

"You say she's headed southwest?" Breamer asked.

"Yes, maybe South America," Parker confirmed. "But that boat does have rudder."

U.S. EMBASSY, TUNIS

It was a few minutes after one in the morning local when Sterling took the call from Gaeta in his office, where he had been looking at the grainy photographs of the *DistalVolente* he'd received earlier this evening. He'd not been able to sleep worrying about Graham breaking out into the Atlantic with a submarine, and his boss's refusal to pass a threat assessment along to Langley.

In fact, Ransom had even refused to send the message even after they'd received a twixt from Langley informing all relevant stations that the Libyans had announced they'd scuttled a surplus Foxtrot. Unless it could be conclusively proven otherwise, he wasn't going out on a limb.

"Good heavens, Russell, do you have any notion what sort of a fright that would cause? Homeland Security would be over the moon." Ransom had shaken his head. "Before we raise the red flag we will make dead certain we have the facts. *All* the facts."

Hopper had been no help, either, and had left early for a party at the Russian embassy where he was working an FSO he suspected was a junior intelligence officer.

"Your Foxtrot's in the Atlantic," Breamer said.

"What happened?"

"We got it from a British ASW frigate patrolling the strait. Your Captain Graham followed the QM 2 out, and it wasn't until the last minute that she was detected. But by then the boat was out of the Brit's area of operations, so her skipper logged the contact. Fortunately he called it home, and the word was passed along to us a few minutes ago."

"I thought your people were going to watch out for us?" Sterling asked. In the old days this would have been called a cluster fuck, but then as now these kinds of screwups usually started from the top.

"Nelson wouldn't budge," Breamer said. "No proof."

"I have the same problem here."

"I'll send you a hard copy," Breamer offered. "But it might be a moot point. The Brits said the sub was heading southwest. They figured South America. They've put their Atlantic Fleet on low alert, though Christ only knows what they think the Libyan navy might want with the Falklands is beyond understanding."

"You didn't tell them about Graham?" Sterling said. "He was one of their own, after all."

"I'll be in enough shit if it comes out I called you," Breamer said. "I'll leave the rest of it to Washington. Anyway, it'll take your Foxtrot ten days or more to make it across. So at least time is on our side."

"Okay, Charlie, thanks for the heads-up. I owe you one."

"What are you going to do?"

"I don't know, yet," Sterling said. "But I'm not going to sit on it."

"Good luck," Breamer said.

"Yeah thanks, you too."

CIA HEADQUARTERS

Rencke was on the verge of admitting failure. There were only three missing or unaccounted for Kilo submarines, although his preliminary sources were sure that all three boats had been cut up for scrap ten years ago. It was now simply a matter of verification.

Yet he couldn't understand what he'd done wrong. Something like this had never happened to him. Not even close. And what was so frustrating was that he knew he was right about everything else. Rupert Graham was the star witness in the case for an al-Quaida submarine mission.

He was at his desk in computer country, racking his brains, all of his screens showing pale lavender, when an incoming call on an outside line lit up in the corner of one of his monitors. His caller ID and search program locked onto the number in less than a half second, and he sat up.

He answered on the second ring. "Commander Daniel Monroe, good evening," he said, careful to keep the excitement out of his voice. "How did the Office of Naval Investigation Middle East get this number?"

Monroe hesitated for just a moment. "It wasn't easy, Mr. Rencke. But the CIA's not the only outfit in town with resources."

"Tell me you're not calling about Gitmo," Rencke said.

"Sir?"

"Then it must be *Unterseeboot*."

"Sir, I'm not following you—" Monroe said, but then he stopped. "You mean a submarine? Yes, sir."

"Bingo," Rencke said softly. "What kind of a submarine? Not a Kilo?"

"No, sir. She's a Foxtrot. The Libyans reported they'd scuttled one of their boats, but she made it through the Strait of Gibraltar about two hours ago."

Rencke brought up a search algorithm for the billions of bytes of data that had come into the Building in the past twenty-four hours. Almost immediately he came up with the announcement that the Libyan government had filed with the UN Security Council early this morning.

He had completely blown it.

"Bad dog, bad, bad dog," he muttered. "Where was she headed, Commander Daniel Monroe, and why did you call me with the glad tidings? What makes you think that I care?"

"Sir, a friend of mine works as the military attaché at our embassy in Tunis. He found out about the boat, but the chief of station there is dragging his feet, and Sixth Fleet wasn't interested. It was a British warship on patrol in the strait that stumbled across the Libyan sub."

"Why'd you call me?" Rencke pressed. He brought up Russell Sterling's file. The man had been a sub driver in a previous life.

"Not you specifically, sir. But he wanted me to pass along this information, plus a name, to someone in the CIA who might be able to do something. And you have the reputation, sir."

Rencke wanted to laugh, but he couldn't. He'd missed so friggin' much. He was so stupid. "Plus a name," he said. "Let me guess. Rupert Graham?"

The line was silent for a long moment. When Commander Monroe came back, he sounded subdued. "Jesus Christ," he said softly.

"Nope. He was the guy who walked on the water, ours sails under the water," Rencke said. "Did the British do a track? Do they know where he was heading?"

"Southwest, sir."

"Thank you," Rencke said. "And thank your old Annapolis pal, Russell Sterling."

He broke the connection, and allowed his mind to go completely blank for a second or two, wiping the slate clean, as if he were rebooting a computer. When he focused again, he began typing, his fingers flying over the keyboard, his frizzy red hair pointing in every direction as if he were a mad prodigy pounding a complex melody on a concert grand piano.

FIFTY-SIX

KARACHI'S FISH HARBOR

With a population of ten million and growing, Pakistan's principal seaport was considered to be one of the most dangerous cities on the planet. More murders, kidnappings, rapes, beatings, thefts, and incidents of street crime and gang violence happened here 24/7 than anywhere else. And only in postwar Baghdad had there been more suicide bombings than in Karachi.

It was bin Laden and al-Quaida. President Musharraf's government publicly opposed the terrorists so that it could continue to receive much-needed financial aid from the United States, while an overwhelming majority of the people supported the *jihad*.

Downtown was bright and modern; tall steel and glass skyscrapers rose from wide boulevards such as M. A. Jinnah Road, named after the father of modern Pakistan, and Raja Ghazanarfar Street, which passed the Saddar Bazaar, the city's main and most colorful shopping center.

But elsewhere, Karachi was mostly a city of incredibly filthy and dangerous slums that coexisted with mosques of delicacy and beauty and museums of exquisite Islamic antiquity. Along the harbor's West Wharf with its fishing fleets, textile and carpet manufacturers and exporters, tanneries and leather works, was the worst slum of all, known as Fish Harbor.

From here, in the middle of cardboard and tarpaper shacks, jumbled rows of rusted-out shipping containers, and the occasional compound of hovels protected behind tall razor-wire-topped concrete block walls, the downtown lights cast an eerie otherworldly glow.

McGarvey, driving a small, dark Fiat he'd rented through the hotel concierge, pulled up and parked in the deeper shadows behind a large warehouse, locked up and dark for the night. He was below the rail line and Mauripur Road, which was the main truck thoroughfare for the commercial district. It was past midnight, and from where he sat, wishing for the first time in a long while that he hadn't quit smoking, he had a clear sightline to a walled compound at the end of the filthy street.

He picked up his sat phone tracker from the seat beside him, and entered three twos and then the pound key. It was the code for the microscopic GPS chip implanted in al-Turabi. Within a second or two the nearest Keyhole satellite picked up the signal and fixed its location within a couple of meters. Overlaid on the sat phone's screen was an electronic street map covering an area two hundred meters on a side. The red dot showing al-Turabi's current location was inside the compound at the end of the block.

It was difficult to believe that bin Laden would actually take refuge in a place like this. But then the man had lived in caves in Afghanistan that were nothing from the outside, while inside they were reasonably well heated and ventilated and more or less comfortable. If this compound were a semipermanent home for the Saudi billionaire, it could very well be fitted out in luxury.

He rolled down the window and held his breath for a long moment to listen. In the far distance there was a siren, but here except for the muffled sound of an electric motor running—perhaps a generator or an air conditioner—the night was almost perfectly still.

Something was wrong.

Just beyond the compound, an open field sloped up to a reinforced embankment on which was one of the railroad spurs that serviced a long line of sprawling brick warehouses. The field was jammed with shacks and shipping containers, home to at least five hundred families, possibly more. A ditch serving as an open sewer ran down the slope and emptied onto the paved road in front of the compound. A thin stream of sewage trickled to a wide iron grate and disappeared, probably to end up emptying directly into the harbor about three blocks away.

There was the stench of a squatters' slum, but there were no lights, no sounds, no movement. It was as if the entire village within the city had been deserted.

Or as if the people were cowering in their hovels, afraid of something.

McGarvey switched off the Fiat's engine, but before he got out he removed the lens from the dome light and took out the bulb. He pocketed the car keys and the GPS tracker, then screwed the silencer on the threaded muzzle of his Walther PPK.

He had changed to dark sneakers, black jeans, and a lightweight dark pullover before he'd left the hotel, and now, keeping to the shadows as he worked his way down the street, he was nearly invisible.

Gloria showing up in Karachi had come as an unpleasant surprise that nagged at him like a dull toothache. She had no idea how badly she had jeopardized the mission. The moment he'd seen her at the hotel, he'd almost decided on the spot to back away, return to Washington, and start the search for bin Laden all over again.

Damned near every woman who'd ever been involved with him had gotten herself killed sooner or later. They'd all thought that they were in love with him, while none of them had the faintest idea what that might mean in terms of their own safety.

Even Gloria, who was a trained field officer, had no idea what she had gotten herself into, or the danger she posed. McGarvey no longer had an absolute freedom of movement. No matter what happened now he was bound to look out for her; he was handicapped because of her and he didn't like it.

But the prize he'd come for was worth everything. If he could get next to bin Laden for even one moment it would be enough. The man would die. And with him would die the one question for which McGarvey had never gotten a satisfactory answer. Why?

He'd come face-to-face with the man several years ago in Afghanistan, and although they'd spoken the same language, spoken about the same issues, McGarvey had not been able to get a real handle on the man.

Bin Laden wasn't some West Bank fanatic, or a religious zealot, or a man with a grudge against the West, which made understanding him all but impossible. The CIA had supported him and his mujahideen in the Afghan war against the Russians. But near the end of that struggle, it was as if a switch had flipped inside bin Laden's head. One day he was America's ally and the next we had become Satan, and he had declared a *jihad* not only against the West, but against Israel and anyone who supported her, and against the members of the Saudi royal family who had sold their people and Islam to the West for the sake of oil without sharing the money with al-Quaida.

There are no innocents in this struggle, he'd told McGarvey. *Infidels, men, women, children, it did not matter. They would all die.*

At the end of the warehouse, McGarvey held up for a moment. Across from an open area that led back to the loading docks, the burned-out wrecks of two cars had been pushed off the side of the road, and were piled in a tangled heap. Twenty meters farther, the wall of the compound rose five meters from the street, the coils of razor wire at the top glinting in the stray light. A set of sturdy-looking double doors, wide enough to admit a car or even a small truck, seemed to be the only way into the compound from this side. From where he stood, he could just make out the roofs of three buildings behind the wall, on one of which was a small satellite dish. Electric wires snaked down from a power pole at the corner.

He looked back the way he had come, and then searched the slum village that covered the sloping field. The stench of human waste was nearly overpowering, but there was no noise, and the silence raised the hairs on the back of his neck.

Taking the GPS tracker out of his pocket, he keyed the three twos and the pound symbol. Within a couple of seconds the display showed al-Turabi's signal still inside the compound.

It did not necessarily mean that bin Laden was here. But al-Turabi was a top lieutenant, and this is where he had come as soon as he had escaped from Camp Delta.

If bin Laden wasn't here, he was probably very close, and al-Turabi was the key to finding him.

McGarvey pocketed the GPS tracker, checked his pistol, and then leaned up against the brick wall to wait for an opportunity to get inside the compound to present itself to him.

PEARL CONTINENTAL

Gloria Ibenez was beside herself with worry. She stood at the window of the tenth-floor suite, looking down at the modern city, its skyscrapers lit in mosaic patterns. Somewhere below a siren was wailing, and twenty minutes ago she'd thought she'd heard gunfire somewhere in the distance.

She had promised Kirk that she would not leave the room until morning. If he hadn't returned by then she was to go immediately to the U.S. Consulate General on Abdullah Haroon Road, which was just a few blocks from the hotel. Dave Coddington, the CIA chief of station there, would be able to help her. If McGarvey had been successful in killing bin Laden, the backlash would be immediate and very big. No American in Pakistan would be safe.

Under no circumstances was she to use the telephone. The opposition would almost certainly be monitoring calls from the hotel, and if they found out that she was alone and vulnerable she would become a target.

"You're here, and there's nothing I can do about it now," he'd told her, his tone harsh. "If we're to have a chance of surviving, you need to keep a low profile."

She nodded her understanding, loving, his eyes and the set of his mouth even when he was angry.

And here and now, more than five thousand miles from home, she could put the notion of McGarvey's wife in a back compartment of her head. She didn't have to think about the other woman in Kirk's life; it was only her waiting for him in his hotel room, only her who had come to Pakistan to help him, only her who cared enough to be at his side, and only her who truly understood what he was, and loved him all the more for it.

A telephone burred softly, bringing Gloria out of her thoughts. She turned away from the window as the phone rang again. It was McGarvey's satellite phone in his overnight bag in the closet.

She got to it on the fourth ring. "Yes?"

"Oh wow, Gloria," Rencke gushed. "Where's Mac?"

"He's going after the man, but I don't know where that is. He told me to stay here."

"Why are you in Karachi? How'd you get there?"

"I booked a flight with my own money," she said defiantly. "I wanted to help."

There was no telling how Kirk would react when he found out that she lied about Otto's help. But she would cross that bridge when she came to it. "Is there something wrong?"

Rencke didn't answer at first.

"Otto?" she prompted. She was becoming alarmed.

"He shoulda taken the phone with him," Rencke said distantly, as if he were doing something else while thinking out loud. "But I shoulda seen it before. Bad dog, bad dog."

"For God's sake, tell me what's wrong."

"He's running into a trap," Rencke told her breathlessly. "The GPS chip hasn't moved in thirty-six hours. Not one meter. Al-Turabi is probably dead, and they might know about the chip somehow."

"Where is he?" Gloria demanded.

"Fish Harbor. I'll send the map to your sat phone display. But you gotta stop him."

Gloria was putting on her sneakers, the phone cradled under her chin. "We'll have to get out of Karachi," she told Rencke. "If they've set a trap for him, it means they know why he's here. Even if I can get to him before he tries to make the hit there's no place he'd be safe in Pakistan."

"I'm working on it," Rencke said. "But keep this phone with you." He had another thought. "Are you armed? Do you have a weapon?"

"No," Gloria said tightly.

"Just get him outta there," Rencke said.

The map came up on the sat phone's display. She saved it, broke the connection, then picked up the hotel phone and called the front desk.

"Good evening, Mrs. McGarvey," the clerk answered pleasantly.

"I need a car out front right now," Gloria said.

"Madam, at this hour that will be difficult—"

"Now!" Gloria shrilled, and she slammed the phone down.

She hurriedly went through McGarvey's luggage, finding his kit of money and passports, but no weapons, or anything else that couldn't be left behind. If she could get to him in time, and pull him out of Fish Harbor, they would not be returning to the hotel, and she didn't want to leave anything incriminating behind.

The lobby was practically deserted at this hour. Two women in maid's uniforms were emptying ashtrays, cleaning tables, and polishing furniture and accessories, while an old man vacuumed the large Persian carpets. There were no hotel guests except for Gloria, who went directly across to the registration counter, where a young man in a smart blue blazer was just getting off the phone.

"Did you get me a car?" Gloria demanded.

"Yes, of course, Mrs. McGarvey. It will be delivered in front very soon. It is coming from the airport."

"Fine," Gloria said. She turned on her heel and stormed across the lobby to the broad automatic doors. There was no bellman on duty this late, and very little traffic on the street. The night air was warm and humid with a mix of unusual odors. Maybe frying fish, she thought, but rancid.

She had been stupid to let him go on his own without backup. It was one of the lessons they'd drummed into her head at the Farm. In these types of operations rely on your partner, and make sure that he can rely on you. Be there.

At the very least she should have arranged for another car and followed him. She'd lost a husband, and then a partner because she hadn't kept her eye on the ball. She had failed both of them. She wasn't about to fail again.

A dark blue battered Toyota van came up the street at a high rate of speed and at the last minute swerved into the hotel's driveway. For an insane second Gloria thought that it was what the stupid hotel clerk had rented for her, but then she realized that she was probably in trouble and she stepped back.

The driver screeched to a halt, the side door crashed open, and three men, balaclavas covering their faces, leaped out and rushed her.

She had a split instant to see that only one of the three was armed, a Kalashnikov held tightly against his chest, and make a decision. They were here to kidnap her, not kill her, which gave her the momentary advantage.

She moved away from the man on her right, and stepped directly toward the armed kidnapper, who'd expected her to try to run away, not attack.

He started to bring his rifle around, but Gloria stiff-armed him to the throat with her fist, driving him backwards, nearly off his feet, and crushing his windpipe.

The man on her left spun around and grabbed her by the neck, pulling her back. But she snatched the rifle and swung the butt stock under her arm, connecting solidly with the kidnapper's ribs. He released his hold and fell to his knees.

The third man had pulled up short and was reaching in his jacket, when Gloria brought the rifle around, switched the safety catch off, and brought her finger to the trigger.

"Don't," she warned.

He yanked what might have been a boxy Glock pistol out of his jacket and started to aim it at Gloria, when she pulled off a single round, hitting him in the middle of the chest, the rifle bucking strongly in her arms, the noise shockingly loud under the hotel driveway canopy.

The kidnapper was slammed backwards off his feet, and even before he hit the pavement Gloria turned toward the van. She reached the open door in a couple of steps at the same time the driver realized that the kidnapping had failed, and he turned back to the wheel to drive away.

"Get out of the van!" Gloria screeched.

The driver looked over his shoulder, directly into the muzzle of the AK-47 Gloria was pointing at him.

"Get out of the van!" Gloria shouted again. "Now!"

The driver shoved open his door, leaped out of the van, and headed down the long driveway in a dead run.

Before he reached the street, Gloria had climbed inside the van, scrambled up to the driver's seat, and laid the Kalashnikov on the hump between the seats. She slammed the Toyota in gear and burned rubber down the driveway and out to the street, passing the frightened driver who looked over his shoulder as she raced by.

I'm on my way, darling, Gloria thought, as she turned the corner at the end of the block and headed toward Fish Harbor.

FIFTY-SEVEN

□

THE WHITE HOUSE

It was after two in the afternoon in Washington when Dick Adkins arrived at the White House. After he signed in, and his attaché case was scanned, he was escorted back to the Oval Office by the president's chief of staff, Cal Beckett.

"Has Joe Puckett gotten here yet?" Adkins asked. Four-star Admiral Joseph Puckett, Jr., was the new chairman of the Joint Chiefs of Staff.

"Five minutes ago, and he wants to know what in damnation—his words—the CIA is playing at now, or something to that effect," Beckett said. He was a serious no-nonsense businessman who, before President Haynes had tapped him for White House duty, had been the CEO of IBM.

"Puckett's always damning something, but he's going to be even less happy when he and the president hear what I have to say."

"Have you guys found the submarine?"

"Yes," Adkins said. "And it gets worse."

"Bad timing," Beckett remarked sourly. "Looks like his energy bill is going down in flames."

"Not a good day to be president," Adkins said.

The president, his suit coat off, was perched against his desk talking to his national security adviser, Dennis Berndt, and the admiral, who was a narrow-faced pale man with thinning white hair whose chest was practically covered with ribbons, including the Medal of Honor. None of the three men seemed happy or comfortable.

"Here he is, Mr. President," Beckett said.

"Leave us," Haynes told his chief of staff, who withdrew and closed the door.

The topic on the table had nothing to do with White House staffing or politics, which were Beckett's purview. Adkins had argued from the start to keep the need-to-know list at the absolute minimum, which had been McGarvey's suggestion, to guard against the media stumbling across the story. What Americans didn't need right now was something else to panic them. But he was surprised that the president had excluded his chief of staff, who was a friend and trusted adviser.

"You've found the submarine?" Haynes asked.

"Yes, sir."

"Good," the president said. "Now explain it to the admiral, because the ball's going to be in his court."

"Yes, sir," Adkins said. He set his attaché case down, opened it, and withdrew a moderately thick briefing book, which he handed to the president. "This is everything as of noon. As you'll see, the situation has become somewhat more complex and urgent in the past twenty-four hours."

The president laid the briefing book behind him on the desk. "I'll look over the details later. For now bring us up to date, Dick. What's the CIA found out?"

"Al-Quaida has managed to get its hands on a submarine, a crew of Iranian ex-navy, we think, and an experienced captain," Adkins said, directing his remarks to Admiral Puckett.

"It's the goddamned Russians and their Kilo boats," Puckett said. "And I suppose the sub driver is a Russkie too."

"It's a Libyan boat, actually," Adkins said. "A Foxtrot. And the captain is a Perisher-trained Brit by the name of Rupert Graham."

The president, who had been contemplative, was angry all of a sudden. "That lying bastard Quaddafi," he said. "Are you sure about this, Dick?"

"Yes, sir," Adkins replied. He quickly brought them up to date on the Indonesian captain's story about Graham, the sinking of the *Distal Volente*, and the Sixth Fleet's confirmation that the freighter was at the bottom of the Mediterranean. "A British NATO frigate tracked a Foxtrot through the

Strait of Gibraltar and out into the open Atlantic a few hours ago, then lost her."

"Why the hell didn't they follow her?" Haynes demanded.

"Not their area of operations, Mr. President," Puckett responded. "Did they get a course?"

"Southwest," Adkins said. "South America, perhaps."

"The Panama Canal again," Berndt spoke up for the first time. "They're persistent. But it won't be so easy for them this time to get into the locks to do any damage. They'll have to run on the surface."

"What about weapons?" Puckett asked.

"At this point we have no idea," Adkins admitted. "We have some assets on the ground in Tripoli and at Ra's al Hilal, one of their major naval installations, but it's not easy to recruit the right people."

"Your vetting standards for Arab speakers are too tough," Puckett said. "You're tossing out the baby with the bathwater."

"We've been burned before, Admiral," Adkins observed dryly. "But for now the situation is what it is."

Puckett shook his head. "At least time is on our side. It'll take them ten days, maybe longer, to get within striking range of the canal, or"—he glanced at the president—"our eastern seaboard."

"What can we do in the meantime?" Haynes asked.

"Look for him in the open Atlantic, but that'll be worse than finding a bug on a gnat's ass. In the meantime we'll set up a blockade off Limón Bay in case he's trying for the canal again."

"What about our coast?" Berndt asked.

Puckett shrugged, a bleak expression crossing his narrow features. "We can cover a few likely targets, but that's about it," he said. "The big problem will be his weapons load. If his boat has been retrofitted he could stand off a couple hundred klicks and fire the Russian Novator Club cruise missile. The weapon was designed as an antiship load, but it could do an appreciable amount of damage to the locks, or anything else, for that matter."

"How about nukes?" Adkins asked. It had been one of Rencke's chief concerns.

"There're all sorts of nasty weapons that can be fired from a standard five-hundred-thirty-three-millimeter torpedo tube," Puckett answered. "The Novator carries a four-hundred-fifty-kilogram payload. Usually high explosives. But that weapon can carry four hundred fifty kilos of just about anything." He turned back to the president. "That's up to the CIA, to find out what weapons the Libyans have got their hands on."

Haynes looked to Adkins.

"We're working on it, Mr. President," Adkins said.

"What's your best guess?"

Three days ago Rencke had voiced a vague concern that if Saddam Hussein had in actuality come up with nuclear weapons, either by Iraqi design and construction, or from the Russians, he might have spirited them out of the country before the U.S.-led invasion. If they had been Russian, then Putin would definitely have arranged for help getting them out of Iraq, and Libya was a possible destination.

But Adkins was not ready to stick his neck out that far. Not for this or any other president.

He shook his head. "We're working on it," he said.

"Where's McGarvey?" the president asked.

Adkins glanced over at Puckett. This was one bit of information that no one in this room needed to know. "I'd rather not say, Mr. President," Adkins replied. It was a matter of plausible deniability for the White House no matter what happened in Pakistan. The president and Berndt understood this.

"If he can be recalled, do it," the president instructed Adkins. He turned to Puckett. "I want our armed forces to find and kill that submarine before it reaches this side of the Atlantic, if that's at all possible. In the meantime I'm giving Kirk McGarvey carte blanche for the possibilities we can't foresee or handle. If he comes to you I want him given whatever he asks for."

It was obvious that Puckett wanted to object, but he nodded. "Of course, Mr. President."

EN ROUTE TO CIA HEADQUARTERS

Crossing the Key Bridge to the Parkway, Adkins got on his encrypted phone to Otto Rencke. "Any word from Mac?"

"None. But Gloria Ibenez followed him to Karachi."

"What?" Adkins demanded, coming half off his seat in the back of the armored Cadillac limousine.

"She's on her own, and it's just as well she's over there, because Mac could be heading into a trap."

"Tell me," Adkins said, a tight knot forming in his stomach. He could think of any number of ways for this entire operation to go south in a heartbeat. No one would come out of it clean, and worst of all al-Quaida's attack would have a much better-than-even chance of succeeding if Mac were to go down. A lot of Americans would lose their lives, and he wasn't at all sure if the nation could handle another massive blow.

Rencke hurriedly explained what was happening in Karachi, especially the part about al-Turabi's GPS chip that hadn't moved in a day and a half. "Gloria's on her way to Fish Harbor to pull him out."

"What then?"

"We'll get them out of Pakistan," Rencke said. "I'm working on that part now. But afterwards, I don't know."

"The president wants him back to help stop Graham," Adkins said. "The navy's agreed to blockade Limón Bay, but I've got a very bad feeling that we're missing something."

"Me too," Rencke said, and he abruptly broke the connection.

FIFTY-EIGHT

□

FISH HARBOR

In the half hour that McGarvey had been watching from the shadows he'd learned that the compound was not deserted and that it was being seriously guarded. Whoever was inside had taken an extreme interest in security that went beyond the locked gate, and the razor-wire-topped wall.

The front of the enclave ran for fifty or sixty meters along the paved street before it disappeared around the corner at the end of the block to the west, and around back halfway up the hill toward the railroad embankment to the east. Every fifteen or twenty meters a closed-circuit television camera was perched in front of the coils of razor wire. At the nearest corner, a pair of insulators, each the size of a liter bottle, led thick electrical wires to a steel mesh that covered the stuccoed wall. And at each corner, powerful spotlights, dark at the moment, were perched well above the wall on aluminum stanchions.

Ten minutes ago, a pair of guards dressed in camos had appeared at the top of the wall, only their heads and shoulders visible as they headed away from each other to the opposite sides of the compound. When they reached the corners they turned and came back to meet at the gate. One of them said something, and the other one laughed.

McGarvey raiséd his pistol and steadied his hand against the corner of the brick warehouse to lead the guard to the left. "Bang," he said softly in the darkness. He switched aim to the other roof guard. "Bang."

The shots were at the extreme range for his pistol, but not impossible.

The guards turned and marched away, but this time they disappeared around the corners, apparently to check the rear of the compound.

A few minutes later they were back above the main gate, where they exchanged a few words, though McGarvey couldn't make out what they were saying, and headed away again.

After they were gone the main gate opened and a guard, also dressed in camos, a Kalashnikov slung muzzle-down over his shoulder, stepped out into the street and lit a cigarette.

McGarvey had found a way inside, but only if the man at the gate didn't go back inside before the two wall guards returned. If he could take out all three of them, he could get inside and find al-Turabi.

After that it was anyone's guess what might go down. But if bin Laden's people didn't know that the enemy had penetrated the wall and was inside the compound—even if it was for only a few minutes—the advantage would be McGarvey's. He could do a lot of damage in that span of time.

Almost as if on cue the two wall guards appeared at the corners and started toward the gate.

McGarvey switched the safety catch to the off position and, steadying his arm against the corner of the building, took aim on the man to the east who would get to the gate first. But suddenly it all felt wrong. Some inner instinct of his was sending an insistent, nagging alarm bell at the back of his head.

He looked up from his gun sight, and studied the situation at the end of the block—the *entire* situation, his attention lingering on the three men who would be in firing range in a few seconds.

In a near perfect firing situation for one man coming to breach the walls.

Too perfect.

McGarvey held perfectly still, not moving a muscle as the wall guards approached the gate. Then he had it. The closed-circuit television cameras had all turned toward the street in front of the gate. Someone inside the compound was watching, waiting to send an army pouring out to spring the trap. A lone attacker wouldn't have a chance of survival. It would be over in a matter of seconds.

He eased back behind the building. Bin Laden's people had known that he'd come to Karachi. And they must have guessed why he'd come. But they had no way of knowing that he would be here this evening, unless they'd discovered the GPS tracker in al-Turabi's body.

Rencke had warned that it was possible, though extremely unlikely, that bin Laden's people would have a receiver sensitive enough to pick up the signal, or even have a suspicion that such a thing was possible.

But it was even less likely in McGarvey's estimation that there was a leak inside the CIA; a direct link somehow to bin Laden. There just weren't that many people in the Building who knew that McGarvey had taken the nanotechnology to Camp Delta, and no reason for any of them to become traitors.

There was no one with a grudge against the United States.

Except for one possibility that McGarvey wanted to reject the instant it came into his head.

He peered around the corner of the warehouse again. The wall guards had reached the gate, and they were evidently talking to the man on the street, because he was looking up at them.

They should have turned by now and started their round along the wall. Unless they were waiting for the attack to come. Unless they'd been telephoned from the hotel that someone was coming.

For a crazy instant in time Gloria Ibenez's face flashed into his mind's eye. He did not want to think that she had betrayed him, yet he found it next to impossible to believe that she could have fallen in love with him so soon and so completely unless it was a setup. She was from a completely different world, and he was old enough to be her father. It made no sense to him.

He thought of Marta and Liese and Jacqueline, three women who had no business falling in love with him. Yet they had. Two of them had lost their lives because of their involvement with him, and the third—Liese Fuelm—had very nearly been killed in Switzerland just last year.

All of them had been traitors to their countries, in one way or another, but none of them had betrayed him.

Headlights flashed in the darkness at the end of the block. The guards on the wall and at the gate turned around, bringing their weapons up.

Seconds later a dark van came around the corner and raced directly toward where McGarvey was crouched against the warehouse wall. He moved farther back into the shadows, and brought his pistol to bear on the rapidly approaching van.

If bin Laden's people had already spotted him, they might just as well have sent an attack to his rear, hoping to catch him in a cross fire. He had no place to go. His only option at this point was to take the van out of play and make it back to his car.

He would go for the driver first, and then the engine.

The van's headlights briefly illuminated the corner where McGarvey was hiding. He slipped the Walther's safety catch to the off position and started to pull the trigger, when the headlights suddenly went out, plunging the street back into darkness.

For just a second McGarvey couldn't make out who was behind the wheel, even though the van was less than ten meters away. But then the interior light came on for just a second, long enough for him to recognize that it was Gloria.

She locked up the brakes and with squealing tires the van slid at an angle down the street.

McGarvey stepped around the corner as the wall guards and the man on the street were taking aim at the van.

"Kirk, it's me!" Gloria shouted at him.

Once again steadying his arm against the building, McGarvey began firing, first toward the wall guards, knocking one of them down with his second shot, and sending the second ducking out of sight.

The guard on the street opened fire with his AK-47, the bullets ricocheting off the pavement as he walked his aim toward McGarvey's position.

Switching targets, McGarvey methodically fired three shots, the second and third catching the guard in the torso and sending him staggering back against the wall.

He raised his sights in time to spot the second wall guard appear behind the razor wire, and he fired three more shots, sending the guard diving for safety again.

The van was sideways in the street where it had screeched to a halt. He ran across to it and Gloria handed the Kalashnikov out the window to him. "I have to turn around," she told him.

McGarvey stuffed his pistol in his belt, stepped clear of the van, and sprayed the open gate and the wall above it, as Gloria did a rapid U-turn, smoke pouring off the tires.

"Come on, Kirk!" Gloria shouted. "It's a trap! They knew you were coming!"

For a moment McGarvey didn't want to believe it. If Gloria hadn't betrayed him, who else in the Building had? Unless it was that pissant Weiss in Gitmo. But the ONI officer had no way of knowing about the nano-GPS tracker.

The only other explanation was that they had once again underestimated the technical abilities of bin Laden as they had in September of 2001. The architects of the World Trade Center towers had never imagined the buildings collapsing because of a strike by airplanes. But al-Quaida's engineers had.

McGarvey emptied the AK-47's magazine, tossed the weapon aside, and leaped into the back of the van. Gloria immediately floored the accelerator and they careened down the darkened street, sliding nearly out of control around the corner before anyone inside the compound could react.

"Are we clear?" Gloria demanded.

"We're clear," McGarvey told her. He shoved the service door shut, and climbed up front into the passenger seat.

They crossed the main railroad line, and headed to the city's center away from the slums. "Are you okay?" Gloria asked, glancing at McGarvey. Traffic was still very light, only the occasional delivery truck and odd car.

"What are you doing down here?" McGarvey demanded.

"Otto called your sat phone to warn you that you were probably walking into a trap. Al-Turabi's GPS chip hasn't moved in the last thirty-six hours. Not one meter. The bastard's probably dead."

"If he's dead they'd have cremated him before the next sunrise," Mc-Garvey said. "It's the Muslim custom."

"Unless they somehow found out about the chip," Gloria said. "But I don't see how that's possible."

"Where'd you get this van?"

Gloria quickly explained what had happened from the moment she'd hung up from talking with Rencke. "Otto's working on getting us out of Karachi."

"Someone inside the hotel must have monitored your call to the front desk," McGarvey said.

Gloria took the sat phone from her jacket pocket and handed it to Mc-Garvey. "I got your money and passports too," she said. "But whatever Otto's planning better happen pretty soon. I don't think it's such a hot idea driving around in this van much longer."

McGarvey powered up the phone, and when it had acquired a satellite he speed-dialed Rencke's number. His old friend answered on the first ring.

"Oh wow, Gloria?"

"It's me," McGarvey said. "What do you have for us?"

"There's a diplomatic flight that was scheduled to leave at six this morning," Rencke said. "Assistant Secretary of State Joyce Fields. She's on the way out to the airport now, and crew is already there prepping the plane. It's a 737, coming back here via Ramstein. They'll take off as soon as you get there."

"What does she know about us?"

"That you're CIA and that you're in a bit of a hurry," Rencke said. "Are you okay, kimo sabe?"

"I'll live," McGarvey said. "I want you to find out what happened to al-Turabi's GPS chip. Could be that Commander Weiss knows something. Soon as Gloria gets home, figure out an excuse for her to get back down to Gitmo and lean on him again. I'm going to hole up here today, and go back in tomorrow. They won't be expecting me a second time."

"Wrong answer, recruit, the prez wants you back ASAP."

McGarvey's gut tightened. "Did you find the submarine?"

"Yeah, but it's not a Kilo boat, it's a Libyan Foxtrot, and it's already on its way across the Atlantic."

"Where's it headed?"

"Apparently back to the canal for Graham to finish the job," Rencke said.

"I don't believe it," McGarvey said. He'd done a lot of thinking about the Brit since their encounter aboard the oil tanker in the Gatun locks. That operation had been important, but it was never meant to be the big strike against us that al-Quaida had been promising since 9/11. In any event, a submarine would not be as effective as a tanker in damaging the canal in a decisive way.

Graham was a highly trained, highly experienced submarine commander, who now had a boat and crew, and presumably weapons. A man like him would not squander such a resource hitting the same target twice. Whatever he was planning would be up close and personal.

Every American remembered the events of 9/11 as if they were etched with acid. This time would be as bad or worse. And after everything that had happened to us since the Trade towers had come down—the wars in Afghanistan and Iraq, the near success of the suicide bombers trying to hit four of our small-town schools, and the terrible seasons of hurricanes and floods—another strike against us, any strike, would be nothing less than devastating.

"How do we get through security?" McGarvey asked.

"Someone will be waiting for you at the air freight entrance," a relieved Rencke said. "It's off Shahrah-e-Faisal Road. There'll be highway signs."

"We're on our way," McGarvey said. He broke the connection and turned to Gloria. "Take us to the airport. We're going home."

"What's happened, Kirk?" she asked.

"Graham's got his hands on a submarine and he's on his way across the Atlantic with it."

"The navy can stop him."

"If they know where to look," McGarvey answered absently. Once again he had the feeling that he was missing something. That all of them were underestimating al-Quaida's ingenuity.

"What are we going to do?" Gloria asked.

"I don't know."

FIFTY-NINE

□

SS *SHEHAB*, IN THE ATLANTIC

It was 2000 GMT when the twenty-four-hundred-ton submarine came to a depth of twenty meters and extended her snorkel above the surface to take in air to run the diesels and recharge their badly depleted batteries. She was well out into the Atlantic now, running at fifteen knots, and by this time tomorrow evening she would be approaching the broad passage between the Maderia Islands to the north and the Canaries to the south.

"The snorkel is clear," Captain Ziyax called from behind al-Abbas at the ballast board.

Graham ducked his head around the corner. "Are we still clear on the surface?" he asked his Libyan chief sonar man.

"The same targets well out ahead, designate them as probable commercial traffic, and the same aft." Ensign Isomil looked up. "Sir, there's nothing closer than ten thousand meters. Nothing that I think might be a warship."

"Well done," Graham said. He went back into the control room and raised the search periscope. The view in the lens was very dim by the standards of the British Trafalgar boats he had skippered, but adequate for him to make sure they were alone. It was a very dark night, no moon.

"You may open the snorkel and start the engines, number two," he said.

"Yes, sir," Ziyax responded immediately and crisply. Graham had spoken with him after the incident coming out of the Strait of Gibraltar, and the Libyan naval officer had come to see the error of his ways. It was Graham's intimate knowledge of the captain's wife and children, supplied by al-Quaida, that had finally convinced the man to cooperate fully.

The three diesels rumbled into life one at a time.

Graham took one last three-sixty, then slapped the handles up and lowered the scope. He turned and looked at his crew. They were well rested now after the long and stressful crossing and emergence from the

Mediterranean. But those thirty-six-plus hours of adversity had melded them into something of a unit. Each of them, Iranian and Libyan, had one common fear, which was retribution by al-Quaida, and one common hate, which was Graham.

He smiled inwardly. They were children, unlike the English crews he'd commanded. Those men had been highly trained and motivated professionals, their equipment state-of-the-art, their weapons as accurate and lethal as those of any nation on earth.

For just an instant he felt a twinge of regret for how he'd thrown away his life, but then the constant image of Jillian's face, contorted in pain, brought his hate back to the surface.

The ship's com buzzed. "Captain, engineering."

Graham pulled the growler phone from its overhead bracket. "This is the captain."

"I think you'd better come back here, sir," Lieutenant Mahdi Chamran, the Iranian chief engineer, said.

"What is it?"

"You need to see this for yourself, sir," Chamran insisted.

Graham's anger spiked, but he brought himself under control. "Very well." He hung up. "Captain, you have the con," he told Ziyax. "Maintain your course and speed. I'll be in engineering."

The Libyan captain looked at him sharply, almost as if he were suddenly afraid of something. But he nodded. "Aye, Captain."

Graham turned, ducked through the open hatch, and headed aft to engineering, which took up nearly one-fourth of the volume of the boat. The three diesel engines, three electric propulsion motors for underwater maneuvering, the huge battery bank, electrical generators, pumps, parts storage, and a complete machine shop were all the responsibility of the chief engineer, who in some ways was even more important than the captain. The control room crew fought the boat, but the chief engineer made sure they had a warship to fight with.

No one was in the crew's mess, or in the passageway. With only a skeleton crew even such a small boat seemed very large and very empty.

Lieutenant Commander Mahdi Chamran, the Iranian chief engineer bin Laden had supplied, was waiting in the electric motor room with Lieutenant Rasal Sayyaf, the chief torpedo man who'd also come from the Distal Volente.

The chi-eng was a short dark Arab with four days' growth on his face, and black grease permanently etching his hands. He wasn't a traditionalist so he didn't wash five times each day before prayers. He'd been kicked out of the Iranian navy because of it; his superiors valued religious practices over good engineering.

Sayyaf, on the other hand, was tall and lanky, with a permanent smirk on his face because he knew that once his military service was completed he would take over from his father as imam at their mosque in Isfahan south of Tehran. He'd gone over to al-Quaida with the blessings of his superiors who thought he was too devout a Muslim. But like Chamran he was good at what he did.

They were all fucking misfits, Graham thought, coming through the hatch. A section of the deck grating had been pulled up and the two men were standing over the opening, looking down at something. No one else was in the compartment and the hatch to the aft torpedo room was closed and dogged.

"What is it?" Graham demanded, approaching them.

Chamran seemed excited, as did Sayyaf, but his voice was oddly subdued. "We've found two new toys for you, Captain," the chi-eng said.

Graham reached the opening, but then pulled up short. Nestled in makeshift wooden cradles between banks of batteries were two metal cylinders, each about twenty inches in diameter and about three feet long. The DANGER: RADIATION symbol was painted on both of them. They were nuclear weapons.

"Are they leaking?" Graham asked.

Sayyaf held up a small Geiger counter. "Not much. But whoever has to handle them, and especially the poor bastard who has to open the packages and arm them, will take a hit."

"They're not Libyan," Graham said. "Russian?"

"Iraqi, but the Russians probably helped get them to Libya," Chamran said. He shook his head in wonderment. "The Americans were right after all. Uncle Saddam actually did it." He laughed. "Quaddafi must have been shitting in his pants all this time. You were Allah-sent, Captain, to take these things off his hands."

"Will they mate to the two Russian cruise missiles we found?" Graham asked, his breath quickening despite his iron will to remain calm in front of these men.

"With some jury-rigging, yes," Sayyaf said.

"They probably won't go critical," Chamran warned.

"What makes you say that?" Graham demanded sharply. This was too good to be true. It was the opportunity that bin Laden had talked about in Karachi and again in Syria, but had refused to give specifics.

You will understand when the time comes, he'd promised. *And your eyes will be opened to the wondrous light.*

Graham understood now. It was Oppenheimer, he thought, in 1945 at Trinity in New Mexico when the Americans exploded the first atomic bomb. He'd called it the "wondrous light."

"I don't think they had the time or the materials to develop the initiator technology," the chi-eng explained. He held up his hand before Graham could object. "But these toys will explode, Captain, if that's what you want. It won't be a nuclear explosion, but when they go off—wherever that might be—they will spread a lot of radioactive dust over a very large area." He nodded solemnly. "More people than the Manhattan attack could die. It will not be another 9/11. It will be much worse."

Graham's soul was singing. He was going to strike back at the bastards in a way that they would never forget.

"That is if you have the stomach for it, Englishman," Chamran said.

Graham smiled again inwardly. Oh, he had the stomach all right. "Disable all the Geiger counters."

CIA HEADQUARTERS

Although Assistant Secretary of State Fields and most of the people in her small entourage recognized McGarvey from his days as DCI, no one questioned why he and Gloria had boarded in the middle of the night in Karachi. Or why they had remained aboard in Ramstein when the aircraft was being refueled.

"Glad to have been of some assistance," she said, shaking his hand after they'd touched down at Andrews.

"Thanks for the lift," he'd said. "But it might be best if you never mentioned this to anyone."

She wanted to say something, he'd seen it in her eyes. But she nodded and left. Afterwards the aircraft was towed from the VIP ramp to an air force hangar where two men from security were waiting with a van to take them directly down to Langley.

McGarvey had slept for only a few hours on the flight over, and he was tired. But it was more than lack of sleep. Fish Harbor had been a trap. He'd been lured to the compound step-by-step all the way from Camp Delta and he hadn't figured out how. The only bit of good fortune to come out of it had been Gloria. If it hadn't been for her he might have bought it.

Yet there was still a nagging thought at the back of his head that he was missing something about her. Lawrence Danielle, his mentor from the early days, had warned that to every spy would eventually come paranoia. For some, the doubts and suspicions became so overwhelming that they were destroyed by their fears. Suicide was an occupational hazard. But the good field officer learned to listen to his or her instincts; they were often the difference between success or failure.

It was morning and rush-hour traffic was in full swing, people going about their business as usual. But McGarvey felt disconnected, as he always did when he returned from the field, and especially from an operation that had fallen apart on him. He would have to go back to finish the job, but for that he would need a new strategy, which at the moment completely eluded him.

"You're going back, aren't you," Gloria said, as if she had read his mind.

They had crossed the Potomac on the Beltway and skirted Alexandria before heading north through Fairfax and Falls Church, the city in the near distance, a jet taking off from Reagan National. "I don't know," Mc-Garvey replied absently as he stared out the window.

"I want to help you."

"I know," he said, turning to her. "Thanks for Karachi. It could have been messy."

She smiled. "I was just doing my job."

From the Beltway they took the George Washington Parkway down to the Building. One of the security officers escorted them up to the seventh floor using the director's private elevator. Dhalia Swanson, Adkins's secretary, passed them straight in.

"Good to see you back, Mr. McGarvey," she said warmly.

"Thanks, but I'm not back," McGarvey told her. She'd been his secretary when he'd served as DCI.

"Yes, sir," she said, smiling.

Dick Adkins was waiting with his number two David Whittaker, Howard McCann, and Otto Rencke.

"Sorry to have to pull you out like that, but from what I understand you may have been walking into a situation," Adkins said. "The president asked that we get you back here pronto."

McCann had a scowl permanently etched on his square features, but Adkins looked like a man who'd gotten some very bad news and was flailing around trying to figure out what he should do about it. Americans had been rubbed raw by the events—natural and manmade—of the last few years, and they were increasingly looking to Washington to do something, or heads would continue to roll.

Counterterrorism had become the political hot potato of the decade.

"It'll take at least ten days for Graham to get across the Atlantic," McGarvey said. "What do you need me for? The navy should be able to handle it."

"A Second Fleet carrier battle group is already on the way to Panama to set up a blockade," Adkins said. "There'll be some tough questions when the media finds out, but that's not our concern for the moment."

"Do we have any idea what weapons are aboard?" Gloria asked. McCann shot her a furious look, but she ignored him.

"Quaddafi won't even admit it's his submarine," Adkins said. "The president talked to him two hours ago. According to the good colonel, his submarine was scuttled in the Bay of Sidra. It's anybody's guess what's aboard."

"Graham's not heading for the canal again," McGarvey said. He'd had time to think about what he would do if he were in Graham's shoes, with a boat and crew, presumably weapons, possibly even some very nasty weapons, and a deep-seated grudge against a system that he figured killed his wife. Graham had become a renegade of the worse kind; intelligent, highly trained, and well motivated.

"Where then?" Adkins asked. "New York? The president wants your best guess."

"Washington," McGarvey said. "They managed to do a number on the World Trade Center in New York, but except for a relatively small amount of damage to the Pentagon, their plans for Washington were a bust. They'll try again."

"They wouldn't even have to get close if they had a couple of cruise missiles," Rencke spoke up. "They could lay a couple hundred miles off and launch from there. We wouldn't have much warning time." He was sitting cross-legged on a chair, his red hair flying everywhere. "Better than even chance he's got 'em, and maybe more bad shit."

"Like what?" McCann asked.

"Anthrax at least. Maybe even a small dirty nuke or two."

"Where the hell would Libya get anything like that?"

Rencke gave McCann an amused, condescending look. "Don't you read the newspapers, Howie? The deserts over there are gushing with oil. And that spells m-o-n-e-y, with which an enterprising soul can buy just about anything."

"The Foxtrot was on a southwest heading," Adkins reiterated.

"Then why did you pull me out of Karachi?" McGarvey asked.

Adkins shook his head. "Maybe we're wrong about Panama. Or, maybe you're wrong about Washington. We could probably come up with a dozen different scenarios that a man like Graham might come up with. But it's the plan that we *haven't* dreamed up is why we wanted you here. You know bin Laden better than anyone else on our side. And right now Panama is our most likely bet, and you are our insurance."

McGarvey turned to Rencke. "Keep me in the loop."

"Will do, kimo sabe," Rencke said.

"I'm going home," he told the others. "We're probably missing something that's important. Let's just hope we can figure out what it is before it's too late." He turned to McCann. "By the way, Ms. Ibenez was working for me. I asked her to backstop me in Karachi, and she did a hell of a job, so if I were you I'd take it easy on her." He smiled. "I'd take it as a personal favor, Howard."

SIXTY

□

SS *SHEHAB,* IN THE ATLANTIC

Graham stepped into the officer's wardroom a few minutes after midnight Greenwich mean time. The three Iranians and two Libyans seated around the cramped table looked up with various degrees of expectation and hate in their eyes. He'd called the meeting, but had not told them why.

He locked the door, and spread a large-scale chart on the table, holding the rolled edges down with teacups, and a couple of ashtrays.

Ziyax was the first to recognize what it was, and he looked up in surprise. "That's the American coast. The Chesapeake Bay."

"Exactly," Graham said. "We'll be there nine days from now."

"Insanity," Ziyax said softly, and he looked at the others around the table. Only al-Abbas, his former XO, nodded, but al-Hari, Chamran, and Sayyaf, all Graham's people, shot him a dark look.

"Why do you say that?" Graham asked mildly. He'd made his final plan the instant his chief engineer had shown him the two nuclear weapons. Bin Laden had kept that part from him in case he was captured by the Western authorities before he could board the sub and make it out into the open Atlantic. But he needed these men to carry out the attack. If there was going to be trouble, which he expected there would be, he wanted it out in the open and dealt with well ahead of time.

"In the first place the water there is too shallow for a submarine, and the entire area is crawling with American military. Especially the navy. Their Second Fleet is based at Norfolk."

"Actually you're wrong about the depth of water, the York River is deep enough to hide us, but you are definitely correct about the military presence, which is exactly why we'll get in without trouble." Graham smiled. "They won't be expecting us."

"For good reason," Ziyax argued. "If we get bottled up in the bay we'd never get out. A few rusty Russian torpedoes are no match for a good ASW warship. Even for a captain with your training and experience."

"You are right again," Graham said. "At least as it concerns us getting out of the bay once we're inside. But the fact of the matter is I have absolutely no intention of trying to escape."

Ziyax opened his mouth, but said nothing.

Al-Abbas leaned forward, his eyes narrow. "You arrogant ass, you're planning on committing suicide with us."

It was exactly how Graham had foreseen this meeting. Not only were they all fools, but they were idiots as well. In fact, in his estimation most of the Arabs he'd dealt, with were scarcely one generation away from being ignorant desert-wandering nomads. Bedouins. Even some of the Saudi royal family he'd met were no different, despite their expensive university educations in the West, and their wealth. Bin Laden himself had once admitted that living the tribal life in the mountains of Afghanistan had been a time of joy and cleansing for his soul. Which was a crock of horseshit.

"I have no intention of committing suicide," Graham said. "Although when we have finished our mission if you would like to die for the glorious cause I won't stand in your way, Lieutenant Commander. In fact, I could probably be persuaded to help."

Chamran chuckled.

"I don't trust you."

Graham laughed out loud. "I don't trust anyone. But for the moment I require your assistance and your loyalty." He leaned forward for emphasis. "If I can't count you, I will kill you."

"You might find that difficult," al-Abbas shot back, despite the warning glance from Ziyax.

"It would be much easier for me than you could possibly imagine," Graham said casually.

The wardroom fell silent for a beat.

"Assuming we make it past Norfolk without detection, and into the York River, what then?" Ziyax asked.

Graham didn't answer at first, his eyes locked on al-Abbas. Finally the Libyan officer blinked and looked away.

"We found the physics packages for two nuclear weapons in the battery room," Graham said. "We're going to mate them with the two cruise missiles and fire them on Washington."

Ziyax turned ashen. He shook his head. "I won't be a party to this insanity. Colonel Quaddafi would never have authorized the transfer of this boat if he'd known your purpose."

"I said that we found the nuclear weapons. We didn't bring them with us, they were already aboard for us to find."

Ziyax was struck dumb.

"It will be up to you to keep your crew in line," Graham warned. "If need be we'll kill them all, and operate the boat ourselves. It would be difficult, but not impossible for us to reach the Chesapeake and launch the missiles."

"What about afterwards?" a subdued Ziyax asked. "Even in the confusion there'll be a more than keen interest by the Americans to find out who launched against them."

"We'll lock out through the escape trunk. A shrimper will be waiting on the surface to pick us up, and take us out to sea where we'll rendezvous with a Syrian freighter." Graham shrugged. "Then it's a very slow boat back to Tripoli where you will be home and I will take my leave."

Ziyax passed a hand across his forehead as if he were trying to ease a headache. "You're living in a world of fantasy," he said tiredly. "We'll all die, and I don't know if I can convince my crew to do this thing. Perhaps they would rather die here fighting you than later in some American river."

"Together we'll convince the crew," al-Hari said, speaking for the first time.

Ziyax turned to him. "How?"

"We've brought a message from Osama bin Laden," al-Hari said.

"They may not care—"

"And from Colonel Quaddafi."

No one said anything for a moment, especially the Libyans, who were struck dumb by the enormity of what they were facing.

"I would like you to pick two volunteers from among your men to mate the nuclear packages to the pair of cruise missiles, and load them into tubes one and two," Graham said. "After all, they are Iraqi weapons, and until recently your Colonel Quaddafi professed an admiration for Saddam Hussein."

CHEVY CHASE

No one had warned Kathleen that her husband was back. When he walked in the front door of the CIA safe house she came to the head of the stairs, a pistol in her hand, her eyes wide.

"My God," she said, swallowing her words. "Kirk." She was in blue jeans and a T-shirt, her feet bare, no makeup yet, her hair not done.

She looked beautiful to McGarvey. He wanted to leave with her right now this morning and return to their new life in Sarasota without ever looking back, never having to look over his shoulder for fear that someone out of his past was gaining on them. Some monster intent on doing them harm, as had happened so many times in the past. He and the people who loved him had endured their own personal tragedies as devastating as 9/11 had been for all Americans. He wanted it to finally end, even though he knew with every fiber of his being that it could never be over for him.

"Hi, Katy, I'm home," he said, and smiled.

She laid the gun on the hall table and raced down the stairs to him, flying into his arms. "Are you all right? Are you all right?"

"Just a little tired. We didn't get much sleep on the flight back. Where'd you get the gun?"

"Elizabeth got it for me, and showed me how to use it." She parted and looked closely at him. "Did you do it?" she asked, her voice soft.

"No."

She digested his answer for a moment then nodded. "Are you hungry?"

"I could eat something," McGarvey said, content for now to let her lead the discussion. But sooner or later they would get around to his next move.

He took off his jacket, hung it on the coat tree, and followed her into the pleasant kitchen where he sat down at the center island. The safe house that the CIA had provided them was not as large as their old house here, or the one in Casey Key, but it was well laid out and furnished. The Company used it to house VIP visitors whom they wanted to keep away from the opposition or out of the public eye. Sometimes a live-in staff was provided, but whenever anyone was in residence, like now, a security detail watched from a second-floor apartment across the street. The house was wired with sophisticated monitoring equipment.

"Where are your things?" Katy asked, pouring him a cup of coffee.

"I had to leave most of it behind," he said. "We were in a hurry."

"We?" Katy asked, setting his cup down in front of him.

"Gloria Ibenez came over to backstop me. Wasn't for her I might have been in some trouble."

Katy arched her left eyebrow. "Handy woman to have around in a pinch. I'll have to thank her." She smiled. "Bacon and eggs?"

"Sounds good," McGarvey told her. His wife had never been much of a cook, but since they had gotten remarried after a long separation she had improved, although she tended to overcook everything. But he wasn't complaining.

She busied herself with the food from the fridge and the pans and dishes, her back to her husband. "How much time do we have until you go back to finish the job?" she asked brightly. She turned to him and smiled. "Or would you have to kill me if you told me?"

"Only if you burned my eggs," he said. "Anyway I won't be going far for the next week or so. Maybe we'll do something with the kids over the weekend. We could rent a boat and take Audrey for her first sailing lesson on the river."

Katy started the bacon, and got out the bread for toast. "You have a timetable, which usually means something nasty is coming our way. Elizabeth refuses to tell me anything."

"We're working on it, Katy."

"And I've never been able to get anything out of Todd," Katy continued. Todd Van Buren was their son-in-law. "Of course Otto's been in his own world lately and Louise claims she doesn't know what's going on." Louise Horn was Rencke's wife. She was working these days for the National Security Agency as director of its Satellite Photo Interpretation shop.

"They can't tell you anything, mostly because, except for Otto, they're not on the list," McGarvey said.

Katy was suddenly brittle. She took a second frying pan out of the cupboard and slammed it on the stove. "I'm in the dark here, darling, and I goddamn well don't like it!" She turned to him. "Toni Talarico's husband came back to her in a body bag. Sorry sweetie, but your hubby died a hero, serving his country. Then they tried to kill her and the children at the funeral. Now what kind of shit is that?" Katy was practically screeching now.

McGarvey got up and went around to her, taking her in his arms. "Bob did die serving his country, and nobody was trying to kill Toni and the kids at Arlington."

"You're right," Katy said, her eyes wild. "They were gunning for you. Why?"

"Because I'm trying to stop them."

"From doing what?" Katy demanded. "For God's sake, if there's a possibility that you're coming back to me in a body bag, I want to know why. What's so fucking important?"

"They're going to attack us again. Maybe here in Washington, in about a week." McGarvey brushed her hair away from her eyes. She was on the verge of crying, but she was no longer spinning out of control. "How about going back to Florida and—"

"Not a chance," she said.

"This time when it's over, it'll really be over for me. I'll stay retired. Promise."

Kathleen managed a small, tight smile. "I've heard that one before, more times than I care to count."

"We'll see," McGarvey said. "Are you okay now?"

"Just peachy," she replied. "Now sit down and have your coffee while I try not to burn your eggs."

SIXTY-ONE

SS *SHEHAB,* MID-ATLANTIC

The attitude that they were all going to die had seeped through the boat like a flu virus. No one spoke above a whisper, and for the past few days everyone had gone about their duties like mindless robots. Even al-Abbas had become docile.

Graham rose from a light sleep around local apparent noon, five days out from Gibraltar, got a glass of tea from the galley, and went forward to the control room.

"Captain on the con," al-Hari called out.

Ziyax, who was leaning over the chart table, looked up, but no one else bothered to respond. For now Graham preferred it that way. A tractable crew was an easily led crew, so long as there was no action. "As you were," he said.

They were running on diesel power at snorkel depth, and the entire boat stank of fuel oil. He stepped back to sonar. "Mr. Isomil, how does it look above?"

The Libyan chief sonar operator looked up, his narrow face drooping, his eyes dull as if he were half-asleep. "We're quite alone out here, Captain," he said.

Graham could see for himself that all three sonar scopes were blank. "Check again," he said. "And if you still detect nothing, run a diagnostic. I want to make absolutely sure there are no targets within range."

"Yes, sir," Isomil said, rousing himself.

Graham went back to the control room, raised the search periscope, and did a slow three-sixty. It was a blustery day, with whitecaps in all directions to the horizon under a partly cloudy sky. But the waves hadn't built up yet, so the motion aboard was still minimal. The conditions on the surface were perfect for what he wanted to do.

A minute later Isomil called from sonar. "Captain, my machines are in good working order, and there are no surface or subsurface targets painting."

"Very well," Graham said. "Keep a sharp eye for the next few hours."

"Aye, sir."

Graham called the ESMs. "Ahmad, we're going to run on the surface all afternoon. I want you to keep a very close eye on all frequencies, but especially on the military radar bands, both surface and air."

"Yes, sir. Cap'n, request permission to raise the Snoop Tray to take a look before we surface."

"Very well, but be smart about it." Graham released the Push-to-Talk button on the intercom phone.

Ziyax and the other officers were looking expectantly at him. He'd gotten their attention.

"Prepare to surface the boat," Graham ordered.

"It's still broad daylight," Ziyax countered.

Graham gave the Libyan captain a bland look. "This will be your last chance," he said. "When I give an order I expect it to be carried out without hesitation or discussion. Is that clear?"

"Yes, but—"

"The next time you question an order of mine I will shoot you, and dump your body overboard. Is that also quite clear?"

Ziyax glanced at al-Abbas at the ballast board.

"Yes, Captain, quite clear," Ziyax said. "Diving Officer, prepare to surface the boat."

"Aye, prepare to surface," al-Abbas repeated the order, with no hesitation.

Graham keyed the phone. "ESMs, are we clear?"

"Yes, we are, Cap'n," Lieutenant Khalia answered.

"Very well, keep a sharp eye," Graham said. He hung up the phone. "Surface the boat, we need some fresh air in here. We stink like a pigsty."

Ziyax stiffened at the insult, but this time he did not delay. "Diving Officer, blow positive."

"Aye, sir, blowing positive," al-Abbas repeated the order, and he began transferring compressed air from a pair of storage tanks into several ballast tanks and they started to slowly rise toward the surface.

"Are we changing course now, sir?" Ziyax asked.

They didn't have a current ephemeris of the American spy satellites over this piece of the ocean, but Graham figured it was a safe bet that if the *Shehab* remained on the surface for the rest of the afternoon, at least one would fly overhead and spot them.

"Negative," he said. "Maintain your present heading, Captain."

CHEVY CHASE

McGarvey and Katy were on their way out the door to catch an early movie and a pizza and beer afterwards, something they hadn't done for a very long time, when the secure telephone rang. The last few days had been quiet, with nothing to do but enjoy their granddaughter and a little taste of their retirement. But McGarvey had been expecting the call. It was Rencke.

"Oh wow, NRO spotted the sub in mid-Atlantic about an hour ago," Rencke gushed excitedly.

"Are we sure it's the right one?" McGarvey asked.

"Louise repositioned a Marvel-two and got a reasonable angle. Unless there's a pair of Foxtrots crossing the big pond, she's our boat." The supersecret Marvel series of spy satellites had been put in high-earth orbit to watch all of Europe in response to the emergence of Germany as a new world power.

"What's her heading?"

"Southwest, same as before," Rencke said. "He's heading for the ditch after all."

"I don't think so," McGarvey said. Last week he had pulled Graham's jacket from the Directorate of Intelligence's current People of Interest file, and spent a few hours studying the man's background. Included were two psych evaluations that Rencke had managed to purloin from British Royal Navy records; the first just prior to Graham's graduation from Perisher, and the second just prior to his discharge under other-than-honorable conditions.

He had learned enough to understand that Graham was driven not only by a strong need for revenge against the people he felt were responsible for his wife's death, but by a deep sense of pride. The man's ego was like a rocket engine on his back with no cut-off switch.

"Where then?" Rencke asked.

"Washington," McGarvey said. Katy was watching him from the doorway, a sad, resigned expression on her pretty face.

"Okay, kimo sabe, what do you want to do? We still have a few days."

"If he's going to try what I think he will, I'll need to borrow a sub driver and a SEAL team from the navy."

"How much can we tell them out of the chute?" Rencke asked.

"Nothing. Not even my name, just that it's a CIA op. We have to keep it away from the ONI in case the leak is at the Pentagon and not down at Gitmo."

"How soon?"

"It'll take at least a couple of days to set it up, so yesterday would be good."

"Keep your cell phone turned on," Rencke said.

"Right."

SS *SHEHAB*, MID-ATLANTIC

The sun was setting a couple of points off the submarine's starboard bow and Graham, standing on the cramped bridge, shielded his eyes against the glare. They'd been running on the surface for a little more than six hours and he was certain that they'd been spotted by at least one American satellite.

Ziyax was on the bridge with him, scanning the horizon with binoculars. The late afternoon was chilly, even invigorating after the stuffiness below.

Graham took one last deep breath, then keyed the ship's intercom. "Con, bridge. Prepare to dive the boat."

"Aye, sir, prepare to dive the boat," al-Abbas replied after only a slight hesitation. The crew had not understood his orders to run on the surface, but now that the boat was well ventilated, and all of them, by fours, had been allowed briefly on deck, they didn't want to submerge.

"What has this afternoon been about?" Ziyax asked respectfully.

Graham glanced at him. The man wasn't a bad officer, limited by his lack of good training. But he wanted to be home with his family, not out here for any cause. Especially not for the Islamic *jihad*. "Insurance."

"I don't understand."

"I wanted to be spotted running on the surface, on this course, by an American satellite."

Ziyax was startled. "They know about us?"

"It's possible."

"Then they'll be waiting for us," Ziyax said. "For the sake of reason, for the sake of Allah we must turn back before we're all killed."

Graham had no real idea why he was bothering to explain anything to the Libyan, especially something so obvious. But he wanted someone to know and appreciate the ruse.

"You're right about one thing, Captain. The Americans will be waiting for us. But we've been on the same heading since we cleared Gibraltar. Southwest, toward Central America. Toward the Panama Canal, which I . . . probed last month. They'll believe that we're trying to hit the canal again." He looked into the Libyan's eyes to see if the man understood the logic. But there was no one home.

Ziyax merely stared at him.

"Insurance," Graham said. He keyed the phone again. "Bridge, con. Dive the boat."

"Aye, Cap'n, dive the boat."

Graham let Ziyax clear the bridge first, then, after one last look at the setting sun, dropped through the hatch, securing it above his head, and descended into the control room.

"I have an all-green board," Ziyax reported.

"All compartments ready in all respects," al-Abbas said.

"Very well, dive the boat," Graham said. "Make your depth four hundred meters."

Everyone in the control room looked up from their duty stations. That depth was well below the safety limits for a boat this age, and everyone knew it.

Graham waited for just a moment. "Captain, if you please."

"Aye, Captain," Ziyax said. "Diving Officer, make your depth four hundred meters."

Al-Abbas repeated the order, and went about the task of submerging the boat.

Graham walked over to the chart table, on which a small-scale chart of the western Atlantic from twenty degrees north to forty degrees north was laid out. As the bow of the submarine began to cant downward, he plotted a great circle course to the mouth of the Chesapeake still two thousand miles away. Five days.

He looked up. "I'm going to the wardroom to have my dinner," he told his crew conversationally. "When we level off—but not before we level off—come right to new course three-zero-five, and make your speed All Ahead Flank."

Graham waited until Ziyax had repeated the order then headed aft to the wardroom. "Mr. Ziyax, you have the con," he called nonchalantly over his shoulder.

SIXTY-TWO

COSMOS CLUB, WASHINGTON

Noon traffic was in full swing along Embassy Row when McGarvey pulled up in front of the Cosmos Club on Massachusetts Avenue and let the valet take his Range Rover. Only a few people in the entire city knew about the threat they were facing, and he figured that they were the lucky ones. At least for now.

He had given a lot of thought to how a missile attack on Washington might unfold, and what could be done to stop it. But although he had what he thought was a fair understanding of Graham, he was going to need a sub driver to lay out the tactics of a strike using a Foxtrot, and he was going to have to keep his ideas *outside* official military channels.

Graham would know U.S. Navy tactics, and how to sidestep them, so they needed to throw him a curveball. Something he would not expect.

The club, which was housed in an elegant three-story Victorian brownstone, had been in existence since the late 1800s, and was the gathering place for movers and shakers; the Nobel prizewinners, the presidents and CEOs of major corporations, the most powerful lawyers and politicians. Merely being wealthy didn't guarantee acceptance, its members had to be people who were doing significant things.

Just inside the elegant entrance, McGarvey gave his name to the receptionist and was directed to the lavishly decorated Smith Dining Room. The tuxedoed maître d' brought him to a corner table where two men, both dressed in civilian clothes, were seated.

McGarvey recognized the older, slightly built man with thinning white hair and pale blue eyes. "Admiral, thanks for agreeing to meet with me on such short notice."

Admiral Joseph Puckett, Jr., glanced up, but didn't offer his hand. "The president said I was to cooperate with you, McGarvey. Sit down."

Puckett had the reputation of being one of the toughest officers ever to chair the Joint Chiefs. McGarvey had never dealt with the man before, but the admiral was also widely known as being a fair, if no-nonsense, man, which meant he was a military officer first and a politician a distant second.

"Fair enough," McGarvey said, taking a seat.

Their waiter came immediately and when he'd left with McGarvey's drink order, Puckett introduced the other man as Navy Captain Frank Dillon, a former Seawolf submarine commander, and now boss of his own squadron in Honolulu. He was a lean, well-muscled man with sandy hair, a thick mustache, and a pleasant, almost handsome face.

He and McGarvey shook hands. "Weren't you the director of the CIA a couple years ago?" he asked.

McGarvey nodded. "I didn't like dealing with politicians so I got out while I still had my hide intact."

Puckett nodded, then put his napkin on the table and pushed away. "I'll leave you gentlemen to it," he said. "Whatever Mr. McGarvey wants, within reason, you're to comply, Captain," he told Dillon.

"Yes, sir," Dillon said, obviously not at all sure what he was getting into.

Puckett turned back to McGarvey. "You may know that I've sent a carrier battle group to screen the canal. Should get down there within the next forty-eight hours. What you might not know is that a couple hours ago a satellite spotted your boy on the surface in the mid-Atlantic, still heading southwest."

"Isn't that unusual?" McGarvey asked. "Running on the surface in broad daylight. He'd have to know he'd be spotted."

"May have had trouble with his snorkel," Puckett said. He gave McGarvey a hard stare. "I know enough about you to know that you're a good man to have around in a pinch. But I also know enough about you to know that whenever you get involved in something, a lot of people, some of them ours, get hurt."

"I don't invent the bad guys, Admiral."

Puckett nodded, turned on his heel, and stalked off.

"I probably could have handled that a little better," McGarvey said wryly. He turned to Dillon. "Captain, have you been told why you're here today?"

"No, sir. Just that you're working on an assignment for the CIA, with the blessing of the White House, and you need someone who knows submarine tactics."

McGarvey glanced around the half full dining room. Their table had been picked so that they would be out of earshot of any other diner. "Al-Quaida has gotten itself a Foxtrot submarine, a Perisher captain, a mixed Iranian-Libyan crew, and an unknown number of weapons, with which I think they mean to strike Washington."

"I see," Dillon said, his eyes widening slightly. "What kind of weapons?"

"We don't know, but it's possible they might have cruise missiles, maybe anthrax, possibly even a nuke. The thing is, I want to stop them before they can launch."

"That's the problem," Dillon said. "If we know when they were coming we could lay a screen and try to intercept them. But they could go silent a couple of hundred miles off and we'd be lucky to stumble across them before they launched."

"What about afterward?" McGarvey asked.

"We'd nail them for sure. The Foxtrot makes a fair amount of noise, especially when the skipper puts the pedal to the metal. They'd have no chance of getting away."

"That's the problem, "McGarvey said. "This guy's not interested in suicide, which means he has a plan to fire his weapons and then get out of there."

"How sure of this are you, sir?" Dillon asked.

"The name's Kirk. And I'm not sure. It's just a hunch. I think he'd like to get up into the Chesapeake somewhere, if that's possible, fire his weapons, and then set his boat to self-destruct while he locks out and disappears ashore. He's done something similar before."

"I did a classified paper for Homeland Security last year outlining just that possibility," Dillon said.

"I know, I read it a couple days ago," McGarvey said. "I need your help to stop them, if you want the job, Captain."

"Name's Frank," Dillon said. "We'll need a SEAL team. Do we have a timetable?"

"Puckett said that the sub was in the mid-Atlantic a couple of hours ago. If he submerges and changes course right now, he could be off the bay in what, five or six days?"

"About that," Dillon said.

"Then let's get on with it," McGarvey said. "How soon can you get a SEAL team together without attracting any notice?"

"Now what are you trying to tell me?"

"There might be a spy in the ONI feeding information to al-Quaida."

Dillon's jaw tightened. "That's just great. The son of a bitch." He took a business card out of his pocket, wrote an address in Alexandria on the back, and handed it to McGarvey. "This is a friend of mine. I stay with him and his wife whenever I'm in Washington. Come over about six tomorrow. We'll have a backyard barbecue."

"No specifics to anybody."

"I'll leave that up to you tomorrow night," Dillon said.

SS *SHEHAB*, HEADING NORTHWEST

Something woke Graham from a sound sleep in his cabin. The only light came from what spilled in around the curtain covering his door, and the dim green illumination of the dials on the clock and compass on the bulkhead above his pull-down desk.

He'd been having the sex dream about Jillian again, but although he could see her naked body lying next to his, her face had faded over the past month or so and it frightened him. He'd known that he'd gone a little crazy after her death, but he was worried now that he might be losing his mind, losing his ability to think clearly, to reason, to act with purpose.

It was a few minutes after 0200 Greenwich mean time, and the boat was quiet, even the deep-throated hum of the electric motors putting out enough power now to run at All Ahead Full were muted, barely discernible. The crew had been given the rig-for-silent-running order when they'd submerged, and so far there'd been no mistakes.

Each time the batteries got below twenty percent, they would rise to snorkel depth and run on diesel long enough for the recharge and then return to four hundred meters in their push for the U.S. East Coast. They'd done that throughout most of the day, and they'd be good now for hours, even at this speed.

Graham had pushed the boat and the crew hard so that none of them would have the time to stop and think about what was going on. If they had, they'd realize that this was going to be a one-way trip for them. Once the missiles were launched, the U.S. Navy would zero in on their position within minutes. There would barely be enough time for one or two men to escape, not the entire crew.

He drifted back to sleep, trying to recapture the same dream about his wife, and it seemed like only seconds had passed when someone came into the cabin.

"Wake up, English," al-Abbas said.

Graham opened his eyes. The Libyan officer stood above him, a 9mm Beretta pistol in his hand. He was out of breath and red in the face as if he had just gotten off a treadmill. Ziyax was behind him at the door, holding the curtain aside. He too looked winded, and angry.

"What is this, a mutiny?" Graham asked calmly. Ziyax was also holding a pistol. The two men had evidently been arguing about just this.

"An execution," al-Abbas said.

"Put the gun down, Assam," Ziyax said.

"It's time to end this here and now. I will kill him, and then we can turn around and go home."

"Think about what his crew will do to us when they find out what you've done. They have more weapons than we do. It would be a bloodbath."

"I would rather die out here like that, than send nuclear missiles raining down on Washington," al-Abbas said. "We're not al-Quaida. It's not our fight now."

"Colonel Quaddafi offered this boat to us, and it was he who ordered the nuclear weapons to be brought aboard," Graham said. He'd reached the Steyr 9mm pistol at his side under the blanket and he eased the safety catch to the off position and slowly began to slide it up over his hip so that he would have a clear shot at the Libyan.

"Two of my men who armed the weapons are sick," al-Abbas said.

"You have Geiger counters. The weapons don't leak," Graham lied smoothly. He had the pistol above his hip, his finger on the trigger.

"But they're sick, and none of your men had the nerve to go anywhere near the missiles," al-Abbas argued. He was getting agitated and he started to wave the pistol around.

Graham began to put pressure on the trigger.

"I'm sorry, Assam, but I'll do whatever it takes to get back to my wife and children," Ziyax said, and he raised his pistol.

"You'll never get home. None of us will unless we stop this madman."

"If I can't go home, then I will do whatever it takes to please Colonel Quaddafi, who will see to it that my family is well cared for."

"Tariq?" al-Abbas said, half-turning.

"Put your gun down," Ziyax said.

Al-Abbas said something in Arabic and started to turn back, but before he could bring his pistol to bear, and before Graham could fire, Ziyax shot the man in the side of the head at point-blank range, blood flying everywhere.

SIXTY-THREE

□

ALEXANDRIA

Liz and Todd had come into town to take Kathleen to dinner, which was one less concern on McGarvey's mind when he showed up at the address Dillon had given him. The house was a small two-story Colonial in a pleasant middle-class neighborhood of shade trees, people washing cars or mowing lawns, kids shooting hoops above the garage doors, and bikes or trikes parked in just about every driveway. It was this kind of a life that had never been possible for McGarvey and Katy, because of his job, but there was nothing he could do now to bring any of it back.

The driveway was full with a BMW convertible, a Corvette, an older Porsche, and a plain gray Taurus with government plates, so McGarvey parked on the street and walked around the side of the house to the backyard.

A man in a chef's hat was tending to a built-in barbecue at the edge of a small brick patio while Dillon, seated at a picnic table, was engaged in conversation with two muscular men and an attractive young woman. All of them were in blue jeans and sweatshirts, and all of them, including the woman, were drinking beer from bottles. One of them said something, and they all laughed.

The man at the barbecue turned and spotted McGarvey. "Frank, the cavalry's arrived."

Dillon looked up and got to his feet. "Glad you could make it," he said, coming across to McGarvey. They shook hands. "Let me introduce you to everyone."

"Holy shit," the woman said. "You're Kirk McGarvey. You used to run the CIA."

McGarvey chuckled. "I must be getting old. I never got that reaction from a woman before."

"Don't mind my wife," the man in the chef's hat said, smiling. "Her handle is Lips, for more than one reason." He came over and shook hands.

"Lieutenant Commander Bill Jackson," Dillon said. "This is his house. "And Lips, Terri, is his wife. She's a lieutenant."

Terri laughed. "Half of it's my house," she said, shaking McGarvey's hand. "I have a feeling this is going to be a real interesting party tonight."

Her grip was firm and her eyes direct. McGarvey got the impression that she was in every bit as good physical shape as the men here. "Nice to meet you."

"The other two are the chiefs, Bob Ercoli and Dale MacKeever," Dillon introduced them.

All four of them appeared to be in outstanding physical condition, and like most of the instructors out at the Farm they exuded self-confidence. "You're Navy SEALs," McGarvey said.

"Does it show?" Jackson asked.

"I wouldn't want to go up against any of you."

"Then no hanky-panky with the boss's wife," Ercoli quipped. "Even we can't get away with it."

Terri leaned over and got McGarvey a beer from a cooler on the patio bricks beside her and tossed it to him. "Frank sure pulled a rabbit out of the hat this time," she said. "You have our attention, Mr. McGarvey, what do you want with us that couldn't have gone through channels?"

McGarvey opened the beer, took a deep drink, and sat down at the table. "Al-Quaida is on its way to the Chesapeake with a Libyan Foxtrot submarine and I think there's a good chance they mean to hit Washington."

"Holy shit," Ercoli said softly.

"Because they didn't hit the White House with the fourth plane like they wanted on 9/11?" Jackson asked.

"Something like that," McGarvey said.

"How soon?"

"Five days, maybe less."

"Send a couple of sub hunters out to look for them," MacKeever suggested.

Dillon shook his head. "Their captain is a Brit, graduated from Perisher. The second he got wind that we were on to him, he'd launch and we couldn't stop it."

"He's got missiles?" Jackson asked.

"We don't know for sure," McGarvey said. "But there's a good chance he could have Russian short-range tube-launched missiles. And possibly even a small nuclear weapon or two."

"That's just peachy," Terri said, and McGarvey shot her a startled look. It was the same expression Katy used sometimes. "What?" she asked.

"Another time," McGarvey said. "This won't be an official mission, and you won't be getting any orders, so the shit could hit the fan."

"But if we pull it off we'll be heroes," Terri said. She turned to her husband. "Gee, dear, looks like we might get our honeymoon after all."

"This is serious," McGarvey warned.

"We wouldn't be much interested if it wasn't," she said, her smile gone. "I assume you have a plan."

"They're going to try to sneak into the bay and get as close to Washington as they can before they launch their missiles, if that's what they have," McGarvey said. "I want to be there, waiting for them."

"Why not offshore?" Jackson asked.

"Because the sub driver wants to escape. Once they launch he can lock out of the boat, come ashore, and disappear," McGarvey said.

"His crew won't have time to get out," Jackson pointed out.

"No," McGarvey agreed. "We need to find the sub before they launch and stop them before they know we're on to them."

"We'd have to know where they're headed," Ercoli suggested.

"The York River," Dillon said. "It's less than one hundred miles from the White House so there'd be almost no warning time, it's deep enough to hide a submarine, and it's well out of Second Fleet's way at Norfolk."

"They'd have to get there first," Jackson said.

"They will if we don't warn anybody," McGarvey said.

"You're taking an awfully big chance."

"I don't want to *react* to an attack," McGarvey said. "I want to stop it."

Jackson looked at his wife and the other two SEAL team members, then back at McGarvey. "I can get the equipment, including a boat, but we'll need a non-navy staging area."

"The Farm," McGarvey said. "It's on the York River and no questions that I can't answer will be asked."

"How soon do you want us there?" Jackson asked.

"The sooner the better. By this time tomorrow?"

Jackson nodded. He turned to Dillon. "You coming along on this one, Frank?"

"Wouldn't miss it."

SS *SHEHAB*, NEARING THE U.S. COAST

It was morning topside when Chamran called Graham aft to the engineering spaces.

They had just finished running on diesel to recharge the batteries and were once again surging west-northwest at four hundred meters.

All the crew, the Iranians included, had become docile after Ziyax had shot his own first officer to death for challenging Graham. They'd not been told the details, except that the shot had been fired by the Libyan captain. It was enough for the time being to make them forget about the two sick crewmen who'd handled the nuclear packages.

Chamran and al-Hari, who'd been Graham's original choice as exec, were waiting in the battery room, one of the floor grates open. Graham stopped a few feet away.

"More nuclear weapons?" he asked. He wasn't about to get close enough to see for himself.

"No, these are the anthrax loads," al-Hari replied. He was grinning. "We're finding all sorts of little toys aboard. The good colonel must have been shitting in his robes to get rid of this stuff before somebody blew the whistle on him."

"What do you want?" Graham asked.

He'd picked al-Hari to be his exec based on the file bin Laden had provided. The man had been born in Syria, but raised by grandparents in London where he'd joined the Royal Navy Submarine Service to earn his U.K. citizenship. He quickly rose in rank to warrant officer, but was finally kicked out of the service for "activities inconsistent with the status as a resident alien."

He'd spent the next few years fighting the *jihad* against the Zionists for no other reason than the thrill of the hunt. He had developed a taste for killing people. When al-Quaida went looking for submarine crewmen, al-Hari's name was near the top of a fairly short list.

"We're seventy-two hours out," al-Hari said. "When do you want to load the missiles into the torpedo tubes and get them ready to fire? I only ask now because the two guys who handled the nuclear packages will be too sick to work by tomorrow, and I don't want to waste anyone else."

"Do it now," Graham said, perfectly understanding al-Hari's cold logic.

"Very well. What about these canisters? We can load them aboard a couple of torpedoes set to explode a thousand meters out. Wouldn't do any damage but the germs might rise to the surface. At the very least they'd contaminate the bay."

Graham shook his head. "I want them to explode inside the boat without breaching the hull as soon as we lock out," he said. "It will be a little surprise for the navy salvage crew."

Chamran nodded. "You're a hard man for an English."

"It's a hard world."

"*Insh'allah,*" al-Hari said. *God willing.*

SIXTY-FOUR

□

THE FARM

Driving up the tree-lined road back to the CIA training facility from I-64 the next afternoon, McGarvey had the strong feeling that whatever happened in the next few days would be nothing more than a prelude to his real mission.

Whether or not they stopped Graham from unleashing whatever weapons he was bringing across the Atlantic, al-Quaida would continue the *jihad* against the West because it was a holy war that had been going on for more than one thousand years.

This submarine attack was only one battle. And even if it succeeded, it would be no more of a decisive blow against the West than the attacks of 9/11 had been.

Only two actions would end the war. The first would be eliminating Osama bin Laden as the quasi-holy figure he'd become across Dar al Islam. Capturing him and bringing him to trial would do no good. He would have a worldwide pulpit from which he could spread his message. Sending the U.S. military to kill him, either by ground forces, or by cruise missiles as Clinton had tried, would only make him a martyr. And Muslims loved martyrs. He would have to be assassinated, quietly and with no fanfare, inside his own lair.

It was what McGarvey did, and he knew that killing bin Laden would be the most satisfying hit he'd ever made, because the terrorist's face in death would never haunt his dreams.

The second thing that had to be done in order to stop the jihad was to interrupt the money. Iran, Syria, and Pakistan were high on the list of prime suspects. But McGarvey was still convinced that ultimately the United States would have to deal with the Saudis, where the bulk of the money to fund thousands of Islamic terrorist organizations around the world— including al-Quaida—was being supplied. Ironically, most of that money came from oil purchases that the United States made.

Before World War II we had sold scrap metal to Japan that had been turned into bullets to kill our soldiers. Now we were sending our money to Saudi Arabia to buy oil that was being turned against us. History had repeated itself.

Last night, after he had come back from meeting with Dillon and the SEAL team, Liz and Todd were still at the house. They'd brought the baby over and it had been a wonderful respite after the tension of the past week or so.

No one asked where he'd been for dinner, but around ten when Liz and Todd bundled the baby into the car seat, McGarvey told them that he would be coming out to the Farm sometime today. But even then no questions had been asked.

Nor had Katy questioned him in bed. She was just happy about their granddaughter. "We'll see her grow up, and maybe get married and have children of her own," Katy said. She looked at her husband, searching for a reaction. "Won't we?"

"We might be a little long of tooth by then," he told her. "But if we don't fall off our sailboat and drown, we should make it." He smiled. "We'll take turns pushing each other's wheelchair. Deal?"

"Deal," she said, and they made love, slowly and gently.

This morning McGarvey took Katy shopping and they had an early lunch in Georgetown before he dropped her back at the safe house and headed down to the Farm.

"Come back to me as soon as you can, darling," was all she'd said to him before he left.

On the way out of town he'd telephoned Rencke at the Building for any updates on the Foxtrot's position, but the submarine had not been spotted since the mid-Atlantic and it was still presumed that she was headed to the canal.

"Dennis Berndt called Dick this morning wanting to know what you were up to," Rencke had said. "The prez is getting worried and he's circling the wagons."

"I got some navy help and they're going to meet me at the Farm this afternoon, but for now I want the White House and Adkins kept out of the loop in case this op goes south. There'll be plenty of blame to go around, no matter what happens."

"I don't think Dick wants to know, anyway he's not been asking any questions," Rencke said. "But Peter has got his hands full." Peter Franza was the CIA's chief press officer. "The Washington Post is storming the gates, wanting to know what's going on at Gitmo. Apparently there was another leak, and the Post found out about the riot."

"Was my name mentioned?"

"Not so far," Rencke said. "Peter's stonewalling them, but that won't last much longer."

"I'll tell you what. Make a blind call to the managing editor at the Post and put a word in his ear about Weiss. Hint that maybe he's under investigation for prisoner abuse."

"Won't Weiss come after you in the press?"

"Only if he's innocent," McGarvey said. "But if he's helping al-Quaida he'll deny the story, and then hunker down until the storm passes. Who knows, he might even try to run."

"I'll get on it," Rencke had promised.

The gate guards at the entrance to the Farm were dressed in BDUs,

Heckler & Koch M8s slung over their shoulders. They were expecting him, and after he showed his ID, they raised the barrier, and passed him through.

His daughter came out of the administration building when he pulled up and got out of the SUV. "Hi, Daddy," she said, giving him a peck on the cheek. "Todd's down at the hand-to-hand barn. We didn't know what time you'd get here."

"Let's take a walk, sweetheart. I've got to ask you to put your neck on the chopping block for the next day or two."

She had to laugh. "That's our thing, isn't it?"

They headed down one of the paths through the woods toward the river. "You're going to have some company this evening, but I don't want anything said about it by anyone. And I mean by anyone."

"What's up, Dad?"

"We're going to try to catch a submarine that might just show up downriver in the next day or two."

Elizabeth's eyes widened slightly. "We'll lock the camp down for the duration," she said. "What can you tell me?"

SS *SHEHAB*, APPROACHING THE U.S. COAST

There was a lot of traffic on the surface. Sonar had forty-seven tracks in its tape recorder in the past twenty-four hours, most of which was commercial traffic inbound or outbound from New York well to the north. But they had detected no U.S. Navy warships.

"Doesn't make sense, unless they're laying a trap for us," al-Hari said.

It was dusk on the surface. They were running the diesel engines on snorkel to recharge the batteries. Graham called back to sonar.

"What's the range and bearing to our nearest target?"

"Fifteen thousand meters, zero-three-zero," Shihabi reported. "She's a large tanker, I think, or maybe a car carrier, heading northwest."

"Very well," Graham said. He glanced at al-Hari. "They think we're heading to the Panama Canal. They probably sent a carrier battle group down there to intercept us."

The Iranian officer shrugged and glanced up at the overhead. "The Coast Guard should be up there somewhere."

"They probably are, but closer in," Graham said.

The ship's com buzzed. "Con, this is the forward torpedo room. Let me talk to the captain." It was Ziyax.

Graham took the phone from its bracket. "This is Graham. You're supposed to be off duty."

"We have a problem up here, Captain. A serious one."

"What is it?"

"It would be better if you saw for yourself," Ziyax said.

Graham was irritated. The next twenty-four hours approaching the mouth of the Chesapeake Bay would be the most crucial. If the Americans had somehow guessed that the *Shehab* was not headed south, and was instead heading toward Washington or New York, the U.S. Navy or Coast Guard could indeed have laid a trap for them. Last night he had ordered Russian conventional free-running HE torpedoes loaded in the remaining four bow tubes, as well as the four stern tubes, in case they got backed into a corner and had to fight their way out.

Winning such a fight one-on-one against an American ASW ship was not likely unless they got lucky, so he meant to avoid a confrontation whatever it took.

That was the major issue facing them, not some glitch in the forward torpedo room.

But if they were cornered he would immediately launch the missiles.

"Go up there and find out what's going on," Graham told al-Hari. "Whatever it is, get it fixed."

"Yes, sir," al-Hari said, and he left the con.

Graham was about to call sonar again, but he stayed his hand from flipping the switch on the com. Something was spooking him; something niggling at the back of his mind. Like al-Hari had done, he glanced up at the overhead as if he could peer through the maze of plumbing and wiring and the inner and outer hulls to the surface, to see what was waiting for them.

He walked over to the periscope pedestal, raised the search scope, and did a quick three-sixty in the fading light. The nearest sonar target was fifteen kilometers away, well over the horizon. They were utterly alone for the moment out here, the skies clear, the seas two meters or less.

He looked away from the eyepieces. The men were docile. They were obeying their orders without question now.

But something was playing with him, as if he were forgetting something important.

He took a second look, then lowered the periscope. The ship's com buzzed.

"Con, this is the torpedo room." It was al-Hari.

Graham answered. "Yes, what's the problem up there, Muhamed?"

"Tube two's inner door will not seal properly. The gasket is shot."

"Do we have a spare?" Graham asked.

"Yes, Cap'n, but that's not the problem. No one wants to open the door, not even at gunpoint, because of the radiation. And without the fix we will not be able to fire that missile."

"Transfer the missile to another tube," Graham ordered. His nerves were beginning to jump all over the place.

"As I said, no one will touch the missile," al-Hari replied. His tone was maddeningly calm. "Do you want me to start shooting people? I can begin with Captain Ziyax."

"No, we need every man aboard," Graham said. He desperately wanted to visualize Jillian's face. It was important to him. She'd known the right words, the right gestures to calm him down whenever he got like this. "You're in charge up there. We need that missile, otherwise this entire exercise was for nothing. If you can't get someone else to work the problem, do it yourself."

Graham slammed the growler phone back in its cradle.

The bastards weren't going to get away with it. They could have broken radio silence to call him home. They hadn't been at war. No big secrets would have been revealed.

They would pay. All the sons of bitches would pay.

SIXTY-FIVE

□

THE FARM

McGarvey stood at the dock waiting for Jackson and his SEAL team to show up with the boat they'd promised for this time yesterday. It was late afternoon, nearly forty-eight hours since the backyard barbecue, and he was acutely conscious that time was not on their side.

There was a light chop on the river, and tonight it was supposed to be overcast with light rain likely. Nearly perfect conditions for a submarine to sneak past Norfolk and make it into the York River. And terrible conditions for a search-and-seize mission.

"Not their fault," Dillon said at McGarvey's shoulder. "NSW Group Three didn't want to part with a boat unless they knew what the mission was." Special Operations boats belonged to Naval Special Warfare Groups Three and Four, and always came complete with their own highly trained crews. They weren't items of military equipment that were usually loaned out.

It had taken a call from Admiral Puckett himself to make the CO of Group Three see things in the proper light. That was last night, and still it had taken until now to find the proper boat in Norfolk, get it fueled and prepped, and bring it across the mouth of the bay and up into the York River.

Jackson had telephoned a couple hours ago that they would be under way within minutes; their estimated time of arrival at the Farm's dock was 1800. It was that time now.

The sharp crack of a small explosion somewhere in the distance behind them was followed by the rattle of small-arms fire. It sounded like M8s to McGarvey's ear. Liz and Todd had kept the batch of new recruits going through the course super-busy and out of the way, and even Gloria Ibenez, who'd come down for a second debriefing, had left for Langley this morning without knowing that McGarvey was here.

He and Dillon were dressed in SEAL night camos, their faces blackened, their weapons and other equipment in satchels at their feet. Their plan was to stay on the river near the only area deep enough to hide a submarine and wait for the Foxtrot to show up.

The approaches to the Panama Canal were being covered in case he was wrong about Graham. And if a missile launch was made from offshore up here, there was little or nothing that could be done about it, other than mount an all-out search along our entire coast. The risk, of course, was that the first whiff Graham got that they were on to him, he'd launch anyway. He had put them in a catch-22.

Adkins had somehow managed to convince the president and his staff to go up to Camp David for a few days. Rencke had called this morning with the news. Most of the key Cabinet members, along with a good portion of Congress, had quietly filtered out of town, not knowing exactly why, except that Don Hamel had quietly spread the word that now might be a good time to visit their constituencies. The media had started to sit up and take notice, but so far they'd come up with little more than speculation.

"It's getting like a ghost town around here, and it's driving them nuts, ya know," Rencke said. "What about Mrs. M?"

"She's far enough from downtown that she'll be able to get out of the way if something happens," McGarvey said. It was the best-case scenario because she had dug in her heels, and nothing he could say would convince her to go to their house in Florida.

He had considered trying to convince the president to order the evacuation of the city, but that would have done no good either. The panic would kill people, and if the attack did not occur, the government's already dismal ratings would fall even lower.

"Good luck," Rencke had said.

"They're here," Dillon said at his side.

McGarvey looked up from his thoughts as a low-slung, dark-hulled boat appeared in the dusk around the bend in the river. It was a Mark V Special Operations Craft used to insert and extract SEAL teams from operational areas where stealth was more important than heavy-duty armament. At eighty-two feet on deck, she displaced fifty-seven tons, and could do fifty knots through the water while making very little noise.

She ran without lights and even as she closed on the dock, it was hard to hear her engines, or make out many details. The delay, Jackson had explained to them, had been needed to fit the boat out with the passive side scan sonar McGarvey had requested, along with a lot of ammunition for the two deck-mounted 7.62mm machine guns, six Dräger closed-circuit rebreathers, enough underwater demolitions material to crack the submarine's hull like an eggshell, and some basic salvage gear.

Terri Jackson was at the helm as the sleek boat eased alongside the dock, the softly grumbling engines at idle. Bill Jackson was on the bridge with her, while MacKeever and Ercoli were on the open stern deck. They did not bother with dock lines.

McGarvey and Dillon tossed their equipment bags across and then scrambled aboard.

The instant they were on deck, Terri gunned the engines and they headed away, making a long looping turn to take them back downriver toward the bay.

"Welcome aboard, gentlemen," Ercoli said. "Soon as you stow your gear below, FX wants to have a word." FX was Jackson's handle, which he'd earned early on in his SEAL career because of the special effects he was fond of using in the field.

"What's up?" Dillon asked.

"We might have pulled some luck," Ercoli said. "An Orion patrol about a hundred klicks off the mouth of the bay thought they picked up a MAD target, but when they went back it was gone." MAD was a Magnetic Anomaly Detector, a device that was able to detect masses of ferrous metal submerged as deep as one thousand feet. "Lots of traffic in the area, so your boy might have detected the overflight, and ducked under one of the surface ships that was in the vicinity."

"When was this?" Dillon asked.

"Two hours ago," Ercoli said. "A friend of FX's gave us a call from Second's ops center just before we shoved off. They're classifying it as a stray hit, but the word was out that we wanted anything that came up no matter how thin it was."

"That's him," McGarvey said.

"That's what we figured," MacKeever said. He was grinning ear to ear. "Tonight's the night, and it's going to be a good one."

SS *SHEHAB*

The Foxtrot eased her way to the west toward the center channel into Chesapeake Bay, her keel occasionally scraping the bottom. It was after ten in the evening and there was no shipping traffic for the moment.

The water was very shallow here, even in the middle of the inbound fairway, so that the submarine was only partially submerged. It would be somewhat deeper once they passed the Bay Bridge-Tunnel, but there would not be enough water to completely submerge until they reached the York River.

Graham and Ziyax stood topside on the bridge, the lapping water less than two meters below them, the boat's hull invisible underwater.

Both missiles were ready to fire now that the gasket on tube two had been replaced. Al-Hari was already beginning to feel the effects of the heavy dose of radiation he'd taken, but he'd been fatalistic about it this morning after he'd vomited for the first time.

"Your story about the shrimper coming to pick us up is a lie," he'd told Graham in the companionway outside the officer's head. No one else had been within earshot at the moment.

"The others don't suspect?"

"No one else cares," al-Hari said. "Like me they're willing to die for the jihad." He coughed up some blood into a rag. "Except for you and Captain Ziyax. You're the only two aboard who think they have anything to live for other than Paradise."

"You'll get your wish," Graham had replied indifferently.

Al-Hari had nodded. "Once the missiles are away, I will set the explosives on the anthrax canisters, so you had best be gone by then." Al-Hari grabbed Graham by the arm. "I ask only two favors. Take Ziyax with you, he's a good man. And leave me a pistol, I'll need time to disable the escape trunk, and then sabotage the engines in case anyone has a change of heart."

Religious mumbo jumbo had always been a puzzlement to Graham. And working closely with the al-Quaida, many of their mujahideen willing to martyr themselves for the cause, had brought him no closer to an understanding. "Why are you so willing to die?" he asked.

Al-Hari had smiled. "You wouldn't understand, English."

"Try me."

"It's simple, my friend. You only have to know God and love Him. The rest is easy."

Graham raised his binoculars and studied the bridge two miles ahead. There didn't seem to be any traffic up there either, though it was difficult to tell with much certainty because of the jumble of multicolored lights ashore and on the channel markers in the water.

One of the Libyan technicians had managed to rig red, green, and white lights on the exposed sail and one of the masts so that from a distance the submarine would appear to be a small fishing boat returning from sea. The fiction would hold for anything but a close inspection, and so far in that regard their luck was holding.

"Al-Hari is sick with radiation poisoning now," Ziyax said. "When it is time to leave what are we going to do with him and my two crewmen who handled the missiles? We cannot take them with us."

"No, we can't," Graham said, continuing to study the bridge. It had been conceived in the brain of a man, not a god. And it had been built by the hand of man, not god. There was proof of man's design everywhere, but so far as Graham had ever been able to detect, there'd never been any concrete sign of the existence of any god, neither the god of the Muslims, nor the gods of the Jews or Christians.

Yet they were willing to die for something they could not see, feel, hear, touch, or smell. All on faith. It was utterly amazing to him.

"What do you suggest?" Ziyax asked.

Graham lowered his binoculars. "Nothing, actually. They'll get their wishes before the others."

"What's that?"

"To die martyrs for the glorious cause, of course," Graham said. He picked up the phone. "Come right five degrees."

"Aye, turning right five degrees to new course three-three-zero," the new COB replied in a subdued voice.

SIXTY—SIX

□

SOC-4

The SEAL Special Operations Craft was drifting well out of the channel outside the mouth of the York River, about five miles east of Yorktown and the Highway 17 Bridge.

McGarvey was on the afterdeck with Ercoli and MacKeever, while Dillon had joined Jackson and Terri on the bridge to operate the side-scan sonar.

The water here was still too shallow for a submarine to completely submerge, but they'd hoped that the passive sonar set would pick up the signature sounds of the Foxtrot's diesel engines.

It was three in the morning. The rain that had threatened had never materialized, but a damp fog had settled in on top of them, making everything wet and reducing visibility to less than fifty yards. Lights ashore were nothing more than very dim halos in the distance, and even the channel markers off the SOC's starboard side were only vague green and red pastels, some of them blinking.

The door to the bridge was open. Dillon was hunched over the sonar display. "I have engine noises," he called softly.

Since they'd arrived on station southeast of Gloucester Point just after dark, they'd tracked nine targets coming upriver, all but one of them noncommercial pleasure boats.

"Where?" McGarvey asked, keeping his voice low.

"Bearing zero-eight-zero about nine miles out," Dillon replied. "Heading upbound, making maybe ten knots." He looked up from the screen and in the dim red light illuminating his face it was obvious he was impressed. "It's our boy."

"You sure?" McGarvey asked.

"Three screws, big diesels. Not one of ours."

MacKeever and Ercoli were looking toward the east through light-intensifying binoculars.

"Anything?" McGarvey asked.

"Still too far," Ercoli said. "But maybe they sent a chase boat ahead to make sure the channel is clear."

"Is there any deep water farther up into the bay?" McGarvey asked.

"Nothing," Dillon called back. "This is the only place." He turned back to the sonar.

"Do you want us to light up the radar?" Jackson asked.

"Negative," Dillon said. "His ESM's gear would recognize it as military." He made an adjustment to the controls. "Hang on."

The night was utterly still for several long moments.

"His aspect ratio is changing," Dillon said. "Stand by."

It seemed for the moment as if the entire world were asleep, yet McGarvey could almost feel an evil presence somewhere in the darkness to the east. Bad people were coming with a dark intent, like monsters stalking in the night, getting set to pounce.

Dillon looked up. "It's turned directly toward us," he said. "It's the Foxtrot heading to where it can submerge."

Jackson came to the open door. "Okay, McGarvey, we've bagged him. Now what? Do you want to call for backup?"

"Will his radar be on?" McGarvey asked.

"I don't think he'll risk it," Dillon answered.

"We'll let him pass and then come in behind him out of visual range," McGarvey said. "As soon as he submerges we'll dive down and knock on the escape trunk hatch."

Jackson's wife laughed. "That'll get their attention," she said. "Won't they fire whatever weapons they have?"

"I'm hoping they'll try," McGarvey said. "If they have missiles what tubes would they load them in?" he asked Dillon.

"They'd probably start with tube one, and go from there depending on how many weapons they have. Wouldn't make any sense to fire them from the stern tubes."

McGarvey's plan suddenly dawned on Ercoli. "Holy shit, the salvage equipment you wanted," he said. "I thought you were going to use it to cut through the hull into the escape trunk. But that's not it." He turned to look up at Jackson on the bridge. "FX, this crazy bastard wants us to weld the torpedo tube outer doors shut."

"Can it be done?" Jackson asked Dillon.

"I don't see why not."

Terri raised an eyebrow. "I thought you and your English captain were either very brave or very crazy," she said. "But I was wrong."

"Which is it?" McGarvey asked.

She laughed. "Both," she said, and she immediately raised a hand. "But I love it. One guy is bringing a Russian submarine up a shallow bay past a major enemy navy base, and the other guy wants to do hand-to-hand combat with the boat." She turned to her husband. "Honey, this sounds like fun. Why didn't we think of it first?"

SS *SHEHAB*

The bottom dropped away once they passed under the Highway 17 Bridge into the York River.

Graham keyed the bridge telephone. "Con, bridge. What's our depth?"

"Bridge, we have fifteen meters under our keel, but it doesn't look like it'll get much deeper," al-Hari responded. He was obviously very sick.

The boat was already partially submerged. Only the top couple of meters plus the masts were above water. Another fifteen meters would do nicely. "Very well, prepare to dive the boat."

"Aye, Cap'n, prepare to dive the boat."

Graham replaced the phone in its bracket under the coaming, and looked at Ziyax, who was studying something to the stern through light-intensifying binoculars. "What do you see?"

"I thought I heard something," Ziyax replied softly. "Engines, but very quiet."

Ziyax might be a Libyan, but he'd been trained by Russians. Graham had developed a grudging respect for the man's abilities, if not his judgment, on the long trip across the Atlantic. He called the control room again.

"Secure the diesel engines and switch to electric power, All Ahead Slow."

Al-Hari hesitated for a second. "Aye, sir. Switching to electric motors."

Within a few seconds the soft rumbling of the three diesels died away, and the night became totally silent except for the delicate sounds of the leading edge of the sail cutting slowly through the water.

Ziyax continued to study the thickening fog behind them.

Graham cocked an ear and held his breath. Their sonar was blind aft, but if a U.S. Navy vessel had spotted them coming into the bay, or turning up into the York River, they would have charged in, radar sets hot, searchlights blazing, the guard frequencies alive with demands to stop and identify, and warning shots fired across their bows. They wouldn't be sneaking around without lights. It made no sense to him.

There was the man on the bridge of the Apurto Devlán with the gray-green eyes. Bin Laden was certain it had been Kirk McGarvey. He is the one man above all others who you must respect and fear.

But there was absolutely no reason to expect that McGarvey were here in this time and place. No reason whatsoever.

Graham held his breath and strained to pick up a sound, any sound, no matter how faint or unlikely, that might indicate someone was behind them.

But he heard nothing.

Ziyax lowered his binoculars. "I must have been mistaken," he said. He shrugged. "Nerves."

They were about four miles upriver from Yorktown here, and there was a certain delicious irony to their position in Graham's mind, because they were only five miles downriver from the CIA's training base.

For a moment he thought about the man on the bridge of the *Apurto Devlán*, but then he called the control room. "Put the boat on the bottom," he ordered.

"Aye, Cap'n," al-Hari responded.

Ziyax was first down the ladder.

Graham cocked an ear to listen one last time, then dropped down into the sail, secured the hatch, and descended the rest of the way into the control room. He took the 1MC mike down from its bracket near the periscope pedestal. "Battle stations, missile," he ordered calmly, his voice transmitted to every compartment aboard the submarine.

Al-Hari was at the ballast control panel, releasing air from the tanks in a carefully controlled sequence, and they started down, cautiously because they had no real idea what was on the bottom.

Ziyax went to the weapons control station and began the process of spinning up the cruise missile guidance systems, making the engines ready to fire once the missiles were ejected from the torpedo tubes and rose to the surface, and arming the nuclear weapons, which would fire at five thousand feet over the capital city.

"All Ahead Stop," al-Hari ordered, as the boat settled.

The angle on the bow was very shallow, and they drifted another two hundred meters, their speed slowly bleeding off until their keel scraped the bottom. The boat lurched forward then came to a complete stop, easing a few degrees over on her port side.

"Secure the motors," Graham said softly. *Shehab* had reached her final resting place. He casually glanced at the men gathered at their stations around him in the control room. This was to be their mausoleum, he thought indifferently. They wanted martyrdom, they would have it.

"Missile one and two are ready in all respects to fire, Captain," Ziyax reported. "Shall I flood the tubes and open the outer doors?"

"Flood the tubes and open the outer doors, but do not fire the missiles," Graham ordered.

"Aye, Captain," Ziyax responded mechanically. He reached up to a control panel and flipped two switches. A few seconds later, two lights blinked green. "The tubes are flooded and the outer doors are open."

Something was wrong. Flooding a torpedo tube and opening its door to the sea was a fairly noisy operation. "I didn't hear a thing," Graham said.

"Captain, my indicators show open doors."

Graham snatched the growler phone. "Forward torpedo room, this is the captain. I want a visual on tubes one and two."

A few seconds later one of Ziyax's people came back. "Captain, tubes one and two are flooded and the outer doors appear to be open."

"Very well," Graham said, and he hung up the phone.

"When will we fire the missiles?" Ziyax asked.

"Soon," Graham said. "First I need to see if our ride is topside and in a safe position. Wouldn't do to hit them with our missiles."

"Isomil, are there any contacts on the surface?" Ziyax called to his sonar man.

"There might have been one briefly off our port stern quarter, but it's gone now, sir," the Libyan junior officer responded.

"Get your crew ready to abandon the boat as soon as I return," Graham said. "We'll set the missiles to launch on a countdown clock. Thirty minutes should give us plenty of time."

"It's already been done, Captain," Ziyax said. He stepped aside from the weapons panel so that they could all see the launch controls for tubes one and two. They were in countdown mode at twenty-nine minutes and eighteen seconds.

Graham shrugged. "Very inventive of you, Captain."

Ziyax pulled out a pistol. "This won't be another *Distal Volente* in which my entire crew is killed," he said. "This time it will be you and your men who die."

Al-Hari fired two shots from Graham's left, both catching Ziyax in the chest and shoving him backwards, his pistol firing once into the chart table.

Graham pulled his Steyr and shot the young Libyan at the diving planes and steering yoke, at the same time al-Hari stepped forward and put bullets into the heads of both sonar operators.

"Best you leave now, Captain," he told Graham. "I fixed the firing circuits so that the timer cannot be shut off."

"I don't think the outer doors are open. You'll have to find a way to get to them."

"I'll do it," al-Hari promised. He was weak, but still able to function.

Graham looked into his eyes. "I don't understand."

"No, and you never will," al-Hari said. "Not until you have come to know God, which I think is too great a leap for you to make."

Someone from forward fired a pistol shot that ricocheted off the deck between them. He and Graham fell back out of the line of fire.

"Get out of here while you still can," al-Hari said. "And may Allah go with you."

Graham shrugged indifferently, and ducked through the aft hatch, to get his things from his cabin and make his way to the escape trunk. "I need three men to lock out with me!" he shouted. It was the only way he figured he'd get off this boat now. He couldn't shoot his way out, so he needed the cooperation of three crewmen who were not so willing to die for the cause after all. He would take care of them once they reached the surface.

SOC-4

"Holy shit, it's gunfire," Dillon said, looking up from the side-scan sonar.

"Sounds like the bad guys are getting cranky," Terri said.

She and the others were donning their black wet suits, equipment packs, and rebreather units. They'd lowered an anchor just aft of the submarine, which was sitting on the bottom in about seventy feet of water, its sail just a few feet beneath the surface.

The two welding sets were on the afterdeck, ready to go into the water. The job of making sure that as many of the forward torpedo tubes as possible would not open had fallen to them.

McGarvey was going to stay topside with the boat in case the others needed help, but the sounds of gunfire changed everything. "You're going to need all the help you can get," he said, pulling on a black wet suit and the rebreather that Terri had to help him with.

"You ever do this before?" she asked.

"Shoot bad guys, or go for a swim in the middle of the night?"

"Both at the same time."

"Once, a long time ago," McGarvey said, thinking about the flooded tunnel beneath a castle in Portugal where he had very nearly lost his life. He shuddered inwardly. It wasn't his most pleasant memory.

His pistol and spare magazine of ammunition went into a waterproof pocket in his suit. Terri handed him an underwater pistol that used CO_2 to fire five-inch steel bolts that were tipped with spring-loaded razor-sharp arrowheads. On impact four blades opened and could do a considerable amount of damage to a human body. Spring-loaded racks held five bolts.

He was given two racks, plus the one loaded into the triangular frame of the eighteen-inch-long weapon.

"We dive the buddy system, Kirk," she said. "For this dive my husband pairs with Frank, and you're mine." She grinned. "Just don't think it means we're going steady or anything."

"Treat him nice, honey," FX said from the stern rail. "He's a VIP."

"I'll keep that in mind, dear," she said. "Ready?" she asked McGarvey, who'd pulled on his dive mask.

"Let's do it," he told her.

"Right," she said. MacKeever and Ercoli went down first with the welding equipment, followed by FX and Dillon, and finally Terri and McGarvey.

The water was pitch-black, though within a few feet the massive sail loomed below and ahead of them like a gigantic black beast. Two small pinpricks of light moved forward toward the bow of the submarine that was completely lost in the darkness, while Jackson and Dillon headed aft toward the escape trunk hatch. McGarvey and Terri followed the lights moving aft.

McGarvey liked diving on the reefs in the Florida Keys, in crystal-clear water, but this was different. The darkness was disorienting, and already a chill was seeping into his bones, though he was sweating with the exertion of fighting the river current.

All of a sudden the bulk of the submarine loomed out of the darkness directly below them. Dillon and Jackson had just reached the aft deck, when a huge stream of air bubbles suddenly escaped from the escape trunk hatch.

Someone was locking out.

McGarvey and the others switched off their dive lights, plunging them into nearly absolute darkness. He pulled out his CO_2 pistol, making sure by feel that the safety catch was in the off position, and swam down a few more feet to a position he thought should be just above and just aft of the hatch, with Dillon and Jackson out of his line of fire.

Terri was behind him. She touched his ankle, and then swam down to him so that their face masks were inches apart. She held up her weapon so that he could see it, and he did the same. She nodded and gave him the thumbs-up, then turned in the direction of the escape hatch.

A very large bubble of air rose past McGarvey and Terri, the current carrying it right over them. All of a sudden he saw a circle of dull red light where he thought the hatch should be. Moments later three ghostly figures, wearing what appeared to be emergency escape hoods, rose one by one from inside the submarine.

Dillon and Jackson switched on their dive lights, illuminating the three figures in harsh white light, and fired their CO_2 guns, taking out the first two men, who flopped backwards, dark, black blood streaming from the massive wounds in their chests where the razor-sharp arrowheads had punctured lungs and severed major arteries.

Terri fired at the third figure who was desperately trying to swim forward, catching him in his left thigh. Jackson was right there, firing a second shot, hitting the man in the middle of the back, severing his spine and causing his body to go completely limp.

McGarvey had been watching the open hatch for a fourth man who'd briefly appeared, but then had ducked back inside the escape trunk when the firing had begun.

He pushed off as fast as he could swim down to the aft deck as the hatch swung shut, getting a brief impression of a pair of eyes behind the clear faceplate of the Steinke hood.

Terri reached him moments later, but the hatch had already been dogged, and they could hear high-pressure air clearing water from the trunk.

McGarvey turned and held up three fingers in front of Terri's faceplate, and pointed toward one of the bodies drifting slowly upwards and downstream.

She got his meaning and together they swam to the first body. McGarvey pulled the Steinke hood off, and shined his light on the face. The man's dark eyes were open in death, his face screwed up in a grimace of pain and terror. He was not Rupert Graham.

Dillon and Jackson understood what McGarvey was doing, and they retrieved the other two bodies, pulling off the Steinke hoods as McGarvey and Terri swam over to take a look. Neither of the dead men was Graham either.

Jackson pulled out a plastic tablet and grease pen. "Graham?" he wrote.

McGarvey shook his head.

Dillon got their attention, and pointed the beam of his dive light back down toward the escape trunk hatch, where bubbles were streaming out.

They switched off their dive lights, and moments later the hatch opened to reveal a dim circle of red light.

No one swam up from inside the submarine.

McGarvey took the tablet and pen from Jackson. "Looks like an invitation to me."

Jackson looked toward the bow of the boat. Just visible, nearly three hundred feet away, were the otherworldly twin glows of the two welding torches. He turned back to McGarvey and nodded, then took the tablet and pen.

"This is our show," he wrote.

McGarvey took the tablet. "I'm coming too. Your wife needs a dive buddy."

SS SHEHAB

Graham was beside himself with rage, crouching in the doorway of the passageway just aft of the escape trunk. Two more of his crew were crouched forward of the hatch that they'd recycled once he'd gotten back aboard.

It was quiet, except for the gentle hush of the scrubbers and fans circulating air that had been recycled and cleaned of its excess CO_2. Earlier he thought he'd heard strange buzzing sounds from somewhere well forward in the boat, but most of his attention had been directed toward escaping before the missiles fired. Now he couldn't hear the sounds.

When the escape trunk hatch had opened and the three crewmen had emerged into the river, Graham had counted three, perhaps four small lights hanging in the water just outside.

Seeing them, and instantly understanding that he had led his boat into a trap, had been the biggest shock of his life. Every detail had been planned. His crew had done exactly what he wanted it to do. They had evaded detection through the Strait of Gilbraltar, had crossed the Atlantic, allowing satellites to spot them heading south, and had sailed into the Chesapeake with not so much as a close call.

But it had been for nothing if he couldn't escape.

The missiles would launch and contaminate Washington if al-Hari had gotten the outer doors open, or fire and destroy the submarine if the doors remained shut. At this point it did not matter to him.

He wanted his life, not merely for the pleasure of it, but to continue striking back at the bastards. Over and over because they . . . because . . . what? He didn't know if he knew the answer now.

But it wasn't going to end here. Not like this.

"There are at least three of them," he called out to his men hiding in the darkness. "Wait until all of them come aboard, and then fire and keep firing."

"We could surrender," someone suggested.

"They'll kill us first so that they can get to the missiles. We have to stop them before we can get out of here."

With the three men presumably dead or captured outside the submarine, plus the four he and al-Hari had killed in the control room and sonar space, the twelve they had shot in their bunks, and the two Libyans who were deathly sick with radiation poisoning, there weren't many men left aboard. What few remained were holed up in various compartments throughout the boat, trying to stay out of the firefight.

But that wouldn't last. Sooner or later some of them would try to reach the escape trunk with whatever weapons they'd managed to find. It was going to get unhealthy back here in a matter of minutes.

He looked up toward the escape trunk hatch, willing himself to get a grip, to remain calm. "Come on," he muttered under his breath. One shot was all he needed and the bastards would be caught in a cross fire. Once his two crewmen had finished the job he would kill them and make his escape.

It all would depend on timing, and on their attackers being lured down into the passageway.

Someone closed the outer hatch, and immediately high-pressure air began to hiss into the escape trunk. They had accepted the bait.

Graham tightened the grip on his 9mm Steyr and eased a little farther back into the shadows, using the bulkhead and edge of the doorway as a shield. "Wait until they all come down the ladder," he called softly.

But he was forgetting something. He could feel it.

The air stopped, and the inner hatch was undogged and pulled up into the escape trunk.

For several seconds nothing happened, but then something small dropped through the hatch and clattered heavily on the deck.

Graham had time enough to realize that it was a flash-bang grenade, the very possibility he had forgotten to consider, and fall the rest of the way back into the generator room, before a tremendous flash of light followed instantly by an ear-shattering boom hammered off the bulkheads.

He caught a glimpse of two black-clad figures dropping through the hatch and immediately spraying the compartment and passageway with automatic weapons fire, before he raced aft, ducked through the hatch into the tiny machine shop and electrical parts storage bins. He had his pistol at the ready, half-expecting to see some of his crew waiting to gun him down.

But he was alone back here for the moment.

The firing stopped, but then started again, farther forward.

He figured that they were U.S. Navy SEALs and that they would make a lightning-fast sweep through the boat, killing anything that moved.

Graham stuffed the pistol in his belt, pulled up a section of floor grating beneath a metal lathe, eased the waterproof bag with his civilian clothing and papers into the bilge, and climbed down into the cold, stinking filthy water.

Someone was coming aft.

He had just enough time to ease the grating back into place, when a black-suited figure appeared at the open hatch.

McGarvey hesitated for a moment just inside a cramped compartment that was equipped with a workbench, a vice, a metal lathe, and other tools, plus bins and bulkhead-mounted cabinets filled with parts.

Terri was right behind him, her Beretta 9mm pistol in hand, her dive mask pushed up on top of her head. "What?" she asked.

He thought that he'd heard a noise. Faint. Metal-on-metal just before he'd come through the hatch, but then Dillon and Jackson, who had headed forward, had opened fire again. "Someone's back here," he said softly.

"Watch yourself," she cautioned.

McGarvey continued aft through the next hatch into the engine room and pulled up short again. The hairs at the nape of his neck were standing up. A slightly built man was sprawled on his face on the deck, a pistol in his hands. He was obviously dead, but there was something wrong with the skin on his hands and neck. He was covered in suppurating wounds or sores.

"That's radiation sickness," he said. "There are nukes aboard and they're leaking badly. You better tell Frank and your husband."

Terri found a growler phone on the bulkhead. She dialed up the 1MC. "FX pick up."

A second later Jackson came on. "Go."

"Trouble. We got a bad guy down in engineering. Already dead when we got here. Mac thinks it's radiation sickness."

"Stay away from the body."

"Have they found Graham?" McGarvey asked Terri, and she relayed the question.

"Negative," Jackson came back. "We've bagged a dozen bad guys, but there are more than that dead in their bunks. Tapped in the heads at close range. Two down in the con, two in sonar."

"Have you reached the forward torpedo room yet?" Terri asked.

"I'm at the hatch, but it's dogged from the inside. How about you?"

"There may be someone else back here. We're going to finish—"

Dillon broke in over the 1MC. "We've got big problems, people," he said. "We need to get off this boat right now."

"Where are you, Frank?" Jackson demanded.

"In the con," Dillon came back. "But you better hurry, we've got less than six minutes."

McGarvey stared at the dead man for a moment longer, then looked up. All the hatches back to the aft torpedo room were open. Nothing moved back here. There were no sounds except for the air circulation fans.

"Mac?" Terri asked.

He had definitely heard something. Someone was hiding back here, but it could take hours to dig him, or them, out. "Right," he said, and he turned and followed Terri forward to the control room.

Jackson got there at the same time they did. Dillon was hunched over the weapons control panel, on which two lights were flashing. A clock was on countdown mode, with five minutes and twenty-eight seconds showing.

"Whatever's in tubes one and two is going to fire in about five minutes unless we do something," Dillon said. "The timing circuits have been sabotaged, so we can't do it from here."

"Did they open the outer doors?" Jackson demanded.

"The indicators on the panel show the tubes flooded and the doors open. They must have opened them before Dale and Bob could reach the bow."

"They were welding something," Jackson said. "The timer was sabotaged, could they have done the same with the indicators for those two tubes?"

"Yes, but I don't know why, unless there was a mutiny."

"We did hear gunfire," Terri said.

"I need two blocks of Semtex, one with a short fuse for the torpedo room hatch, and the other with a longer fuse to destroy the compartment," McGarvey said. "We can't let those missiles fire. If they explode even inside the tubes they'd spread radiation through the river and all of the lower bay."

"That compartment will be hot," Jackson said.

"I'll blow the door, shoot anything that moves, and toss the second block inside."

Terri had taken a brick of plastic explosive from her pack and was hurriedly molding a small block of it for the torpedo room hatch. "What do we have to wreck inside to make sure the missiles won't fire?"

"Take out the inner doors," Dillon said. "Should break the firing circuitry between there and here."

"You can't go inside," Jackson cautioned.

"Neither of us are, honey," Terri said. "I'll toss a big enough block to take out the door and the entire compartment. Stand by at the escape trunk, we're probably going to be in a big hurry." She gave McGarvey a grin. "For a first date, you're not half-bad."

"Terri," Jackson said softly.

She turned to her husband and a look of complete understanding passed between them. "Be back in a flash," she said.

McGarvey. The single thought crystallized in Graham's head as he noiselessly climbed up into the escape trunk. His sneakers were slippery with oil from the bilge, and he nearly fell.

The son of a bitch was aboard. But no matter how the man had gotten this far, he was going to die down here in just a few minutes. Graham only wished that he could somehow see the look on McGarvey's face when the escape trunk was blown apart and the wall of black water came rushing through the boat.

There would only be a brief moment between the time McGarvey knew he was going to die and the instant when his consciousness was blotted out. But Graham wished he could see it.

He closed the inner hatch, dogged it, and opened the seawater valve to flood the compartment. As the water rose, he donned his Steinke hood.

Within ninety seconds the chamber was filled with water. He un-dogged the outer hatch and swung it open. He waited for a few seconds, to make sure that no one was waiting outside, then cautiously eased out of the escape trunk.

Somewhere forward, possibly at the bows, two very dim violet lights flickered in the pitch-black water.

It came to him all at once that he knew what the buzzing sounds he'd heard earlier were. Someone was up there welding the torpedo doors shut.

The missiles would fire inside the tubes and when they did, the entire bow section of the submarine would be destroyed.

It was another failed operation, and he was bitter about it. But this time McGarvey would die for certain.

Graham jammed the ten-kilo brick of plastic explosive against the in-ner hull just inside the escape trunk, set the timer for four minutes, and, holding his waterproof satchel against his chest, kicked off for the surface.

"Fifteen-second fuse," McGarvey said.

Terri had molded the small block of Semtex around the dogging wheel at the center of the forward torpedo room door. She nodded, inserted the acid fuse into the plastique, and she and McGarvey ducked back around a bulkhead.

"Get the big charge ready to toss," he told her. He switched his Walther's safety catch to the off position.

Someone fired a pistol from behind them, the first shot ricocheting off the deck, a piece of the shrapnel catching McGarvey in the left foot. He turned in time to see a tall, slender man waving a large pistol stagger up the passageway from where he had apparently been hiding. He was rav-aged by radiation sickness, open, running sores distorting his face so badly that he looked like something out of a horror movie.

McGarvey started to bring his pistol to bear when the dying man fired a second shot, this one caching Terri in her forehead just above her left eye, and she fell back.

"No!" McGarvey shouted, and fired three shots in rapid succession, all of them striking the Arab in the middle of his chest, sending him back-wards, dead before he hit the deck.

The Semtex Terri had set blew with a sharp bang, and the torpedo room hatch locks came loose, the door swinging open a few inches.

McGarvey ducked across the passageway to Terri, who was crumpled against the bulkhead. Her blood-filled left eye was open in surprise but she was dead, and there was no power on earth that could bring her back.

He looked up toward the torpedo room, his heart like granite, willing with everything in his soul for someone to come charging out of there. But no one came.

Terri Jackson, whose handle was Lips, was a pretty young woman, who McGarvey thought looked a little like the movie actress Kim Basinger. He shook his head. So goddamned senseless. All of it. All the killing. All the suicide bombers. All the attacks.

And for what? Religion? He sincerely hoped not, because that would mean the entire world would be at war with itself forever.

McGarvey picked up the heavy charge, darted down the passageway, and shoved the torpedo room hatch open with a foot. The body of one man dangled half out of his bunk. He too had advanced radiation poisoning.

There was no one else inside the narrow, very cramped compartment. Six torpedo doors, three to the right of the boat's centerline and three to the left, were arrayed in the forward bulkhead about thirty feet from the hatch. There were at least six torpedoes still in their racks.

McGarvey only took a split second to look before he set the acid fuse to three minutes, and tossed the heavy package into the compartment with all of his might.

He did not bother to see where the package landed before he pulled the hatch shut, went back to Terri's body, picked it up, and headed in a run back to the control room.

Dillon had gone aft to get the escape trunk ready. Jackson was the only one there, waiting for his wife and McGarvey. He didn't say a word, nor did he look at McGarvey as he took his wife's body in his arms. He studied her face for several long moments, his expression completely unreadable.

"I'm sorry," McGarvey said. "We missed one."

Jackson looked up. "Did you kill him?" he asked, his voice soft as if he were whispering a secret.

"Yes," McGarvey said. "But we need to hustle. I set the fuse for three minutes." He glanced over at the weapons control board, which showed the missiles were set to launch in three minutes and ten seconds.

"Time to go," Jackson said. He turned and headed aft in a run, McGarvey right behind him.

When they reached the escape trunk, Dillon was there, wrestling with the controls. "Somebody locked out and left the outer hatch open," he said, as he turned around. When he spotted Terri's body in her husband's arms, his face fell. "My God," he said.

McGarvey was looking up at the escape hatch. "It was Graham," he said. The noise he'd heard in the workshop aft. The bastard had been hiding back there after all.

"Dale and Bob are out there, they might have spotted him," Dillon said, not able to take his eyes off of Terri's body.

"Not unless they came aft," Jackson replied mechanically. There was no animation in his face.

"As it stands there's no way we're going to get out from here," Dillon cautioned.

"We've got to get away from this compartment," McGarvey said, suddenly realizing that Graham wouldn't have simply jumped ship without first making sure that no one else could follow him. "The forward torpedo room is going to blow in less than two minutes, and I think this hatch is going to blow too."

"Son of a bitch, you're right," Jackson said.

McGarvey hustled them aft into the generator room, and tried to close the waterproof door, but it wouldn't budge.

"What's wrong?" Dillon demanded.

"It's been welded open," McGarvey said. "All the doors to the aft torpedo room have been welded open."

"It's going to get real hairy here in about one minute," Jackson said.

"It's worse than that," Dillon told them. "I took off my rebreather and left it in the control room—"

A very large explosion in the forward torpedo room shook the entire boat as if she were a child's toy.

McGarvey and the others ducked back behind the bulkhead on either side of the open hatch, the sounds of water rushing forward as loud as a 747 coming in for a landing, bringing with it every piece of loose debris or equipment or bodies like deadly shrapnel from a powerful bomb.

All the lights aboard the submarine went out, plunging them into absolute darkness.

A second explosion, this one practically on top of them, opened up the hull at the escape trunk. Water immediately came pouring into the boat as if from a hundred fire hoses, acting as a temporary cushion against the water and debris racing forward from the wrecked torpedo room.

Water had already risen to their waists and would flood the entire boat within seconds.

Jackson saw their chance at the same time McGarvey did. "We're going out the hole where the escape trunk was!" he shouted.

"Go!" Dillon shouted over the tremendous din. "I'll be right behind you!"

"You're coming with me and Terri!" Jackson shouted. "You need to use her rebreather."

McGarvey switched on his dive light, pulled his mask over his face, and took a deep breath from the rebreather as the water rose up over their heads.

Jackson had his own mask on, and moments later Dillon had donned Terri's mask. He and Jackson had to hold her body between them because there had been no time to take the dive equipment from her body.

Within a couple more seconds the entire boat was flooded and the in-rushing water stopped.

McGarvey swam out of the generator room first to survey the damage and see if they could get out of the boat. The entire escape trunk had been obliterated, as had a fifteen-foot-wide section of the hull. Except for some dangling wires and piping the boat was open to the river here.

McGarvey helped Jackson and Dillon maneuver Terri's body out of the generator room, and up through the debris and out into the open water.

MacKeever and Ercoli appeared out of the gloom from forward and above, but they moved slowly, their bodies battered by the massive concussion of the explosion in the forward torpedo room.

Together the five of them rose slowly to the surface, Terri's body cradled in her husband's and Dillon's arms until they reached the surface.

"Son of a bitch," MacKeever said. "Someone stole our boat."

PART
FOUR

SIXTY-SEVEN

□

THE WHITE HOUSE

Dick Adkins was ten minutes late for his 9:00 A.M. briefing to the president, and an impatient Dennis Berndt met him at the west entrance for the walk down the connecting corridor to the Oval Office. "Well?"

"He did it," the DCI said.

Berndt heaved the first sigh of relief in ten days. "Thank God."

Don Hamel and his National Intelligence apparatus had been purposely kept out of the loop on the McGarvey–bin Laden operation, to give the intelligence community plausible deniability. It meant that if something went wrong, the blame would not fall on the White House. But Adkins was bringing good news, and Berndt figured they had dodged the bullet for the second time in as many weeks. First the Panama Canal, and now the submarine.

"It was right where he said it would be," Adkins said, with a little awe in his voice. He shook his head. "I worked with the man for years, Dennis. I was his assistant DCI for the couple of years he ran the show. I know the mechanics of what he does. But I still haven't a clue *how* he pulls it off."

"He's never been afraid of stepping up to the plate."

President Haynes, his jacket off, tie loose, was sitting at his desk, talking on the telephone, while his staff came and went, depositing files and other paperwork in front of him. He was working Congress to get enough votes for passage of his controversial energy bill, and neither he nor anyone else seemed very happy.

"He needs this lift," Berndt said.

The president looked up and waved them in.

"There were some problems," Adkins cautioned as he and Berndt entered the Oval Office.

"Good morning, Mr. Director," the president's secretary said, going out.

"Morning," he mumbled.

"Casualties?" Berndt asked.

"One of our people was killed, but there are a lot of dead bodies at the bottom of the York River we're trying to get to. Plus a big mess. Could be an ecological disaster."

The president finished his call, and ordered everyone except Berndt and Adkins out. When the door was closed he came around his desk. "What ecological disaster?"

"The sub was where McGarvey figured it would be, and he and a SEAL team managed to stop the attack, but the boat was badly damaged," Adkins said. "The Coast Guard is on site to evaluate the situation, but at the very least there's a significant diesel oil spill into the river. The media is already down there wanting to know what's going on. Problem is that nobody other than us and McGarvey's team has the answers."

"What about nuclear weapons?" the president asked.

"At least one, possibly more," Adkins reported. "Mac thinks there's a good chance we'll also be facing a nuclear materials spill, which we had to warn the Coast Guard about."

The president turned and looked out the thick Lexan windows toward the Rose Garden. "Were any of our people injured?" he asked.

"One of the SEAL team members was shot to death," Adkins said.

"How about the terrorists?"

"We've recovered three bodies so far, but everyone aboard the sub is dead," Adkins said. He glanced at Berndt who had a strong feeling what was coming next.

"What about Graham?"

"Somebody escaped from the sub, got past Mac and the others, and stole the Special Operations boat the SEAL team borrowed from the navy."

The president turned back. "Was it Graham?"

Adkins shrugged. "Unknown, Mr. President," he said.

"How'd Mac and the SEAL team get back to the Farm?" Berndt asked. "It's a long swim."

"His daughter and son-in-law run the facility. Mac and the others swam ashore just above Yorktown and used a cell phone to call for help. They were picked up in a van and brought back to Camp Peary. It was the middle of the night and apparently no one saw a thing. That's national parkland along the river there."

"What about the boat?" Berndt asked.

"A Matthews County Sheriff's deputy found it abandoned at a commercial dock between Newport News and Hampton."

The president was surprised. "That's just across from the navy base."

"I think McGarvey was right about the Brit all along," Berndt said, not surprised at all. "He did the same thing in Panama, abandoning his crew when the mission fell apart. By the time anybody realized he was gone he'd made his escape."

"Well, unless he has help, he won't get out of the country," the president said.

"Don't count on it, sir," Adkins said. "The man has been ahead of us every step of the way."

"But only one step," the president said. "McGarvey's stopped him twice."

"There'll be a third time, unless we get to bin Laden first," Berndt said. He could feel it in his bones. No matter what else they would have to face in the near term, bin Laden was the key.

"I agree," President Haynes said. "Will McGarvey go back to Pakistan and finish the job?"

"Mr. President, I don't think any power on earth could stop him," Adkins replied.

SIXTY-EIGHT

□

THE FARM

McGarvey got off the phone with Adkins a few minutes before ten, and walked across the compound from the BOQ to the five-bed field hospital housed in a World War II–style Quonset hut. It was operations as normal at the training camp, and so far no one had taken undue notice of him or the SEAL team that Todd had rescued early this morning.

A doctor had come down from Bethesda to tend to MacKeever's and Ercoli's concussion injuries. They'd started to swim aft toward the escape trunk hatch when the bow section of the boat had exploded. It was the only reason they'd survived. Both men had sustained damage to their ears and eyes, and Ercoli's left hip and knee had been severely dislocated.

But that small bit of luck was nothing against Terri Jackson's death and the growing probability that it was Graham who had escaped from the sub, sabotaged the escape trunk, and had made off with the SOC. The Coast Guard had found a small inflatable with Libyan navy markings drifting downriver. Whoever had locked out of the submarine had probably intended to use it to make their escape, but had seized the opportunity of taking the SEALs' boat. The entire operation had Graham's signature written all over it.

"The boat was found near Newport News," Adkins had told him.

"Get an FBI team down there right away to look for trace evidence," McGarvey suggested.

"The county cops found it tied up at a sightseeing dock, and from what I understand they found no evidence of a crime so they turned it over to the navy. Figured someone on base had gotten drunk and took it for a joy ride."

"Get Puckett to run interference for Jackson and his people. I have a feeling they're going to be in a tight spot as soon as they report in."

"How's Jackson taking it?" Adkins asked.

"I don't know, Dick," McGarvey said. He could put himself in Jackson's shoes, he'd almost lost Katy on more than one occasion, but the man had become a blank slate from the moment McGarvey had brought Terri's body back to the control room. There'd been no rage, no tears, no blame. Jackson had carried on as a fire-team leader, making sure that MacKeever and Ercoli were well taken care of, and then retreated with Dillon to write the end-of-mission report.

Nor had he been able to get a read on Dillon or the other two. They had pulled together as a unit, them against everyone else, including McGarvey.

"Well, you'd better keep them isolated for now," Adkins said. "The Coast Guard has taken over just downriver from you, and they're stonewalling the media. Won't be long before some wise guy realizes that the Farm is less than five miles away, and they come knocking at our door."

"I'll give Todd and Liz the heads-up, but any minute now the navy is going to get real interested in talking to Jackson and Dillon."

"I'll talk to Puckett right away," Adkins said. "In the meantime, the Bureau has put out an APB on Graham, but I have a feeling it's already too late."

"If it was Graham, and I'm betting it was, he had his escape worked out before he ever set foot on that submarine," McGarvey said, but then stopped. The last word had caught in his throat. Suddenly he had it. He knew how Graham meant to escape and where he was going. "We might get lucky this time, as long as nobody gets in his way," McGarvey added, not really believing it, or wanting it.

He needed Graham to escape. It was the only way now to get to bin Laden. The Brit was going to trade his life for the al-Quaida leader's.

"How about you?" Adkins asked, apparently not catching the change in McGarvey's voice. "The president sends his thanks."

"And he wants to know if I'm going back to Pakistan to finish the job."

"Something like that."

"I'm coming up to the Building this afternoon," McGarvey said. "Have Gloria Ibenez meet me in Otto's office, and we'll work it out."

"It?" Adkins asked.

"I'm going after bin Laden again," McGarvey said.

"I see," Adkins had said, and he'd sounded like a man caught up in the middle of something that terrified him. "Do you know where he's hiding?"

"No, but I know how to find out."

Dillon was alone, nursing a cup of coffee in the break room, when McGarvey went in and sat down across from him.

"How's FX?"

Dillon shook his head. "I thought I knew him pretty well, but I just don't know. At any minute I expect him to blow sky-high. I would. But there's nothing."

"I don't think I'd care to be around any of them when it hits home," McGarvey said.

"I know what you mean," Dillon said.

"The boat was found downriver near Newport News, apparently in good shape, but there was no sign of Graham," McGarvey said.

"He won't get far on foot, will he?"

"He had it all planned ahead of time. By now I expect he's either out of the country or on his way out."

"The FBI will at least cover the airports, for God's sake," Dillon said. He was having a hard time believing what he was hearing. "They know what he looks like, don't they? A man like that can't just waltz onto an airplane and fly away. That's one of the reasons Homeland Security was created."

McGarvey shook his head. It never ceased to amaze him just how naïve most Americans really were. Even after 9/11. "You can't imagine how easy it is for a pro," he said.

Dillon looked away.

"Anyway, I have to get back to Washington, but I want you guys to lay low here for the time being. Admiral Puckett will send for you when the time is right."

Dillon turned back. "We're all sorry about Terri, but no one thinks it was your fault."

"Thanks," McGarvey replied, but he didn't know what else to say. Her death was, in his mind, his fault. He should have been better at covering her back.

WASHINGTON DULLES INTERNATIONAL AIRPORT

A tall man with longish blond hair, a crumpled but stylish linen suit, and thick glasses presented his British diplomatic passport and the return portion of his first-class ticket on Lufthansa's noon flight to Berlin to one of the security officers at the international departures lounge.

The airport was busy this morning. Arriving by cab from the city, Graham had spotted the extra security measures that had obviously been only recently put into place. A dozen Virginia Highway Patrol and Loudon County radio cars were stationed along the departing passengers unloading area, and the deputies were scrutinizing the faces of every white male who entered the terminal.

Maintaining a neutral expression, Graham got out of the cab and marched directly past one of the cops, who gave him a once-over with no sign of recognition.

Inside, there were more police, and several National Guard troops with bomb-sniffing dogs where passengers were checking their bags.

Walking down the corridor to the international lounge, Graham was able to see that airliners pulled up to jetways were being guarded by other National Guard and law enforcement officers.

Yet he'd been allowed to walk past them all without a question. Homeland Security was an even bigger joke than he thought it would be. America's borders had always been even more porous than those of Canada and Great Britain. Security had always been one of the more serious faults of a free and open democracy. But it amazed him how little had actually changed in the United States after 9/11.

They still didn't get it. Only one man did, and thinking about McGarvey gave him almost as terrible an empty feeling in his chest as missing Jillian did.

The day of reckoning would come. He had twice underestimated McGarvey, and there would not be a third time, because for Graham there was no longer a *jihad*. The next time they met, Graham would kill him.

And arranging such a meeting would be as simple as offering the former DCI exactly what he wanted.

"Good morning, Sir Thomas," the security officer said, looking up from the passport photograph into Graham's eyes that were now blue. "Do you have any other baggage?"

"No, just this one," Graham said. His passport identified him as Sir Thomas Means, the third assistant to the British ambassador to Germany. "Just popped over for a day and a wake-up. Have to get back into the fray, you know."

The security officer handed back the passport, while a second officer passed Graham's overnight bag through a hazardous materials scanner. Since he was traveling under diplomatic papers his luggage could not be searched unless something showed up on the scanner.

It did not. Nor did anything on his body set off the security arch when he walked through it.

"Have a good flight, sir," the officer said, as Graham collected his bag.

"Thank you, I will," Graham said, smiling, and he sauntered across to the bar to have a glass of wine, despite the hour, and wait for his flight to be called.

SIXTY-NINE

□

CIA HEADQUARTERS

Just after lunch Gloria Ibenez took the elevator up to Rencke's office across the corridor from the Watch. He'd phoned her around eleven to tell her that McGarvey would be coming to the Building in a few hours and wanted to talk to her. Since then her stomach had been aflutter with anticipation.

Despite his repeated denials of her and despite the obvious fact that he was happily married, she was in love with him. And for the past few days she had been miserable because, although he had protected her from Howard McCann, he'd been avoiding her.

Until now.

The pass around her neck did not authorize entry into Rencke's inner sanctum, so she had to be buzzed in. He was seated in front of one of the several wide-screen monitors that were arrayed in a broad U formation. Some of them displayed satellite images of what looked like a large city, a seaport, which Gloria recognized as Karachi, and the slum section of Fish Harbor where bin Laden was supposedly hiding in the compound. A series of figures and mathematical equations crossed the screen directly in front of Rencke, his fingers racing over the keyboard. The background was lavender.

"Oh, wow, Mac just came through the gate," he said without looking up.

His office was a mess; classified files, photographs, and maps covered the small conference table in the middle of the room and were stacked on chairs and in piles on the floor along with empty plastic Twinkie packages and empty cartons of cream. Despite his marriage to Louise Horn, who'd tried to change his horrible eating habits, he reverted to his old ways whenever he had the bit in his teeth, as he apparently had now.

"What does he want with me?" Gloria asked, perching on the edge of the conference table to Rencke's left.

"Unless I'm way off base, I think he's going back to badland to finish the job, and I think he's going to ask you to tag along again."

Gloria lost her breath for a moment. She could almost feel Kirk's arms around her, smell his scent. It was a good, safe feeling. Comfortable, but exciting. "Will Mr. McCann sign off on the assignment?"

Rencke chuckled. "I don't think that'll be a problem," he said without missing a keystroke or looking away from the monitor.

"I meant that I want to have a career here after this assignment," she said. She couldn't think of any other job she'd rather have.

"I don't think that's gonna be a problem either," Rencke said. He suddenly stopped typing, but it took several seconds for the equations and diagrams to catch up. When they did, the background color deepened sharply.

"What is it?" she asked.

Rencke turned to her. "It's a threat assessment. They failed again because of Mac, and now they're going to drop everything to find him and kill him."

"Did he find the submarine?"

Rencke nodded. "Last night. Actually early this morning. That part's a nonissue now, except that Graham managed to escape."

As irrational as it was, being left out of anything McGarvey was involved with stung. "Why didn't someone tell me? Maybe I could have helped."

"It was Mac's call," Rencke said. His bemused genius persona was gone, replaced now by someone who seemed genuinely concerned about her. "Look, you're in love with Mac. Well, so are a lot of us. You're not the first, and I suspect you won't be the last."

Gloria lowered her eyes, but she refused to cry. "It hurts."

"I know," Rencke replied gently. "But Mrs. M is the sun and the moon to him, and you'd better come to terms with it or you're going to be miserable for the rest of your life." He smiled. "You're a pretty girl. You could probably get just about any guy you wanted."

"I want him."

"I know," Rencke said. He glanced up at a small black-and-white closed-circuit monitor that showed a half-dozen pictures-in-picture from various cameras in the building. McGarvey was just getting on an elevator in the executive parking garage. "He's on his way up, so you're going to have to make up your mind now. You're going to love him and try to seduce him away from his wife, or you're going to love him and help him."

There was no real choice, of course, but it hurt all the more knowing she could never have him. She nodded. "Whatever he wants."

A couple of minutes later, Rencke buzzed McGarvey in.

"I'm going after bin Laden again, and I'm going to need your help."

"Me too?" Gloria asked.

McGarvey nodded. "Especially you."

CHEVY CHASE

On the way back to the safe house McGarvey played over in his mind the instructions he had given to Rencke and Gloria, which were going to put them in harm's way no matter if he were right or wrong. Otto had agreed that his plan gave them the best shot at finding bin Laden and eliminating him. Gloria, on the other hand, would have agreed to anything.

They both were relying on his judgment, and he had based his plan on one very narrow—and on the surface, unlikely—possibility, which depended on Graham making his escape from the United States.

Traffic was heavy on the Beltway as he got off at Connecticut Avenue and headed south. But the summer afternoon was warm and beautiful, and Washington was in its quiet mode. Yet McGarvey couldn't shake the feeling of impending disaster.

Some rough beast was slinking its way toward us, and would strike again unless it could be stopped soon.

It was exactly what he had to explain to Katy. He needed to make her understand that it would be impossible for them to go to Florida until this challenge was met once and for all. Even though he had promised time and again to finally get out of the business, he couldn't walk away now even if his marriage depended on it.

He was going to kill bin Laden and nothing on earth was going to stop him.

He parked in the driveway and Katy came from the kitchen as he walked through the front door. He'd called early this morning to tell her that he was okay, but she pulled up short the moment she saw his face. She raised a hand to her mouth.

"It's still not finished, is it?" she said, her voice small.

"One last thing, sweetheart."

She turned away and made to go back into the kitchen, but he caught up with her and took her in his arms.

"One last thing, I promise," he told her. "But it has to be done."

She looked into his eyes. "Bin Laden?"

He nodded.

"When?"

"In the morning," McGarvey said. Katy wanted to pull away in anger, but he held her all the tighter until she calmed down a little. "I can't walk away from it, no matter how much I'd like to."

She considered what he was telling her, but then shook her head. "You like it. You always have."

"It's my job—"

"No, goddammit, you love it!" she screeched. "You did when you went to Chile, that time just before you walked out, and nothing has changed." She slapped his chest with the flat of her hand. "You love it, goddammit."

"It's something that needs doing, and I've always been the one to do it," McGarvey told his wife. "But I've never loved it."

"Yes—"

"I've killed people, Katy."

"I've seen you in action," she said bitterly.

He released his hold on her and let her step back, a heavy bitterness descending upon him like a death shroud. "I'm sorry, Katy. But you're wrong, I've never enjoyed it." He turned to go, but this time it was she who stopped him, and she fell weeping into his arms.

"Oh, Kirk, I'm sorry," she sobbed. "I didn't mean to hurt you."

He held her, his heart still impossibly heavy for this and for all the other times he had driven her half-crazy with fear and anger. It had never been her fault, it had always been his.

"You should never have married her in the first place," his sister had told him years ago after he'd sold their parents' ranch in Kansas. She'd despised him for doing it, and every chance she had of hurting him, she took it. "You'll end up destroying the poor girl."

There'd been no answer to his sister's charge then, nor was there one now. Except that he loved his wife with every fiber of his being, and he always had.

"I know, Katy," he said softly. "It'll turn out okay. Promise."

SEVENTY

□

KARACHI

It was nearly noon by the time McGarvey and Gloria cleared customs and walked out of the terminal to find a cab. This time they had flown commercial, Delta from Washington and Emirates from Dubai, and with layovers it had taken the better part of two days to get here.

Rencke had assured them that neither Karachi police nor Pakistani ISI had warrants for their arrests following their last trip here, even though both Mac and Gloria had been involved in incidents in which blood had been shed.

McGarvey wanted their arrival to be as transparent as possible. He wanted anyone who was the least bit interested in his movements to know he was here.

And the two-day travel delay getting here had given Rencke extra time to make all the necessary arrangements.

There would be only one very narrow window of opportunity between the time that Graham made contact and when the Pakistani government sat up and took notice that something was going down. They wouldn't have a second chance.

Joe Bernstein, the CIA's contract cabbie, was waiting for them. He took their bags without a word and hustled them back to his taxi. Five minutes later, they had cleared the airport and were heading into the city on Shahrah-e-Faisal Road, the weekday traffic very heavy.

"I did not expect to see you back so soon," he said, glancing at them in the rearview mirror. "I don't think this is a very safe place for you right now."

"It won't be safe for anyone seen with me," McGarvey said. "Maybe you shouldn't have picked us up."

"Your son-in-law is a friend," Bernstein replied. He chuckled. "Anyway you're an open secret now. Best show in town. I wouldn't miss it for all the poppies in Afghanistan."

"Did you talk to Todd?"

"No, but Otto and I had a long and fruitful conversation," Bernstein said. "I'm to be the bagman." He chuckled again. "I'll admit that all that money will be a real temptation."

"That's what we're hoping," McGarvey said.

On the long flight over, McGarvey had gone over all the details of the operation with Gloria, so that she knew exactly what she would have to do.

The details had also been worked out with a reluctant Dave Coddington, who was the Company's Karachi chief of station. There was a lot at stake this time, not the least of which was five million U.S. in cash, as a down payment on the twenty-five-million-dollar reward for the capture or killing of Osama bin Laden. In the five years the reward had been offered, there'd been no authentic takers.

This time, however, McGarvey was betting that someone would finally come forward with information that would lead to bin Laden. It would be a trap, of course, to lure McGarvey to a place where he could be killed. Bin Laden would be nowhere near, but his mujahideen would be.

"You'll be gambling with five million of Uncle's money, and if you lose it there'll be some people seriously pissed off at you," Rencke had offered.

"Won't be the first time," McGarvey said.

"We could give them counterfeit money," Gloria suggested.

"None of our people would take the deal seriously," McGarvey told her. "The word would get out."

"You're talking about leaks," Gloria said. "In Karachi? I know Coddington, he's a good guy."

"I'm sure he is," McGarvey said. "But are you willing to bet your life that his shop is airtight? We're talking about five million cash. A lot of people are going to want a piece of the action."

"What if we do lose the money?" she asked.

McGarvey had shrugged. "The Company can afford it."

Bernstein glanced over his shoulder. "From what I heard, Coddington had a hell of a time coming up with that much cash in such a short time. And the word is already out on the street. It's like somebody tossed a big boulder into a small pond."

"Any takers yet?" McGarvey asked.

"No, but our guys are in place and ready to go at a moment's notice."

"It'll happen tonight," McGarvey said.

"How can you be so sure?" Bernstein asked.

"Because I'm here. And as soon as they find out that I am, they'll move."

Once they were checked in at the Pearl Continental and their bags were brought up to their tenth-floor executive suite, Gloria ordered lunch from room service while McGarvey used his sat phone to call Rencke.

The number rang once in Rencke's office before it was automatically rolled over to his sat phone. "You're in place?"

"We just checked in," McGarvey said. "Where are you?"

"On the move," Rencke said. "The opposition knows you're there. A half hour ago just about every al-Quaida Web site went quiet. Not so much as a symbol. The sites are all blank, and I haven't been able to get into any of them, which means their computers were disconnected."

"They knew that we would be looking. That's good."

"That's very good, kimo sabe. Now we just have to wait until they take the bait."

"How about you?" McGarvey asked.

"No matter what happens, I'll be at this number until it's over."

SEVENTY-ONE

DOWNTOWN KARACHI

The entire twenty-fifth floor of the M. A. Jinnah commercial tower was in darkness. Osama bin Laden walked to one of the floor-to-ceiling windows and looked out at the city. Below, the streets were alive with activity. And out there somewhere Kirk McGarvey was coming.

Bin Laden had no fear, although he did have a great deal of respect for the American's abilities. They had first come face-to-face in Afghanistan before 9/11, and every day since then he regretted with everything in his soul that he'd not killed the man when he'd had the chance. McGarvey had thwarted nearly every al-Quaida initiative, except for the attacks of 9/11, and now the assassin was here.

But this time McGarvey would surely die, because an al-Quaida traitor would accept the reward money that the Americans were offering and a trap so exquisitely believable for them would be set.

Kamal Tayyhib, bin Laden's chief bodyguard, knocked softly at the open door. "Contact has been made, Imam."

"Have the Americans agreed to the meeting?" bin Laden asked, without turning away from the window.

"Yes, and our people are in place."

Bin Laden nodded. "Very well. But under no circumstances must the American deliverymen come to any harm."

"It will be as you have ordered," Tayyhib promised. "But what of the money? It would be of inestimable assistance to the jihad."

Bin Laden smiled inwardly. In the early days of the struggle, money had been of no concern, because he was a rich man. And later, after most of his personal fortune was gone, some of the very Saudi princes he vowed to depose had supported him and the cause. "Destroy it," he said softly.

"But surely that's not necessary, Imam."

Bin Laden turned around, an infinite patience welling up in his chest. "Has my double arrived at the compound?"

Tayyhib wanted to press the point. Five million dollars was a great deal of money. At the very least it could be used to finance the continuing struggle in Afghanistan, Iraq, and Syria. Or it could be sent to the West Bank to help support the families impoverished by the Jews. But he lowered his eyes. "He arrived two hours ago."

"Has Colonel Sarwar been notified?" Obaid Sarwar was the chief liaison among Pakistani intelligence, the U.S. Embassy in Islamabad, and the U.S.Consul General here in Karachi. He was also a strong supporter of al-Quaida and the jihad. Pakistan was walking a narrow line between appearing to be hunting the jihadists while all the while secretly supporting them.

"Yes. He promises to give us forty-eight hours. If McGarvey hasn't made his move by then, the ISI will ask the Americans to help raid the compound. But of course by then no one will be there."

"McGarvey will take the bait," bin Laden said.

"If he's as smart as you say he is, won't he suspect a trap?"

Bin Laden smiled. "He'll be certain that it's a trap. But that won't stop him. He'll do it tonight. I'm sure of it. And then he will be dead."

Tayyhib nodded respectfully. "As you say, Imam."

"Now leave me," bin Laden ordered, his voice as soft as a breeze in a field of grass. "But do not go far, I want to know the moment the handover takes place."

"Yes, Sayyid," Tayyhib said. It was a term of deep religious respect, most often used for descendants of Mohammed himself.

"Not Sayyid," bin Laden corrected, although he was secretly pleased. "Imam will do."

He turned back to the window as his chief bodyguard withdrew, and turned his mind to a second problem, that of Rupert Graham and what had to be done with the man who'd become a serious liability to the jihad.

CHAKIWARL ROAD

"You should let me make the handover," Joe Bernstein insisted.

He was at the wheel of a consulate red Mercedes 300 diesel sedan, parked in the rear of a tall concrete apartment building on the outskirts of the city across the Lyarl River. It was after nine in the evening, and it had started to rain a half hour ago. Before it had been hot and muggy. Now it was hot and steamy, and Bernstein's filthy white shirt was plastered to his back.

"This is my money and my operation," David Coddington said from the backseat.

It came down to a matter of trust, Bernstein thought. Five million dollars was a lot of money to let walk out the door. But it rankled, because he had given four dangerous years of his life to Company operations here and up in Islamabad. More than once he could have sold his services to Indian intelligence. Word on the street was that they paid twice as much as the CIA for items of interest. But he'd been loyal the entire time.

"We could run into some serious shit. It wasn't such a good idea to drive out here all alone."

"They'll want the money," Coddington replied in his maddeningly calm voice. "But if they get a decent look at your face you'll be worthless to us on the street." The COS patted Bernstein on the shoulder. "This could be the big one. If we can bag bin Laden we'll all go home heroes."

There were lights on in some of the apartments, and the parking lot was more than half-filled with decent-looking cars, most of them Fiats, VWs, and a few small Mercedes, plus a plain white windowless van, but Bernstein had parked in darkness near the trash Dumpsters. Their instructions, which they had received at the consulate's primary contact telephone, had been very specific. No more than two people would be used to deliver the money. They would not be armed. And they would park directly beneath the one inoperable light stanchion in this lot no later than 9:10 P.M. It was that time now.

Headlights flashed around the corner of the building, and moments later a battered green Toyota pickup truck came into view and parked twenty meters away to the right of the white van.

"I can only see the driver," Bernstein said.

The pickup's headlights went out.

"Maybe it's not our man," Coddington suggested, and Bernstein could hear the first hint of tension in his voice.

"He's just sitting there."

"Can you tell if his engine is running?"

"No," Bernstein replied. Suddenly he didn't like the setup. They were boxed in back here. The only way out took them directly past the Toyota. He looked over his shoulder. A broad ditch, half-filled with water, separated the rear of the parking lot from the access road to another apartment block a couple hundred meters away. From there they could probably reach Chakiwarl Road. But if they got stuck in the ditch, they would be out of luck.

"I think we should get out of here," he said.

The driver got out of the pickup truck.

"Hold on," Coddington said. "This is it."

The driver made no move to come across the parking lot, but he was staring at them. He was dressed in baggy dark trousers, a light shirt, and baseball cap. He was holding something about the size of a book in his hand. It did not look like a weapon.

"I'm going over," Coddington said. "If this falls apart call for backup right away."

"If it falls apart you'll be dead," Bernstein said. "Let him come to us."

"No," Coddington said. He got out of the car with the big aluminum case containing the five million and headed across the parking lot.

"Jesus H. Christ," Bernstein swore. The hair at the nape of his neck was standing on end. He reached under the seat, brought out his 9mm Beretta, and switched the safety to the off position.

Coddington reached the pickup truck and for a minute or two nothing seemed to be happening. But then the informant handed the book, or whatever it was, to Coddington, who gave the man the aluminum case.

"Come on," Bernstein murmured.

Coddington waited until the driver laid the aluminum case on the pavement and opened it, then turned around and headed back.

Bernstein tightened his grip on the pistol. If it went bad, it would be right now. He kept his eye on the informant, watching for the man to pull out a weapon, but it didn't happen.

Coddington reached the car and climbed in the backseat. "Fish Harbor," he said triumphantly. "Bin Laden's at Fish Harbor in a compound. Now get us the hell out of here."

Bernstein dropped the car in gear and started toward the exit, when four men armed with Kalashnikov rifles leaped out of the white van, and opened fire on the informant.

"Son of a bitch," Coddington swore.

Bernstein floored it, spun the car around, and headed for the ditch. "Hang on!" he shouted.

A big explosion lit up the night behind them, and then the car, still accelerating, slammed into the ditch, the shocks bottoming out, the rear end fishtailing wildly, water and mud flying everywhere.

For just a moment it seemed as if they were going to be bogged down, but then they were rocketing up the other side and Bernstein hauled the heavy car down the access road toward the next apartment building.

"Are they coming after us?" he demanded.

"No!" Coddington shouted. "Christ, they shot him, and then tossed a bomb or something right on top of his body."

The access road crossed behind the apartment block, and opened two hundred meters later back on Chakiwarl Road. There was no traffic and speeding away Bernstein checked his rearview mirror to make sure that they were not being followed.

"What about the money?" he asked.

"Gone," Coddington said. "It proves that he wasn't lying."

"Yeah, doesn't it now," Bernstein replied. "But why didn't they stop us?"

"Because you were too goddamned fast for them," Coddington said. He was hyper. "And now we've got the bastard."

"When are you going to let McGarvey know?"

"Right now," Coddington said, pulling out his cell phone.

SEVENTY-TWO

□

PEARL CONTINENTAL

It was 9:15 P.M. The afternoon had dragged for McGarvey and Gloria after Coddington's initial call that contact had been made and the handover would take place sometime after nine o'clock. The bait had been taken, and now a major portion of the puzzle would be solved by al-Quaida's reaction.

McGarvey had tried to warn the chief of station to bring plenty of backup in case he found himself in the middle of a firefight, or at the very least to insist on a rendezvous site somewhere very public. But he'd been told that this part of the mission would be strictly a local CIA operation.

He was in the bathroom, splashing water on his face, when his cell phone rang. He dried off and walked back into the bedroom to answer the phone on the third ring. Gloria stood at the window, an expectant look on her face.

"Yes?"

"We made the handover," Coddington said. He was excited, all out of breath as if he had just run up a flight of stairs. "He's at a compound in Fish Harbor. We've got the bastard now. This time we've really got him."

"Listen to me, David. He's not there, but the CIA is going to act as if they believe he is—"

"No, goddammit, you listen to me!" Coddington shouted. "They gave me a videotape. And that's not all. Right after the handover we came under attack. The informant was killed and the money destroyed."

McGarvey glanced at Gloria, who was staring at him, trying to gauge what was going on.

"Christ, they figured out someone was coming for the money, and where the handover was going to take place, and they were waiting for us," Coddington said.

"Did they fire at your car?" McGarvey asked.

"No," Coddington said. "We got out of there too fast."

It never ceased to amaze McGarvey how people could believe what they wanted to believe, tossing out any fact that didn't fit. The problem was especially bad in the intelligence community that was tasked with trying to come up with the right facts to fit whatever the current administration's position was.

These were bright people, many of them even brilliant. But they were very often blinded by their own set of preconceived notions, and by a general bureaucratic malaise that seemed to affect nearly everyone the moment they got anywhere near Washington, D.C. Every single agency had its own unique culture, the primary driving force of which was nothing more than the survival of the agency.

In any given situation, if a piece of intelligence information promoted the agency's survival, then it was branded as fact, whether it was true or not.

"That's good news," McGarvey said. "You might want to contact the ISI right away. If bin Laden is actually at the compound, he'll probably try to get out of there tonight, so you'll have to move fast."

"That's what I thought," Coddington said. "But what about you?"

"We'll backstop you in case you're too late," McGarvey said.

The COS was silent for a moment. It wasn't the answer he'd expected. "That's a good idea," he said.

"Yeah, good luck."

McGarvey broke the connection. "Bin Laden is not at the Fish Harbor compound. It's a setup."

"It's just what you figured," Gloria said. "So what's next?"

"Get dressed. We're going to the lounge for a drink."

Pakistan was a Muslim nation, and alcohol was forbidden except in special circumstances. In most hotels, guests could order beer, wine, and liquor, night or day, but only to drink in their rooms. And major hotels usually provided a concierge floor of executive suites, generally reserved for foreign, non-Muslim visitors. A cocktail lounge was one of the perks.

A half-dozen businessmen and two women were seated at the bar and at tables in the small, tastefully modern lounge when McGarvey and Gloria walked in. Tall windows on two sides looked out on the city, and at the governor's palatial mansion next door. A man in a tuxedo was playing American standards on a piano. The lighting was subdued.

They took a table in a corner from where they could watch the door and the bar. A cocktail waiter came and took their order, a cognac neat for McGarvey and a dark rum neat for Gloria, and when he left, Rupert Graham walked in the door and went to the bar.

McGarvey stiffened imperceptibly. He had suspected that Graham was the one who'd escaped from the sub and made off with the SOC, just as he suspected that Graham was here in Karachi and knew that McGarvey had come here too.

He'd even suspected that sooner or later the Brit would make contact to suggest a trade; bin Laden's whereabouts, something McGarvey wanted to know, for a head start so that Graham could lose himself somewhere not only away from Western authorities, but from al-Quaida. He'd almost lost his life twice in the past weeks; first in Panama and second five miles downriver from the Farm. He would want some breathing room.

Or at least that's what he wanted everyone to believe.

But McGarvey hadn't counted on the man actually showing up in person. He'd expected a telephone call or perhaps a messenger to suggest a meeting somewhere safe for both of them, though he'd known that Graham had the balls to come here like this.

It would be so easy to get up as if he and Gloria were leaving, pull out his pistol, and as they passed behind Graham, put a bullet into the man's head. In the confusion he and Gloria could make their way out of the hotel, and depend again on Otto to get them out of the country.

McGarvey smiled. Graham would be dead, but it would leave bin Laden's whereabouts still a mystery.

"What's so funny?" Gloria asked.

McGarvey nodded toward Graham at the bar. "It's him."

Gloria nearly came out of her seat, but McGarvey reached out and laid a hand on her arm. "Easy. He's here to talk, not shoot. So we'll talk to him."

Their waiter brought the drinks, and as soon as he'd gone, Graham got up from the bar, a glass of what looked to be champagne in hand, and sauntered back to their table. He was dressed in a conservative dark blazer, with club tie and gray slacks, his grooming perfect, his manner supremely confident.

McGarvey pulled out his pistol and held it under the table on his lap, the safety catch in the off position.

Gloria noticed, but she held her cool.

"Mr. McGarvey, we meet again," the Brit said pleasantly. "May I join you and Ms. Ibenez?"

"No," McGarvey said harshly, but without raising his voice. "What do you want?"

A momentary flash of anger passed across Graham's eyes. But he recovered nicely and smiled. "Why, to talk, same as you."

"No," McGarvey said. "I'm here to kill you and bin Laden. At the moment I have a pistol aimed at you from under the table. Tell me why I shouldn't kill you here and now."

"Unsporting, old—"

"Has anyone taken notice of us?" McGarvey asked Gloria.

She looked past Graham at the other patrons, and shook her head. "No."

"Get your purse, we're leaving now."

"Wait," Graham said, the first hint of uncertainty creeping into his demeanor. "Bin Laden's not at Fish Harbor."

"I know that."

"But you don't know where he's hiding."

"Somewhere here in the city."

"So right," Graham said. "I'll tell you where he is, and you'll give me forty-eight hours to make my escape."

"You could have escaped after Norfolk," McGarvey said. "Yet you came back here, practically led me here. Why?"

"Looking over my shoulder for you is bad enough. But looking over my shoulder for al-Quaida as well is too much." Graham managed another tight smile. "Besides, you may get killed trying to get out of Pakistan. The man does have his supporters. I might bag myself a twofer."

"Okay," McGarvey said. "Where is he?"

Graham laughed. "What do you take me for?"

"A traitor," McGarvey said matter-of-factly. "A coward. A fucking rabid dog. Shall I go on?"

Graham held himself in check, the strain obvious in his eyes, which narrowed slightly. "Perhaps you should kill me now, while you have the chance," he said, his voice soft. "Because sooner or later I will kill you."

"It's a thought," McGarvey replied. He raised his pistol. "But I want bin Laden first."

Graham nodded. "And I'll give him to you."

"How and when?"

"Tonight. Two A.M. I'll meet you downstairs in the lobby."

"And take me to him?"

Graham shook his head. "No, of course not. I'll tell you where he's hiding—and you're right, he's here in the city. You'll suspect it's a trap, so I'll remain here with Ms. Ibenez. We can hold each other hostage. When you return, having got what you came for, I'll walk out of the hotel and you'll give me a forty-eight-hour head start."

"What makes you think that I won't just kill you?" McGarvey asked.

"You're an American, and your sense of honor and fair play is nearly as strong as a Brit's. If you give your word, you'll keep it."

McGarvey said nothing.

"Well?"

"You have my word," McGarvey said.

"I'll see you at two," Graham said. He started to leave, but then turned back. "I do have connections, you know. If I find that you've involved the Company with anything other than the Fish Harbor operation I'll put out the word why you're here. Fair enough?"

"Fair enough."

Graham walked away, setting his champagne glass on the bar before he left the lounge.

"It'll be a trap," Gloria said.

"Yup," McGarvey said. He put his gun away, took out his sat phone, and speed-dialed Rencke's number. It took a few seconds to acquire, but Otto answered on the first ring.

"Yes?"

"He's here in the hotel. He just left the lounge."

"I'm on it."

Graham's new driver, Tony Sampson, leaned up against the right fender of the Mercedes S500 sedan parked in front of the Pearl Continental Hotel, smoking a cigarette as he waited for his boss. He'd been a British SAS sergeant until he was arrested for smuggling drugs out of Afghanistan. He'd come to bin Laden's attention, who had him rescued from a convoy transporting him to the airbase at Bagram for transport back to England, and brought him here to work with Graham.

This was a pisshole of a city and a pisshole of a country, but it was better than Afghanistan and decidedly better than England. Anyway, Sampson had always thought of himself as a man of opportunity. And already he could see any number of possibilities working for Graham. For the moment, then, he was the loyal soldier.

A drunk in rumpled jeans and a filthy, torn sweatshirt stumbled across the busy Club Road, horns blaring, traffic flowing around him.

Sampson looked over his shoulder in time to see the man collapse on the pavement right behind the Mercedes. "Bleedin' Christ," he muttered. He tossed his cigarette away and went around to the rear of the car.

The drunk had his hands on the molded rear bumper and was awkwardly trying to pull himself to his feet.

"Here, what the fuck do you think you're all about," Sampson said. He grabbed the man's arm, hauled him to his feet, and shoved him away. "Get the fuck out of here before I start breaking bones."

"*Entschuldigen, mein herr,*" Rencke said, bleary-eyed.

"Fucking Kraut," Sampson said. "Cops catch you drunk, you'll be going to jail before you can say *bitte.*"

Rencke turned and walked away, leaving Sampson with an odd feeling that something hadn't been quite right about the encounter.

SEVENTY-THREE

KARACHI CITY CENTER

Graham emerged from the hotel in a hurry and climbed into the backseat of the black Mercedes. He was torn in two directions; his intense need to kill Kirk McGarvey, and the elemental instinct of survival. Bin Laden and his fanatical al-Quaida mujahideen were right in the middle of both forces. No matter whatever else went down in the next few hours, he needed bin Laden, McGarvey, and the Ibenez woman to be dead.

Afterwards he would make his way out of Pakistan to someplace neutral, where he would have time to figure out what would be next for him.

"Where do you want to go, sir?" Sampson asked.

"Back to bin Laden," Graham said, looking at the bellmen at the front doors. "But we'll be leaving again in a few hours, so stay on your toes."

"Yes, sir," Sampson said, and he pulled out into traffic.

"And, Tony, make bloody well sure that we're not followed."

Sampson glanced in the rearview mirror. "Is that a possibility tonight, sir?"

"Oh, yes," Graham said. "A very real possibility. I don't want you to take anything for granted. Do you understand?"

"Yes, of course, sir."

Graham sat back and closed his eyes, trying hard to bring up an image of Jillian in his mind's eye. But it was impossible tonight as it had been for some weeks. His head was filled with nothing more than thoughts of revenge; getting back at all the bastards of the world who had forced him to take a path he'd never wanted. Admiral Holmes, Osama bin Laden, and Kirk McGarvey; all men cut of the same rotten cloth.

The admiral, who had given the order that Graham was not to be recalled from patrol, had died of cancer a few years ago, so he was out of Graham's reach. But bin Laden and McGarvey would come together this night in a dance of death that Graham had choreographed to the last detail.

"Will it be the Pakis or the CIA?" Sampson asked.

Graham opened his eyes. "Is someone on our tail now?"

"No, sir. I'd just like to know who the opposition is, that's all."

Sampson was new, and Graham didn't know if he should be trusted, despite bin Laden's opinion. But he'd seen the man's SAS record, which looked good, and his question now was a valid one.

"Probably the CIA," he said. "I don't think they've involved the local cops or the ISI yet."

"Yes, sir," Sampson said. He'd passed the National Tourist Office but instead of turning left on Abdullah Haroon Road, he'd headed straight across to Shahrah-e-Faisal toward the airport.

This route would take them well away from the city center, and the M. A. Jinnah Commercial Centre, but once they were on the airport road outside of the city with sparse traffic at this hour of the evening, it would be virtually impossible for anyone to follow them undetected. As soon as they were clear, Sampson would double back into the city center.

Graham laid his head back and closed his eyes again, content for the moment to let his driver make the decisions. He'd been continuously on the go, it seemed, since Cabimas, with McGarvey right there over his shoulder the entire time. He was weary, and he wanted to be done with the entire business; McGarvey, al-Quaida, the jihad.

He'd come up with a notion for continuing the fight on his own, but over the past few days, with his thoughts focused almost exclusively on McGarvey and bin Laden, another idea had begun to niggle at the back of his mind: Why? Why bother going on, when nothing he'd ever done or ever could, would bring his wife back from the grave?

Jillian was dead, and that was more of an immutable truth than all the gods, Jahweh, Christ, and Allah included. Every man, woman, and child on earth was some religion's infidel. Killing them all wouldn't bring back his wife.

Graham let his mind drift to the Panama Canal operation where he'd come face-to-face with McGarvey, then to the York River where once again McGarvey had shown up, and finally tonight at the hotel where the arrogant bastard had been waiting with his girlfriend.

He could not simply walk away as he had in Panama and the York River. Not again tonight.

"We're clear," Sampson said.

Graham opened his eyes. They were back downtown. "You're certain?" he asked, sitting up.

"Yes, sir."

A couple of blocks later they turned onto A. R. Kayani Road, and entered the underground parking garage of the M. A. Jinnah Commercial Centre. The steel mesh security gate opened for them with a code card. Sampson drove all the way down to the fifth level where he pulled up at the private elevator for the twenty-fifth floor.

"I want you back here at one thirty," Graham told his driver. "We have a lot to do this morning, and I'm going to need your help."

Sampson nodded tightly, and Graham got out of the car and took the elevator up to the twenty-fifth floor.

Sometime after two this morning, when McGarvey showed up, the security system for entry to the parking garage would be disabled, as would the closed-circuit television cameras protecting bin Laden's lair, and his personal bodyguards would be sent on a wild-goose chase.

McGarvey would make it far enough to kill bin Laden, but he wouldn't leave the building alive. Because by then his girlfriend would be dead, and Graham and Sampson would be waiting in the parking garage for him to descend from the twenty-fifth floor.

PEARL CONTINENTAL

"What the hell kept you?" McGarvey asked, letting Rencke into the hotel room.

"Trying to keep myself from being arrested," Rencke said, going directly across to the desk and setting up his laptop computer to the WiFi network.

"Did you get the tracker attached?"

"Yeah, that was a piece of cake," Rencke said. He brought up a GPS program that displayed a map of downtown Karachi on the monitor. "But I had to bug out for a while. It was probably one of the bellmen who spotted me behind Graham's car and called the cops. Before I could make it around back, they were all over the place."

"Did you get back here clean?" McGarvey asked.

"I think so," Rencke said.

Gloria was at the window looking down at the street. "It's quiet," she said.

Rencke had come over to Riyadh on the Aurora, and from there on a diplomatic passport flying a Gulfstream bizjet. He had stationed himself across the street from the hotel with a laptop and WiFi equipment that could hack into the hotel's switchboard as well as McGarvey's cell phone and sat phone. If and when Graham made the phone call Rencke could trace it. But he was also in a position to attach a tracking device to Graham's car in case the man showed up in person.

"I never thought he'd have the guts to face you," Rencke said, his fingers flying over the keyboard.

"What's the tracker's range?" McGarvey asked. He tried to keep himself in check. They were close now, and he could almost feel bin Laden's presence.

"It's uplinked to one of our Jupiters. Anywhere on earth from eighty degrees north to eighty south."

The map display shifted to a much narrower area of downtown within just a few blocks from the hotel. A small red dot appeared near the center of the display, a blinking cursor next to it.

"The unit's shielded," Rencke called out.

McGarvey was looking over Otto's shoulder. "Have we lost him?"

"I don't think so." Rencke centered the search area directly adjacent to the red dot and cursor, which showed the last location within one meter where the uplink was lost. He overlaid the street map with a satellite view of that specific downtown block which showed a tall building on A. R. Kayani Street.

"Underground parking?" McGarvey asked.

"Probably," Rencke said absently. He brought up a Principal Places of Interest directory, and overlaid it on the double display. "Bingo," he said, looking up. He clicked on the building, and an info box popped up with M. A. Jinnah Commercial Centre, an address, and a brief description.

"Can you get more?" McGarvey asked. He looked up. Gloria was watching him from the window, her eyes bright. She was excited for him, and yet it was obvious she was a little frightened. If they had actually found out where bin Laden was hiding, it meant McGarvey would be going after him sometime before two this morning when Graham was supposed to come back to the hotel. Almost anything could happen.

"I don't know if they've gone digital yet," Rencke mumbled, his fingers once again flying over the keyboard. The street map overlaid with the satellite image disappeared and a logo that looked like the Masons' symbol came up with an Arabic inscription around a compass rose. "City Engineer's office," Rencke said.

He pulled up an Arabic-to-English translation program, went to the City Engineer's home page, and from there, a directory of major buildings and structures within the city proper. Scrolling down a dozen pages, he came to the M. A. Jinnah Commercial Centre. He looked up with a big grin. "Am I good, or what, kimo sabe?"

"You're good," McGarvey agreed.

Rencke clicked on the blueprint icon. A page came up asking for a password. He took a CD from his laptop bag, loaded it, and a few seconds later an enable icon came up onscreen. He clicked on it and his program bypassed the password block. Moments later a directory of blueprint pages came up. "Okay, if he's in there, he wouldn't have his name painted on the door. How do you want to do this?"

"Floor by floor. First let's see what we can eliminate."

Gloria came over to watch. "This could take a while," she said. "We've only got a little more than three hours before Graham comes back."

"It'll be something obvious," McGarvey said. "Something you can look at a thousand times and still not see."

Rencke started with the ground floor that housed a security post at the front entrance, as well as a monitoring command post. A large atrium was bounded by shops, a travel agency, a storefront banking service, rest rooms, and a first-aid station. At the rear of the building were the service entrances and loading docks.

The second floor contained mostly attorneys' offices, along with a small consulting service that apparently helped promote foreign investments, especially those from eastern Europe.

The third, fourth, and fifth floors were taken up by something called PHI Telecommunications Co., LLC, the sixth and seventh by Hassan Aly Publications, and the eighth through eleventh, businesses that were involved with port of Karachi operations and the shipping industry.

There were other consulting firms, doctors' offices, financial advisers, and investment counselors, plus a number of other businesses whose purposes couldn't be guessed from their names. One of them, Amin House, which took up more than half of the twentieth floor, looked promising. Rencke minimized the City Engineer's site, and pulled up the City Directory, which listed Amin House as the private investment service center for Naimat Amin, who apparently was a Pakistani multimillionaire.

Rencke looked up. "It's a possibility," he said. "Bin Laden could be using it as a conduit for funds from his Saudi Arabian pals."

"So far as I know most of that money is going through Prague," McGarvey said. "But if we don't find anything else, we'll come back to it."

Fifteen minutes later they came to the twenty-fifth floor, and Rencke sat up. There was no listing for the entire floor. The twenty-fourth contained an investment house, as did the twenty-sixth, but the twenty-fifth was blank.

There was no other information in any of the building's directories, or in the City Directory, Karachi Utilities, or Karachi City District Taxing Authority. The twenty-fifth floor simply did not exist.

"He's there," McGarvey said.

"How can you be so sure?" Gloria asked.

Rencke was going through the directory for the remaining twenty-three floors, and when he was finished he looked up. "If bin Laden is in that building, he's on the twenty-fifth. How're you going to get through security? They know you're here, and if Graham is setting you up you could be walking into a trap."

"Not until two," McGarvey said. He pulled out his cell phone.

"Who're you calling?" Rencke asked.

"Joe Bernstein. I'm going to need a few things."

SEVENTY-FOUR

M. A. JINNAH COMMERCIAL CENTRE

It was one in the morning. Osama bin Laden sat alone in his sanctuary, a well-worn copy of the Qur'an open to Al-Nisa in chapter four to his right, and the Kalashnikov rifle he'd taken from the hands of a dead Russian soldier in Afghanistan to his left.

If they turn away from Allah, then seize them and kill them wherever you find them.

He was weary from the long struggle, especially after the attacks on Manhattan and Washington, which hadn't really worked the way they'd hoped. The American people had not risen up against their government as they had to end the war in Vietnam.

His engineering advisers had been correct about bringing down the World Trade Center towers, but his political advisers had been wrong about everything else.

He had been wrong then about the aftermath of the attacks, as he was now about Rupert Graham, his infidel sword, his Allah's scorpion. His man at the Pearl Continental had telephoned him an hour ago with the disturbing news that Graham had met with Kirk McGarvey and a woman presumed either to be his wife or perhaps a mistress. The meeting in the tenth-floor lounge had been brief, and what had been said was unknown, but immediately after Graham walked off, McGarvey and the woman had returned to their hotel room.

Possibly the most disturbing news was an event that occurred in front of the hotel when a man, apparently intoxicated, had an encounter with Graham's driver. An hour later, the same man showed up at the hotel and had gone directly to McGarvey's suite.

The CIA had some devilishly clever people working for it, and some of the technology they were able to come up with was truly frightening, making secure cell phone use impossible, and even the Internet unsafe.

It was only a matter of time before the infidels found him. Even with the help of a number of key ministers in the Pakistani government and its intelligence service, the ISI, that he been getting all along, the U.S. government's financial and military aid packages to Musharraf were siren songs, impossible to resist.

So far McGarvey had not taken the Fish Harbor bait, even though he had approached the compound on his earlier visit, but the CIA had already contacted Colonel Obaid Sarwar, who was chief of ISI operations in the Karachi region, with the information it had purchased for five million dollars.

His time here in Karachi was running out. But before he left he hoped to solve the most vexing problem he'd ever faced. McGarvey.

Someone knocked softly at the door.

"Come," he said, and he looked up as Graham's driver, Tony Sampson, came in. The man was extremely ill at ease, nevertheless he rudely looked bin Laden in the eye.

"You were right, sir, it's there where you said it might be."

Bin Laden nodded. So it would begin and end tonight. "You did not disturb it?"

"No, sir, I left it under the bumper where the bugger must have put it." Sampson looked away for just a moment. "I swear to God I'm sorry. I should have known . . ."

There was no doubt which god the infidel was swearing to, but before this night was over, he too would be joining his maker, though on which hand he would be seated would certainly come as a horrible shock.

"Where is Captain Graham at this moment?"

"I don't know, sir. But he asked me to be ready to leave by one thirty."

"Find him, please, and tell him that I wish to speak to him."

"Yes, sir," Sampson said and he turned to leave, but bin Laden stopped him.

"Sergeant, are you armed?"

"Not at the moment, sir. Not up here."

"Get your pistol. You may be needing it this evening."

"Yes, sir."

It was a few minutes after one when the blue and white Toyota van that Joe Bernstein was driving pulled up and parked on A. R. Kayani Road, directly in front of the main entrance to the soaring M. A. Jinnah Commercial Centre front plaza. There was very little traffic at this hour, only the occasional truck or cab; in fact the entire sprawling city seemed to be asleep, or at the very least holding its breath in anticipation of something happening.

McGarvey and Rencke sat in the back, waiting for Bernstein to give them the all-clear. They'd agreed that they wouldn't go in until the street was totally free of innocent bystanders. Too many Pakistani civilians had already been killed by the U.S. military trying to run down and wipe out al-Quaida leaders. McGarvey did not want to add more bodies to the carnage.

Gloria was parked at the end of the block across from the building's underground parking entrance in a Fiat she had rented from the hotel. She wasn't going inside with them, despite her best arguments. In the end she understood that she would be more valuable helping Bernstein as a backup in case they had to get out in a hurry, or if for some reason they got stuck inside.

It had taken Bernstein the better part of two hours to gather the uniforms and equipment McGarvey had requested, and make it back to the Pearl, and now they were on the verge of running out of time. Graham had promised to return to the hotel at two, which meant he would probably be leaving the building within the next half hour or forty-five minutes. If he got to the hotel and found that McGarvey and Gloria had gone, he might guess something had gone wrong and warn bin Laden.

But bin Laden almost certainly knew that McGarvey was here in the city, so he would be on his guard in any event.

A garbage truck lumbered by, and moments later Bernstein turned back to them. "Okay, it's clear now," he said.

Rencke's eyes were round, but he was determined. He wasn't a field officer, but over the past few days he'd learned enough Urdu, which was Pakistan's major language, to give them a slight edge when they first entered the building. He had darkened his face and hands, and wore a cap to hide his long, out-of-control frizzy hair. The slight disguise wouldn't hold up much beyond a first impression, but hopefully it would be enough, combined with a few phrases in Urdu, to give them the time to take control of the building's security people before an alarm was sounded.

"Ready?" McGarvey asked him.

Rencke nodded. "Let's do it."

"If everything goes okay we should be out of there in fifteen minutes," McGarvey told Bernstein. "If it's much longer than that, it'll mean we ran into trouble. Get word to Coddington."

"Good luck," Bernstein said.

McGarvey slid the side door open, grabbed the black nylon bag with the equipment Bernstein had brought, and jumped out of the van, Rencke right behind him. They were both dressed in dark slacks and windbreakers with the ISI logo across the back.

Rencke closed the door and together he and McGarvey crossed the broad plaza in front of the tower. The automatic glass doors were locked, but the night service door was equipped with a card reader.

Two guards in uniform were stationed behind a counter in the middle of the atrium lobby. They stood up and watched nervously as McGarvey held up a red ISI identification booklet while Rencke swiped a universal keycard through the reader and the door buzzed open.

Rencke slipped inside first, and held up his ISI booklet as he walked to the security desk. "Good evening," he said in Urdu.

One of the security officers had a hand on a telephone, the other had unsnapped the restraining strap on the pistol holstered at his side. They both were suspicious.

One of them said something in Urdu, and Rencke laughed.

"Of course I will explain," he replied.

McGarvey pulled out his pistol, stepped to the side, and pointed it at the guards.

"You will surely reach Paradise this very evening unless you cooperate fully with us," Rencke told them.

The one guard started to pick up the telephone, but McGarvey gestured at him with the pistol, and the man backed off.

"We mean you no harm, brothers," Rencke said. "I promise this in Allah's name."

The one guard carefully moved his gun hand away from his pistol.

Rencke pocketed his ISI booklet and went around behind the counter. "Get down on the floor, please," he said. When they complied, he bound their hands and feet with plastic wire ties, and duct-taped their mouths and eyes.

McGarvey holstered his pistol and came around the counter with Rencke, who took just a moment to figure out the control panel for the building's monitoring system. A bank of six television screens plus a flat panel monitor for the computer were laid out just beneath the lip of the countertop.

Rencke brought up the directory to see if there were any closed-circuit television cameras on the twenty-fifth floor, but if there were any they did not show up in the file.

"Try the parking garage," McGarvey said. He glanced over his shoulder to make sure that no one was coming.

Rencke brought up the five underground levels one at a time. Most of them were free of parked cars, but a half-dozen were parked on the lowest level, including Graham's Mercedes. "Bingo."

McGarvey moved closer as a man stepped out of the deeper shadows across from an elevator. He was dressed in loose trousers, a dark shirt, a light-colored long vest, and he was armed with the boxy Ingram MAC-10 submachine gun, fitted with a suppressor.

A moment later the elevator door opened and a man dressed in dark slacks and a dark pullover came out. A second armed guard stepped out from behind the Mercedes and said something.

"The guy from the elevator is Graham's driver," Rencke said. He looked up. "Could be they're expecting trouble."

"Can you find out what floor that elevator came from?"

Rencke brought up the building's elevator panel. "Twenty-five," he said triumphantly. "You were right."

McGarvey keyed his lapel mike. "Gloria, set?"

"Set," she said in his earpiece.

"Joe?"

"Set."

"I'm going in," McGarvey radioed. Their communications units were encrypted, so there was little chance that their transmissions had been monitored. Nevertheless he watched the guards in the subbasement for any sort of a reaction. But one of them laughed, and the other lit a cigarette.

They might have been planning for trouble, but they weren't expecting anything immediate.

"Can you lock down just that elevator?" McGarvey asked.

"No problem," Rencke said. He entered a few commands into the computer, and a small red tab popped up beneath the elevator command display. "If they want to get back to the twenty-fifth floor they'll have to use the stairs."

McGarvey hefted his nylon bag, and nodded toward the main elevators across the atrium. "Those still work?"

"Yes."

"I'm going up to the twenty-sixth floor," McGarvey said. "Once I'm there lock these elevators down too. I don't want anyone sneaking up behind me."

"You got it," Rencke said. "And Mac? Good luck. Okay?"

"If anything goes wrong, call Gloria and get the hell out of here," McGarvey said, and he stepped out from around the counter and sprinted across the atrium.

Graham hesitated for a moment at the end of the long corridor that led back to bin Laden's prayer sanctuary and held his breath to listen. But the building was deathly still. The hair at the nape of his neck bristled, and his gut was tight, though he didn't exactly know why.

Something was coming; something was about to happen. The air was pregnant with possibilities.

He had sent Sampson down to the garage to wait for him until it was time to meet with McGarvey, and he had delayed answering bin Laden's summons for as long as possible. Something had been odd about his driver since shortly after they'd returned from the Pearl, and when the man had relayed bin Laden's order ten minutes ago, Graham had been sure the bastard was hiding something.

In the meantime all but a handful of the mujahideen usually up here had been sent over to the Fish Harbor compound on a show of force guarding the bin Laden double. Depending upon how quickly ISI reacted, the imposter would either be allowed to get out and make a run for the mountains, or he and his freedom fighters and whoever managed to get inside the compound would all be destroyed in a series of powerful suicide bombs.

It was a ruse they had used before. The CIA was convinced that bin Laden and most of his key lieutenants were hiding in the mountains along the border with Afghanistan. It was a fiction that the Pakistani government was willing to maintain for the gullible Americans.

All but one American.

Around the corner, Graham used a house phone to call Sampson. "Get the car ready, we're leaving in a few minutes."

"Yes, sir," Sampson said. "But there's something wrong with the elevator. Do you have it locked?"

For just an instant it made no sense to Graham, but then all of a sudden he had it. McGarvey was already here. Somehow the son of a bitch had followed them from the hotel.

"Get the car ready, but send the others up here."

"How?" Sampson demanded.

"The west stairwell, you idiot!" Graham bellowed. "McGarvey is here." He slammed down the phone, checked the load on his Steyr, and started to the east stairwell.

Bin Laden came to the door of his prayer room. He was dressed now in his traditional Arab garb of headdress and flowing white robes. "Captain Graham," he called.

Graham stopped in his tracks and turned back, the pistol hidden at his side behind his leg.

"I would like a word with you about Mr. McGarvey," bin Laden said. He was flanked by his two mujahideen personal bodyguards, armed with Kalashnikov rifles.

"What about him?"

"There is a possibility that he traced you here after your meeting this evening," bin Laden said, his voice soft as if he were talking to a schoolboy. He stepped aside. "Please join me. We'll have tea and discuss how you will deal with this problem. And with your next assignment."

"First let me fetch something from my room," Graham said.

"If it's your weapon you're after, you will not be needing it. I have sent for help."

"Okay," Graham said, but he spun on his heel and ducked around the corner before bin Laden's bodyguards could react.

At the end of the corridor, he tore open the stairwell door just as the first of the two mujahideen opened fire from the end of the corridor, but by then he was racing down the stairs, taking them three at a time.

He had no idea how McGarvey had found this place, but with a little bit of luck the bastard would be coming through the garage, that by now was unguarded except for Sampson, whose pistol's firing pin was missing.

He wanted McGarvey dead, but first he wanted the American to kill bin Laden, because the worldwide repercussions would be so great that no one from the CIA or al-Quaida would bother looking for one British ex-pat.

SEVENTY-FIVE

M. A. JINNAH COMMERCIAL CENTRE

Stepping off the elevator on the twenty-sixth floor, McGarvey heard the brief burst of automatic weapons fire directly below. It was a single Kalashnikov and very close, no more than one or two floors down, which at least meant that Otto wasn't involved.

He stopped in his tracks for just a moment, to wait for more gunfire, but the building fell silent again; no screams, no shouts, nothing.

He could think of any number of possibilities, not the least of which involved Graham, who might have outlived his usefulness to al-Quaida. He keyed his lapel mike as he crossed the corridor to a pair of highly polished oak doors. The brass plaque on the wall identified the offices as MI-RANI TRADING COMPANY: KARACHI, BERLIN, PARIS, LONDON.

"Otto, I'm on twenty-sixth, somebody's shooting just below me."

"I didn't hear anything," Rencke radioed back. "But you're going to have company. Two guys from the garage are on their way up the stairs. The only one left is Graham's driver, and it looks as if he's getting set to get out of there. He found the tracker and destroyed it. What do you want me to do?"

"Graham's probably on his way down. Make sure Gloria and Bernstein have the heads-up. But tell them to be careful."

"I read you," Bernstein radioed.

The channel was silent for a moment. "Gloria?" McGarvey radioed.

There was no answer.

"Check on her, Joe," McGarvey ordered.

"You got it."

"Otto, I want you to shut down the main elevators. If you don't hear from me sooner, turn them back on in ten minutes and get the hell out of the building." McGarvey set his bag down, and using the same universal card key Rencke had used downstairs, unlocked the door and let himself in.

"It's done," Rencke radioed.

"I'm in, shut down the alarm system for the entire floor."

"Stand by," Rencke said.

The anteroom was large and expensively decorated with ornately framed seascapes on the walls, several tall plants, and a tasteful grouping of dark wine leather furniture on an Oriental rug facing a receptionist's desk.

"Done," Rencke radioed.

"Start the clock now," McGarvey said. He crossed to the door beyond the reception room, let himself into a plushly carpeted corridor, and hurried to the palatial office at the end. This one was at the rear of the building, opposite from the M. R. Kayani Road's main entrance, and was furnished like the reception room with massive, dark leather and oak furniture, including a very large executive's desk and credenza in front of tall glass windows.

He opened the nylon bag on the desk, took out a Kevlar vest and black jumpsuit, and quickly pulled them on. Next he donned a rappelling harness with caribiners, and stuffed his zippered pockets with several small blocks of Semtex plastic explosive and pencil fuses, three spare magazines of ammunition for his 9 mm Walther pistol and three for a Heckler & Koch M8 short-barrelled carbine, and several H & W E182 flash-bang grenades, plus an evidence kit.

Next he took out a 150-foot coil of nylon rope from the bag, and quickly tied a double loop around the massive desk, which would serve as an anchor, and then swept the credenza clear of a stack of files, a half-dozen books held in place by heavy stone bookends, and a water carafe and several glasses on a silver tray.

He attached two suction cup window glass handholds onto the window, and then using a battery-powered glass cutter, removed a four-foot-round section from the window, careful to make sure that the lower edge was below the top of the credenza so that the sharp glass would not cut the rope.

He set the heavy piece of windowpane aside, the warm, humid night air wafting in on a light breeze, the sound of a siren in the distance. He slung the M8 carbine over his shoulder, then threaded the rope through the snap rings attached to his harness, paid the long end out the window, climbed up on the credenza, and slipped backwards through the hole in the glass.

Balancing 250 feet above the city, his feet on the window ledge at the floor level, McGarvey paused for just a moment to take stock. The two guards from the basement were on their way up to the twenty-fifth floor because Rencke's GPS tracker had been found. They knew someone was coming, and they would be getting ready to spring their trap.

But they couldn't know yet from what direction the attack would come.

McGarvey gingerly rappelled down a few feet to a point where he could lean over and look into the window below. The room was mostly in darkness except for a dim light spilling through a partially open door. From what little he could make out there were bare mattresses scattered on the floor, and perhaps knapsacks and other things piled here and there. The room was being used as a dormitory for bin Laden's mujahideen. For the moment, however, it was empty, which was a bit of luck.

He lowered himself the rest of the way down, and then holding that position, took out a small block of Semtex, which he plastered to the center of the window. He inserted one of the pencil fuses, set it for ten seconds, then scrambled twenty feet to the left, beyond the edge of the glass.

The plastique blew with a small, sharp bang, spraying shards of glass inside the room as well as outward into the night air like a million diamonds suspended for just a second until they began to rain down onto the backstreet below.

The countdown had just begun.

McGarvey unslung the M8, switched the safety catch to the off position, and kicked away from the side of the building, swinging in a short arc to fly through the shattered window into the dormitory.

As he landed inside, a dark figure flung open the door and raised a Kalashnikov rifle. McGarvey fired a short burst from the hip with one hand, stitching two shots into the mujahideen's chest, slamming the man off his feet back into the corridor.

He disengaged himself from the rope, then threw off the rappelling harness, and crossed the room to the door. Someone was shouting something in Arabic, and at least two people were coming up the hall.

McGarvey pulled out a flash-bang grenade, pulled the pin, waited for just a couple seconds, and then tossed it around the door frame out into the corridor.

Someone shouted a warning just as the grenade went off with an eye-searing flash of intense light and a tremendous bang.

McGarvey stuck the carbine around the corner and sprayed the corridor. Pulling back, he ejected the spent magazine, popped in another one, and rolled left through the door.

Three mujahideen were down, blood splattered on the walls and ceiling, and pooling up beneath two of the bodies. The third man, blood pumping from a neck wound, had grappled a pistol out of his tunic and was raising it.

"Don't," McGarvey warned, but the man managed to pull the hammer back. McGarvey shot him in the head, killing him instantly, then sprinted down the corridor.

There was no way to know how many of bin Laden's freedom fighters had been holed up with him, but the dormitory room had mattresses for at least ten. By now they knew that they were under assault, and if bin Laden were actually here right now, they would have called for help, and would be barricading themselves somewhere. Or they would be trying to make a run for it. Either way there were probably other well-armed, well-motivated men up here perfectly willing to give their lives for the cause.

But there'd been gunfire, so there'd already been some sort of trouble here tonight.

The end of the corridor opened to a large room decorated only with prayer rugs facing a raised platform on which lounging pillows were piled. McGarvey held up around the corner, waiting for someone else to show up. But the building had fallen deathly silent.

He glanced over his shoulder to make sure that no one was coming up behind him, then, girding himself, stepped around the corner and zigzagged his way across the big prayer room to a pair of doors, one of them partially ajar.

He looked through in time to see a mujahideen just a few feet away down a short corridor, a Kalashnikov pointed at the door. A second armed man was waiting farther down the corridor at an open door, he too held a Kalashnikov in the ready-fire position.

McGarvey fell back, away from the doors, an instant before the nearest freedom fighter opened fire, the 7.62mm rounds slamming through the door, fragments hitting McGarvey in his right hip, and left arm, causing him to lose his grip on the carbine, and two striking him in the chest, shoving him backwards off his feet.

The Kevlar vest had saved his life, but the wind had been knocked out of him, and a wave of dizziness and nausea washed over him. For just a moment he saw spots and jagged bolts of black lightning in front of his face.

He managed to pull out his pistol and push the safety catch to the off position, as the half-destroyed door slowly opened and the mujahideen extended the Kalashnikov around the corner. A moment later the freedom fighter ducked his head through the opening and McGarvey fired one shot, catching the man in the middle of the forehead.

The man's head snapped back and his legs collapsed under him.

McGarvey scrambled away from the doorway as the second mujahideen opened fire from the end of the corridor, bullet fragments and pieces from the door flying all around him.

At six hundred rounds per minute, it took only a few seconds for the rifle to run out of ammunition.

Despite his injuries, McGarvey scrambled to the open door in time to see the mujahideen at the end of the corridor slam a fresh magazine into the weapon. The man looked up as McGarvey fired three shots, two catching him in the chest, and the third in the throat, shoving him backwards into the room.

The building fell silent again. McGarvey braced himself against the door frame as he cocked his head to listen. But there was nothing. No sounds to indicate that anyone else was alive up here.

Rencke and Gloria were not to initiate radio contact, lest it be a distraction at a critical time. And for a few seconds McGarvey felt a tremendous wave of loneliness and depression wash over him. Everything, every person and place he knew and loved seemed to be a million miles away, completely inaccessible. He had been in situations like these countless times in his career, so this was nothing new—coming out of the night, an assassin stalking his prey—but there'd never been anything glamorous or exciting about what he did.

He lowered his head and closed his eyes for just a moment. He wanted to think about Katy, bring a picture of her face into his mind's eye, but he shoved that thought away. He could not afford the distraction, not until this business was over.

Pushing away from the door frame, McGarvey hobbled slowly down the corridor, stepping over the body of the first mujahideen, careful to keep out of the blood that was soaking into the carpeting.

All of his senses were alert for the slightest sign that he was walking into a trap. He stopped a few feet from the open door. The second mujahideen was lying on his back beneath a single light bulb hanging from the ceiling. His rifle was on the floor within reach beside him, but he posed no further threat. He was obviously dead.

McGarvey went the rest of the way, holding up just at the threshold before he leaned forward to see inside, and he almost fired his pistol on instinct alone.

A clean-shaven Osama bin Laden, dressed in white robes, sitting cross-legged on a large prayer rug, an open Qur'an lying on his lap, his Kalashnikov propped against the wall behind him, looked up, and smiled sadly. "Good morning, Mr. McGarvey," he said softly. "It seems as if Allah has intertwined our destinies against all odds."

McGarvey peered around the corner to make sure no one else was in the room before he stepped through the doorway, over the mujahideen's body.

"Congratulations for a job well done. You have been a formidable opponent."

McGarvey glanced over his shoulder. It wouldn't take the two men from the parking garage much longer to get up here. It was something bin Laden probably knew, so he was stalling for time.

"I presume that you mean to take me away so that I can stand trial," bin Laden said. He seemed to be amused. "So that a mockery will be made of me before the entire world."

"No," McGarvey said softly, not sure if bin Laden had heard him. By now the Pakistani authorities had probably been alerted to the explosion and the gunfire up here, and were likely on their way.

"In any event I would welcome a public trial," bin Laden said, a smug expression on his long face. "Your lawyers will not be able to prove a thing against me, because in Allah's eyes, I am innocent."

McGarvey keyed his communications unit. "Otto, unlock the main elevators, and get ready to move. I think we'll be having company any minute."

"Will do," Rencke radioed back.

"As an innocent man I have nothing to fear from your American justice," bin Laden said.

McGarvey shook his head. He didn't know if there was any clear definition of what evil was. Soldiers opposing each other on a battlefield couldn't be included. But if any man fit the notion of evil, bin Laden was one. "Wrong answer," McGarvey said, with great difficulty. "Just before 9/11 you told me that no one was innocent in this war. That includes you." He raised his pistol.

The smile faded from bin Laden's lips. "The money to fund the *jihad* comes from Saudi Arabia."

"I know."

"I can give you the names, and—"

"I don't care," McGarvey said. He squeezed off a shot, striking the terrorist leader in the middle of the forehead, driving him backwards, the Qur'an sliding off his lap.

Bin Laden was dead and the war was over. Or at least it was for him.

McGarvey went the rest of the way into the room, and unloaded his pistol, one careful shot after the other, into bin Laden's face, his neck, and his chest.

For several long seconds he stood over the terrorist leader's body, a tremendous sense of sadness coming over him. It had been the same after every kill. He could remember all the faces of his victims. Now bin Laden's would be added to his nightmares.

He ejected the spent magazine from his pistol, pocketed it, and loaded a fresh one into the handle, cycling a round into the firing chamber.

Next he took a cotton swab and small plastic Baggie from one of his pockets, dabbed some blood from bin Laden's head wound, and sealed the cotton swab in the Baggie.

They would want proof.

He took one last long look at bin Laden's lifeless body, then turned and sprinted down the corridor toward the main elevators at the front of the building, the wound in his hip getting steadily worse with each step.

He keyed his radio. "I'm heading to the elevators."

"Hustle, kimo sabe," Rencke replied. "I'm picking up chatter on the local ISI channel. They're on their way here. And Graham showed up in the parking garage five minutes ago. He and his driver are gone."

"I'll be with you in two minutes," McGarvey radioed. "What about Gloria?"

"I can't raise her," Otto said. "The main elevators are unlocked."

"How about Joe?"

"Nothing from him either."

"Christ," McGarvey muttered. He went through the large prayer room and took the corridor in the opposite direction from the dormitory. At the far end, a plain steel door opened to a small lobby across which were two elevators, one of the cars standing open.

He was in a quandary if he should go back and take out the two mujahideen coming up the stairs, which would delay the authorities finding bin Laden's body, or just leave now. But they were not worth the risk or the extra time.

He stepped aboard the elevator and punched the button for the ground floor. Something was wrong on the street out front, and the hairs stood up on the nape of his neck as the doors closed and the car started down.

But Otto would have warned Bernstein and Gloria that trouble was coming their way. They would have been prepared.

It was an express elevator and it took less than one minute to reach the ground floor. McGarvey stepped to one side and raised his pistol as the doors opened. But except for Rencke and the two trussed-up guards behind the security console, the atrium lobby was empty.

"Shut down all the elevators!" McGarvey shouted, hobbling across the lobby. "We're getting out of here right now."

Before McGarvey reached the main doors, Rencke had locked down the elevators and was right behind him, his pistol in hand.

Outside, the night air was warm, and extremely humid. In the not too far distance they could hear a lot of sirens, but there was no traffic here for the moment. The blue and white Toyota van that Bernstein was driving was still parked across the street, and Gloria's Fiat hadn't moved from the end of the block across from the entrance to the building's underground garage. There was no sign of Graham's Mercedes, or that there'd been any trouble. But if he'd emerged from the garage he would have driven directly past Gloria.

McGarvey hurried across the broad plaza and then across the street where he approached the driver's side door of the van from the rear, and looked inside. The window was down and Bernstein was slumped over, blood all over the seat from a gunshot wound in the back of his head. There was no doubt he was dead.

"What do we do?" Rencke asked, his voice still steady despite the fact that he was not a trained field officer.

"We have to leave him," McGarvey said tersely, and he headed as fast as his legs would carry him back to Gloria's Fiat, sick at heart by what he thought he would find. Somehow Graham had managed to get past her and take Bernstein unawares. Christ, he had warned them both about the bastard.

Gloria was also slumped over the seat, blood matting the hair on the left side of her head, but she was starting to come around and trying to sit up. "What happened?" she stammered.

The sirens were very close now.

McGarvey pocketed his pistol, tore open the door, and helped Gloria to sit up and slide over the gearshift lever to the passenger side. He got behind the wheel and as soon as Rencke was in the backseat, started the engine and took off. Just as they were turning the corner at the end of the block, McGarvey looked in the rearview mirror in time to see three pickup trucks filled with armed men pulling up in front of the building. They were bin Laden's security forces, responding to a call for help.

How it would play out between them and the Pakistani intelligence officers who were closing in was anyone's guess, but McGarvey was certain that the ISI had been cooperating with bin Laden and al-Quaida all along.

"Call your people at the airport and tell them that we're on our way," McGarvey told Rencke.

"Already did. The jet will be ready and cleared for takeoff when we get there," Rencke said. He gave his handkerchief to Gloria to stanch the blood seeping from a gash in the side of her head.

"What happened?" McGarvey asked her.

Her eyes were slightly crossed, the pupils dilated. She had probably suffered a concussion. She shook her head. "I don't know," she mumbled.

She seemed to pull herself together a little. "What's going on? Did you get him?"

Something niggled at the back of McGarvey's head, but he nodded. "He's dead, and we're on our way out."

Gloria closed her eyes. "Thank God, darling," she said. "I was desperately worried about you getting away alive." She opened her eyes again, and managed a smile. "Let's go home now, okay?"

EPILOGUE

☐

HONG KONG

Ten days later, on an early Friday evening, Rupert Graham was finishing dressing for dinner in the palatial bathroom in his suite at the super-luxurious Conrad Hotel on Queensway Road with its magnificent views of the harbor and the city. He had thought that after the Panama Canal, the York River, and finally Karachi, being beaten three times by McGarvey, that he would be filled with the overwhelming need to go after the bastard and destroy him. But it hadn't happened. He was at peace with himself for the moment, though he knew that mood wouldn't last forever.

He evened out his bow tie, and walked back into the bedroom to put on his Armani white dinner jacket. Four nights ago he had begun seeing Jillian's face in his dreams again, and for the first time in possibly more than a year he had actually enjoyed a day of sightseeing as an ordinary tourist.

Ignoring the television that was tuned to CNN, he poured a glass of Krug champagne that the room service waiter had opened and put on ice, and went to the floor-to-ceiling windows overlooking the harbor. He raised the glass. "To Kirk McGarvey," he spoke softly. "We will meet again in due time and when you least expect it."

He smiled broadly, but then something intruded on his pleasant reverie. He turned back in time to see a photograph of a bearded bin Laden on the television screen. Three days ago a pair of U.S. Predator drones had fired two missiles into a compound in the Fish Harbor section of Karachi on a tip from unnamed sources that bin Laden had been attending a meeting there. It was presumed that he had been killed in the attack, but the Al Jazeera network had received an audiotape this morning that was identified as the voice of bin Laden, who claimed to be very much alive and planning the next major strike against America.

Graham raised his glass again, and drank. "But you are dead, old boy. There isn't a chance that McGarvey could have missed." He chuckled. "The king is dead, long live the king."

There was no way of knowing what would come next, but it was a safe bet in Graham's mind that the *jihad* was far from being over. Very far from being over.

CIA HEADQUARTERS

"It's not over, Mr. President," McGarvey said. He and Adkins were having a teleconference with the president and Dennis Berndt, his national security adviser, in the Oval Office.

"But bin Laden is dead," the president said. "The DNA from the blood you brought back is a match."

"Yes, sir."

"The problem we're faced with now is how to handle the news," Berndt cautioned. "There could be a tremendous backlash throughout the entire Muslim world if we announced that bin Laden is dead."

"What do you think, Mac?" the president asked.

"I'm not a politician, it's one of the reasons I made such a lousy DCI, but like I said it's not over, and won't be until we can find a political solution."

"Like getting out of Saudi Arabia, or pulling our support from Israel?" the president asked, a touch of edginess in his voice.

McGarvey shrugged. "That might help, Mr. President, but I doubt it. The only way al-Quaida is going to be reigned in is for countries like Saudi Arabia and Pakistan and Syria and Iran to withdraw their support. Once they stop their funding, and close down the training bases, al-Quaida will feel the squeeze. But even more than that, we need to make sure they've got nobody to recruit."

Berndt chuckled. "How do you propose we do that?"

"That's your job," McGarvey said. "But you might start with education."

"Reforming their school systems is just not possible," the president said.

"Not theirs, Mr. President, ours," McGarvey said. "Half the people in our own country couldn't have found Afghanistan or Iraq on a map until we invaded, and they were all over the news."

"More than half," Berndt said.

"Almost every ambassador we send out can't speak the language of the country they've been assigned to. And damn few of them have the slightest idea of the cultures they're expected to deal with on a rational basis."

"You don't know what you're asking," the president said.

"No, sir, you're probably right."

CHEVY CHASE

It was late and the safe house was finally quiet after Otto and Louise had gone home, and Todd and Liz had left with the baby. McGarvey stood at the open patio door looking out at the night. It was warm and humid, though not as bad as Karachi. And the Washington suburbs certainly smelled better.

Katy had stayed up here with him until he was finished with his debriefings. Lieutenant Commander Weiss turned out to be nothing more than a guy who had inherited a small fortune from an aunt. He was only guilty of being an asshole. Which left someone at Guantanamo who was on al-Quaida's payroll. The FBI was working with the ONI on the problem, and it would only be a matter of time before they caught the bastard.

Two days ago, Gloria had come out to the Farm where McGarvey had been going through the three scenarios—the Panama Canal, the York River, and the M. A. Jinnah Centre—as a training exercise. She was being reassigned to the U.S. Embassy in Mexico City and wanted to say goodbye. They had gone for a walk through the woods by the river, the morning bright and beautiful.

"I just wanted to say goodbye, and thanks for everything you did for me," she said. "McCann wanted to stick me on the Cuban desk."

"You would have done a good job there," McGarvey said. He wasn't sure how he felt about her. She was a beautiful woman, bright, well trained, not a complainer, but there was something about her that he couldn't quite put his finger on. She had a chip on her shoulder, and she had a desperate need to prove herself, but he had worked with people like that before. It was something else.

"I'm a field officer," she said. "It's all I ever wanted to do." She turned away for a moment, and when she looked back, her eyes were bright. "I love you, and that will never change. I just wanted you to know that I won't make trouble for you. It's my problem, not yours."

There was nothing to say.

She reached over and kissed him lightly on the cheek. "Goodbye," she said.

"Penny for your thoughts," Katy said behind him.

McGarvey turned. "I didn't hear you coming." He drew her close. "I was thinking about Gloria Ibenez. She's on her way to Mexico City."

"She's in love with you."

"Yeah," McGarvey said.

Katy smiled and gave her husband a squeeze. "Can't fault the girl's taste," she said. "What's she going to do down there?"

"I don't know. I'm out of the loop now. I'm retired, remember?"

Katy laughed. "Yeah, right," she said. "Just give me long enough to finally get settled in our new house. Deal?"

"Deal," McGarvey promised, and he kissed her.